JINNAH VS. GANDHI

Jinnah vs. Gandhi

Roderick Matthews

First published in 2012 by Hachette India
(Registered name: Hachette Book Publishing India Pvt. Ltd)
An Hachette UK company
www.hachetteindia.com

1

ISBN 978-81-9061-739-0

Hachette Book Publishing India Pvt. Ltd
4th & 5th Floors, Corporate Centre,
Plot no. 94, Sector 44,
Gurgaon-122003, India

Typeset in Berthold Baskerville 11/14
by InoSoft Systems Noida

Printed and bound in India by
Gopsons Papers Ltd., Noida

Contents

CONTENTS

Prologue

Two men are sitting in the back seat of a slow-moving car. They are both politicians. Far away a war has been declared, and neither man yet knows how this will affect his prospects. No words pass between the two. The taller man is legendarily averse to small talk, and the shorter one has nothing useful to say to his taciturn neighbour. They have known each other for decades and were once allies, but conflicting ideas and ambitions estranged them long ago.

The car glides silently on through the quiet streets of Simla, the summer capital of British India, built as a hilltop sanctuary from the debilitating heat of the plains. Despite its importance, Simla does not look like an imperial city. Instead it has the air of a model village, its wooden houses calmly expressing much of what the British like to think about themselves in India – functional, orderly, well turned out. Imperial airs and graces are reserved for the great administrative capital of New Delhi, half a day's drive away to the south. New Delhi is self-consciously massive, designed to impart a sense of permanence and authority. The British will not be slow to mock Hitler's upstart ambition when a few years later they find his plans to magnify Berlin beyond any human scale, but they themselves have already built New Delhi's massive classical colonnades and Indo–Saracenic cupolas as a vast, pidgin expression of dominance. Simla is the boudoir version of this imperial vocabulary, with its confident, fake naturalism, well-tended lawns and neat chalets, all surrounded by meadows filled with wild flowers, entrance to which is reserved for picnicking sahibs. Even the railway that runs up to Simla is scarcely more than a toy, a narrow-gauge joyride quite unlike the lowland, broad-gauge railways that carry grain to the ports, or drag long lines of carriages barnacled with India's ticketless poor.

The car creeps on towards Viceregal Lodge, where its two occupants are due to meet the Viceroy, Lord Linlithgow, to discuss the changes that war with Germany might bring to India. The previous day Linlithgow had informed 390 million Indians via the radio that they were now living in 'a belligerent country'. In thus committing them to a distant war without a word of consultation, the Viceroy gave his listeners an uncomfortably sharp reminder that India, as a colony of Great Britain, was bound in foreign affairs by the decisions of His Majesty's Government in London. This highhanded action will bring the Viceroy much criticism later, but he was under no constitutional requirement to confer with any Indian politician, and he chose not to.

The two men in the car, both experienced lawyers, are perfectly aware of the constitutional position and of their relative powerlessness. However, the Viceroy has asked to speak to them, and together they must now work out what the war will mean for India. In the back seat the pair sit closer than they have ever been before, looking strangely ill-matched. One is immaculately dressed in a suit of smooth-finished fabric, the other wears nothing grander than a two-piece ensemble of loincloth and shawl, both of coarse khadi cloth. One coughs occasionally, the other does not. They share, perhaps, only one thing – an unnatural thinness. Like a crane and a chaffinch, the two most recognizable men in India are perched so closely together that the contrasts between them seem almost absurd, but this is no more than an unfortunate moment, born of grave circumstance. Usually, they possess a dignified air that enables them to dominate the stage of national politics. British India offers no place for these men to wield real power, but nonetheless they are looked up to by millions as leaders, spokesmen and exemplars. They possess many strengths that later generations will come to praise and even envy.

The taller man is Mohammed Ali Jinnah, life-president of the All-India Muslim League. As a young man he had been an idealistic liberal, dreaming of Indian self-government and the life of a gentleman-politician.

Now, aged 64, his prime motivation is fear – fear of the domination of India's Muslims by the country's Hindu majority. To avoid this he has long been attempting to unite India's disparate Muslim community and place himself at its head. He relishes the authority he has so far acquired and is keen to extend it, his ambition still not sated after 30 frustrating years in national politics. He lives in Bombay, where his considerable earnings from the law have allowed him to create his own little Simla on top of Malabar Hill. His friends call him elegant and dignified; his enemies consider him arrogant and aloof. No one doubts his determination.

The smaller man is Mohandas Karamchand Gandhi, ascetic, moral reformer and political maverick. He does not look like a leader, and he is in many ways uncomfortable with the power he wields. Now 71, he has been in retirement from national politics for the last five years, but his pre-eminent stature is still unchallenged, and he remains the conscience and centre of gravity of the Indian National Congress. In this time of crisis, the Viceroy has had no hesitation in calling Gandhi to his presence; no one else can speak for India in the way that he can, despite the fact that no Indian has ever voted him into public office.

Jinnah sits still, but Gandhi fidgets, tugging at his shawl. He is accustomed to working long hours at the spinning wheel, and his hands crave useful labour after the enforced idleness of the journey from his ashram at Wardha in the dusty centre of the country, where he received the Viceroy's summons. He came as soon as he could, but it has taken him days. Jinnah was luckier. He was in Delhi, attending a session of the Legislative Assembly, and had only to make a short journey up to his elegant home in Simla, a fine two-storeyed house named The Yarrows.

Jinnah's outer stillness conceals a state of intense mental turmoil. Politicians must recognize and seize opportunities – he has lived his life by this code – but he has yet to identify the precise advantages that the new war might offer him. He has always opposed imperial rule but he knows that it is wise to maintain good relations with the British, because he is beginning to believe that political rights for Muslims can only be assured in a separate Muslim homeland, and after years of unsuccessful wrangling with the Congress he is now convinced that only British power can give him that homeland.

Gandhi has been unable to detect a silver lining as the war clouds gather. The complex relationship between his dislike of Hitler's racist militarism and his aversion to British imperialism remains to be worked out. The British need help, but perhaps they can be persuaded to ask for that help from equals, not subordinates. Twenty-five years earlier he had supported the British in their last great war, hoping for concessions and liberty, but he had been disappointed. This time he will not be so unguarded.

A hard political struggle between the two men lies ahead, but as they sit in the car Jinnah, ever alert to details, has already won a small victory. He was delighted when Gandhi suggested that they go to Viceregal Lodge together, and even more so when the Mahatma offered to pick him up on the way. It seemed a satisfactory kind of deference for Gandhi to come to him. So Gandhi, who had been staying further away at Summer Hill with a wealthy supporter, drove to The Yarrows in a borrowed car, expecting Jinnah to climb in. But when he arrived Jinnah insisted that they then drive on in *his* car. Gandhi, typically, was completely indifferent to such niceties and was happy to get into any car with anyone in order to further the cause of swaraj for Indians. So Jinnah pulled away from his own house in his own car, driven by his chauffeur, with Gandhi as his guest.

Jinnah thus already had some cause for satisfaction as the car murmured its way up the Mall, but neither he nor Gandhi was ultimately to gain much else from their trip that day.

Gandhi was closeted with the Viceroy for around two hours, during which he offered his (moral) support for the Allied cause against Hitlerism. But he stressed that he spoke as an individual, not for the Congress. This was his usual line and it was sincere enough, though it regularly frustrated those with whom he was dealing, because it made it hard for them to know whether they were in the process of agreeing a deal with the Indian National Congress, or were listening to no more than personal opinions. This was how Gandhi always conducted his indoor politics, quietly and simply.

Jinnah had a much shorter meeting with Linlithgow, who immediately beforehand had received a message from Sikandar Hayat Khan, premier of the province of Punjab, asking him not to 'inflate' Jinnah or do anything that might make him harder to handle within the world of Muslim politics. Jinnah was still obliged to endure such humiliations because he had yet to work out his destiny as undisputed leader of all India's Muslims. He told the Viceroy flatly that the Congress would not stand by the British during the war, advised him to turn out the eight Congress provincial ministries and asked for some concessions to secure Muslim loyalties.

The contrast was clear. Gandhi was left indecisive by the outbreak of hostilities, and all through the war he remained mired in moral paradoxes arising from his commitment to non-violence and his opposition to both imperialism and fascism. Jinnah, however, was immediately looking for ways to turn the situation to his advantage. Then, with the flexibility of one mind against many, he out-bluffed, out-waited and out-thought his opponents. Over the next seven years Gandhi slowly lost a national political party while Jinnah built one.

The centrepiece of Congress philosophy had always been that the march towards Independence was a collective journey towards a collective destination. The Second World War advanced this common cause only indirectly, but six years of global conflict allowed Jinnah the opportunity to turn that cause into a personal journey, in a vehicle of his own choosing, with himself at the wheel.

The two met for the last time on 5 May 1947 at Jinnah's house in Delhi, but by then both had lost control of the wider political agenda. Gandhi's writ no longer ran in Congress circles, and Jinnah, though the undisputed leader of his own party, had lost a series of crucial arguments once the Viceroy, Lord Mountbatten, and the Congress leader, Jawaharlal Nehru, had both accepted that Partition was inevitable and best done quickly. This last meeting of Gandhi and Jinnah was, therefore, their least significant. As the old adversaries talked that day, a plan for the division of India was lying on a table in London awaiting Cabinet approval, and that plan did not conform to the aspirations of either man – Gandhi opposed Partition with all his being, and Jinnah was not to be given the six provinces he had originally demanded for the Muslims.

Soon afterwards, in a process that had elements of both triumph and tragedy, two new countries that came to embody the most fundamental differences between the two men were born, differences that concerned much more than the basic fact that one was born a Hindu and the other a Muslim.

Gandhi always defined himself by his opposition to colonialism, while Jinnah was defined primarily by his opposition to Gandhi. A clear hierarchy of constructive and reactive purposes has distinguished India and Pakistan ever since their foundation – Jinnah's narrower focus left Pakistan crucially short of positive aspirations, other than not to be a colonial or a Hindu state. This was hardly enough; by 1950, neither was India. The new Indian Constitution, agreed upon that year, grew naturally out of the anti-colonial struggle waged by the Congress. Pakistan still awaits a stable political structure, mostly because a natural constitutional extension of the country's founding principle – national self-determination for Muslims – has been hard to find. Gandhi's optimism gave India a broad and inclusive conception of nationhood, whereas Jinnah's pessimism bequeathed to Pakistan a narrow and defensive brand of nationalism. Jinnah was a sincere liberal, but too few among his wider following were natural liberals or had any interest in or sympathy for liberalism. All this has left Pakistan insufficiently defended against a tendency to revert to forms of autocratic government.

India, created by collective leadership and built on principles of diversity and tolerance, has become a country addicted to debate; Pakistan, the product of fear, single-mindedness and hero-worship, has become a country marked by intolerance and inclined to authoritarianism.

India was fortunate to inherit the best of Gandhi. Pakistan has had to make do with the worst of Jinnah.

Part 1
Political Foundations

The extended confrontation between Mohammed Ali Jinnah (1876–1948) and Mohandas Karamchand Gandhi (1869–1948) was one of the great dramas of the twentieth century. For nearly three decades these two remarkable men were locked in a series of political battles that involved opposing views of individuals, communities, states and nations – even the cosmos. The two had contrasting styles of leadership, lifestyle and presentation that reflected very different attitudes towards political power, and to what it can and cannot do. The stakes were high, and the eventual outcome not only created South Asia's two principal nation states, but also shaped their political and social character, and has had a direct influence on wider geopolitical concerns, including superpower relations, nuclear proliferation and the development of international terrorism.

This extraordinary tale has generated an enormous amount of historical commentary, much of which has been unashamedly biased and has simply sustained the conflicts it retells. In the process, the two characters at the centre of the story are regularly robbed of their humanity in various ways, becoming anything from saintly and infallible heroes to scheming villains, or witless stooges of foreign powers and sinister vested interests. In other words, they are often turned into much more or much less than the real human beings that they actually were.

As leaders and thinkers, Jinnah and Gandhi deserve full appreciation of their talents, clear assessments of their objectives and measured criticism of their weaknesses. Sadly, these basic courtesies have been denied them rather too often. Gandhi has been relentlessly over-praised and Jinnah has attracted few apologists outside circles as willing to rewrite history as to understand its complexities.

The differences between the two as personalities and leaders were real and deep, but they can easily become lost in the specifics of particular political controversies. Their opposing positions over Pakistan were not based purely on incompatible definitions of nationalism, but rested on massive supporting structures of conflicting ideas about the nature of liberation and the appropriate place of politics within the life of the individual and the nation. The existence of these very important, though often overlooked, philosophical systems indicate that the enduring antagonism between Jinnah and Gandhi was not determined purely by the struggle for Indian Independence. That struggle elevated the two men to national status and became the theatre in which they played out their political lives. But it did not create their differences; it merely served to exacerbate them. The two men were distinct and fully fashioned characters that would have disagreed on a wide range of topics in any place or era.

How, then, can we build an understanding of them? Gandhi was always keen to explain himself, and his *Collected Works*, in 92 printed volumes[1], give a candid picture of the man and his ideas.[2] But where Gandhi was prolific and self-critical, Jinnah was reticent and defensive. The keys to Jinnah's thoughts and deeds lie buried in more than 600 volumes of Muslim League documentation. He left no autobiography or political testament that might reveal the private thoughts behind the public persona, and his letters, which might be expected to give glimpses of the inner man, were generally written to convey instructions or to recap recent events in a particular light. Nearly everything he said or wrote was highly 'political', and many of his words were designed by their clever author to defy exact interpretation. Our understanding of him, therefore, has to be based largely on his recorded public actions and the speeches he used to justify them.

This book seeks to provide angles of approach to the massive body of historical data that has accumulated around the Jinnah–Gandhi struggle, and to suggest ways of clarifying rather than complicating or distorting the various official narratives and the frequently contradictory personal accounts from contemporaries that have come down to us. It will attempt to show that Jinnah was more principled but less gifted as a leader than he is conventionally portrayed, and that Gandhi's significance was much more political than his image suggested. It will also show how the two men made their way to the centre of Indian politics in very different ways, how those journeys affected their actions and decisions and eventually determined the very different things they wanted by the end of British rule.

Fundamentals

How did a moralist and social reformer like Gandhi ever become a national political leader? How could Jinnah start out as an admirer of John Morley's *On Compromise*[3], an eloquent exposition of secular Western liberalism, yet end up as an obdurate Muslim nationalist? The answers do not lie in fine details.

The essential point about Gandhi is that he anchored his thinking at a very personal level. 'The individual is the one supreme consideration,' he wrote in *Young India* in 1924.[4] His great national campaigns were rooted in common personal experience, not high political principle. Self-reliance, self-sufficiency and self-control were always at the heart of his political activities. He was profoundly uninterested in the details of grandiose political structures and he always focused on the individual elements in any political situation. This explains his faith in personal appeals, to viceroys, to Jinnah and even Hitler. If Hitler could be made to change his mind then war could be avoided. This was quite logical to Gandhi, and he felt no shame in trying to avert war in Europe by writing a personal letter. It was not only not absurd, but it was also absolutely consistent with everything he ever did. He was a pioneer of the idea that the personal is the political, though he never used those words. Here lies the reason why he always talked of the importance of a 'change of heart'. Quite correctly, he supposed that all political actions have a personal dimension and originate in individual hearts and minds.

Gandhi worked forwards and upwards from the microscopic, personal level; hence all his worries about sexual behaviour and diet. Jinnah, however, worked backwards and downwards from grand notions and, like most modern politicians, he had no great concern with the personal realm. In line with these contrasting approaches, Gandhi tended to sustain warm friendships with many people across the political spectrum. Jinnah, by contrast, made few close bonds, and seemed almost unconcerned about maintaining the few that he had. This indifference damaged him enormously in the longer term, because reminiscences about Gandhi that have come down to us have been generally favourable, whereas Jinnah tended to accumulate more and more detractors.

One can represent this as simply the indifference of a great man to the small details of social conviviality, but it demonstrates a real difference between the two men. Gandhi was grounded, a man who literally sat on the floor to eat with guests, to whom he was unfailingly courteous, were they friend or foe. Jinnah remained aloof, in his house on Malabar Hill, untroubled by what others thought about him. India can be a dusty, windy place, and the two men were like earth and air; Gandhi understood the dust that Jinnah, for the most part, was only concerned to blow around.

One popular perception of Gandhi is that of a mystic dreamer who blithely wandered into the harsh world of politics, in which he strove to remain fastidiously holy and which he ultimately failed to understand. This view is mistaken. Gandhi understood politics very well, but he also had an acute sense of the limitations of political action. The idea that he had no grasp of politics is at heart a Western view, born of an inability to classify his thinking in Western terms. It would be an error rooted in chauvinism to assume that because he had no specific Western political locus, he was not a proper politician.

Gandhi stood at a good distance from any recognizable Western '-isms'. He was only concerned with personal and national reformation, which in his view were the same thing. He disliked party politics as divisive, and as a political leader he always insisted that he was representing himself rather than anybody else. He listened inwards to his conscience, not outwards to his supporters; he never sought office. Political opponents were often unable to make sense of this strange mixture of egocentricity and selflessness. Most of them considered him to be either a saint who had stumbled into public life by mistake, or a crafty charlatan who could not be trusted because he was not trying to do the usual sorts of deals.

Jinnah on the other hand was a highly conventional politician, and can take no credit for original political thinking at any point. His -isms were nationalism and liberalism. He began his career thinking within an 'Indian' framework, in the sense of nationalist opposition to British rule; later, he renamed India's Muslim community a 'nation' and continued his opposition from a narrower base. His resistance to colonialism, then Hindu majority rule, were both for the sake of liberal values – self-determination and political rights. It is thus entirely possible to read Jinnah in Western terms, despite the Muslim label, while it is absolutely not possible to read Gandhi in this way. Ironically, it is Gandhi that has generally attracted more Western attention.

The exact relationship between Gandhi's spiritual beliefs and his desire to achieve concrete political ends is certainly hard to define precisely, and he struggled to do this himself. In his own words, he was 'a politician trying my hardest to be a saint', and not vice versa. The key to the Mahatma's political outlook lies in understanding that he was not concerned with states and nations so much as in the moral reform of individuals. This sets his political aims well apart from those of Jinnah, who habitually thought in terms of constitutions and states. These themes run through the whole of the careers and philosophies of the two men, and it is essential to state this and lay out its implications at the start of any attempt to understand the narrative of their interactions.

In common with the academic physics of the times, which dealt with the smallest particles of matter, Gandhi's 'experiments with truth' were aimed at the smallest scale of human experience. Thinkers such as John Locke, Jean-Jacques Rousseau or Karl Marx were like the Isaac Newtons of political thought, laying down laws about the behaviour of humanity in large groups, whereas Gandhi was concerned with the small human interactions that combined to produce larger effects. He was always trying to get to the quantum level of politics, which was personal, ethical reform.

Where others were thinking about the Indian 'nation', Gandhi was always thinking about individual Indians. Where others simply believed that Indians should be 'free', Gandhi was passionately concerned with what that freedom would actually mean, in practical terms, for the people that were about to receive it. Liberation is what Gandhi preached; liberation from the British, but also the release of individuals from their lower nature. The political objective was swaraj – self-rule, with the associated and deeper meaning of personal self-control. He was determined that any freedom won by the nation should also amount to individual liberation. To drive out the British in the name of freedom only to continue to live in an exploitative, materialistic society did not strike him as a victory worth the winning. To create a new India in which Indians only oppressed one another like the British had oppressed them, to perpetuate the same system except run by Indians, would only be to build what Gandhi dismissively called 'Englistan'[5]. Of what use was political liberation if it brought no spiritual benefits? For him, the Independence struggle was to allow rediscovery of the virtues of simple rural society, in which individuals were not driven to compete, but instead looked after one another.

Gandhi always worked from small to large, from inside to outside, from personal issues and moral reformation to practical political measures. This is why he seemed so amenable in detailed negotiations, while holding on to what other politicians thought of as rather dreamy generalities. Jinnah always worked backwards from structures because he had a standard liberal faith in human progress through correct laws and institutions, though he was fairly modest in his ambitions. He expected Pakistan to be a better place than a Congress-run India, but mostly in the sense that Muslims would not be oppressed by Hindus. He did not expect Muslims to behave very differently in Pakistan.

This would never have been Gandhi's way. He thought human beings would get a better government by behaving better. Jinnah saw all this from the other end of the telescope, and was therefore always at the mercy of the liberal politician's standard cry in times of stress and failure: 'Bring me some better people so that I may improve their lives!' Gandhi would not have recognized that as any kind of sensible strategy. When he found that his people were not good enough in 1922 he did not complain, but merely called off the Non-Cooperation

Movement and resolved to work harder to create the better people he needed to recruit.

The appreciation of small things was the principle that gave Gandhi such a strong feeling of the profound connection between means and ends. Most politicians, and certainly all great exponents of high causes, are equivocal about this; Jinnah certainly was. But for Gandhi this was an issue of prime and central importance, touching on the deepest of 'natural' laws. No good thing could grow out of bad, and truth was indivisible. Therefore, good ends could only ever result from good means. Good means might not always succeed quickly or completely, but this was not sufficient reason to embrace evil or to stray from the path of truth.

Jinnah was committed to ends without great regard to means. His 'end' was always the protection of the Muslim community, but his chosen means changed as British India was dismantled. Initially, he placed his trust in electoral safeguards and weighted representative bodies; later, in separatism. A correct appreciation of this long-term flexibility resolves the difficulties surrounding his change of allegiance from the Congress to the Muslim League, which should never have become a riddle that could only be resolved by imputing a deep level of perfidy to the man. At no point after 1909 did Jinnah not represent Muslims and he never abandoned his obligations to them. This is a basic consistency running through his career. The central point is that in 1937 he changed his tactics, not his objective. He intended to protect the Muslims of India, to develop their interests as a community, and in this he never wavered. The betrayal, or reversal, or desertion in his life was the rejection of broad Indian nationalism as a means to promote the best interests of Muslims; this only occurred after direct personal experience had convinced him that Congress-style nationalism was not broad, but 'Hindu'.

This aspect has been repeatedly overlooked by two main types of observers. First, those Indian patriots who blame him for Partition and can see no good in him, and who therefore label him a turncoat or a calculating demagogue. Second, the broad group of Pakistani patriots who are unwilling to believe that the country they admire could have been anything but the creation of a man who saw it as a vehicle for the will of God. But Jinnah did not have to see Pakistan as anything much more than a haven for Muslims, where they would be free of Hindu raj. This bolthole was not necessary under a British-led non-democratic regime, and it was not necessary within some sort of devolved federal Indian Union. But under the heavily centralized model of India pursued by the Congress he felt that the only way to preserve Muslim security was somewhere outside Congress control.

He was in equal measure an advocate and a politician. Both callings require the presentation of opinions with which one does not necessarily identify, heart and soul. Both are about jockeying for position with words, pushing or even bending the rules and making deals or bargains. This means that it has become all too easy to discredit or undermine almost anything Jinnah ever said, and to accuse him of insincerity, deception or ambition. There are inconsistencies in his career – it would be hard not to make the odd loop in 40 years of exceptionally complicated politics in a rapidly changing world – but his conduct can be represented as possessing a recognizable inner coherence.

Jinnah can be understood as a Muslim community leader from the very start of his political career. He was always, in some sense, on the Muslim side of the fence. He was born a Muslim; he sat for a Muslim constituency from 1909; he introduced a bill relating to Muslim family interests in 1911; he joined the Muslim League in 1913, after reassurances that it had adopted truly nationalist objectives. The fact that he was determined to promote and secure good relations with Hindus does not invalidate his original concerns. On the contrary, it reinforces the case for his sincerity.

He started out strongly committed to the idea of a multi-faith, modern Indian nation, as visualized by Congress leaders such as Dadabhai Naoroji and Gopal Krishna Gokhale, both of whom he came to know well. As a young man he preferred this Congress vision to either the archaic, feudal conception of India still retained by many Muslims who stayed away from the Congress's modernism and wished to live in traditional Islamic purity, or the conservative view promoted by Vedic enthusiasts who were pressing for a spiritual revival and the expulsion of foreign influences. Liberal nationalism was his creed, and like most of his fellow Congress members he hoped to see his country run by Indian gentlemen who would build a tolerant, diverse, modern country. Hidden in this broad picture was his own particular niche, as a defender of and spokesman for the sectional community he represented.

The causes Jinnah took up through his career were based on movable definitions of identity (Indian, Muslim), or on free personal choices (liberalism). Gandhi, on the other hand, never addressed some variable or voluntary quality in his listener; he aimed his words at their spiritual core, whether they were peasants or viceroys. As a religious man he believed in the existence of a soul within everyone, and he spoke to that part, seeking that all-important change of heart. Jinnah was by choice a liberal, and liberalism is not prescriptive; it speaks to the self-interest of individuals and relies on the aggregated rational choices of whole populations to create good outcomes. Self-interest was always at the heart of Jinnah's schemes. Gandhi was not a liberal. He expected truth to be the driver of beneficial change – his concept of truth included 'love' and 'God', and the motivation he wished to awaken was never a narrow or a selfish thing.

Both men were, in a sense, preoccupied with liberation from injustice, but the words meant very different things to them. Gandhi was concerned with the injustice of all men to all others, whereas Jinnah was concerned with the injustices of a particular majority to a particular minority. Gandhi's methods meant that his style of liberation – dharma raj – could be found anywhere. Jinnah's guaranteed that his could only be found in Pakistan.

Gandhi was perhaps the twentieth century's greatest anti-collectivist thinker. This is why his teachings have proved so transportable. All over the world people have found inspiration in his thoughts and actions because of the inclusiveness of his classifications – humanity as one whole, but with each individual also autonomous and responsible. His ideas relate to anyone, anywhere. His credentials as an 'Indian nationalist' are therefore somewhat misleading. He was a sort of nationalist, but only insofar as he thought that India should be ruled by Indians. This, however, was not a dogmatic or theoretical commitment, but a natural and necessary part of moral responsibility and self-control. Swaraj always had a greater and a lesser meaning for him.

GANDHI, INDIA AND ECONOMICS

Gandhi took a radically alternative approach to nationality. The British constantly told the people of India that there was no such thing as 'an Indian', but he was able to show them a new sort of nationality in visual form. Hitherto the British had been content with their own version of 'Indianness'. They liked India's princes and palaces, ancientness and complexity, all of which had been seized on by scholars and awarded seriousness and dignity. But these things were of no use to Gandhi in his attempt to offer accessible unity to the masses. So Gandhi's new Indianness was something that ordinary people could easily recognize. He would have nothing to do with silk or jewels, elephants or howdahs, tulwars or durbars, tigers or shikar. Instead Gandhi elevated to public view the most simple, unornamented thing about India that he could find: homespun cloth, of which he then wore as little as possible, in a visual statement that avoided all excess and luxury – two things that the British also associated with the Orient.

By doing this he managed to avoid the European style of historic and ethnic nationalism that so easily becomes mired in tortuous definitions. Instead, he adopted a contemporary, geographical approach, and simply accepted that the Indian nation was made up of the people who lived in India. He did not seek to define Indianness in anything but the widest sense, charting a course between two more exclusive definitions that appeared in Indian political life through this period – the 'Hindutva' philosophy that first appeared in Vinayak Savarkar's 1923 pamphlet *Hindutva: Who is a Hindu?*, and Jinnah's new local Muslim identity, which hardened into a version of 'nationality' somewhere around 1937–38.

There was no discriminatory force at work within Gandhi's nationalism. He did not even dislike the British on any abstract or generalized basis. He just thought that they had no right to be governing India and were doing a great deal of harm by continuing to do so. Nor did he have any strong denominational sense of religion, and he chose to pick up the best of what the world could offer. The Hinduism he practised was a form of world syncretism; if a spiritual idea were of any value it would be found in 'his' Hinduism. At his prayer meetings he insisted on having readings from the Qur'an, and this was one of the features that enraged his eventual assassin. He worked backwards from the idea of one God within us all, and felt that the imperfections of Man were written into all religions. No people were perfect, therefore no religion was perfect, and there could be no scale of merit between them.

Although a passionate believer in justice and social equity, he avoided standard Western forms of these ideas as defined in political creeds such as socialism. Indeed he denied the idea at the very heart of socialism, namely, that the poor should share in the uneven gains that industrial society produces. Gandhi simply thought that material prosperity was a snare. Whereas socialism embraces economic complexity and requires social micro-engineering to run it, Gandhi replaced all these technicalities with an admiration for the uncomplicated lifestyle of the rural poor, or what he called 'voluntary simplicity'. Were this adopted, then sarvodaya – general uplift – would result, both materially (a little) and spiritually (a lot). Following Gandhi's way was not going to make the masses wealthy, and he never gave out that message. He was not preaching Western-style redemption through material accumulation; he was promoting a path towards contentment without reference to material conditions. In his view poverty, in the sense of deprivation, was not good – and was indeed a form of violence – but material prosperity was not a great deal better. Simplicity, community and contentment with small things were his messages. He had no wish to pursue industrial and materialistic models in a free India.

Gandhi made no distinction between economics and ethics, which paralleled his view of the inseparable connection of means and ends. This constant blurring of lines and redefinition of political concepts challenged and recast conventional political wisdom. Gandhism as a system of ideas is radically holistic, and carries the stamp of genius, in that it is irrefutable within its own terms.

Politics without economics is considered an impossibility in modern democracies, in which the bulk of the electorate wishes to be richer. But Gandhi was not attempting to woo an enfranchised mass electorate; he was trying to speak for a mass constituency of rural poverty. Gandhi's politics were not specifically electoral politics, but they were *mass* politics. Individual reformation is simply that – individual. Millions of individual reformations, however, must add up to massive social change. That was his aim.

JINNAH, PAKISTAN AND LIBERTY

The question is often asked how the main advocate of Pakistan – Jinnah – could ever have taken up such a cause after starting his political career as a convinced Indian nationalist, garlanded by Hindus and Parsis within the Congress for his lack of sectarian feeling. This question can be answered all through the narrative of Jinnah's life in small steps. There was no abrupt break, turning point or conversion. Most importantly, the course of his career is distorted if we neglect to see him as approaching Congress politics from the Muslim side. His origin in the Muslim community was the one aspect of himself that he could never change, and at no stage did he attempt to hide his concern for the advancement of the conditions of Muslims, specifically for the attainment of *equality* for Muslims. This was not the side of his politics that fell away. It was his trust in the good faith of Hindus at large that failed him.

Jinnah becomes rather more consistent if we reframe his lifelong ideals by emphasizing that he was an anti-imperialist. There was much that he loved about Britain and British culture – like liberalism, Shakespeare and marmalade – but this did nothing to undermine his conviction that British rule in India was unjust and insupportable. The best way to be rid of it was to unite the Indian nation. This was his Congress side, his general side. But he also insisted on the full inclusion of all Indians in the new dispensation, and from a personal angle he was a natural advocate of Muslim interests. He was anti-colonial and pro-Muslim all his life. Everything else became a matter of tactical assessment.

Pushing the personal angle a little further, we can see that he did not wish to be ruled by other people – the British, feudal Muslims, Hindus – at any point in his career. He wanted to be free. This was the quality of Islam that he always emphasized above all others – that under Islam a man was free, whereas under Hinduism, with its rules of caste and dharma, a man was not. Under Islam everyone was equal; under brahmin rule they were not. Jinnah gradually became unable to see India as an open field for liberal ideas. He began to fear that with the advance of democratic institutions, and especially after the British were gone, it would become a closed system under a regime that threatened to be unequal and unfree. This can serve well enough as a consistent motivation to explain the train of events that resulted.

Satyagraha

Gandhi tried to avoid dogmatism when it came to politics, economics, nationalism and religion. But there was one overarching idea about which he would not compromise – non-violence or ahimsa. It has remained the idea most closely associated with him.

All the lines of Gandhi's thinking converge on the concept of non-violence. For him it was the key to moral elevation. It opened up a complete way of life, because the violence he wished to avoid was not just the direct gross assaults perpetrated by individuals or institutions – it included poverty, industrialization and the mistreatment of animals. In 1939 he called it 'the law of regenerate man'[6]. Correctly understood and assiduously practised, non-violence would produce answers to all the world's problems more surely and more directly than any messianic political or sectarian religious creed could hope to. From the small, a large entity would grow; the good would bring forth more good things. Non-violence was a comprehensive concept that conditioned his attitude to every other aspect of his work. It directly connected the spheres of political protest and revolutionary social change.

The people, he believed, would be elevated and educated by the desire for Independence and would eventually overcome not just their oppressors but also oppressive parts of themselves. It was this that would create the new India. He was sure that through a just struggle waged in a spiritually pure manner the masses could rid themselves of their base instincts – to compete, accumulate, copulate and drink alcohol. A simpler life would result, and it would be more than enough. Most importantly, there would be no step change between the struggle and the world that emerged from it. There would be no weapons to lay down, no passions to put aside and no stores of vengeance laid up.

Gandhi acknowledged a debt to Henry David Thoreau and Leo Tolstoy for the idea of 'passive resistance', but he took the concept rather further because he did not wish resistance to remain purely passive. Silent acquiescence in the face of injustice was to be avoided, as too similar to cowardice, for which he reserved a special contempt. He believed that protest should be active and vigorous. To resist injustice without doing further harm was the objective. The creation of political pressure through non-violent means was his aim, and his activism in South Africa led him to develop satyagraha – mass protest designed not only to accomplish political ends, but to achieve spiritual transformation too.

Satyagraha – 'truth force' – used ahimsa to challenge injustice in an organized, disciplined way. It required a body of men and women committed to the principles of non-violence, who had the strength of character to endure suffering for the greater good. Satyagraha was a route to liberation from colonial oppression, but it was also a purpose in itself. It was a pilgrimage, a sacrifice, an education. This style of mass mobilization was consciously intended to lay the groundwork for social revolution, and in this he profoundly differed from Jinnah.

Gandhi conceived of violence as an offence against truth, a view that had deep roots in Hindu spiritual traditions. The Sanskrit word 'satya' – truth – is linked to the word 'sat' – 'to be'. Philosophically, he accepted that what is, is true. In religious terms he believed that what is, is God. In sum, this means that 'Truth is another form of God'[7]. God is in us all and we can only save ourselves by remaining in concert with divine truth, which he also understood as love: 'Love and truth are two faces of the same coin'[8]. None of the standard justifications for violent action in pursuit of political ends moved him in the least. He thought that the Congress 'Extremists', who believed violence was justified as part of the liberation struggle, were misguided. Fighting violence with violence is like fighting wrong with more wrong, thus compounding the evil without introducing the good. For Gandhi, evil could only be conquered by superior virtue, not superior force. All the excuses for violent actions – that they are only in self-defence, that they are essential remedies to reverse injustice, that nations are entitled to fight for freedom – did not address the central point. These kinds of arguments were, and still are, largely expansions of the theme: 'They started it.' Gandhi's point was that, regardless of who started it, it should be our concern to finish it.

Gandhian non-violence was part of a wide, interconnected set of views about the world and the universe, including vegetarianism, celibacy, pacifism, animal husbandry and mechanization. It was not a narrow 'strategy' because it did not actually matter whether it was 'successful' or not, although he believed that it always would be successful, because non-violence touches the essential humanity in all of us, oppressors and oppressed alike. The discipline of non-violence was reaching for the good in a good way and was therefore a direct path to self-improvement, even if political progress was not an immediate result. Lack of instant political results did not matter because Gandhi was utterly committed to the idea that ends and means are connected at a very deep level. Sincere non-violence cannot possibly produce any harm because anger, evil and revenge are neutralized and dissolved by non-violence, and are only sustained by violence. For him, non-violence was 'complete innocence', and in its 'active form' nothing less than 'pure love'[9].

In a wider context, to achieve national liberation through violence was to risk a range of negative and destructive outcomes. Gandhi fervently wanted a better India than the one the British had created. The seed and the tree are connected, and the India he wished to live in could not be born from violence; that would not ennoble the liberated people and would leave a residue of malevolent consequences.

Gandhi, therefore, absolutely required moral purity among his disciples in action. Through their struggle they would be reborn spiritually, and not only them – the true wonder of correctly executed satyagraha was that it would also eventually win over the enemy and make him aware of his sin. When violence met true spiritual love, wickedness would drain away and moral reform could begin. Thus mass disobedience was not just a way to expel the British, it would regenerate the former colonial masters too, while morally elevating the Indian people.

All this was deeply original thinking and challenged several contemporary Western ideas. It was a detailed mirror image of fascism, which worshipped violence, stressed the ennobling effects of war and taught that the weak should be extirpated. Gandhi reversed all these concepts. In what he called the 'dictionary'[10] of satyagraha, he also redefined the meanings of success, failure and enemy.

Gandhi's non-violence resembles the Christian doctrine of 'turning the other cheek', and he fully recognized the parallel. He enjoyed pointing out that Jesus was an Asiatic,[11] like himself. But Gandhi was not a Christian, and was never close to adopting formal Christianity, although the ethical teachings of Jesus were completely to his taste. Committed Christians, such as Charles Freer Andrews, tended to see signs of Christianity within him. Andrews, an Anglican priest and Congress sympathiser, became a lifelong friend and companion after meeting Gandhi in South Africa, and was instrumental in persuading Gandhi to return to India in 1915. Andrews understood non-violence from a Christian perspective, and was sufficiently dedicated to the idea to oppose Gandhi's recruiting activities during the First World War.

Apart from the basic message of love though, there is no evidence that Gandhi ever took to the complicated superstructure of Christian doctrine. Any overlap between Christian Puritanism and Gandhi's ascetic life and general revulsion from sex were purely coincidental; Puritans have always been quite happy about sex within marriage, whereas Gandhi was not.

His concept of 'sin', a word he used a great deal, was nothing like the Christian view. He simply equated sin with gratification of the senses, with selfishness and uselessness – a degradation of the higher motivations available to all. This sense of the harmfulness of self-indulgence crossed the whole spectrum of human experience, from consumerism, to pride, to lust. He believed that carnal urges were a distraction from public service and an aberration from the ideal life of universal love for all. A world built around a closed relationship between two people was not a worthy or estimable thing; it was no more than self-indulgence.

He had absolutely no belief in the tainted or 'fallen' nature of Man. On the contrary, he persistently expounded his faith in human nature and humanity.

It was this absolutely immovable faith that so often led him into what looked like strange concessions to opponents, because he believed that the best must be brought out of people, and that fighting could never do this. To give power to someone else was to allow them to act better, to *be* better. Thus he was quite happy to offer Jinnah the premiership of the Interim Government in 1947, for he had no fear of the consequences. Non-violence was the best way to reveal and empower people's better natures. Oppressed people should resist their oppressors, not solely to 'defeat' them but also to show them their errors. This profound conviction underlay all of his political thinking.

Non-violence as a political programme had the merit of being both simple and largely self-explanatory. But it was not without its detractors. Ahimsa is a recognizable part of traditional Indian culture, inherited primarily from Jains and Buddhists, but it is not a canonical Hindu virtue or obligation. It is a matter of some sensitivity to Hindu nationalists that the tradition of martial vigour within Hinduism has been lost, swamped by the Gandhian interpretation. Certainly, the Extremists within the Congress had no trouble accommodating the idea of violent struggle into their vision of national revival. For instance, Bal Gangadhar Tilak was fully prepared to use violence as part of the liberation struggle, and to emphasize the tradition of Shivaji alongside that of the saints and sages more frequently associated with Hinduism, at least by the British. The dharma of a kshatriya is of course to be a warrior, and a non-violent warrior would have certain potentially contradictory issues to resolve. Nationalist and philosopher Aurobindo Ghose also felt, on a more conceptual level, that a fully mature philosophy must have the courage to encounter, absorb and co-opt violence before it could consider itself complete. His 'Integral Yoga' accepted that violence was part of the natural order of things, and he considered that to ignore it or to refuse to understand it would only produce a lopsided philosophy that was neither complete – 'integrated' – nor truly courageous.

The whole concept of non-violence also opened Gandhi up to a set of accusations about inconsistency. The most obvious of these was his support for Britain in the First World War, during which he worked actively to recruit soldiers for the King–Emperor's armies. This he defended on two grounds: that accepting the benefits of living within the Empire imposed an obligation to fight for its cause and that rallying to the defence of the Empire was a way to win swaraj more quickly. How this fitted with the notion that only bad things can come out of violence was not clear, but he thought that the greater good was being served by fighting for the Empire, which stood, in his judgement, for freedom. But in general, he dismissed all accusations of inconsistency on this subject by pointing out that he did not believe, like Tolstoy, that non-violence was a rigid code. He clarified his position by saying that non-violence was always better than violence, without being mandatory in all cases. This was tied to his insistence that the use of violence was preferable to cowardice, under all circumstances. Cowardice was more a betrayal of truth than the use of violence, because in the heart of a coward, ethical priorities have already died, whereas they have at least a chance to outlive and overcome violent actions. Abhayata – lack of cowardice – allows the growth of truthfulness. Fearlessness brings strength.

A more serious charge against non-violence as a political tool was that it was unrealistic, that ruthless opponents would surely overwhelm it. Gandhi thought that if tyrants and dictators were genuinely confronted with non-violent resistance on a sufficiently massive scale then they could have no power. As a practical argument this would, of course, be correct, but he also believed that no one could remain unaffected in an encounter with genuine ahimsa. He was entirely consistent in this, and in the case of India he could claim to have been proved right by events. The British did leave, though not immediately, and they were less violent than perhaps they might have been if confronted with more force. How things might have gone elsewhere is hard to know because at the time no other leader had deployed ahimsa on remotely the same scale.

Proof of the power of non-violent political action, however, is not to be found on paper. It has its vindication in the non-violent reform movements that have succeeded at various times since his death, in America, South Africa, all over Eastern Europe at the time of the fall of the Berlin Wall, in the 2011 Spring Revolt in Egypt, and more mundanely in the thousands of demonstrations, sit-ins, mass trespasses and peaceful protests that have been staged for all sorts of political, environmental and social causes all over the world. It is, in most cases, now the norm for protests.

The Two-Nation Theory

While Gandhi pitched his ideas at the universal level, Jinnah only laid claim to one great truth – and it was markedly local in time and place. He maintained that India contained two distinct 'nations', Hindu and Muslim, and that they were incapable of living together.

This idea can be traced at least as far back as the late nineteenth century and the thoughts of educator and politician Sir Syed Ahmad Khan (1817–98), who used the word 'nation' to describe the Muslims of India. However, he never followed through to Jinnah's conclusions about the impossibility of cohabitation, and was happy to conclude that India's two 'nations' should share the land they lived in. Syed Ahmad's main concern was to point out the unhelpful nature, for Muslims, of any demand for mass democracy, and his separatism largely confined itself to the need to provide special education for Muslims to give them access to the benefits of employment within the government of British India.

From 1909 to 1935, a great deal of Indian politics was concerned with designing constitutional arrangements to relieve the permanent minority status of Muslims (and others) in the new electoral systems that the British were introducing. This was a time during which Jinnah never spoke of separateness or separation. On the contrary, he made a long series of attempts to reach an agreement with the Congress to ensure that the minority status of Muslims would not be institutionalized into permanent exclusion from influence and office. Various schemes for forms of separation began to appear from the early 1930s, notably by poet–philosopher Muhammad Iqbal, and Jinnah referred to the

Muslim minority as a 'separate entity in the state'[12] in a speech in the Legislative Assembly in early 1935. But it was only in 1937 that Jinnah himself publicly adopted the language of Two Nations.

The theory itself was very simple. It was five words, Jinnah told the British writer Beverley Nichols in 1942: 'The Muslims are a nation.'[13] Muslims, the theory claimed, were so different in terms of language, custom, law, dress, calendar, inheritance, architecture, disposal of the dead, music, diet – and, of course, religious beliefs – that they could not live together with other faiths, particularly not Hindus. Jinnah claimed that by all standards of international recognition, India's Muslims were entitled to the status and dignity of a nation. That was about as far as the positive argument went, and the theory never explored the trickier areas that this line of reasoning opened up. The most obvious of these was that its central concept of 'nationality' was divorced from territory, and therefore did not easily permit the creation of international borders, a central element of statehood. This was glossed over by saying that the new Muslim nation would apply not wherever there was a Muslim but wherever Muslims were in a majority, although this did not deliver a consolidated national space either. The two major Muslim-majority areas were territorially compact, in the northwest, and in Bengal and parts of Assam in the northeast, but the insoluble problem in the 'majority nation' thesis was that it did not cater for India's other Muslims, at least a third, who lived in non-majority provinces. These Muslims would either not receive the protection required by their 'nationality', or they would have to move. This problem was not addressed when the first full political incarnation of the theory appeared in a resolution moved by Jinnah at the Muslim League's conference at Lahore in March 1940.

The Muslim minorities would have been the uppermost, immediate problem, had the British and the Congress ever agreed to any plan for local political separation, but there were other objections that greeted the theory the moment it reached the unforgiving arena of public examination. Some questions were intellectual – was its essence political or religious? – and some were strategic – did it require complete separation or was it only a bid for federation? Jinnah was never very clear on the practicalities, and remained so until around 1946 when the Cabinet Mission put some very searching questions to him along exactly these lines.

Through the intervening six years, an air of unreality surrounded the theory. Politicians could see that if Jinnah wanted to get Muslims away from Hindu domination then this was no comprehensive solution to the problem, because those Muslims left outside any newly created 'homeland' would be more outnumbered than before, while those in majority provinces were not at risk of Hindu domination in the first place. The geography of Muslim-majority areas was not contiguous, and this promised to make any new national state a patchwork that did not bode well for economic viability or rational defence.

But the theory had active political effects. Taken at face value, it was a direct declaration that Muslims simply *could not* live alongside their Hindu neighbours. This was not an accurate description of the past, but rather a warning for the future, because if, under democratic rule, Muslims came to believe that their lives were insupportable and that they were now permanently and necessarily at odds with those around them, then the consequences were incalculable. If Jinnah was demanding a Muslim space 'outside' India, then there would be all manner of problems, as outlined above. But if he was prepared to stay in, then the theory seemed over-pitched and dangerously divisive.

Congress leaders were highly critical. Jawaharlal Nehru pointed out that because Islam was a choice for individuals, two brothers in the same village might end up in different nations. But the theory did not just do violence to the unity of Indian nationality; 'Muslims' were not easily recognizable as a nation when regional variations were also considered. Most Bengalis felt that they had a distinct type of sub-nationality, based on culture and language, that was strong enough to elide Hindu–Muslim distinctions. In the northwest, the Pathans and Sindhis were extremely wary of possible domination by the populous Punjab, while Punjabis considered they had little in common with Bengalis. Then there was also a substratum of minority Muslim sects, which presented another form of potential division overlooked within the wider concept.

So the theory looked weak as a true description of Muslims in India, and it bore only a tenuous relation to the territorial 'Pakistan' that was being demanded from 1940 onwards. It also ran into problems over the relative claims of ethnicity and faith. Jinnah needed to place religious identity above ethnicity in order to counter the fact that most Indian Muslims were descended from converts and were, therefore, of identical stock to their Hindu neighbours. Jinnah was also forced to define his Muslim 'nation' broadly enough to include all of India's Muslims, who were a diverse lot, yet also narrowly enough so that he was not involved in some kind of supranational pan-Islamic movement. He was always in the tight corner of having to argue that, in international terms, his Muslims and his alone were in need of special treatment. But within India he had an opposite difficulty. In launching a religious model of nationality, he also opened up a channel for demands by other communities, principally the Sikhs, for separate political rights. These he disallowed, by referring to such other groups simply as 'sub-national'. Jinnah's Muslim nation was too distinct to fit into India, but remained scarcely visible internationally.

If these problems with the theory were so clear, then we need to ask two questions: why did Jinnah pursue it so vigorously, and why did the theory's expression – Pakistan – eventually attract such wide support within the Muslim community?

It is relatively easy to see the immediate political value of the Pakistan demand to Jinnah. Pakistan gave him a powerful cause and a prominent position as its leader, but it also offered opportunities to a host of other Muslims notables keen to be rid of Hindu competition. Arthur Lall, a distinguished former Indian diplomat, reveals in *The Emergence of Modern India* that Sir Firoz Khan Noon, a Punjabi grandee and eventual Prime Minster of Pakistan, told the author that 'he had not been in favour of the creation of Pakistan' but had hoped to do well out of it in terms of appointments.[14] Businessmen were also drawn to the opportunities presented by the new state, which offered the prospect of freeing themselves from the great Parsi–Hindu industrial complex. A new country that promised reserved employment and protected markets was attractive to a broad cross-section of ambitious Muslims all across India. Many of the landless middle classes were quite prepared to migrate, and did so in the event, especially from the United Provinces and Bihar.

And to simpler minds or more devout souls the idea of Muslim rule over Muslims had an irresistible attraction, no matter what the political small print in the deal.

In a wider sense, separatism, despite all its complications, became an attractive option as a potential Phase Three of the Muslim political experience in India. Most Muslims on the subcontinent had always been ruled either by other Muslims, or the British. But all Muslims now faced being ruled by Hindus, and many, for religious, political and economic reasons, did not savour the idea. Pakistan offered a way out.

Though Pakistan had its allure, Jinnah did not get an easy ride from all Muslims. Some scholars were unhappy with the idea that a 'homeland' for Muslims could be marked out in this political way. Within orthodox Islam, all the earth was God's, and to divide it up was effectively to deprive Him of His due in the rest of India, where there would still be Muslims. Some ulema therefore deemed it unacceptable, and possibly blasphemous. Others of a more pan-Islamic bent considered that the creation of Pakistan was a betrayal of the dream of a greater Islamic community. Conventionally, the 'nation' of Islam stands globally against the 'nation' of unbelievers. As such, Muslims could never constitute so narrow a concept as one nation among plural others. Yet another school of Islamic scholarship opposed Pakistan from the Congress side. Congress leader Maulana Azad thought that Pakistan would not solve the real problems experienced by Muslims in their daily lives, and that the creation of a separate country was not the best answer to poverty and underdevelopment. Staying in a Congress-led, religiously tolerant India, he believed, was a more promising way forward for India's disadvantaged Muslim masses.

Jinnah remained determined to rise above the critics and doubters by presenting his case in terms of national self-determination, as established by President Wilson's Fourteen Points of 1919, and this was why he was so insistent on using the word 'nation'. But deploying the word 'nation' did more than that. It solved the problem of minorities. If Muslims were actually a 'nation' trapped within British India, then they were entitled to special treatment, meaning separate representation. This was an insurance against being outvoted on a simple head count. But the extra attraction to the idea of a nation was that all nations are equal, regardless of their size. This was a key concept in international law, and one that was to legitimize Jinnah's demands after 1940 for not only separate electorates but for equal representation in any central Indian government. So for him the Muslims of India were, as he put it, 'a nation, miscalled a minority'[15] – a tenable idea as long as the concept of a nation could be applied with certainty to India's Muslims. This is what Jinnah fought so hard to establish. It was a way of safeguarding his people and of marking out equal rights for himself as their leader, at one stroke.

Jinnah produced a great many parallel cases for why the sort of separation he was demanding was feasible, and even beneficial. Spain and Portugal, Norway and Sweden, British India and Burma and, rather incongruously, Ireland were all pressed into service as witnesses that partitions created no ill effects and that separate states could coexist happily within larger geographical units. He also maintained that 'India' was a British myth, that India was not a country but a continent. Most cleverly, he confronted the question of captive minorities – Muslims left under Hindu rule, and Hindus and Sikhs stranded within Pakistan. These substantial 'hostage' communities, he claimed, were actually a strong point of the scheme and would ensure the smooth working of the entire project. They would, he believed, be a guarantee of good behaviour by both sides.

Ultimately, for all its quirks, the Two-Nation Theory turned out to be more of a self-fulfilling prophecy than an intellectually compelling idea. It held a deep attraction for enough of its intended audience to ensure that once it became familiar it acquired a force beyond intellectual persuasion. It also gradually lost correspondence with objective reality, and though undoubtedly convincing (and useful) in the short term, in the longer view it was proved conclusively wrong. Jinnah was compelled to insist that the Muslims of India possessed a single real identity, but he was mistaken. Pakistan has been ravaged by divisions, and the release from Hindu domination did not unearth a primal unity long buried by minority status. On the contrary, Muslim solidarity has been conspicuously lacking since 1947, perpetuated by the tendency for scholars to disagree, especially when given time to reflect and licence to differ.

The convenience of the theory was in its premise that India's Muslims were different from the Hindus. India's Muslims may well have been distinguishable from India's Hindus, but they were not all the same as each other. The idea that India's Muslims were a 'nation', proved tragically misguided. Jinnah's Two-Nation Theory was just strong enough to make two states out of British India, but by 1971 it proved too weak to prevent the creation of two states out of Pakistan.

Politics and Religion

Religion, as defined by communities, was formally introduced to Indian politics as the result of the 'democratization' of British rule after 1909. The new electorates created by the Morley–Minto reforms of that year recognized religious groupings in an attempt to ensure that minority interests were adequately represented. Religious electorates then remained part of British India until 1947.

The 1909 system represented a minimum grant of electoral democracy. Its main function was not to provide candidates for executive office but merely to reflect opinion, and that opinion, though purely advisory, was communal. Indians were not being asked to exercise their political imaginations; they were expected to vote according to what they *were*. This ensured that religious identity came before policy in Indian electoral politics from the very start.

The reforms were also designed to exclude Indian politicians, no matter how popular, from any share of executive political power. This meant that political parties in India were forced to grow up outside a system of responsible self-government, and not inside it as they had in Britain. This removed any direct connection between the popular vote and the exercise of real authority, so that Indian politics took on an abstract quality. Politicians lacked loyalty to the system and remained divorced from the main political measures under discussion, which they had not originated and could not modify or reject.

Religion, as a personal and community identifier, came to play an exaggerated part in filling this vacuum, in a way that ultimately suited Jinnah, but which never appealed to Gandhi. Despite his avowed religious tendencies, Gandhi's mission was to bring spirituality, not sectarian religion, to Indian politics.

Multiple shades of religious–political opinion existed in British India, and a crude Hindu–Muslim divide was never the whole of it; each community was subdivided by region, class and sect, and there were other faiths, including Sikhs and Parsis. But despite the repeated efforts of many of India's most prominent leaders, including Jinnah and Gandhi, after 1909 national political issues tended to harden into a contest between the two largest communities, Hindus and Muslims. The Congress always fought to rise above this simple polarity and constantly promoted itself as a non-denominational body. This was technically true, and the Congress leadership did contain representatives of many faith traditions. But this was not enough to take the religion out of Indian politics, because most of the high-profile Congress leaders – Tilak, Gokhale, Gandhi, C.R. Das, Sardar Patel, Rajendra Prasad, S.C. Bose, C. Rajagopalachari – were undeniably Hindus. Some were more 'Hindu' than others, but any future Congress government would be led by Hindus, and supported by the Hindu majority in the Congress rank and file. How, then, would 'Hindu raj' look any different? Thus, despite all its secular aspirations, playing the religious card against the Congress was an easy and effective way for Muslim leaders to rally support.

Paradoxically, the refusal of the Congress to align itself in religious terms did not protect Indian politics from religion; it simply left room for others to pursue more overtly religious politics. The most organized expressions of this tendency was the Hindu Mahasabha, which was formed in response to the creation of another religious party, the Muslim League, founded in 1906. The Mahasabha was organized on a national scale by 1915, and it became increasingly militant through the 1920s. In purely religious terms, therefore, the Mahasabha, not the Congress, was the League's 'natural' opponent.

It is important to emphasize here that Gandhi never viewed the Congress as a narrow 'party' that should attract partisan loyalty. In 1920 he wrote: 'I do not consider the Congress as a party organization, even as the British Parliament, though it contains all parties and has one party or other dominating it from time to time, is not a party organization.'

He saw the Congress as a forum for the nation, and pledged to try to preserve its 'non-party national character'.[16]

The Congress remained by far the broadest church in Indian politics, but the Muslim League was home to a considerable degree of diversity too, and was not nearly as monolithic as its name might suggest. It did not represent all Muslim opinion at any point in its history, and it repeatedly split into factions before Jinnah became its unchallenged leader in 1934. But the Muslim League could never deny its religious basis, and it always attracted lines of attack that were explicitly religious. Once Pakistan had begun to acquire shape and currency, it became easy for Congress leaders to insist that Pakistan was to be a theocratic state, using this claim to rally support in provinces destined for inclusion in Pakistan. The charge was hard to refute, because Jinnah generally remained reticent about details of the new state's structure and policies. Nor would the question go away, because it benefited the Congress to keep asking it, no matter how it was answered. If Pakistan was to be a primarily religious state, then liberal-minded Muslims could be deterred from supporting it. If not, then there seemed little point in having Pakistan at all.

Thus the two leadership cliques, no matter how secular, could draw real political benefits from exaggerating the religious character of their opponents.

RELIGIOUS BLINKERS

Gandhi began his career looking for a way to realize his religious aims in political terms, while Jinnah ended his career looking for a way to fulfil his political aims in religious terms. Both mixtures, of religion with politics and means with ends, produced drastic and momentous decisions that can only be described as misjudgements.

In Gandhi's case his decision in 1919 to bring together the Congress's political demand for swaraj with the Muslim religious demand for protection of the Sultan of Turkey's Khilafat (Caliphate) had damaging consequences for the development of Indian politics. It broadened political activity enormously, but it also drew an emotional response that both excited and divided the population. The immediate result was to drive moderates, including Jinnah, out of the Congress and to leave Gandhi with a movement he could propel but not steer. Gandhi's religious sensitivities also led him to the extraordinary misapprehension that the Khilafat was safe in the hands of Kemal Ataturk, who abolished it shortly afterwards in 1924.

Rabindranath Tagore heavily criticized Gandhi at the time in private letters to Gandhi's friend C.F. Andrews, who released them for publication. They reveal Tagore's belief that Gandhi had committed the Indian political nation to a cause that was mistakenly anti-Western and fundamentally negative, a decision that threatened to unleash the 'anarchy of mere emptiness'.[17] Tagore favoured cooperation over non-cooperation, and was firmly opposed to what he called 'non-education', which he saw as one of the movement's most direct results.

Tagore proved to have had a more realistic view of the mixture of religion and rebellion than Gandhi, for the 'orgy of frightfulness' that he feared appeared shortly afterwards when Malabar's Muslim minority, the Mapillahs, rose in violent revolt in August 1921 in support of the Khilafat, and against Hindu landlords and moneylenders. Gandhi's reaction, that they were religious men fighting for their religion in a way they considered religious, seems irresponsible. It is very hard to lay that statement comfortably alongside his belief in the necessity of non-violence in the attainment of political goals, or even his declaration in July 1919 that 'a Civil Resister never seeks to embarrass the government'.[18]

Congress ideology was nationalist and secular, so why did Gandhi persuade the party to take up a cause that was internationalist and religious? The answer is because he wanted to find a plainly moral issue upon which to unite the Hindu and Muslim communities, and he took (or mistook) himself as the standard of measurement of religious emotion and moral outrage. He felt strongly about the threat to the Ottoman Sultan's spiritual leadership of the world's Muslims, and this deep feeling seemed to present an ideal opportunity to find unity. Twice he described the vital importance of the Khilafat to Muslims as a matter of 'life and death'.[19] The leap to associating this feeling with a demand for Indian swaraj was not necessarily a connection made in the minds of the Muslims at the head of the Khilafat movement that had built up since Turkey's First World War defeat in 1918. Jinnah thought this whole linkage was a mistake, that it would lead to strife and that it would not help India's national cause one bit. In these judgements he must be considered to have been correct.

The second, and permanent, entry of religion into Indian politics came when Jinnah began to demand Pakistan based on the Two-Nation Theory, thus overlaying a national and a religious demand without any attempt to distinguish the two. He developed an entire political campaign around the scarcely tenable idea that the nationalistic demand he was making was only a religious demand by coincidence. But the slogan 'The Muslims are a nation' was inherently and inescapably a religious statement. Jinnah remained in denial about this, and the confusion that resulted has come down to our own times in the disputes in Pakistan over his constitutional legacy, and in the problems of interpretation faced by writers who constantly have to assess Jinnah's actions within conflicting categories, as 'secular', 'nationalist' or 'Islamic'.

Jinnah did his utmost to keep the link between Pakistan and religion as vague as he could, by treating Hindus and Muslims not as separate bodies defined in religious terms but as 'different and distinct social orders'[20], a phrase he used at Lahore in 1940. This kept the whole discussion within a political frame, which was where he wanted it. He was always concerned with *political*, not religious rights; he took it as read that everyone in Pakistan would have full religious rights. What he was worried about was that Muslims in a Congress-led India would not have their full complement of political rights.

Jinnah was not a cynic when it came to Islam. He really did believe that an Islamic society would be freer than a Hindu one; he had his own understanding of what the message of the Prophet was about and how it related to social relations. For him Islam was an 'ideology', and its principal elements were about human dignity, social justice and equality, which very definitely included the equality of women. His interpretation may have been idiosyncratic and rather modernist, but it does not have to be thought of as insincere. It was as useful to him as his liberalism, with which he clearly did not think it incompatible. He spoke much too often about the virtues of Muslim society, particularly its freedom, for him to be labelled a hypocrite just because he enjoyed ham sandwiches.

Another way to see this is to underline how he felt that Islam was more compatible with politics than Hinduism. He was sure that Muslims could understand and maintain the balance between religion and politics, which were closely allied within their faith. The point was that he feared that Hindus could not. Therefore, in one way his religious concerns were less about Muslims than about Hindus.

Jinnah held Muslim society as a lofty political vision, but he never clearly separated the political and religious elements of the Pakistan demand, something that involved a great deal of agility on his part. His political shifts on this issue have generated ample evidence for all interested parties to interpret as they wish. In 1938 he was pleased to be rid of the 'unwholesome influence'[21] of maulvis and maulanas, but he was courting whatever sections of the scholarly community he could rally by 1945. In February 1939 he publicly agreed with the respected scholar Ashraf Ali Thanwi that it was not possible to separate religion and politics within Islam – a very orthodox position – yet he persisted in underplaying precisely this linkage up to and beyond the creation of Pakistan. He managed to find support within the religious community, but in an uneven and fluctuating manner. Barelvi Muslims, followers of Ahmed Raza Khan Barelvi, were primarily traditional and spiritual in emphasis and tended to welcome Pakistan, but he also experienced opposition from more politically conscious hardliners such as Maulana Maududi, who thought the concept and especially the personnel involved were insufficiently religious. Meanwhile the Deobandi tradition, led by Maulana Husain Ahmad Madani, combined conservative observance with a broad Indian nationalism, and therefore opposed the division of India on a purportedly Islamic pretext. Though Jinnah's opponents continually represented the Pakistan demand as a religious cause, for devout Muslims it could be either not Islamic enough, as for Maududi, or essentially unIslamic, as for Madani.

Jinnah had to steer a course through the narrow passage that remained, and he preferred to say as little in the religious sphere as possible. In the 1930s he even restrained the Raja of Mahmudabad, his main lieutenant in the United Provinces, from making religiously themed speeches. But gradually his public stance became more Islamic and the Islamic scholars became more pro-Pakistan. It is possible that Jinnah became more sincerely religious during this process, but more likely that he yielded to the political realities of his mission and did what he needed to do to keep moving forwards. He probably judged this pretty well, for the 1945 elections were a triumph, with the Muslim League trouncing all the religious parties at the poll. This boost gave him the final platform from which to demand Pakistan with real authority.

The Pakistan issue is much harder to reconcile with Jinnah's general political outlook than the Khilafat was with Gandhi's. Jinnah consistently opposed the introduction of religion into Indian politics, stating on many occasions that religion had no place in politics, that religion was a matter between man and God, and that the state had no business in this relationship. These statements led up to his famous speech of 11 August 1947 in Karachi,[22] in which he reiterated these exact sentiments while explaining his vision of the new Pakistan.

So how, then, are we to understand his constant advocacy of the necessity for Pakistan? Was he simply opportunistic and manipulative? No. Pakistan was intended to achieve a real objective – to protect the political rights of Muslims by ensuring that they were not permanently outnumbered. He tried repeatedly to broker constitutional deals at the national level to ensure this, but he was frustrated on every occasion. Muslims were free to worship as they pleased in British India, but he became increasingly worried that they could not be guaranteed this right in a post-colonial Hindu-majority India, and Congress leaders seemed unconcerned to reassure him after 1929.

By 1937 it seems clear that he thought he was championing the cause of Muslims primarily in the socio-economic sense. He did not explore 'Muslim' identity very deeply, and he never attempted to refine it, or set out a preferred version of it. He pressed ahead in the cause of the people he wished to help under a banner they could all recognize.

Eventually his definition of 'Muslim' became not a religious identity meaning a follower of the Prophet Muhammad; from 1938 he began to define a Muslim as someone that followed him in politics. Those who did not were branded 'traitors', 'show-boys' or 'trophy Muslims' of the Congress. Yet how could Jinnah deny that a Congress leader like Maulana Abul Kalam Azad was not a proper Muslim? If he obeyed the five requirements of an Islamic life then surely the issue was beyond doubt. But for Jinnah the definition of 'a Muslim' became a matter of politics, and of who would and would not allow him to speak for them. Religion may have been a matter between man and God, but politics was between leader and follower. Jinnah led the Muslims – they could worship as they wished.

Gandhi, at the head of an avowedly secular organization, brought religion into politics to a rather more modest degree. It must be emphasized that it is not true that Gandhi envisaged a secular state: he did not. He did not want a religious state either. What he advocated was a tolerant state. He did not want a secular state because he did not want secular *people*.

In March 1915 he told a student gathering in Calcutta[23] that politics and religion should not be 'divorced', and he was so willing to see politics as a seamless mix of morality and social issues that his apparently neutral principles of non-violence and tolerance appeared rather more religious than he realized. He was endlessly concerned to reassure Muslims that he was not an advocate of any specifically Hindu form of government, which was always the Muslim League's easiest and most damaging accusation against him. But no matter how he defined what he was doing, it always seemed to some others that he was importing a faith dimension. He looked and sounded like a Hindu. Certainly, his constant references to 'Ram Rajya' could hardly fail to raise communal hackles. Even without the later promptings of Jinnah, the idea that Islam was in danger was not hard to pick up. Gandhi may have been less 'political' than the standard Muslim divine, and more tolerant, but he could easily be represented as being the Muslims' opposition as much as the government's.

Gandhi never acknowledged that his overall approach to politics was not secular enough to establish the broad base he needed to achieve his aims. The anti-British part of his policy was closely connected with moral regeneration and his plans for the reform of Indian society, which became increasingly centred on the abolition of untouchability. He expended a great deal of energy on this issue, which could not fail to persuade Muslims that his concerns were primarily Hindu concerns. Nor was his belief that independence would produce spiritual transformation an attractive idea to the mass of Muslims, who already had a well-understood way of intertwining their politics and their religion. Perhaps if Gandhi had been dealing with a substantial minority from another religious tradition he might have been able to establish a common purpose. But Islam, with its strong discipline and its textual and legal centre of gravity, could not easily ally with the Mahatma's project. To Islamic minds, it was a spiritually purer course to be rid of the skinny sadhu than to follow him.

So while Gandhi underestimated the importance of religion, Jinnah's willingness to demand some form of partition was doing the same thing. He never foresaw the absolute desperation of so many people to escape the new arrangements that he was foisting on them. Had he realized the enormity of the impact of his years of warnings then he might have been more willing to settle for some kind of federated system – and indeed, perhaps that is what he wanted to do all along. As Partition loomed, he did try to lessen the anxieties of the populations affected, and he clearly stated that there would be no persecution or oppression of minorities in the new Pakistan. He made this abundantly clear on 13 July 1947 in Delhi to the whole Indian press corps,[24] and again on 11 August in Karachi.[25] But the years of corrosive fear-mongering came home to roost. Neither side wished to take the risk of putting themselves at the mercy of a hostile majority: chaos ensued.

And so another irony can be set out: that both Gandhi and Jinnah, by underestimating the importance of religion, managed to make it the key deciding factor in the final shaping of South Asia. This happened because one man was so spiritual that he never considered sectarianism as a serious viewpoint, and the other because he was essentially unmoved by religion, while a great many of his supporters were.

In truth, neither Gandhi nor Jinnah was a particularly vigorous advocate for the religious tradition he was supposed to champion. Gandhi's unorthodoxy over untouchability even led Pandit Sen, a Bengali brahmin, to declare that the Mahatma was 'not a proper Hindu' in the legislative assembly in January 1934. Jinnah was not a keen mosque-goer, was a regular drinker of alcohol and was certainly no Islamic scholar.

The politics of British India tended to fall into religious alignments partly because there was so little real power at stake in the argument until much later on. Until then the discussion remained unhelpfully abstract, with promises too easily made, too far from the point of redemption. Add to this the tremendous enthusiasm that the prospect of Independence could generate, and politics became all too volatile in the lives of individuals and communities. The standard accompaniment to party politics in the West – cynicism, disillusionment and disengagement resulting from years of voting and seeing no change – were largely absent from British India. Religious demands and expectations became competitive community aspirations. These were inherent in the system and were even actively encouraged by the structures the British put in place. A secular political culture was never likely to grow up within such a system, at either its roots or its higher levels, and it did not.

Leadership

There are two distinct types of political leaders: those that acquire a position by outlining a vision which attracts mass support, and those that acquire office and then become a mouthpiece for sectional interests. Gandhi was of the first type, bringing something distinct and original into Indian politics as if from nowhere. Jinnah was of the second type, emerging out of the Muslim community as the one man who could speak for them at a national level.

This difference lay at the root of their very different styles of leadership. Gandhi spent years organizing mass protests or sitting in jail in South Africa, while Jinnah took a smoother and more comfortable path to national prominence. While Gandhi excelled as an active protestor, Jinnah was the most skilful of passive opponents: Gandhi a leader by example, Jinnah a leader by inspiration. For Gandhi, leadership was a burden willingly shouldered for the sake of others; for Jinnah it was a necessary exhilaration.

Gandhi trusted people and expected them to behave well. In consequence he held the reins of power very lightly. His leadership could safely remain loose because his followers were in such awe of him personally. This allowed him to make his decisions without wide consultation, and to maintain the impression that his leadership was diffident – that he was personally unconcerned whether people listened to him or not.

Gandhi's humility, though, was a strange creation. He never laid claim to authority by virtue of election, and he either set up his own organizations, or became the leader of others by acclamation, sometimes in rather irregular ways. These techniques ensured that he could never be ousted. His power relied on the voluntary submission of his followers, and their devotion was stronger and more resilient than any purely political alignment of interests. He effectively built up a personal cult, as much as a political movement. He set up a leader–follower relationship in which his disciples, weak as individuals, could exercise great power collectively, but only through him. And as reward they received not money or power or office, but merely his praise, and a standing among the wider public that was purely honorific.

As a man of unquestioned virtue, Gandhi remained a leader who could not be superseded or replaced. His entire approach to leadership allowed him to give orders based on declared moral precepts, which he expected would be obeyed. Whenever those orders were not carried out – ignored, defied or simply left unfulfilled – he could withdraw the instruction, claiming either that his people were not up to the task of doing his bidding, or that superior numbers against him must be recognized and permitted to win the day. So he was an autocratic leader, except when he chose not to be.

In effect he was always seeking to reject, overlook or dismantle his own status as leader, but with the luxury of knowing all the while that his position was unassailable. His own moral authority went unquestioned within the Congress, and those rare souls who did question it were soon eased out. Gandhi understood this process with exceptional clarity. In 1925 he said, very neatly, that moral authority 'comes without seeking and is retained without effort'.[26]

By contrast, Jinnah constantly had to exploit such status as he could credibly claim for himself to build the authority he wished to exercise. This involved striking a delicate balance between inspiring devotees, cajoling sceptics and impressing opponents. He was always seeking to tighten his grip on command, but until around 1945 he enjoyed no comfort in his eminence. He was so regularly undermined and betrayed by close colleagues and allies that avoiding such treachery remained a primary concern throughout his career. Leaving the Home Rule League, the organization leading the demand for self-government, in October 1920, and the Congress two months later, were traumatic experiences. These upheavals were more about principles and methods than persons, and they did not determine the entire course of the rest of his life, as some historians have maintained, but they made him wary of popular causes and Congress cliques. Although both defeats in 1920 were nominally at the hands of Gandhi, the degree to which these permanently soured relations with him is debatable. Jinnah was certainly very opposed to Gandhi's populist programme at the time, but he seems not to have harboured any permanent aversion to the man himself at this stage. They shared a platform a year later at Ahmedabad and cooperated several times through the 1920s on different issues.

More than the events of 1920 it was the jockeying within Muslim politics after that date that really scarred Jinnah. The betrayal he felt at the hands of his deputy M.C. Chagla over the latter's acceptance of the Nehru Report in 1928 was a severe lesson. Concern to buttress his leadership became his main focus all through the 1940s, because his ability to ask for Pakistan with authority was closely tied to his personal eminence. This demand, after all, was by then the sole purpose of the Muslim League's existence. If he did not lead the Muslims unchallenged, as the continued high status and popularity of other significant Muslim figures suggested, or if he did not speak for all Muslims, as the Congress insisted, then there was no chance of presenting a compelling case to the British that Pakistan was either wanted or workable. If the community was divided then the new country was not required, and would clearly not work, were it ever set up. Jinnah hated dissent in the ranks and was vigilant in seeing off every threat to his standing within the Muslim community. This is why so much argument from 1938 onwards revolved around Jinnah's absolute insistence that the Congress should not be allowed to appoint Muslims to national bodies.

He became convinced that the only way to win Pakistan – to obtain adequate safeguards for the Muslim community – was for him to exercise maximum personal authority within Muslim politics and to enjoy complete freedom during negotiations. It was this combination of liberty for himself and discipline among his followers that led Clement Attlee, the British prime minister, to remark that Jinnah was the only fascist he had ever met.[27]

The unity that Jinnah eventually achieved depended heavily upon his own person, and remained highly vulnerable if he were ever to be eliminated by illness, accident, scandal or other misfortune. Solidarity was maintained by his titanic stature within the Muslim League, but the intense concentration of power that his drive for unity created was duly exposed. Within little more than a year, newborn Pakistan lost its Quaid-i-Azam (Great Leader), and it turned out that there was no statesman in waiting, no spiritual heir, to take over and mould Pakistan into a successful political entity. Jinnah created a coalition strong enough to reach the goal of the new homeland, but it was very narrow at the top, weak in agreed ideals, and lacking real social cohesion.

His death in 1948 was not unexpected, but he left no clear signposts set out in speeches and literature. He seemed to have considered the relationship between Pakistan and Islamic culture as something in no need of definition. It has often been suggested that he did not want a 'Muslim state', but simply a state for Muslims; we cannot know for sure because the explicit words are not to be found. In terms of a true political legacy, Jinnah died intestate.

Faced with such a striking lack of material, there have to be serious doubts over whether a completely independent Pakistan was Jinnah's sole and exclusive aim. Did he really have no alternative positions? He became so personally responsible for the conduct of negotiations that it is difficult to determine what his exact intentions were, without running the risk of projecting one's own perception of him onto a series of highly complex transactions, the outcome of which no one at the time could have foreseen. His failure, deliberate or otherwise, to write about his own political life means that we can get no nearer to him than his contemporaries did, which isn't very close. He was always reluctant to reveal his hand and this concealment has lasted to this day, allowing, as is so often the case, for this space to be filled by whomever with whatever they wish to place there.

As a philosopher of his actions, Jinnah seriously lacked substance. Because his style of leadership was so personal, and because his mass support was not mobilized by detailed reasoning, he felt little pressure to explain what exactly he was thinking. The general rhetoric of Muslim identity was enough to set out his case for him, at least in terms of mustering an emotional attachment to his cause. He never had a pressing need to specify, and after 1938 he exploited this advantage brilliantly, casting responsibility on his opponents. So it was always the Congress that had to issue soothing words or to invent safeguards, or the British who had to bring forward increasingly complex constitutional structures. It was his deftness in throwing the burden onto others that led British officials to joke that he was the man with a problem for every solution.

He was not a paragon of constancy. He changed his mind on a number of issues, notably over separate electorates and the necessity of Dominion Status for Pakistan, and he constantly extended or withdrew his approval for various constitutional plans during the 1945–47 period. Others called him a man of principle, but he never claimed any such title. In his later career he described himself simply as a 'realist'.

The case for Jinnah as a visionary is not strong. If he was a visionary then he was unique in never setting forth or writing down that vision. By contrast, Gandhi did – at length, very clearly and in the face of all opposition, derision and scepticism. This is more like the characteristic behaviour of visionaries. Jinnah had all the characteristics of a politician who wished to keep his options open, his position flexible and his opponents guessing. Without the obligation to prove that Jinnah had a 'dream' we can get on with assessing him as a flesh-and-blood political being. We need not sympathize with him as a man. Admiration should be a luxury for an observer, not a requirement, and a by-product of analysis, not its foundation.

Gandhi really was a visionary, but he was still a politician, and one with a perfectly normal degree of fallibility. Though he remained broadly consistent in his political aims, it is not difficult to find apparent contradictions in his positions: his recruiting campaigns during the First World War would seem incompatible with the doctrine of non-violence; his condemnation of hunger strikers in 1931 sits oddly with his own use of fasts for political ends. Consistency is an ever-present problem in assessing Gandhi because he seemed to approach each issue piecemeal. 'Consistency is a hobgoblin,'[28] he explained. We have to understand that while his overarching spiritual views never changed, his political reactions and recommendations did, because his immediate reasoning was always influenced by the wider, developing context. This was what in the final analysis made him a politician, not simply a swami. His politics were much more relative than his spiritual direction, which was increasingly absolute during his life. His faith in the fundamental goodness of people, the efficacy of non-violence, and the primacy of loving-kindness exhibited through voluntary service and suffering, only deepened. Specific issues prompted him to pick out different aspects of truth. 'My aim is not to be consistent with my previous statements on a given question, but to be consistent with the truth as it may present itself to me at a given moment. The result is that I have grown from truth to truth...'[29] This is Gandhi-ese for 'When the facts change, my opinions change.'

The mature Gandhi had a relatively unchanging conception of what he wanted and how he would get it. This is perhaps a surprise to those who see Jinnah as the stubborn one and Gandhi as the flexible conciliator. Gandhi was surprisingly invariant on major issues. He set out his demand for swaraj in 1920 and never really deviated from it. He was never willing to be drawn on the details of any post-Independence settlement until Independence was definitively granted. This objection lay behind his refusal of Lord Reading's invitation to talks in the spring of 1921, and Lord Irwin's in late 1929. It also rendered indecisive the Round Table Conference sessions he attended in 1931, and provided one of the reasons to reject both the Viceroy's August Offer of 1940 and the Cripps Mission's proposals in 1942. But he did have a clearer vision of his India than Jinnah had of his Pakistan. Gandhi did not wish to see a 'Hindu' India in the narrow sense – he wanted a pious and spiritually sensitive India. He believed that India was the world's great spiritual reservoir and that India would quite literally save the world by bestowing her spiritual bounty on others in need of it. He wrote at great length about the wickedness of Western 'civilization', meaning industrial modernity, with its emphasis on the body and its immediate needs. He was repelled by the barbarity of machines like railway engines and cotton gins. Indian civilization also had its failings, he accepted, but these were aberrations, and were superficial and reversible. The great weakness of the Western model was that its failings were identical with its central objectives – consumption, self-indulgence, materialism, sensual gratification – and were fully admitted to be so by its 'votaries'.[30]

In terms of political detail Gandhi was never very clear about the India he hoped to build, although he expected the majority of Indians to live in self-governing villages, and preferred them there rather than in the filthy, sinful cities that drained human interactions of their goodness and where men were enslaved to consumerism, intoxicants and carnal pursuits. In 1921 Sir Valentine Chirol, for the London *Times*, asked Gandhi what swaraj would bring. He would not be drawn and merely said that British courts would go, to be replaced by village panchayats. India would dispense justice 'in accordance with her inner conscience,' he said. There would be no universities, just traditional gurus teaching in 'shaded groves open to God's air and light'.[31]

The truth was that most of the Congress leadership did not actually share this archaic, pastoral vision. Certainly, Jawaharlal Nehru was an advocate of modernization and industrialization, and had no romantic attachment to the nobility and purity of poverty, which was Gandhi's main political idea. Neither C.R. Das nor Subhas Chandra Bose was a natural Gandhian, but they were removed by death and expulsion respectively. There were groupings in the Congress to both left and right of Gandhi's perceived position, but his massive popular appeal allowed him to moderate between them rather than to become a casualty of their rivalry. In this he was helped by the fact that Congress leaders remained clear of the stress and responsibility of high office.

One last point of comparison can be made concerning the way the two leaders presented themselves visually. Jinnah's time in London from 1893 to 1896 seems to have given him a taste for high London style. In 1946 George E. Jones described Jinnah in a *New York Times* feature as 'one of the best dressed men in the British Empire'.[32] Gandhi, by contrast, was one of the least dressed. His middle-class upbringing left no visible marks on him, and he permanently abandoned any thoughts of comfortable living while in South Africa. His lifelong infatuation with poverty does, however, bear distinct middle-class traces. He invented a sort of peasant look that peasants could recognize, but which they would probably not choose to emulate. He had enormous faith in the dignity of 'voluntary simplicity', but involuntary, inescapable poverty confers only the simplicity of deprivation and does not confer any dignity on anyone. It was Gandhi's intention to make a statement about India's indigence, the injustices of colonialism and the pressing moral obligation on the British to listen to civil, unarmed protests. This led him to dress in a style that made him look like a man trying to look poor. The point about poor men is that they never *want* to look poor. It's just that they cannot avoid looking as poor as they are. Gandhi's visual image was for the consumption of the illiterate masses in India and eventually, a worldwide public. Though it was not a particularly accurate reflection of 'poor' India, nevertheless it was brilliantly, wordlessly effective.

Even the British Army appreciated this, as evidenced by a doggerel circulating during the Second World War among the troops in India:

Mussolini with his Blackshirts, backs against the wall,
Hitler with his Brownshirts, heading for a fall,
Churchill in his dress shirt dominates them all.
Three cheers for Gandhi – no shirt at all!

This pauperism had its effect on Jinnah too. After his permanent return from London in 1935, his attempt to appeal to the Muslim public enfranchised by the new reforms could not be undertaken in his old dapper, Edwardian style. Gandhi had changed the whole appearance of the Congress leadership, who all now wore khadi, but Jinnah's tailoring spoke in a different accent. He too went native. We even have a specific, attested date for the change: Jinnah adopted the sherwani on 15 October 1937, at a Muslim League meeting at Lucknow.

No leader ever dressed like Gandhi in India afterwards. His appearance was an essential part of the appropriate message at the crucial time. To look like that in 1950 would have been to remind Indians of something they were keen to rise above. By then, sleek but modest tailoring was the aspiration.

THREE ISSUES

As leaders, Jinnah and Gandhi shared one major objective – the expulsion of the British – but this common ground also threw up significant differences between them.

Jinnah wanted the details of any independence settlement to be put in place by the British before they went. He trusted the British to maintain an impartial stance between the Muslim League and the Congress, and it was therefore preferable to finalize as much of the post-Independence arrangements under their aegis as possible. If the British went, leaving minorities at the mercy of the majority, Muslims would be left with insufficient defences. Jinnah feared the possible chaos that might follow a British withdrawal without prior agreement on all contentious subjects. He wanted the British to go, but he was not in any great hurry to see them leave.

Gandhi took an opposite stance. The British Raj represented almost everything bad he could think of, and he was impatient to be rid of it. Western influence meant modernity, industrialization, lawyers, surgery, vaccinations, railways and urbanization. All these things were not in need of better management – they were in need of complete removal. His *Hind Swaraj* (1909), written on a boat returning from London, exposed the false prospectus that Western civilization rested upon; its science had discovered nothing worth knowing, while its medical men practised vivisection and relied on cures based on animal fats and spirituous liquors, repellent to both Hindus and Muslims. His view of bodily illness was that it resulted from sin – meaning personal weakness and vice – and because Western medicine set out to cure the results of these lapses, it encouraged the sinner to sin again. This is why he considered Western medicine a barrier to freedom from imperial oppression, and why he viewed hospitals as the Devil's attempt 'to keep his hold on his kingdom'. He stoutly maintained that Indian 'quackery' was better, because it addressed the drive towards sinfulness.[33] All these elements underpinned Gandhi's view that the British presence was a real moral evil, one that had distorted Indian society. It is striking how often he used a word as strong as 'satanic' in his description of the

British government and its doings. The rediscovery of self-sufficiency, the reform of the abuses of caste, the rekindling of village life, all these things could only come once the British were gone. There should be no long goodbye. Stewardship was over, trusteeship betrayed. 'Go, and go now' was his unequivocal message. He explicitly linked the moral and spiritual regeneration of the country with the expulsion of the British. All detailed arrangements for the reform of Indian society and government could be addressed afterwards. This sequencing of independence, then reform, set him completely at odds with Jinnah, who preferred the reverse, and this became much more than a theoretical issue between 1944 and 1947.

Another issue that took on very serious aspects was the dispute between them about 'spokesmanship'. Each felt that the other was falsely claiming to speak for a wider public. Gandhi felt that Jinnah was not the voice of all Muslims, and furthermore, that Muslims did not need to be represented as a separate interest group at all. Jinnah was infuriated that Gandhi could so effortlessly switch between speaking for the entire nation on some occasions, and abjuring this role at others. Throughout their talks in Bombay in 1944 he was never sure whether Gandhi was negotiating with him as a private individual or as a plenipotentiary envoy from the Congress. Neither man felt able to take the other as what he claimed to be, and this had serious consequences.

The two men also disagreed profoundly about the very nature of the country they were seeking to liberate. Jinnah believed that the British had erected a façade of unity that was quite unreal. After 1937 he insisted that India was really 'Two Nations' – the Muslim and the Hindu, two real national entities. Gandhi, on the other hand, was passionately committed to the idea that India was one, and always had been. He believed that the British had artificially created and fostered divisions in India. If only the British would go then all would be well. Historic national unity would reassert itself and brotherhood among Indians would remake the whole community.

Lastly, there was a chasm between the two men on the subject of political method. Jinnah was essentially a social conservative. He liked orderliness; he was comfortable with the superior status that his abilities assured him. Nevertheless he was paternally concerned to protect poor Muslim cultivators and hoped to improve their lot over time, especially via education. Peasant uplift was a main part of the Congress programme and he had no quarrel with it. But he was a substantial property owner himself, as were many of his principal supporters, and he always fought shy of anti-landlord rhetoric and the redistribution schemes favoured on the Congress left. Instead, he favoured measured change, brought about by top–down reform of the law and the arrival of gradually increasing prosperity, founded in self-government. When he was in England in the early 1930s he actually joined the Fabian Society, an organization committed to the gradual, peaceful introduction of socialism. But though he had a social conscience, he was really an evolutionary conservative.

Gandhi's post-1920 Congress party was rather different. Gandhi was a conservative revolutionary, in that he advocated ancient values, not new ones, but was more than happy to remake society in order to reinstall older ideals. He advocated restoration not innovation, because he felt that the modern world had brought no discoveries worth making. Nothing in science or political theory impressed him. Old ways, slow ways, ancient insights, eternal virtues – these were his bedrock.

At the most fundamental level, therefore, the two men did not agree about the nature of the country they lived in, or the correct procedure to end colonial rule, or the methods that should be used to persuade the colonialists to leave. These three vital issues were never resolved.

Part 2
Interactions

Jinnah and Gandhi were very different kinds of politicians, but they had one remarkable feature in common: Each essentially created his own political world. Jinnah shaped and mobilized the Muslim community into a new political entity, and Gandhi virtually invented mass politics in India. Though this partly resulted from the restricted nature of colonial politics, both men were sufficiently atypical to ensure that neither had a career that was preordained in its course or destination. This is perhaps more easily appreciated in the case of Gandhi, whose entry to Indian politics came not via the Congress, but through successful direct action on behalf of India's poorer classes in the years 1917 and 1918. He brought an independently acquired status into Congress leadership circles with him, and never laid it aside in favour of alliances within the organization. He remained in some ways, therefore, a cuckoo in the nest. This, along with his disinterest in the day-to-day details of conventional political life, granted him an unusual degree of independence in both thought and deed that he was able to exploit over a very long period, frequently to the exasperation of his colleagues.

Jinnah was more conventional than Gandhi in almost every way, but he was still an unlikely candidate to acquire the leadership of India's Muslims, whose leaders at that time were generally rich and aristocratic. The young Jinnah was neither. He started out in politics with a natural Congress profile, as a bright lawyer with secular views, and he made more than satisfactory progress through Congress ranks before 1909. But it was not his background, profession or beliefs that made Jinnah so different in Muslim circles – it was his lack of regional identity and support, coupled with his ambition to speak nationally on behalf of India's Muslims in secular and political terms. This set him apart from other 'national' Muslim leaders such as Muhammad Ali and Maulana Azad, who had primarily religious concerns, or Fazl-i-Husain in the Punjab, whose aspirations to self-government expressed themselves in distinctly regional terms. Jinnah was always pursuing nationalist objectives of self-government, with special concern for the full inclusion of Muslims as a political minority. He never changed this view substantially. Throughout his lifelong opposition to colonial rule, he was always mindful of what self-government might mean politically for his own community.

That two men, so far to the fringes of their respective constituencies, could achieve the prominence they attained was not only not inevitable, it was also extraordinary, and we need to bear this in mind when recounting Indian history in terms of a simple struggle between the Congress and the Muslim League. Both organizations suffered from chronic internal tensions, which hinted that, as political 'parties', they were almost too broad for the purposes they were being asked to serve.

The role that Jinnah and Gandhi played within those parties is, above all, the story of how the two men shaped the parties more than how the parties shaped them.

Towards Unity: 1900–19

In 1900, British India was a ramshackle military dictatorship, brimming with good intentions but hamstrung by lack of funds. The army was the principal prop of the regime, and remained its greatest expense. At the centre ruled the Viceroy, who had small executive and legislative councils to deal with all-India matters. Below the Viceroy, there was a layer of provincial Governors and Lieutenant Governors who had their own executive and legislative councils, and below them were smaller local establishments. The overall purpose of the system was to keep power in the hands of as few people as possible. The elective principle was not entirely absent from British India, because some Indian members on the provincial councils were indirectly elected from local representative bodies. But direct elections existed only at the lowest, local level where it had been introduced for some members of municipal and district boards by Lord Ripon, Viceroy from 1880 to 1884.

Outside the British provincial structure, India was still ruled by hereditary princes. The general support given by native rulers during the 1857 Uprising had prompted the British to confirm them in their privileges, and after that date there was no pressing military or political need to dispossess them. They were denied the right to maintain large standing armies and were restricted in their capacity to conduct independent diplomacy, but the princes were left in charge of their traditional states, free to reform or atrophy politically as they pleased. 'Good' government was all that was expected of them. Whenever standards were reckoned to have slipped, the British put in ministers, or tutors to a princely minor, to steer the ship of state back to an approved course. India outside direct British control, therefore, remained atomized and regionalized.

INDIAN POLITICS

Although political activity in India around 1900 was very restricted in scope and scale, there were issues to discuss and plenty of educated Indians willing to discuss them. Standard grievances were that India's wealth was being 'drained' away to Britain by heavy taxation and unfair commercial policies, and that government expenditure on the army and the administration was too high. There was also the demand for 'council entry', that more Indians should be included in government business.

In 1900 there was only one nationwide organization in the field to express Indian opinion – the Indian National Congress (INC). This was not a political 'party' in the modern sense; it was an annual assembly of gifted, motivated men, who came together to discuss issues of national concern. The first such meeting had been in 1885 and was the brainchild of a sympathetic British official, Allan Octavian Hume (1829–1912), a keen birdwatcher and Indophile who thought such gatherings would benefit the general running of the Raj. At this stage the Congress was not a particularly disciplined organization, or one with deep roots in popular culture, but it fizzed with energy that had little room to express itself within the very narrow confines of political life in British India. Gradually, it adopted a more combative tone through the next 20 years, during which time it developed from a broadly loyal body to one recognizably in opposition. The Viceroy who supervised its birth, Lord Dufferin (1884–88), had smiled benignly upon it, but by 1905, Lord Curzon (1899–1905) had come to loathe it, and was hoping to assist it into an early and unlamented grave.

The first real crisis of loyalty for the Congress came in 1905 when Curzon decided to split the very large province of Bengal into two. The furious popular opposition this scheme generated helped to give the rather elitist Congress a connection with a wider public that it had previously lacked, and the party used this leverage to develop real political muscle through the use of an economic boycott in the cause of swadeshi, or home-produced, goods, particularly cloth; the great swadeshi drive of 1905–09 reduced Indian textile imports by about a quarter. This campaign prefigured much of the opposition that Gandhi was to fashion after 1919, with its mass disobedience and import replacement.

The Congress was an avowedly non-communal body at its inception, and through its early years it had a rainbow of religious affiliations in its leadership, with Christians such as Hume and William Wedderburn, Parsis such as Ferozeshah Mehta and Dadabhai Naoroji, and plenty of Hindus of all descriptions, including Tilak, Gokhale, Surendranath Banerjea and Womesh Chandra Bonnerjee. There were also Muslims, including Badruddin Tyabji and Nawab Syed Muhammad, but Muslims were much less well represented, principally because Sir Syed Ahmad Khan, the most senior Muslim political spokesman of the previous generation, had considered democratic politics a dead-end for the minority community. He therefore shunned the Congress, and advised his fellow Muslims to do the same. Syed Ahmad, who died in 1898, represented the more traditional, aristocratic element in Muslim society, and the congeries of largely Hindu lawyers and journalists from Bengal and Maharashtra that made up the Congress at the time did not speak his political language. He spoke for Muslims who had no need of government jobs or political office, and who were content to deal with the British from their existing social base. The wealthier, more conservative elements in Muslim society declined to join what appeared to be a progressive, middle-class institution, especially after it started to contemplate self-government as a goal and began heading for a confrontation with the British.

This communal alignment was greatly exacerbated by the partition of Bengal, because the measure was perceived by both major communities as having sectarian implications. The overwhelmingly Muslim population of the new province of East Bengal seemed to have been granted privileges on a religious basis, while the most vocal, sophisticated and politically active section of the Bengali population, the Hindus of Calcutta, found themselves in a linguistic and ethnic minority among Biharis and Oriyas in the new West Bengal. The official line was that the changes were purely a matter of administrative efficiency, but the suspicion that the whole scheme was politically motivated took a deep hold, and was not entirely mistaken.

As the protests against the partition of Bengal continued, strident voices began to be heard attacking British rule from within the Congress, and the session of 1907 at Surat saw an open split between Moderates, such as Gokhale and Mehta, and Extremists, led by Tilak. What was 'extreme' about the Extremists was that they sought a definitive break with British rule, as opposed to merely demanding a role in self-government. They also differed in their preferred methods, openly advocating the use of violence, a stance that landed most of their leaders in various kinds of trouble with the authorities. Tilak, Lala Lajpat Rai and Bipin Chandra Pal were all imprisoned or deported, and Aurobindo Ghose, though acquitted of sedition in 1908, was forced out of British India. The Extremists were also more explicitly 'Hindu' in their conception of India as a nation. This was obviously a barrier to a wider acceptance of their philosophy within an organization that constantly struggled to retain its non-communal credentials.

Jinnah was a committed Moderate, and remained so. Gandhi, still in South·Africa, was less partisan. He differed on various points with both sides, and set out his reservations in *Hind Swaraj*. He thought the Extremists went too far in their flirtation with violent methods, and that the Moderates were too admiring of Western ways. Eventually he adopted a position that was nearer to the Extremist line, but shorn of its combative rhetoric.

The Extremists lost the day at Surat, and the Congress remained divided for another eight years. Jinnah was to take a leading role in the reconciliation.

THE 1909 REFORMS

Political change was in the air in Britain after the election of a Liberal government in 1906, ending 20 years of Conservative domination. The new Cabinet was decidedly reformist in its outlook, with John Morley

(1838–1923), a long-time anti-imperialist, as the new Secretary of State for India. Morley, in tandem with Curzon's successor, Lord Minto, set about devising constitutional changes for India from mid-1906. The result was the 1909 Indian Councils Act, known as the 'Morley–Minto' reforms.

This Act introduced the principle of election to both national and local institutions. At the centre, the Viceroy was now to preside over an Imperial Legislative Council for all India that contained a substantial element of elected members, but these remained in a minority. Provincial legislative councils now contained small 'non-official' majorities, made up of members either nominated by the administration or chosen by limited electorates, but remained primarily consultative bodies. The changes, therefore, were largely cosmetic. The executive powers of the Viceroy and the provincial Governors survived intact, and the government of the country was not made responsible to elected representatives at any level. There was, however, a real shift of political policy. From 1907 the Secretary of State's Council of India in London contained two Indian members, and the Viceroy's executive council in Calcutta admitted an Indian for the first time in 1909, with the appointment of S.P. Sinha (1863–1928). He was deemed suitable because he was a brilliant lawyer, a firm loyalist and, as Morley put it, 'comparatively white'[34].

When news of the proposed changes got out in 1906, a delegation of senior Muslim figures approached Lord Minto and petitioned that in any new electoral system the Muslim community should not be placed at a permanent numerical disadvantage. This group, led by the Aga Khan, met Lord Minto on 1 October 1906, and asked that some form of protection, or 'weightage' as it became known, should be put in place to assure Muslims of a degree of representation in line with the quality of their 'importance',[35] as opposed to their quantity in bald arithmetical terms. Minto agreed, and the principle of separate electorates was established at the same moment that electorates on any scale came into being in British India. This was to have momentous long-term consequences for India's development.

In order to take advantage of these new arrangements, the All-India Muslim League (AIML) was then founded in December 1906. It had three declared objectives: to promote loyalty to the (British) Government of India; to protect and advance the political rights and interests of India's Muslims; and to prevent among Muslims the rise of feelings of hostility towards other communities. In 1906, this programme set the League well apart from the Congress, which remained the only national forum for those concerned to win India an increased degree of self-government.

The 1909 Act was designed to court Congress Moderates, to appease the Muslim elite, and to admit sober men into what Morley was only prepared to call 'cooperation' in government. In its political aims it was a short-term success, but it left a long list of wider issues untouched, particularly regarding the introduction of responsible government at the national 'centre'. The elective principle was conceded, but Morley himself was at pains to deny that there was any intention in the 1909 Act of moving towards a Parliamentary model in India. If there had been, he told the House of Lords, he would have had 'nothing to do with it'.[36]

After 1909, public life in British India remained more administrative than political. This was quite deliberate, and reflected the common belief among British officials that it was not votes that Indians wanted but good government and even-handed justice. Such political life as the 1909 reforms allowed was built around institutions that were deeply unrepresentative by modern standards, and Indian politicians were left with only one broad choice – to cooperate with the government or not.

THE HOLLOW CENTRE

The reforms of 1909 marked the beginning of an extended imperial rearguard action, continued in 1919 and 1935, in which 'responsibility' was granted not at the centre but in the provinces. India's representative opposition was thus distributed to the regions and any effective challenge was literally removed from the central, 'national' stage. Such a system, without real political power on offer at its centre, reduced India's political talent to an essentially ornamental role, and few of India's politicians were truly national figures after this restructuring; all, except Jinnah, were in the Congress. Gandhi deliberately built his support outside the British establishment, and thus avoided being limited by it. His constituency was the whole people.

Jinnah's political project was very different. He chose, at least at the beginning, to stay within the areas defined by the British view of what Indian politics was about, meaning the steadily increasing involvement of prominent Indians in the processes of Indian administration. But having decided to play politics in a formal way, Jinnah often found himself very isolated. The British could mostly afford to ignore him as an individual, and he was often considered unimportant by other politicians, nearly all of whom had pre-existing power bases independent of party politics. At this time the typical Muslim League member was a rich landowner. The typical Congressman was a lawyer or journalist who had, at the very least, a regional following, although some Congress politicians, especially the Extremists, had begun to reach a little further by preaching wider causes of social and religious reform.

Jinnah was different. He was no rabble-rouser, and he had a pronounced distaste for religious politics. He also had what has often been described as a 'double minority status'. He was a Muslim in a Hindu land, and he was also a Khoja, a member of a Muslim sub-sect that constituted less than 1 per cent of the 20 per cent Muslim minority in the Bombay Presidency. Thus he was not starting from a place of advantage in terms of the new Indian politics that opened up after 1909. He was overqualified to be a politician in terms of personal ambition, ardour and ability, but time and again his lack of a strong regional base undermined his attempts to build unchallenged positions of leadership.

THE RISE OF JINNAH

Much of Jinnah's early life remains obscure, and there is disagreement even over where and when he was born. Some sources say his birthplace was Karachi, others that his family moved there when he was a small child and that he was born at Gondal, in the Gujarati princely state of Kathiawar. There is also some confusion as to the exact date of his birth. This is conventionally placed on Christmas Day, 1876, the date Jinnah himself used, although it may have been in the previous October. Little is certain about his early years as he seems never to have written or spoken on the subject. Such information as we do have comes from acquaintances with real or imaginary connections to his family, a body of witnesses who disagree on many important details. Jinnah stories were socially useful in newly independent Pakistan, and the market became flooded early on. About the sum total of what is known for sure is that his father was a merchant, that the boy Jinnah was clever, that he loved horses and that he grew up in Karachi. This enigmatic, incomplete quality characterizes much of the evidence we have about the rest of his life.

Young Jinnah was ambitious and was sent to London, possibly to take up a place in a merchant firm. Whatever the original plan, he took events into his own hands shortly after he arrived in 1893 by enrolling at Lincoln's Inn to read for the Bar; three years later he was admitted. This was a period of intense excitement for him, and he appears to have involved himself in a variety of activities, including amateur dramatics and professional politics. The latter was to be his life's work and he was blessed with an extraordinarily propitious beginning. He came to know Dadabhai Naoroji (1825–1917), who at the time was attempting to become Member for the London constituency of Finsbury Central, and formed a personal bond with him. Jinnah helped 'The Grand Old Man' to get elected as the first ever Indian Member of Parliament in 1893, and then sat and watched Parliamentary debates from the public gallery of the Commons. The oratory, the verbal sparring and the spectacle of constitutional lawmaking enthralled him. His respect for the spoken word, his mastery of the adversarial process and his belief in the necessity for constitutional procedure never left him.

He returned to India in 1897 and set up a legal practice in Bombay, where he struggled for several years. Eventually his eloquence and confident manner brought him success, and he was regularly described

as among the best, if not the best, barrister in British India. For the
rest of his life he could always rely on the law to provide him with
a substantial income, but this was not his prime interest. He wanted
to succeed in politics, and not local politics either. He had become a
convinced nationalist and he wished to lead on the national stage. The
young Mohammed Ali Jinnah was not cut from the same cloth as Sir
Syed Ahmad Khan, and he was attracted to Congress ideals. He attended
the 1904 Congress session and joined the party in 1906. When the Aga
Khan's delegation met Viceroy Minto in 1906, Jinnah responded by
demanding to know what right 'these gentlemen' possessed to speak for
Bombay. Who had elected them? He also intensely disliked the mixing
of religious and political affiliations, and opposed the separate electorates
the delegation had asked for as 'an obnoxious virus' introduced into the
body politic of India 'with evil designs'. He had a standard liberal faith
in institutions that inclined him to see the government, even the colonial
government of India, as a neutral force. In 1913 he told the Islington
Committee on administrative reform that: 'I do not see why a Hindu
should not be in charge of a district where the majority happens to be
Mohammedan'.[37] He even married a Parsi, against the wishes of her
family. All this was pure, copper-bottomed Congress philosophy.

His status in Congress circles rose steadily through the years 1904–09.
His name was put forward to be part of a Congress delegation to London
in 1905 with Gokhale, but he was not chosen; either he was as yet
too little known, or he may have been too closely associated with the
Moderate faction to have balanced Gokhale. He then served as political
secretary to Dadabhai Naoroji from 1906 to 1910 and even helped Tilak
fight a sedition charge in 1907, although he did not actually defend him
in court. Finally, his election to the new Imperial Legislative Council
in late 1909 was an undoubted step into the national arena. He took
up his seat as the Muslim member for Bombay, with Gokhale beside
him as the general member for the city.

In his early thirties, Jinnah was now a successful lawyer and established
Congressman, newly admitted to the first national political forum in
British Indian history. From this point his education in national politics
really began, and he started to experience his first real difficulties as he

worked to create a unified national political vehicle by reuniting the two factions of Congress and bringing them together with the Muslim League, a feat he achieved within seven years.

JINNAH AND NATIONAL UNITY

Jinnah's first notable act on the national stage was to clash with Viceroy Minto in the Imperial Council over the treatment of Indian indentured labourers in South Africa – Gandhi's pet subject. His next was to introduce the first Indian-sponsored legislation of the British era – the Waqf Validating Bill, eventually enacted in 1913, which defined the status of Islamic religious trusts. But Jinnah soon became disillusioned with the formality and irrelevance of Council business, and he did not stand again at the 1912 election. Instead, he threw himself into an ambitious campaign to bring together the Indian political nation.

This was standard Congress policy, but he went about it in a slightly different way. He stepped outside the central arena and ceased to demand concessions from the British there. Instead, he worked directly to forge unity among Indian politicians and preferred to speak to the imperial power in London rather than on Indian soil. When reform of the Indian bureaucracy was mooted, he went to Westminster in 1913 to give evidence to the Islington Commission, and took an impeccably non-sectarian line about the appointment and deployment of officials in India. When ideas for reform of the upper levels of the Indian executive began to circulate in 1914, he went to London again to lobby Lord Crewe, the India Secretary. He suggested the inclusion of more Indians in the London-based Council of India, the abolition of the office of Secretary, and the payment of all officials from the British exchequer, not the Indian.

But this was mere window-dressing compared to the wider project he had in mind. From 1910 onwards he attended sessions of the Muslim League, and when the League changed to a more nationalist stance in 1912, he joined it.

He was able to do this because a profound change in the outlook of the League had come about through the years 1911–13. During this time Britain refused to support Turkey, the greatest Muslim power in the world, in a series of small wars with other Western powers. Within India, the British also alienated Muslim opinion with the reunification of Bengal announced at the Durbar of 1911, a move that was felt to disadvantage Muslims to much the same degree as the original partition in 1905 had benefited them. These developments led the League to abandon its habitual loyalism and adopt Home Rule as its prime political objective in December 1912. This allowed Jinnah to join the organization with an assurance that doing so involved 'no shadow of disloyalty to the larger national cause to which he had dedicated his life'.[38] His nationalist conscience remained undisturbed.

The period 1913–16 then saw him working hard to bring the two main parties closer together. Most nationalists understood the necessity for unity as a way to counter the British accusation that Indians were chronically unable to agree among themselves and were thus unfit to receive any further degree of self-government. The question, though, was always on what terms unity could be achieved. Congress Moderates were keenest on brokering national Hindu–Muslim unity, while the stiffest resistance came from within the more religious and conservative sections of the Muslim League. The main issue at stake was the separate electorates introduced in 1909. Weightage and the detailed distribution of seats had generally favoured Muslim communities, and most League members were in favour of retaining separate constituencies. Jinnah strongly opposed them, arguing that all they did was to reduce Indian politics to two 'watertight compartments'.[39] Both ideologically and politically, Congress members were generally against any kind of communally based representation, and Jinnah was still taking this line until sometime in 1916.

Jinnah's entry to the League should not be seen as an early desertion of the Congress cause. Indeed, it is more appropriate to see it as an aspect of Jinnah's Congress orthodoxy, for it placed him in a uniquely favourable position, as a uniquely favoured individual, to pull the two bodies together. It was during this phase that Jinnah revealed his ambition to become 'the Muslim Gokhale'. Gokhale was aware of the younger man's political talents and praised him highly, famously dubbing him 'the best ambassador for Hindu–Muslim unity'.[40]

WAR

The outbreak of global conflict in 1914 brought a halt to all schemes for reform, and changed political conditions by making opposition rather more dangerous. But Jinnah set about using the war as an opportunity. He successfully stood again for the legislature in 1915, and made a giant stride towards setting up a united political front when he persuaded both the League and the Congress to hold their annual sessions in Bombay that year, the first time they had held their meetings at the same time in the same city. This move met with opposition both from loyalist and more traditionally religious members of the League, who were unhappy about the liberal–nationalist direction being plotted by the 'Lucknow' clique, within which Jinnah was now a prominent figure. The League session was disrupted by religious hardliners who opposed any form of a joint front with the Congress, forcing the meeting to be adjourned. Jinnah carried his resolutions the next day in a closed session held in Bombay's exclusive Taj Mahal Hotel, where security could be more effectively enforced. As a result, the League abandoned loyalism, stepped away from religious issues and became committed to developing a joint programme with the Congress.

India's unstinting contributions to the war effort soon prompted her leaders to ask for something in return, and the demand for swaraj reappeared more forcefully than ever. Tilak, newly returned from prison in Burma, formed a Home Rule League in April 1916, and Annie Besant, the Anglo-Irish Congress sympathizer, set up another in September. Both still restrained their demands, asking merely for self-government within the Empire, and this remained the standard line until Gandhi dared to go further in 1920.

Jinnah joined Besant's Home Rule League, thus placing himself handily in all India's active nationalist bodies. He further ramped up the pressure on the British in October 1916 by drafting a memorandum supported by 19 members of the 25-man Imperial Legislative Council. This document, agreed on largely with Congress leader Motilal Nehru, then served as the basis for the pact reached that December in Lucknow, where the two parties had again agreed to hold simultaneous sessions, with Jinnah presiding over the League. Both organizations were in an unusually united condition that year; the leading religious militants within the Muslim League were defeated or interned, while the Congress had healed the Moderate–Extremist schism after the return of Tilak.

The Lucknow Pact was a plan of constitutional reform leading to self-government at the earliest opportunity. It demanded a much wider franchise, with an agreement that the separate electorates established in 1909 should remain. It also contained provisions for a third of the seats in a central legislature to be set aside for Muslims, and for various proportions of seats in every province, many of which were very generous to Muslim minorities. As a further safeguard, no proposal that affected any one religious community could be passed if three quarters of that community's representatives opposed it. India's politicians had boiled down three factions into one united front, and for this Jinnah must take an enormous share of the credit.

The most surprising element in the Pact was the preservation of separate electorates, which represented not just a volte-face for Jinnah, but was also his first significant departure from the standard Congress line. Why he did this is disputed, but one important factor may be the voices from within the League that were telling him forcefully that separate electorates were an absolute necessity to preserve Muslim representation. Research seems to show that within the 'open' electorates of UP, Muslims had been doing consistently badly, and if this is true, he cannot but have been told about the situation. Nevertheless, at the cost of this one small concession to special interests, Jinnah could have told himself, with some truth, that he had pulled off a spectacular coup on the national level.

But events overtook the Pact. In one way it was almost too successful. Faced with a united Indian front, the British made concessions within eight months that refocused the minds of the Congress leadership. The year 1917 also saw the emergence as a national figure of a skinny man from Kathiawar, and this brought yet more new elements into the national picture.

THE RISE OF GANDHI

Mohandas Karamchand Gandhi was born in 1869 to a middle-class family in the small state of Porbandar on the west coast of India. His grandfather had been diwan, or chief minister, of the Raja of Porbandar, and his father diwan of Rajkot, another small state nearby. By religion Gandhi was a Hindu with a discernible degree of Jain influence; by caste he was a vaishya, or merchant–trader. A shy and gangly youth, he did not excel at school, and his chief formative teenage experience seems to have been his marriage at the age of 13 to Kasturba. The young groom liked nothing better than making love to his wife, and in his autobiography Gandhi confesses his shame for this juvenile lustfulness.[41] His first mature act was to travel to London in 1888 to study law at the Inner Temple, a decision that put him at odds with his local community, who were prepared to outcaste him for crossing the black water. Undeterred, he sailed, and qualified three years later.

His time in London was of great significance in his development as it convinced him of the limitations of Western civilization. One exception was his discovery of Christianity, and he remained deeply impressed by the ethical teachings of Jesus, especially the short list of injunctions and promises known as the Sermon on the Mount. The humanity of that Sermon, its prophecy that the meek shall inherit the earth and its assurance that the peacemakers shall be blessed were to remain foundational principles of his thinking throughout his political career.

He also explored the Bhagavad Gita in depth for the first time, and was comforted by its complex teachings about courage, strength and duty. Two key themes of the Gita were to inspire him for the rest of his life. The first was its message that one must accept whatever is unavoidable without regret. This played a major part in his acceptance of the Partition Plan of 1947. The other was the Gita's teaching that one should do one's own work well and not engage in that of others.

This allowed him to use his background as a bania, or trader, as a valid basis for a political career. Many times he proudly evoked this relatively humble heritage as a prime justification for what he was doing, describing himself as a 'trader in ahimsa'.[42] But for much of his time in London he was perplexed, hungry and isolated. When he finally found fellow vegetarians, the food and the cause gave him company, nourishment and purpose. The rest of his experiences – the violin lessons, the suits and the dancing – literally left him cold.

He returned to India but struggled to establish himself professionally, eventually taking up an invitation to practise in South Africa. It was during his work there on behalf of the expatriate Indian community, from 1893 to 1914, that he developed the various techniques of exerting political pressure he was later to employ in India. He started newspapers in order to influence wider opinion and wrote for them constantly. He organized labour strikes and later, a type of non-violent mass protest that he called satyagraha, literally 'holding to truth', which he translated into English variously as 'truth force' or 'soul force'.

His repeated successes against the South African colonial authorities attracted notice in England, where the press began to follow the details of South African debates about the rights of Indian immigrants and the various battles fought by Gandhi against overtly racist legislation. As part of that struggle he visited London in 1909 as a member of a delegation to Parliament, during which he met Winston Churchill, then the Colonial Under-Secretary, for the first and only time. When he finally decided to leave South Africa in 1914 he travelled to London first, to see Gokhale, and was received with honour in (liberal) political circles. He even met Jinnah for the first time at a dinner given in his honour at a London hotel. The First World War broke out just days before he arrived in England and he volunteered for service in the Ambulance Corps. At this point he was still convinced that the liberties assured by the British Empire made it an institution worth defending.

But the food and the climate in London did not suit him, and he became increasingly ill through the autumn of 1914. Eventually his pleurisy was so bad that his friends advised him to return to India. He boarded ship in December and arrived in Bombay in early January 1915.

JINNAH, GANDHI AND THE TEA PARTY

Upon Gandhi's return, the Bombay Gurjar Sabha (Gujarati Society) gave a reception for him. Presiding was a local dignitary, Mohammed Ali Jinnah, who made a speech of welcome in English. Gandhi replied in Gujarati and, among other things, expressed pleasure that a Mohammedan was chairing the proceedings. These are the bare facts of the meeting, but fuller accounts of this event differ enormously, and with them the significance it has been accorded. In one version Gandhi actually stops Jinnah in mid-flow and insists that he should speak in Gujarati, thus deliberately embarrassing him. A further refinement has it that Jinnah then tried to speak in Gujarati but failed. These different versions lead on to totally conflicting claims over whether Jinnah could or could not speak Gujarati (he could – it was his mother tongue), and a whole wealth of interpretation about Gandhi's need to cut Jinnah down to size, while Jinnah's determination to carry on is seen as evidence of his indomitable will. This is all grist to the mill of anyone who wishes to set up antipathy, rivalry and irreconcilable differences between the two men at the earliest possible date.

This is only the first of many times in the Jinnah–Gandhi story when less interpretation is required, not more. The events of the evening are clearly set out in a report dated 15 January 1915 in the *Bombay Chronicle*, an eyewitness account. It tells us that Jinnah's speech was followed by one from K.M. Munshi, a young nationalist lawyer, who also spoke in English. No interruption is mentioned. Gandhi then replied, but did not openly chide Jinnah for speaking in English, although he himself chose to address the assembled Gujarati dignitaries in his – and their – own language. He did refer to Jinnah's religion, but only as a way of expressing his pleasure. He said that in South Africa, when it came to talk of Gujaratis, usually 'Parsis and Mahomedans were not thought of', but now he had returned to find a Muslim chairing the meeting.[43] Here was the proof that not all Gujaratis were Hindus.

Gandhi also refers to this incident in his autobiography, describing his decision to speak in Gujarati as a 'humble protest'. He was, as ever, leading by example. That Indians should speak to Indians in Indian languages in India was a central part of his version of the nationalist message. Despite worrying that he might appear 'discourteous' that night, he records that the audience did not take his decision amiss. Nor was it a protest against Jinnah alone. On the day it was as much a rebuke to Munshi, and indeed to himself. When he had addressed a grand gathering at the house of Bombay magnate Jehangir Petit a few days earlier, he had not been able to summon the nerve to speak in Gujarati, and this more intimate occasion afforded him a chance to redress this failing.[44]

The whole incident was not a clash of titans, but a commonplace outing in polite society. Reading manipulative psychology, power politics and the destiny of nations into the affair is uncalled for. Stanley Wolpert is tempted to foresee the rest of the Partition story in the encounter, detecting an early crackling of tension between the two men, a recognition that they were 'natural enemies'.[45] He also describes Gandhi's reference to Jinnah's 'minority identity' in public as 'a barb', meaning that it was designed to wound. This is unwarranted. How calling attention to Jinnah's religion would have helped Gandhi is not clear, nor is it obvious why Gandhi would think it worth any effort to point out to an audience of Bombayites that a man named Mohammed Ali, who was a prominent member of the Muslim League, was a Muslim.

The real story was surely much simpler. There was a friendly reception given for Gandhi and his wife that passed off well. Gandhi was pleased to speak to an audience of Gujaratis in his native land in his native tongue. Everyone was polite to each other and Gandhi took an early step in the promotion of one of his long-term concerns – the use of vernaculars. He was duly welcomed, and the local Bombayites met the celebrity. Nothing was achieved, nothing was decided; everyone went home happy.

GANDHI FINDS HIS FEET

Gandhi spent the rest of 1915 travelling all over India to acquaint himself with the people and their lives. He had spent most of his adult life out of the country and had much to learn about conditions in India. This tour, during which he spent a week with Rabindranath Tagore in Bengal, was the fulfilment of a promise he had made to Gokhale, that he would not engage in politics until a year after his return to India. Gokhale was a shrewd man and he extracted this promise to curb Gandhi's enthusiasm and to embed him in the causes he was keen to champion.

Gandhi shared a great deal of Gokhale's general outlook about rendering service to the poor, but after the latter's death in February 1915 he soon began to exhibit a much deeper radicalism than his mentor had ever espoused. Gokhale expected Gandhi to take on the mantle of his leadership in time, but after his arrival in India, Gandhi showed no interest in the kind of formal politics in which Gokhale had spent his life. His first gesture was to set up an ashram in 1915 at Sabarmati near Ahmedabad, where untouchables were welcomed from the beginning, despite the scandalized reactions this prompted.

Gandhi duly served his year's silent apprenticeship, but when he began to speak out it was in an altogether different register from Gokhale's Moderate, gradualist tone. The first full airing of this new voice came at a gala opening of the Hindu University Central College in Benares (Varanasi) on 4 February 1916. This institution had been founded in 1892 by Annie Besant, but the original school had since been elevated to university status. Congress luminaries, wealthy benefactors and the local aristocracy were present at the grand inauguration, as was Viceroy Lord Hardinge. It was in front of this Westernized, privileged, Raj-friendly audience that Gandhi launched a thoroughgoing attack on Westernization, privilege and the Raj. His speech[46] had little immediate impact and was not widely reported at the time, partly for its content but also because the mass national media was as yet underdeveloped. Nevertheless, that speech is worth examining in some detail because it served notice on the powers-that-were that a new style of radical criticism was coming in from an unfamiliar angle.

That day, Gandhi set out what was in effect a manifesto for his next three decades' work. His hosts might have expected some remarks about the South African struggle, which had given him such renown in India as he then possessed, but he chose to level a series of devastating, and at times highly personal, criticisms at virtually everyone in his audience.

He berated the rajas and aristocrats for their ostentatious jewellery; he regretted that the educated elite chose to learn and conduct their politics in English; he criticized the heavy security that surrounded the Viceroy, asking whether this was any way to build trust, or for the Viceroy, trapped in such a 'living death', to not have any kind of contact with the Indian people in his charge; he bemoaned the dirty state of India's temples and asked what good it would do such places if the British left tomorrow – would they somehow suddenly become clean and wholesome? In response to this verbal attack, there were howls of dissent from the floor and the podium, but also cheers from some of the students. Offended dignitaries walked out and Annie Besant begged him to stop. Eventually he did, but the message had been delivered.

This inflammatory speech previews almost the entirety of Gandhi's subsequent political concerns, and it further developed the philosophy he had set out in *Hind Swaraj*. He touched on the poison of mistrust, the obscenity of the way poverty in India coexisted so closely with vast wealth, the need for politicians to speak to the poor in their own languages, and the shameful lack of selflessness, moral stringency and high-mindedness in public affairs. His criticisms clearly set out what he thought the effective Indian politician should be – a modest person living a life as much like the people he sought to represent as was possible. How could India be freed if her leaders never met real Indians, could not understand what they said, did not share their concerns, and had no knowledge of their lives and their needs?

Gandhi had not yet found his niche, but he had unambiguously set out what he wanted to achieve. As 1916 ended, he had served notice that he would not be put into some convenient, pre-existing box that the Congress, or even Gokhale, had designed for him.

THE MONTAGU DECLARATION

By the time the Lucknow Pact was agreed, the First World War had been grinding on for over two years, and had begun to affect India profoundly. There was much economic hardship, especially due to inflation and high prices. The British were worried by terrorist plots, both real and imaginary, and were facing acute embarrassment over the disastrous Mesopotamia Campaign, in which the lives of many Indian soldiers had been squandered. The atmosphere was further soured when Annie Besant was interned for sedition in June 1917, with Jinnah stepping up to take her place at the head of her Home Rule League.

Events in the wider British context then played a vital part. Ministerial resignations over Mesopotamia brought the sympathetic Edwin Montagu to the India Office. Under his influence the British Government, recognizing the new unity of India's political classes, made a gesture of appeasement to the nationalists that was intended to acknowledge the fearless loyalty with which Indian soldiers of all ranks were giving their lives all over the world for the Empire. On 20 August 1917, Montagu read a carefully prepared statement to the House of Commons, announcing that further constitutional reform would be coming to India at the end of the war.[47] The statement was artfully vague, but its overall thrust was clear. Change was coming and it would include a greater involvement of Indians in their own affairs. The key words were 'responsible government', which seemed to be the appropriate promise, and loyalty's expected and merited reward. Details were not provided, but Montagu went out to India in late 1917 for a round of investigations and consultations.

Unspecific though it was, the Montagu Declaration permanently changed the Indian political agenda. Instead of demanding adjustments to the existing arrangements, Indian politicians could now imagine new systems, which undermined the Lucknow Pact. But much more significantly for the future of India, the prospect of self-government turned the Congress, as by far the largest national body, from an opposition into a government-in-waiting. If at this point the Muslim League was not absorbed into the Congress, and if Muslims could not be persuaded to feel that Congress politicians were acting in their interests, the Muslim League faced potential marginalization. Were Congress leaders to feel that they no longer needed to put up the united front that had seemed so necessary to extract concessions, the Muslim League would have to remain a permanent junior partner in the game. Of all Indian politicians, this development threatened to strike most directly at

Jinnah, by downgrading his status as the central channel of nationalist cooperation. And as the Congress grew in stature and self-regard, it also threatened to undermine the ability of Muslims as a community to safeguard their interests.

GANDHI'S FIRST PEAK

Gandhi's star, meanwhile, was rising as rapidly as Jinnah's had in 1915–16. He was not interested in constitutional details, and his general support for the war led him away from the usual run of nationalist politics. Instead, he concentrated on developing his own more direct, personal swaraj campaign. Over the years 1917–18, he established himself as a fighter for the underprivileged, and his popularity soared.

It began in December 1916, when he was approached at the Lucknow Congress by a peasant who told him about the injustices inflicted by indigo planters. This encounter led him to Champaran (Bihar) in March 1917, where he spent a year, on and off, fighting on behalf of the local farmers who had been reduced to poverty by the powerful indigo interests in the area. For the first time Gandhi came face to face with British officialdom in India, and his steady resolve forced it to back down. Involvement in a mill workers' strike in Ahmedabad the next year further enhanced his reputation as the champion of the downtrodden. It was during this strike that he first used the device of fasting. Between March and June 1918 he then led a protest against high taxes in the Kheda district in Gujarat. When the authorities finally caved in, he had racked up a third successful campaign.

These confrontations were very important in building Gandhi's reputation as a warrior–saint in the cause of the oppressed peasantry, and in allowing him to develop a range of effective protest methods. They also gave him something more politically valuable than either tactics or reputation; they gave him access to mass support independent of the Congress. The local links he established, such as with Rajendra Prasad in Bihar and Vallabhbhai Patel in Gujarat, lasted for the rest of his life.

By mid-1918 Gandhi was not just a leader, he was a leader with his own programme, his own methods and his own men.

GANDHI'S FIRST CRISIS

While India waited for Secretary Montagu to dream up a new scheme of government, the Raj asked for yet more effort. In April 1918, Viceroy Chelmsford invited India's leaders, including Jinnah and Gandhi, to Delhi for a War Conference. Here for the first time Jinnah came into open conflict with Gandhi, over the issue of recruitment. Jinnah was determined that the war should present opportunities for India and he brought up a list of grievances, especially the denial of commissioned rank to Indians. He wanted these grievances to be addressed before India provided more men. Gandhi took a more trusting line, and was prepared to defend the Empire as it was, not only because of the ideals of freedom it stood for, but because military service and the profession of arms was a stepping stone to the personal swaraj – self-discipline – that particularly concerned him. In direct contradiction to his pacifism, his political instinct told him that loyalty would persuade the British of the justice of Indian demands for self-government, and that Indians should enlist willingly because the British would be sure to reward them for their loyalty. In this respect he seems to have underestimated the capacity of the British for meanness and overestimated the appetite of Indians for self-sacrifice. And as he did so, he effectively cut the ground from under Jinnah's feet.

Stimulated by the Viceroy's request, Gandhi decided to go to familiar parts of Gujarat to raise men, but when he arrived there in July he found that his revered status among India's peasantry was no guarantee of success. The farmers of Kheda, who had completely understood his non-violent campaign against economic and social injustice, failed to grasp why he was now trying to get 12,000 of them to go to the Western Front. Where three months before they had loved and admired him, now they refused to enlist, or even to let him hire a cart to travel in. The shock was so great that his overworked and undernourished body collapsed into illness for most of the rest of 1918. He only began to recover when news of the defeat of Germany finally resolved the various ethical and political dilemmas that the war had imposed on him.

ROWLATT TO AMRITSAR: 1918–19

With the war finally won, the political climate should have improved, but the British contrived ways to ensure that it did not. All the optimism born of the Lucknow Pact and the Montagu Declaration had evaporated by then, because of the ungenerous and paranoid reaction to the end of the war by Raj officials.

During 1917, fears about 'criminal conspiracies' between hostile foreign powers and terrorist networks across India had led to the setting up of an enquiry under a senior British judge, Sir Sidney Rowlatt, to consider what changes, if any, needed to be made to the laws on sedition and general security when hostilities ceased. The Rowlatt Committee reported in July 1918 and recommended that the special wartime powers of the courts to try men without juries, defence counsel or appeals, should be extended beyond the end of the war. The legal authority resting in government hands under the 1915 Defence of India Act was to be extended by an initial six months, while permanent changes were to be made to criminal procedure in cases of sedition. These recommendations horrified the Indian political establishment. They seemed unreasonably harsh – a calculated snub to Indian expectations of better post-war relations with the British, and a monstrous piece of ingratitude for India's wartime sacrifices and unfailing loyalty.

Rowlatt's work ran simultaneously with that of Montagu, but was pulling in the opposite direction. Montagu finished his fact-finding mission in April 1918, and then drew up a set of proposed reforms with the Viceroy, Lord Chelmsford. These were published in July 1918, but were overshadowed by the near simultaneous appearance of the Rowlatt Report, after which public reaction to the two Reports became inextricably entangled.

The immediate political effect of the Montagu–Chelmsford Report was to spark a divisive debate within the Congress over whether to cooperate with the new system or to oppose it, an argument that eventually led to another Congress split, with the Liberals leaving permanently to set up on their own. Jinnah was reluctantly prepared to accept the Montagu–Chelmsford package as a temporary measure, while Gandhi was happy to 'work' the new system.

As for the Rowlatt proposals, the Indian political nation rejected them unanimously. Yet despite all the protests, they were passed into law as two Acts in March 1919. Jinnah was scandalized and resigned from his seat on the legislative council, telling Viceroy Chelmsford in a letter that his government had forfeited the right to call itself 'civilised'.[48]

Gandhi informed the Viceroy in February that if the Acts were passed into law, he would call for non-violent action to register India's displeasure. The first wave of protests duly took place on 30 March 1919, in the form of a hartal, or general strike, during which the city of Delhi came to a complete standstill. The protest passed off peacefully there, although there were deaths in Ahmedabad. Violence also broke out in Amritsar in the Punjab, where two nationalist leaders, Satya Pal and Saifuddin Kitchlew, were expelled from the city, leading to further rioting. The situation then appeared to have calmed down, but General Dyer, the local officer commanding, feared for the safety of the town's European population. He decided to teach the locals a lesson and fired on an unarmed crowd of several thousand assembled in Jallianwala Bagh, a small piece of open ground surrounded by buildings and walls. Sustained fire from Dyer's small contingent killed at least 379 people and wounded around 1,200 more.

The Indian public was outraged, as were some on the British side; in the House of Commons Winston Churchill called it a 'monstrous event'[49]. Explanations were required, and a Commission of Enquiry was set up that October under the chairmanship of Lord William Hunter. Dyer explained to Hunter that he thought there were exits from the Bagh and that the crowd was simply being stubborn. Hunter's Report, eventually delivered in March 1920, found no evidence of a plot to raise the Punjab in revolt, but delivered only a lukewarm condemnation of Dyer's actions: he had not issued due warning; he had continued to fire for an unnecessarily long period; he had not tended to the wounded. Back in England the public rallied to Dyer's cause. Though he was forced to retire, a large sum of money was collected for his upkeep. Even worse, a substantial faction in Parliament approved of his actions and said so, while a motion of support was passed in the House of Lords.

All this was deeply distressing and unsatisfactory to Indians. The Rowlatt Acts looked like tyranny writ enormously large and the mistrust they embodied was inexplicable to moderate Indian opinion. The Amritsar massacre seemed barbaric and indefensible, yet there were voices raised to support it in Britain. Dyer shot away any hope of a new 'liberal' consensus between India and Britain, and even between Indians. What hope, then, was there that any new constitutional tinkering would bring better government to British India, if injustice in the courts and slaughter on the streets were to be the hallmarks of British rule?

Eight months after the horrors of Amritsar, the shape of the new India was determined. The proposals of Secretary Montagu and Viceroy Chelmsford passed into law as the Government of India Act, 1919. With it came a proclamation from George V himself on 23 December, in which the King–Emperor expressed his hopes that bitterness would be left behind and that future relations would be more cordial. He was to be disappointed.

JINNAH, GANDHI AND THE FIRST IMPERIAL WAR

In 1914, Gandhi urged Indians to 'think imperially' as a way to establish a store of goodwill in British hearts that could only help to win swaraj. He then stayed loyal to the Empire throughout the war, as he had done twice before, in wars against the Boers and the Zulus in South Africa. The champion of ahimsa supported the war because it was a potential path to good outcomes, both in terms of the relationship with Britain and in offering Indians a chance to discipline themselves.

Jinnah's reaction was rather different – it was dictated by a desire to make bargains. He was prepared to support the war, partly because to do otherwise was hazardous, but he wanted something specific in return. He repeatedly pointed out the injustices done to serving Indian soldiers, and skilfully demonstrated how British actions were often fundamentally in breach of the principles they claimed to be fighting to protect. The temporary slackening in the political tension between Indians was a great help to him in his attempts to form a united nationalist bloc and once unity was achieved, he expected a reasonable response from the British. This put him in direct opposition to Gandhi's attitude, which seemed to become increasingly compliant as the war went on.

The first open breach between the two men was at the War Conference of April 1918, when Gandhi played the loyalist, keen to help raise volunteers, while Jinnah demanded the immediate introduction of a Parliamentary Bill to set up Home Rule as laid out in the Lucknow Pact. He wanted to see Indians fighting in the war as equal citizens of the Empire, not mercenaries. Jinnah's priorities were clear – concessions before enlistment. Gandhi took the opposite view – enlistment would bring concessions.

This disagreement was based on the very different understanding the two men had of swaraj. In Jinnah's world, swaraj meant responsible Home Rule on the Canadian model. It was a political arrangement that could be argued over in detail and arrived at in stages. The war presented a real opportunity to get it. Even after the Amritsar shootings, he was still prepared to go to London and appear before Lord Selbourne's Joint Parliamentary Committee to discuss details of the new India Bill. He carried on pulling conventional political levers, expecting conventional political responses.

Gandhi's approach to politics was always less mechanistic, and for him swaraj was a matter of deep personal reformation, which would in time produce its own correct implementation. *Hind Swaraj* sets out at length his definition of self-government, which is not remotely technical or constitutional. Swaraj, he wrote, is 'when we rule ourselves', and by this he meant morally as well as politically, and individually as well as collectively. Swaraj was something everyone could achieve for themselves at any time. He was so mistrustful of political processes that he explicitly stated: 'What others get for me is not Home Rule but foreign rule'.[50] This indifference to external forms, which persisted throughout his career, allowed him to maintain a surface loyalty to the British Empire at a time when Jinnah was becoming exasperated.

Governor Willingdon of Bombay held his own war conference in June 1918, and Jinnah again demanded not words but 'action and immediate deeds'[51] on the matter of granting Indians self-government, and trusting them as soldiers to carry arms in defence of their own land.

The impatience, even the passion, that is discernible in Jinnah through 1918 led him to his one period of radical opposition to the British. After the Delhi and Bombay conferences, he maintained his public opposition to the Raj when the Montagu–Chelmsford scheme and the Rowlatt Report were published in July. This phase peaked in December, when he led a mass protest against a civic function to mark the end of Governor Willingdon's term. After the successful disruption of the event Jinnah seems, uncharacteristically, to have got rather carried away with the emotion of the moment, instructing his audience to 'rejoice over the day that has secured us the triumph of democracy'.[52]

This was only one of many false dawns on the road to Independence, but it marked a rare moment when Jinnah's popularity eclipsed that of Gandhi. Jinnah was then at his peak. Handsome, energetic and imperious, newly married to the beautiful heiress Rattanbai Petit, he was India's chief political broker, acclaimed as the uncrowned king of Bombay. Gandhi, in stark contrast, spent the end of 1918 demoralized, unpopular and ill. His health did not return until 1920, but he managed a political recovery before then, riding the wave of outrage against the Rowlatt Acts and the massacre at Amritsar. He took control of two magazines – *Navajivan* in Gujarati and *Young India* in English, which he intended to use to educate the wider public in satyagraha. In a much bolder move he also managed to reach out to the one constituency beyond Jinnah's reach – the religious Muslims.

Gandhi Raj: 1919–29

Jinnah and Gandhi had always agreed about the necessity for national unity, and Jinnah, as the senior figure, was better placed to bring this about in the 1915–19 period. The Lucknow Pact and the coordinated response to both the Rowlatt and Montagu–Chelmsford proposals were the results. Jinnah went about building national unity in a conventional manner within the political class, and succeeded well enough. But events conspired to undo most of this work, and Gandhi then managed to build a national alliance of much greater potency by avoiding the political classes and exploring issues that were less conventionally political.

THE GULF OPENS

By the middle of 1919, Jinnah and Gandhi disagreed on several areas of policy and tactics. The two were soon to engage in a contest for the leadership of the Congress and over the very nature of the organization.

Though Jinnah was still a prominent member of the Muslim League, in many ways he was actually more of a typical Congressman than Gandhi. He was not so far from the position of, for instance, Motilal Nehru within the Congress fold – with his gradual reformism and patrician, non-sectarian views built around faith in a British-style executive centre. The Congress believed in 'big' government to go with the big nation, which set it apart from the Muslim League, whose leadership was very prone to provincial leanings. Congress leaders had always assumed that they would inherit the imperial governmental machine and use it to make economic and social progress. This, again, was nearer to Jinnah's position than that of conservative or religious League leaders.

But Gandhi was of a new type. He had never subscribed to Moderate beliefs that: 1) the British presence was the best guarantee of national unity and order; 2) that they should not be forced out too quickly; and 3) that they were in effect partners in reform and progress. Until the war, Gandhi had wanted the British out as soon as possible, because he directly connected their continued presence with all the moral ills within Indian society. He took a 'No swaraj, no progress' line, while Jinnah held to Gokhale's 'Reform now, British out later' approach. Conditions during the war had gone some way towards reversing these stances, but after Rowlatt and Amritsar the two reverted to their previous positions.

They were soon also deeply divided over methods, and it was here that Gandhi was to make his greatest contribution, by moving the Congress into a new, more radical era of mass agitation. He realigned the party behind full self-government, social reform and local self-sufficiency, while adorning these policies with semi-spiritual trappings. Jinnah was highly uncomfortable with several aspects of the new Gandhian direction. As a believer in leadership, he was wary of mass agitation and preferred gradualist, institutional reforms to revolutionary change. He also disliked the mixing of religious feelings with politics, fearing that this might open the way to intensified communal tensions. To put the two together, which seemed to be (and was) Gandhi's intention, he considered unwise.

GANDHI AND THE KHILAFAT

Gandhi recovered from illness through early 1919 and restored his public standing through the Rowlatt protests of that spring. When he was arrested and prevented from travelling to Amritsar a few days before the massacre, Rabindranath Tagore wrote an open letter to him on 12 April, dignifying him with the title of 'Mahatma' (great soul).[53] This new status neatly matched the new energy he discovered once the end of the war had left him free to lead a wave of nationalist moral outrage against the Raj. The passing of the Rowlatt 'black Acts', the shootings in Amritsar, the half-hearted British attempts to criticize or make amends for them, and the high-handed treatment of Turkey by the British at the end of the war all propelled Gandhi into the kind of struggle he understood and was best equipped to fight.

Although a nationwide campaign of 'non-cooperation' was the eventual result, Gandhi's radicalism had a rather slow burn to it across 1919. His first national political act as Mahatma was to persuade the Congress, at its December 1919 session in Amritsar, to accept the Montagu–Chelmsford reforms and to 'work' them. The meeting acquiesced but also passed a motion declaring them to be 'inadequate and unsatisfactory'. But within a few months, largely in the light of his own investigations, as a member of a Congress enquiry into the 'Punjab atrocities', Gandhi turned against the Raj and decided to lead India into a nationwide non-violent protest, against the reforms and British policy towards Turkey. Resentment at the treatment of the Turkish Sultan had provoked protest among India's Muslims – the Khilafat Movement, which grew up during the final stages of the First World War, as Turkey came under military occupation and faced dismemberment at the hands of Britain, France, Italy and Greece. In an extraordinarily bold move, Gandhi decided to join and then to lead this movement, alongside the brothers Shaukat and Muhammad Ali, and Maulana Azad, all three of whom were freed from internment in late 1919.

Where Jinnah resigned from the central legislature over Rowlatt, where Tagore renounced his knighthood after the Amritsar shooting, Gandhi took a much more active stance and in the early months of 1920, he incited the nation to non-violent protests on an unprecedented scale. Again, he informed the Viceroy of his intentions and the action began on 1 August 1920.

Uniting the religious Khilafat Movement and the non-sectarian Non-Cooperation protest was entirely Gandhi's achievement, undertaken outside the boundaries of Congress politics; in 1919 he held no Congress office or position. Having made a personal alliance with the Khilafat leadership, he then asked the Congress to join him in the protests. Action was already under way that September when he persuaded a special Congress session at Calcutta to recommend joining the movement, and the full Congress session in Nagpur that December eventually agreed. It was only at this point that the Congress officially adopted Non-Cooperation.

This was a remarkable series of developments, one that brought an irreversible change to Indian politics. It lifted Gandhi into unprecedented prominence, radicalized the masses of the subcontinent and introduced a specifically religious element into national issues. As a short-term bid for national unity it was highly successful, but the alliance it created was fragile. Gandhi adopted the Khilafat because he was personally able to sympathize with the outraged religious sensibilities of Muslims. To cement his pact with them he had merely required that the Khilafat organizers were to join the Non-Cooperation movement with full enthusiasm, and that protests were to be non-violent. He obtained agreement to these conditions in mid-1920, although the Khilafat Committee accepted non-violence only as a tactic and not as a binding principle. A national alliance was thus created that superficially embodied the Congress ideal of undifferentiated Indianness; at the same time it marked the abandonment of constitutional proceeding and of the secular, liberal agenda. It was also highly dependent on the person of Gandhi himself, because large sections of the established Congress leadership harboured serious reservations about supporting a cause that, if successful, would advance the Sultan's authority rather more than the prospects of Indian swaraj. But Gandhi was determined that it was the duty of Hindus and Muslims 'to share one another's sorrow'.[54]

As the Non-Cooperation agitation began, the old-style Congress, educated and legalistic, finally disappeared. Gandhi had been asked at the Amritsar Congress of 1919 to revise the party's constitution and within a year he had expanded its popular base, moralized its programme and radicalized its methods. Having done all this he managed, from 1920 to 1922, to deliver a brief glimpse of the power of unity to India's politicians. But confused objectives and indiscipline in the ranks were to render that glimpse all too fleeting. It ended in defeat; the Khilafat was abolished by the Turks, and the reforms survived.

THE MONTAGU–CHELMSFORD CONSTITUTION, 1919

What was in the new reform package? The main developments were that the electoral principle was now widely distributed across India's institutions, and 'responsibility' came to provincial government for the first time.

At the national level, at least three Indians were henceforward to sit on the Viceroy's executive council and there was a new central legislative assembly of 146 members, elected every three years, and a Council of State of 61, elected every five years. This looked a little like a Westminster-style government, with an upper and lower chamber and a Cabinet, but the catch was that the chief executive and his ministers were not responsible to the central assembly; they were appointed by and answerable to elected politicians in London. In effect this meant that Indian politicians at the centre wielded a minimal amount of political leverage. The future of Indian politics under the Montagu–Chelmsford reforms lay in the provinces.

At the provincial level, enlarged legislative assemblies now had non-official, elected majorities on a slightly wider franchise, and ministers in charge of certain government departments were now to be nominated by, and responsible to, these assemblies. This was called dyarchy, implying a twofold holding of power. The basis of this power-sharing was a careful division of provincial government into transferred and reserved subjects, with elected ministers given charge only of transferred subjects. These included health, public works, education and agriculture; in other words the less strategic, 'nation-building' departments. The reserved departments covered the vital concerns of government, such as the police, judiciary and finance, and were run, as previously, by nominated British officials. The Governor retained a veto over all legislative proposals and could force through, or 'certify' any measure he pleased.

The British tried to represent the new system as a training ground for responsible government. More realistically it could be seen as a sop to local notables, who were bought off with responsibility for minor administrative functions. Significantly, the reforms did nothing to clarify the exact relationship between national and local powers within India, and potential tensions between an autocratic centre and democratic provinces were not addressed. This left fertile ground for the centralizing, 'national' Congress to clash with other organizations more wedded to provincial identities and aims.

THE RISE OF PROVINCIAL POLITICS

It was in the provinces that the new system placed its most subtle checks and balances, for it was here that the largest concessions had been made. The 1919 electorate was small and still segregated along religious lines, but 'weightage' ensured that no single community could dominate any provincial electoral body. This looked like a safeguard for Muslims, and it did indeed work in that way in some provinces, but more broadly it meant that any politician who wished to build an effective power base had to make coalitions across communities. There was also a strong bias in the way the constituencies were drawn, giving rural voters a preponderant voice. This may have reflected the rural character of India but it also brought that character right into the heart of the new politics. Rather like eighteenth-century England, the new franchise put landlords in a prime position to build political influence. It was no accident that the most powerful parties in Punjab and the United Provinces were directly based on rural power. Punjab's Unionist Party and the UP's Agriculturalist Party were to dominate their respective provinces until the next reforms in 1935. The effects in Bengal were more complex, producing a large bloc of Muslim peasant voters, which opened the way for a more class-based approach to politics. The ramifications of weighting in the province and the jealousies among both the larger Hindu and smaller Muslim elites lent a fluidity, or chronic instability, to Bengali politics. But in all these cases, as with the Justice Party in Madras, which was formed to combat brahmin domination, it was local issues and loyalties that were the key drivers of politics

Under the 1919 Act the prime devolution of political authority was to governors, not ministers, and so power remained only loosely dependent upon electoral results. However, there were still opportunities for strong individuals to find a role at the central level – not to wield direct power, from which they were still insulated, but to attain public prominence. A central all-India platform was now a permanent feature of Indian political life, and Jinnah set out to use it to advance the cause of constitutional reform.

The Congress remained split on how to use the new assembly, but Jinnah had no hesitation in building his own status through speaking and serving on select committees in an attempt to advance the nationalist cause. He remained the hardest worker and the loudest spokesman for national unity throughout the mid-1920s. He had only one weakness, but it was a very serious one – the community that he actually represented was not particularly supportive of him, or unified within itself. Gandhi, on the other hand, took his own route to national prominence, bypassing British institutions entirely.

The Montagu–Chelmsford system was not designed to nurture the ambitions of men like these, but their determination forced them through. They were two fish that the net was not designed to catch.

GANDHI TAKES THE REINS

Although there was much at stake politically through 1920, personal relations between the two men do not seem to have been particularly strained. Although some historians are keen to ramp up the tension between the two of them at this stage, which makes for a good story, there is no direct evidence that there was any real animus between them, even after the Congress adopted Non-Cooperation. But several converging narratives were conspiring to set them directly against each other.

One of these was that the Congress was looking for new leadership. The last of the older generation finally departed with the death of Tilak in August 1920, after which new men were needed to deal with new issues. It was not clear who these would be, but they would come from among a pool of younger contenders that included Jinnah, Gandhi, Chittaranjan Das and Motilal Nehru. To some degree, the politics of the next few years were determined by the relationships of these main players and the rise and fall of the causes they stood for. Neither Jinnah nor Gandhi had as solid a base in conventional Congress politics as Nehru or Das, but Jinnah as arch-unifier and Gandhi as moral authority could both lay claims to national status that Bengal's Das and UP's Nehru could not easily match.

Another strand was the long-running demand for swaraj. In April 1920, Jinnah proposed Gandhi as his successor for the presidency of the Bombay Home Rule League, which had been founded in 1916 and ran parallel with the Congress in its demand for Home Rule within the British Empire. M.R. Jayakar, its secretary, opposed Gandhi's candidacy and wrote to him that he was concerned that he might bring to the organization some of his 'pet theories' or 'fantastic fads'[55] – meaning satyagraha and hand-spinning, which Gandhi had been promoting vigorously since he learned the skill in early 1919. But Gandhi had enough political momentum to win the presidency, and in an important public statement he set out his intentions, reassuring the League's members that he had joined the organization purely to advance his preferred 'causes', which he listed as 'swadeshi, Hindu–Moslem unity with special reference to Khilafat, the acceptance of Hindustani as the lingua franca and a linguistic redistribution of the Provinces'.[56] But that October, with Non-Cooperation already running, he decided to change the Home Rule League's name to the more patriotic Swarajya Sabha, and to propose that its basic constitution be amended, abandoning the milder Home Rule demand in favour of complete self-government. Jinnah and Annie Besant then resigned along with a number of others.

Gandhi asked Jinnah to reconsider, but Jinnah declined to rejoin, stating that he could not accept the Mahatma's methods or his programme, which he was sure would 'lead to disaster' and 'chaos'.[57] Instead, he called for an agreed programme among nationalists to bring responsible government to India.

To Jinnah, the whole direction of national politics seemed to be going off track. He was clear that resorting to extra-constitutional methods – whipping up 'mob hysteria' – was a mistake. Along with Tagore, he also had serious reservations about the sacrifices that Non-Cooperation demanded of individuals. He saw no benefit in Indians denying themselves education, and he saw only suffering in the spectacle of poor people burning cheap foreign garments when they were barely able to clothe themselves. He saw no Indian interests at stake in the Khilafat issue, and he thought it ill advised to turn it into a Muslim League cause, let alone a Congress one. But by late 1920, the national mood was militant.

Having withdrawn from the Home Rule League, Jinnah could only challenge Gandhi within the Congress, but his prospects of changing the national direction were not good. There had been an enormous upsurge of interest in the Congress among Muslims, so that audiences at that year's session at Nagpur were larger and more vociferous than usual. This did not bode well for moderate, secular voices. Jinnah spoke against Non-Cooperation but was constantly interrupted and even booed. He took the hint and walked out of the meeting, leaving Gandhi to carry the resolution adopting Non-Cooperation.

It is tempting to interpret the proceedings at Nagpur as a clash of ambitions between the two men, and there is an element of truth in such a reading, but there is also a connection to the longer view of Jinnah that should not be neglected. It was the events of 1920 that convinced him that there was no longer a way forward to Muslim equality through the Congress. It is not correct to say that he permanently severed all ties with the Congress at this point; he attended the next year's session at Ahmedabad. But the Nagpur session clearly demonstrated that the Congress was going to be a mass-based party, and a mass-based party *had* to be a Hindu party, Gandhi or no Gandhi. The popular Muslim element within the Congress that year was temporary and contingent, and it was not the constituency to which Jinnah wished to appeal.

GANDHI'S FIRST NATIONAL MOVEMENT

Having persuaded the Congress to back Non-Cooperation, Gandhi promised swaraj within a year. This was an ambitious boast, one that he redeemed by repeatedly redefining what swaraj meant. Through that year it became less political as a goal, and slowly metamorphosed into forms of self-respect and, eventually, freedom from fear. These were worthy enough objectives in themselves and they harmonized exactly with the overall thrust of his wider spiritual concerns, but as real political gains such redefinitions fell a little short. Meanwhile, students boycotted schools and colleges, government employees left their jobs and lawyers withdrew from the courts. But the Raj did not fall. Instead it struck back vigorously, imprisoning the firebrand Ali brothers in July 1921 for exhorting Muslims not to join the armed forces. The controlled energy of the campaign's early months was followed by various kinds of uncontrolled chaos. In August 1921, the Muslim Mapillah community of Malabar decided to start a jihad against wealthy Hindus in the region; murder and forced conversions followed. The Prince of Wales was sent to drum up loyal support, but his visit, in November 1921, only produced protests and boycotts. Black flags greeted him at the docks and he drove through streets empty of admirers. Riots followed in which over 50 people were killed. A peace offer came from the new Viceroy, Lord Reading, to try to make a success of the Prince's visit, but Gandhi turned down the chance of talks – an act for which he was roundly criticized afterwards by C.R. Das and S.C. Bose. By the close of 1921, several important Congress leaders were in prison, including Motilal Nehru and his son Jawaharlal. In all, around 20,000 persons were in custody as the new year began.

Gandhi was trapped. There was no progress to be made by negotiation because the British could not concede; they could hardly expect to hold India for another week if the protests were seen to be effective. On the other hand, Gandhi could not call off the campaign. He would be left with nowhere to go politically if he did and, more importantly, he was not sure that he actually could. In the end he decided to raise the stakes, and announced a projected satyagraha in the region of Bardoli in Gujarat. This district was small enough to be controllable, under the watchful eye of Vallabhbhai Patel, but it was also large enough, with around 90,000 people, to make a serious impression if a tax strike could be kept solid. Gandhi, as was his wont, informed Lord Reading of his plan, but the whole enterprise was aborted when word came that 22 policemen had been killed in the small town of Chauri Chaura (UP).

Tension between local peasants and police had been running high in the area, and after a confused series of violent incidents, a large crowd of protesters had surrounded and burned down the police station. Gandhi was devastated at the news. This was not the only fatal incident in the campaign, but it somehow spoke to the Mahatma as the voice of God, telling him that he was on the wrong course. Shortly afterwards he called off the entire Non-Cooperation movement and went on a fast to atone personally for the failure of the nation to maintain self-discipline. The British intended to extract their own idea of penance and arrested him in early March for a series of articles in his English language magazine, *Young India*, which they considered seditious.

GANDHI ON TRIAL

Gandhi answered these charges at Ahmedabad in what became known as the Great Trial. This was a hyperbolic title, considering that he put up no defence, pleaded guilty with all his heart and actually requested that he be given the 'severest penalty'.[58] But as a trial of the man and his cause in the court of wider opinion, it was a sensation. Gandhi had faced a court in India once before – in Champaran in 1917, when he had deliberately flouted an official order to quit the district. That incident never came to a full hearing because the magistrate was so intimidated by thousands of peasants sitting around the courthouse to show solidarity with the saintly stranger that he asked for advice from his superiors, who decided not to press the issue. In this first face-off with British justice in India, Gandhi had won hands down.

It was very different in Ahmedabad. This time the defendant insisted that he was guilty as charged. He had preached sedition against the government and he was extremely proud to have done so. To deny it would be to render himself not only a liar but also a coward, and thus negate all his fine words about self-respect and fearlessness. It was his duty and his privilege to oppose an evil government that had done so much harm. Furthermore, he actually felt so conscience-stricken about the deaths of the policemen and others that he had no wish, on a personal level, to do anything other than to submit himself to punishment. By refusing to evade the charges in any way, Gandhi reversed the roles of prosecutor and defendant. By claiming it was his bounden duty to resist the government set over him, he was goading it into an act of petty vengeance, shaming it with its willingness to crush a defenceless man striving for liberty.

He did not seek to dispute the authority of the court; he was merely showing its basis in injustice. This could as easily be highlighted by accepting the law as by opposing it. In accepting the court and the verdict, Gandhi was essentially demonstrating his own highly localized swaraj. By willingly accepting his guilt under British law with a clean conscience, he managed, in his own eyes, to condemn the law and acquit himself.

But under the veneer of defiance, he was mortified that his people had not proved equal to the task of struggling against their iniquitous government without descending to rancour and bitterness, that they had not absorbed the lessons that non-violent struggle was designed to teach, that they had not been able to stand firm and show their oppressors, through the medium of loving kindness, the error of their brutal ways. After the 1919 protests against the Rowlatt Acts descended into violence he had accused himself of a 'Himalayan miscalculation',[59] but this was worse. More important issues had been at stake this time, greater numbers of people had been involved, and more had in some ways been lost because the government was stronger than ever and the people had learned nothing but discouraging lessons. He accepted the six-year jail term he received and resolved to make better plans for the future. He did not lead another national satyagraha until 1930, fully eight years away. On the plus side, the British never dared put him on trial again. Though they imprisoned him several more times, they knew after 1922 that a man of his unique abilities could turn any trial into a triumph, no matter where they sent him afterwards.

CALM RETURNS

The defeat of Non-Cooperation delivered a severe blow to the cause of national unity. Radicals, like the young Jawaharlal Nehru, felt betrayed by Gandhi, while conservative Hindus were thoroughly alarmed by the show of Muslim strength and passion. With Gandhi in jail, the Congress was left leaderless, and spent the rest of the decade working through a long-running split over whether to work inside Raj institutions or outside. The Muslim League hardly fared better, because the only clearly Islamic religious issue – the Khilafat – quickly faded out of national politics as the new Turkish state under Mustapha Kemal Pasha gradually divested itself of its Ottoman legacy, leaving no Khalifa to support. This actually suited Jinnah, who was able to redirect the League towards more pressing, more Indian, more secular issues. The League had effectively lapsed during the Khilafat agitation, but by 1924 he had raised sufficient enthusiasm to resume annual sessions.

While its most dangerous opponents all suffered, the Raj survived largely intact, and even prospered politically. Law and order, finance and foreign affairs were still entirely in the hands of the British, and national politics remained a sideshow for most elite Indians. If the idea of the reforms had been to pull attention away from the centre, it generally seemed to be working through the mid-1920s. India began to fall under the spell of provincial politics as the ambitious classes moved into positions of responsibility tied to the new assemblies. The Congress remained in opposition, but prominent Muslim League leaders like Sir Muhammad Shafi and the Aga Khan were generally loyalists, and were rewarded for it.

Jinnah maintained the nationalist cause in the assembly, pressing for reform and greater inclusion of Indians in all branches of government and the military, but he cooperated with the government as he saw fit and maintained sufficiently cordial relations with the Raj to be offered a knighthood in 1925. He refused it curtly, saying he preferred to remain 'plain Mr. Jinnah'[60] till he died.

The next great national issue was to be the appointment of the Simon Commission in 1927, but the years till then were not entirely dormant for either Jinnah or Gandhi.

GANDHI AND THE COMMUNAL PROBLEM

Gandhi remained in prison till February 1924, when the authorities set him free four years early, after an attack of appendicitis had threatened his life. Somewhat reluctantly he returned to Congress politics, determined to work for unity and reconciliation.

The solidarity achieved during the first days of the Khilafat–Non-Cooperation alliance was long gone, and intercommunal relations had seriously deteriorated. At the end of May 1924 Gandhi penned an article in *Young India* in which he reiterated his belief in the importance of harmony between the communities. Friendship, he declared, was essential for India's future and for the prospects of swaraj 'because it is so natural, so necessary for both [communities] and because I believe in human nature'.[61] But too few humans were listening at this point. At a meeting of the All-India Congress Committee (AICC) in June it became clear that his hold over the party was waning, and he wept publicly as he felt the commitment to non-violence draining away in the country. Unfortunately, he was right. Where there had been around 16 major communal incidents between 1900 and 1922, there were 72 between 1923 and 1926.

When serious communal riots broke out on 9 September 1924 in Kohat (North-West Frontier Province), the Sikhs and Hindus of the town were driven out in two days of arson and murder. Gandhi was appalled. To try to expiate the nation's guilt, to bring the offenders back to their senses and to prevent further outbreaks, he announced he would embark on a 21-day fast for peace. This he would undertake under the roof of Muhammad Ali, his old colleague from the Khilafat campaign. Leading Muslim members of Congress attended him throughout, and care was taken to publicize the inclusion of readings from the Qur'an in the daily prayer meetings held at the house. The Mahatma announced that his purpose was to end 'this quarrel which is a disgrace to religion and to humanity. It seems as if God has been dethroned. Let us reinstate him in our hearts.'[62] He fulfilled the 21 days and was in good enough health to be in no hurry to take the glass of orange juice that would end his privations.

The fast was not noticeably successful in permanently halting religious violence, but it marks an important shift in Gandhi's preoccupations. He had been let down by the people in 1922 and again in 1924. Though he remained as convinced as ever that communal harmony was essential, he felt that the nation was not yet ready to lay aside its differences. So he diverted his attention from the communal issue to wider social criticism.

He did not absolve the British of responsibility, for he fervently believed that it was the oppression of colonial rule that brought a wide range of evil consequences to India. But by exhorting Indians to look at themselves he hoped to alleviate the moral diseases that colonial government incubated, and at the same time make it more likely that swaraj would come, because it was being demanded by a spiritually clean and self-respecting people. His writings of this period are full of the benefits of fearlessness and self-respect. Resistance to unjust government was the essence of swaraj, which people could grasp for themselves once sufficient spiritual consciousness had taken root within individuals. It was important to show that the people created government, not the other way around.

His return to national politics was thus brief. After serving as Congress president in December 1924, he spent a year promoting unity, then slipped out of the national picture as he turned his attention to the other great internal Indian split – the institution and practice of untouchability. His focus shifted from direct confrontation with the British to thoughts of Indian self-improvement, to what he called 'constructive work'. He pressed hard for the entire Congress membership to spend more time spinning, which he viewed as the cornerstone of personal and national swaraj. Economic and spiritual salvation were to be found through the spinning wheel, its rhythm, its products and the meditation it allowed.

But the times were not propitious for unity. The mid-1920s saw the rise of organized and militant communalism within the Hindu community, largely as a reaction to the Khilafat agitation. In 1922 the Hindu Mahasabha, with its forthright Hindu agenda, was revitalized under the leadership of Madan Mohan Malaviya and Lala Lajpat

Rai, both Congressmen, a Moderate and an Extremist respectively. Then in 1923 a pamphlet appeared entitled *Hindutva: Who is a Hindu?* written by V.D. Savarkar, a passionate nationalist, who took up armed struggle against British rule, was captured in 1910, and then wrote the paper secretly while in jail. Savarkar's main concern was to promote a form of Indian nationality restricted to those who were prepared to accept India as both homeland and holy land. This could easily include Hindus, Sikhs, Jains and Buddhists, but would exclude Christians, Jews and Muslims.

That same year the Mahasabha reached out to the untouchable community and proposed that they be given more rights, such as access to roads, temples and wells. This offer was rather less liberal than it seemed and was an attempt to prevent the wholesale desertion of untouchables to other religions. Meanwhile, the Arya Samaj, a reforming Hindu body founded in the late nineteenth century, had revitalized itself and was promoting re-conversion to Hinduism for the first time, and even began to contemplate forced conversions if necessary. Finally, in 1925, the even more forthright Rashtriya Swayamsevak Sangh (RSS) was founded by Dr K.B. Hedgewar to pursue an agenda of assertive nationalism centred on the concept of a Hindu 'nation'. Along with the divergences within Congress, there were now considerable differences across the spectrum of Hindu opinion.

JINNAH, GANDHI AND THE FACTIONS

Jinnah made a slow sort of progress through the mid-1920s. He resumed his legal practice after the debacle at the Nagpur Congress, and observed the Non-Cooperation campaign from a disapproving distance. Once he had been proved substantially right in his pessimistic views of its prospects, he decided to return to politics in 1923, when he successfully stood for the Bombay Muslim seat in the Central Legislative Assembly.

His next challenge was to revive the Muslim League – which was no simple task. The Muslim constituency was at one time both easier to define than that of the broadly based Congress, but it was much more regionally fragmented. Once the powerful anti-British feeling in the Muslim community, which had been prompted during the Amritsar–Khilafat period, had died down, local concerns predominated again. Jinnah was forced to confront this parochialism during the All-India Muslim League session at Lahore in May 1924, when the Punjabi delegates expressed a general disinterest in Jinnah's demands for full independence. Living in a Muslim-majority province, they were happy to bless any Indian state that would allow them extensive local self-government and were not very interested in independence as conceived by Jinnah, which revolved around a strong central authority. Only with a certain reluctance were the Punjabis persuaded to take on board the political needs of their co-religionists in Muslim-minority provinces. This issue raised its head repeatedly over the next 20 years and was always a serious weakness in Jinnah's overall drive to create a unified and effective Muslim political voice. It was an uncomfortable truth that, without a clear religious issue to unite them, India's Muslim community was a diverse and fissiparous entity. Nevertheless, this 1924 meeting laid out four fundamental concerns that remained central parts of Jinnah's political life for the next two decades. The League resolved to demand provincial autonomy, separate electorates, full religious liberty and, recalling the Lucknow Pact, a provision that any legislative proposal which affected any Indian religious community must be approved by a minimum of three quarters of that community's elected representatives. Jinnah was not entirely in sympathy with the first two of these demands, and although he accepted the first as the necessary price of Muslim unity, he then spent the rest of the decade trying to set up deals with the Congress to find ways to guarantee Muslim rights and opportunities without resorting to separate electorates. This search was doomed to failure because Congress always thought his price was too high.

Jinnah's quest for these deals was outside the ambit of regular government, and the series of All-India Party conferences that stretched across the 1920s are a reminder that the most vital strand within Indian politics was oppositional. But there was a high degree of fluidity that tended to work against clear national trends, including a good deal of overlap in party membership. Several leaders of the Hindu Mahasabha, such as M.R. Jayakar and M.M. Malaviya, were also in the Congress, and some Congress members, such as Dr Ansari and Muhammad Ali, were also in the Muslim League.

The opposition groupings that formed within the assembly after the 1923 election lacked a clear structure. The National Liberal Federation sat on the politically moderate side of Congress, while the Hindu Mahasabha sat on the more conservative 'Hindu' side. At the same time, they faced the Muslim League across the religious divide. Meanwhile the Congress, without the leadership of the imprisoned Gandhi, was split over the issue of continued Non-Cooperation. The Congress session of 1922, held at Gaya in Bihar, had been divided on whether to boycott the up-coming elections in a spirit of Non-Cooperation or whether to enter the new system and disrupt it from within. Those who wished to abstain from involvement were Gandhians such as Chakravarthi Rajagopalachari and Rajendra Prasad, nicknamed 'No Changers', while those that wished to 'collaborate' were led by Motilal Nehru and C.R. Das. These latter lost the conference vote and chose to withdraw from the Congress and form their own Swaraj Party.

Jinnah, newly re-elected, found himself leading a faction of 'Independents' in the assembly large enough to hold the balance. He then worked alternately with the Congress and against it, and adopted the same approach with the government. The Swarajists did well in the 1923 elections, winning 42 out of 101 seats in the assembly, where they took their places alongside Jinnah and the Independents. An informal alliance sprang up between them, and when they voted together they called themselves the Nationalist Party. But it was not a stable alliance. The Swaraj Party was dedicated to wrecking the system from within, while Jinnah's Independents were not committed to opposition; Jinnah preferred to take each measure on its merits. Although together they could command a majority in the assembly of 1923–26, the reservation of powers to the government neutralized this advantage. Over time the cooperation between the two bodies fell away as factions multiplied at the central level of Indian politics. After 1926 another branch of dissident Congressmen, notably M.R. Jayakar and N.C. Kelkar, formed the Responsivist Party, which intended to counterbalance Muslim influence by closer cooperation with the British.

Jinnah, however, was as active in the mid-1920s as he had ever been. In 1924 he was appointed to the Muddiman Committee, a body set up by the Viceroy after pressure from the opposition to assess the working of the new 1919 Constitution. This nine-man committee sat through the second half of 1924, reported in September 1925, and eventually delivered two verdicts. The majority report found that dyarchy was working well and needed no improvements. The minority report, largely penned by Jinnah, was scathing; it recommended scrapping the whole system and introducing wider popular representation.

Gandhi had tried hard to avoid the Congress–Swarajist split and had put together a pact with Das at the 1924 Congress session in an attempt to avoid further recrimination. But as time passed it became plain that the overall Swarajist premise, that the Raj could be brought down from within, was mistaken. The business of government continued as normal, apart from the occasional heated exchange across the assembly floor. After the 1926 elections the party was gradually reabsorbed into the wider Congress, as other issues came to prominence. Gandhi had been proved right.

Across the years 1923–27, national politics remained fragmented. It is perhaps no coincidence that the peak of this fragmentation occurred in the time that Gandhi chose as a year of political silence (1925–26), during which he sat quietly in his ashram and spun. His health was poor, as it often was when he felt politically sidelined, so he took no active part in Congress politics. He finished his autobiography, and wrote letters and articles for print – many of them about stray dogs.

THE DELHI PROPOSALS

Jinnah, meanwhile, maintained an active commitment to find a basis for Hindu–Muslim cooperation. He had always thought of separate electorates as no more than a temporary expedient and he was prepared to forsake them within an overall settlement. To this end he proposed four points to Congress on 20 March 1927 in what became known as the Delhi Proposals.

He wanted to create more Muslim-majority provinces in order to help balance the number of Hindu–majority provinces represented in the central assembly. He therefore proposed that Sind be separated from the Bombay Presidency and made a full province, and that Baluchistan and the North-West Frontier Province be brought up to provincial status. He also wanted protection for Muslim minorities, with complementary safeguards for other minorities in the Muslim-majority provinces of Punjab and Bengal. One third of seats in a central legislature were to be set aside for Muslims, and no law affecting communal interests was to be passed if three quarters of the community concerned opposed it. Last, he was prepared to explore the possibility of reserved seats rather than separate electorates. The proposals were favourably received by the Congress in May, but then pressure from the Mahasabha through the year led to a withdrawal of support.

Towards the end of 1927, the prospects for national unity and communal harmony appeared as bleak as ever. Gandhi was in retirement, waiting for his health to mend and for the times to smile on the prospects for unity. Jinnah, too, was isolated. He had become estranged from his wife, who was more than 20 years his junior, and he was unsupported by the most powerful elements in the community whose interests he was trying to protect and advance.

THE SIMON COMMISSION

The whole national picture was then dramatically altered with the British government's nomination of the Simon Commission in November 1927.

The 1919 Government of India Act provided for a review of the new system after 10 years, but a nervous Conservative government decided to bring this review forward, to ensure that the next British General Election, due in 1929, would not permit an incoming Labour administration to send its own men to India. This prospect had been of particular concern to Lord Birkenhead, Secretary for India, who among all British politicians has to rank as particularly Jurassic. He was still clinging to attitudes that were outmoded decades earlier, and compounded the fault by expressing himself on Indian topics quite indiscreetly. In a distant echo of Lord Curzon 30 years before, he found it difficult to take Indian politicians 'very seriously'[63], and privately he wrote to Viceroy Reading that he saw no prospect of Indians being fit for self-government 'in a hundred years'[64]. Such a die-hard could only dread the prospect of a sympathetic Labour government (which did in fact arrive in 1929) being allowed to determine the constitutional future of British India.

So in November 1927, Viceroy Lord Irwin announced to a small meeting, which included Gandhi, that a statutory commission to review the Constitution of India had been appointed a full two years early under the chairmanship of Sir John Simon, a Liberal MP and former Home Secretary. That much at least was encouraging, but the generous impression created by the early review was rather spoiled by the revelation that the Commission was to contain no Indian members. It was a Parliamentary body and Indians were thin on the ground at Westminster, numbering only two. In the Commons there was Shapurji Saklatwala (1874–1936), the Parsi Communist MP for Battersea, but he was an unappetizing choice for any Conservative government. Nor would he have served if asked. 'Any saint or scoundrel appointed to [the Commission] will be in the wrong place,'[65] he declared. The other possible Indian nominee was Lord Sinha, the first, and at that time the only, Indian peer, but he was terminally ill, and died in March 1928.

This 'all-white' line up was a tactical mistake that united the Indian political nation in a way it had not since Amritsar. Yet again the British undercut the liberal, moderate elements in India, which could never show adequate responses to their polite and reasonable requests. Such misjudgements were perhaps an inevitable side-effect of a colonial relationship in which it was never easy for Indians to move the political agenda along at any speed, so thoroughly were the British provided with powers to deflect political pressure. The only time the British Government was forced to listen to Indians was when they were united and angry, and only British officialdom seemed to possess the ability to get them into such a condition. Thus the Simon Commission was able to do more for Indian national unity in an instant than all the work Jinnah and Gandhi had done over the previous decade.

The Simon Commission had a 4:3 Conservative majority and was not as unsympathetic as Birkenhead could have made it, but this mattered not at all to India's outraged politicians, who began to recombine to oppose it. The only substantial body prepared to deal with the visitors was a loyalist minority of the Muslim League under the leadership of Sir Muhammad Shafi. Jinnah stayed hostile, although he did make suggestions to Lord Irwin as to how the storm of protest might be appeased. He proposed a Mixed Commission, or a Twin Commission running in parallel with Simon's. Irwin thanked him and moved on to other business.

Out on the streets Indian opinion was more difficult to ignore. When the seven Parliamentarians eventually stepped ashore at Bombay, in February 1928, they were bombarded with abuse, and wherever they went they were greeted with black flags and chants of 'Simon, go back!' The seven struggled on and after two trips to India they submitted a lengthy report in 1930, which recommended the abandonment of dyarchy, the introduction of provincial autonomy, the temporary retention of separate electorates, and the creation of a federal constitution to include the princely states. Despite all the distraction of the Round Table Conferences through 1931–33, this is broadly what the Government of India Act, 1935, eventually contained.

From an Indian point of view the agitation against the Simon Commission had some very positive effects. Stung by Birkenhead's declared conviction that Indians were unable to agree among themselves, the Indian political nation, prompted by the Liberal Sir Tej Bahadur Sapru (1875–1949), arranged an All Parties Conference for Indians to discuss their country's future governance on their own terms. The initial meeting was held in February 1928 and another followed in May, at which a committee under Motilal Nehru was set up to prepare proposals for a new constitution. Its report was delivered that August.

THE NEHRU REPORT

The Nehru Report's main recommendation regarding the imperial relationship was that India be given immediate Dominion Status within the British Empire, on a par with Canada. Domestically, it proposed a number of points that went on to be included in the eventual constitution of independent India. These included a bicameral central legislature, universal suffrage, and adjustments to provincial boundaries in line with linguistic distribution. More contentiously, it rejected all special representation in the central assembly for Muslims or other minorities and it proposed the abolition of separate electorates at both the national and provincial levels. The Congress, unsurprisingly, welcomed the Report. More unexpectedly, so did the Muslim League, but this was not Jinnah's doing. He had been touring Europe since May 1928, spending time with his wife, whose health was rapidly deteriorating. M.C. Chagla, his deputy, had been left in charge, and it was he who approved the Report, without referring either to Jinnah or to official League bodies. When Jinnah returned that October he was furious with Chagla for flouting party discipline, and for accepting what he considered the 'Hindu position'.[66] The Report was given full consideration at another meeting of the All Parties Conference in Calcutta that December. Jinnah moved two amendments but was defeated on both, whereupon he walked out, reportedly declaring that this was 'the parting of the ways'.[67]

The Congress also met in Calcutta that December. Gandhi, re-entering national politics, attended the session, which adopted the Nehru Report as policy, but not without some opposition. The more radical wing of the party, led by Jawaharlal Nehru and Subhas Chandra Bose, was unwilling to settle for Dominion Status and wanted to press for full independence – purna swaraj. Gandhi headed off this potential split by proposing that the British be given two years to adopt the Nehru Report; if they did not, then a national satyagraha would be started. Satyagraha had gained recently in potency after a campaign in Bardoli, where local farmers had successfully defeated a tax increase. The two years' grace in the motion was whittled down to one, and the motion was carried. The Congress was now holding a loaded gun to the head of the Viceroy.

The Muslim issue was disregarded. Jinnah's attempt at constructive engagement had failed and his fortunes were in decline. He had been edged out of 'big tent' politics in 1920; now he was about to be marginalized within the Muslim community too, handicapped by his attachment to a strong central authority within India and his lack of a regional support base. The power in Muslim politics lay very much with the leaders of the Punjab, who had little interest in central Indian affairs and were content to press for provincial autonomy within as loose a federation as could be constructed. The Punjabi leader Fazl-i-Husain formed his own version of an All-India Muslim party, called it the Muslim Conference, and recruited the Aga Khan to head it. The All-India Muslim Conference of January 1929, which Jinnah did not attend, rejected the Nehru Report and continued to demand weighted representation at the centre and separate electorates in the provinces.

JINNAH IN RETREAT

Jinnah, however, was not ready to admit defeat and doggedly continued to press for the formation of a united nationalist front. He drew up a list of demands, known as the Fourteen Points, in an attempt to create a new national pact. The Points were basically an elaboration of the Delhi Proposals of two years before, but were rather more detailed in light of the Nehru Report. They included a demand for a federal government, with residuary powers vested in the provinces, and a uniform degree of autonomy for all provinces. Minorities had to be represented in 'adequate and effective' ways in all provinces, but majorities – of any kind – should not be reduced to minority status or even parity. Muslim representation in the central legislative body had to be at least one third. Any government had to contain at least one third Muslim ministers. Freedom of worship and belief had to be guaranteed. Separate electorates were to continue but could be amended or revised by agreement. Possible future boundary changes were not to affect Muslim majorities where they already existed. Muslims were to be given a reasonable share of government jobs and preferment, and Muslim culture, language, education, charitable foundations, etc., were to be respected and protected.

Jinnah took the Points to a chaotic Muslim League meeting in Delhi in March 1929, but was unable to get them adopted. This was a much more damaging blow than the defeat at Calcutta the previous December, and Jinnah did not recover from it until he took control of a revitalized Muslim League more than five years later.

The Congress took a very high-handed view through this period and ignored all Jinnah's various proposals. In a letter to Gandhi, Motilal Nehru described the Fourteen Points as 'preposterous'[68] and advised that Jinnah could be safely ignored. Motilal was aware that Jinnah was, in fact, not in a strong position even within his own party. It was not just Chagla who had approved of the Nehru Report; the League's president, the Raja of Mahmudabad, was only one among many others who saw it as a constructive way forward, and the Congress leadership gradually came to consider Jinnah to be more famous than representative. They also felt strong because by the middle of 1929 the Congress was more united than it had been for a decade, while Jinnah's League was still a small body, tolerated but not unduly respected by the Muslim communities in Punjab and Bengal.

At this time, there were a large number of influential Muslims in the Congress leadership, including Maulana Azad, Dr Ansari, Syed Hasan Imam and, most improbably, the giant Pathan Abdul Ghaffar Khan – 'the Frontier Gandhi' – whose Red Shirts dominated the politics of the NWFP. To this confident Congress, Jinnah looked like an isolated and quarrelsome man who was too stubborn to rejoin the party he had once served with distinction. Basic Congress ideology denied that there was any need for separate Muslim political representation, and with a nationwide organization and a national leader who had a weapon of increasing efficacy in his power, there seemed no pressing reason to make deals with a man so out of step with everyone else.

Gandhi, however, saw fit to travel to Bombay in August that year for private talks with Jinnah. Nothing resulted, but the fact that the meeting happened at all, at a time when Jinnah was at his most isolated, emphasizes that it was still these two men who were the most committed to finding a national settlement.

THE PROMISE OF DOMINION STATUS

Soon enough, however, the situation changed again with the advent in Britain of a Labour government in May 1929. A change of tone was expected in Indian affairs and Viceroy Irwin, a Conservative appointed by Conservatives, was recalled for consultations in June. When he returned on 31 October he announced that, in the light of the Simon Commission's difficulties, His Majesty's Government (HMG) were seeking the broadest possible measure of agreement 'for the final proposals' to be put to Parliament. He also stated that: 'it is implicit in the Declaration of 1917 that the natural issue of India's constitutional progress, as then contemplated, is the attainment of Dominion Status'.[69] This was a long overdue clarification of Montagu's 1917 statement, and it sounded encouraging. Irwin then announced that there would be a Round Table Conference, including the Indian princes, to discuss the constitutional issues arising from the Simon Commission's findings.

This development was less unexpected to Jinnah than anyone else, because when news of the new Labour government's election had reached him in May he had travelled to Simla immediately to speak to Irwin, and had worked closely with him and the new prime minister, Ramsay MacDonald, over succeeding months to bring about exactly this announcement.

Indian politicians were unsure how to react and met in Delhi to work out a response. On 4 November, a cross-party gathering of Gandhi, Dr Ansari, Annie Besant, Sir Tej Bahadur Sapru, Motilal Nehru, M.M. Malaviya, Srinivasa Sastri and Jawaharlal Nehru put their names to a 'Leader's Manifesto', in which they welcomed the new initiative and what it seemed to promise, while also demanding the largest representation at the proposed Conference for the Congress, and the release of political prisoners. They also made it clear that they considered that the Viceroy had effectively announced the granting of Dominion Status, and that the Conference should not, therefore, be about when self-government was to be delivered, but about its specific details.

Jinnah was not involved but he forced his way into the picture by travelling to Gandhi's ashram in Ahmedabad on 12 December for several days of secluded, private talks. Nothing resulted. Meanwhile, there was an uproar in the more hardline Congress faction, with Bose and the younger Nehru keen to announce immediate independence with no further talking. Gandhi held them back. There was also outrage in London, where empire hardliners, led by Liberal ex-Viceroy Reading, demanded that the government grant no new liberties to India. The Labour government was a minority administration and was unsure how far it could push its Liberal allies. Concessions suddenly seemed less likely.

The Viceroy called a meeting for 23 December in Delhi with, among others, Gandhi, the elder Nehru, and Sapru in attendance. This time Jinnah was also invited. Gandhi asked the Viceroy to assure him that the upcoming Conference would grant Dominion Status immediately. Irwin, whose train had been bombed that very morning, replied that he could not 'prejudge or commit'[70] the proposed Conference, nor could he forestall the findings of the Simon Commission, whose recommendations were as yet unpublished. The Viceroy did not, and could not, budge.

India's political classes, however, would not be baulked. If the British did not grant Dominion Status immediately they were in danger of being left behind by events. Gandhi's deadline was only days away, but of swaraj, purna or otherwise, there was still no sign. The Congress met on 28 December in Lahore under the presidency of Jawaharlal Nehru. No last minute offer came and the final step was boldly taken. A new Indian tricolour flag was unfurled as the new year opened, and Independence was declared amid jubilation – 26 January was fixed as the new annual date for the celebration of India's freedom, and was duly observed just over three weeks later. But the political realities had not changed, nor would they for another 17 years. Indeed, the gusto with which the event was marked, and the unilateral way it was decided upon, did much to alarm many Muslims, who felt they were being railroaded into a Congress India.

The Remaking of Jinnah: 1930–39

As the new decade dawned, Jinnah – isolated and ignored – was at a personal and political low point, perhaps his very lowest. His wife had died in February 1929 and although they had been estranged at the end, he felt her loss deeply. Their early years together had been an intense and sustained exercise in intimacy and he was never to recover this closeness with anyone else. After Ruttie's death his closest companions were his sister, Fatima, and his daughter, Dina. Politically he had little to look forward to. His pleas for the creation of a unified platform based on Hindu–Muslim unity had been swatted aside by a confident Congress. There were negotiations in prospect on the subject of self-government, but there was no honoured place reserved for him at the table; he was expected to tag along behind the Punjabis and the Aga Khan. Motilal Nehru was correct that Jinnah, circa 1929, could safely be ignored, because the general absence of Muslim unity meant that he was only one voice among many. Traditional leaders with regional power bases, such as Fazl-i-Husain, were bigger tigers than Jinnah in the jungle of politics. Less able they may have been, less passionate about Muslim safeguards they may have been, but in their ability to get the British and their own co-religionists to listen to them, they outranked the clever man from the minority within a minority.

Gandhi by contrast was on an upward curve and would soon reach a new peak of popularity. But there was an air of false achievement in Congress politics at this time, brought about by the self-declared swaraj of 31 December. Nothing had actually changed, and despite the personal warmth between Gandhi and Viceroy Irwin, and the apparently favourable stance of the Labour government, the underlying realities of the Anglo–Indian relationship remained unaltered.

SALT AND SATYAGRAHA

The newly militant Congress was now poised for action, waiting for the Mahatma to choose a time, place and reason to launch the promised satyagraha. As January passed, he received no insights in prayer, but in February he decided to flout the government's monopoly on the manufacture and sale of salt, an old imposition stretching back well before British rule. It was a flat-rate tax on one of life's necessities, and as such it fell most heavily on the poor. Gandhi thus crystallized the larger issue of the nation's need for swaraj into the smaller issue of everyman's need for salt. As a piece of demagoguery it was a brilliant move, avoiding abstractions and touching directly on matters of concern to ordinary people. It was a complaint against unfair taxation, oppression of the poor and the absurdity that something so naturally abundant should be the exclusive property of the government.

The British considered the salt monopoly to be beneficial in that it was a guarantee of quality. They also took the general absence of illicitly made salt as proof that the tax did not lift official salt out of the reach of ordinary people. But the monopoly meant that poor people living by the seashore could not pick up what lay at their feet without incurring the wrath of the colonial possessors of India. Gandhi resolved to do exactly this and made sure that the prerequisites for a successful satyagraha were in place. He first informed the authorities that he was about to break their laws. This was essential, as a clandestine act of defiance would have no value and would be equivalent to a vulgar crime, not a political statement. So he wrote to the Viceroy on 2 March, serving notice of his intentions. Next, he needed to garner maximum publicity, so he alerted the press, who then followed his activities on a daily basis and reported them to the world. Lastly, he undertook the actions in a spirit of humility, accompanied by supporters similarly dedicated to non-violent action. The point was not to overthrow the government directly, but to chasten it as the world looked on, and to embolden the masses to defy a law that had no moral basis.

On 11 March Gandhi set off from his ashram to walk to the seashore at Dandi, a distance of 240 miles; he covered the ground in 26 days. His original entourage of around 70 satyagrahis swelled to thousands, while millions read about his progress and watched it on newsreels. On 6 April he waded into the sea, then picked up some salt crystals. Soon thousands of others were doing the same, first on the beach at Dandi then all over India. The government held back, caught in a cleft stick: to arrest him was to do exactly what he wanted them to do, but to leave him free was to show weakness in the face of deliberate rebellion. To try him was to give him a platform for yet more homilies on the Raj's satanic behaviour, while to ignore him would result in nationwide defiance and a serious loss of revenue. The government's first response was to start arresting those that copied him. Jawaharlal Nehru and thousands of others were detained in the week that followed. Eventually the Governor of Bombay acted on 4 May, sending a contingent of policemen to arrest Gandhi at night, detaining him under a British Indian law of 1827 that allowed persons engaged in 'unlawful activities' to be placed 'under surveillance' at the discretion of the authorities. This avoided the necessity for a trial.

The movement was not decapitated, nor were its participants dismayed by Gandhi's imprisonment. Later in May, Sarojini Naidu and Vallabhbhai Patel led a mass picket of the Dharasana Salt Works, an action that lasted over several days and involved thousands of protesters. This was a high spot in the Independence struggle and a complete vindication of satyagraha as a tactic. Literally hundreds of unarmed protesters were clubbed with lathis in full view of appalled reporters, including several from the foreign press. Two deaths and hundreds of serious injuries resulted, but not a hand was raised in retaliation. The moral effect of this outcome was more or less as Gandhi had foreseen, with demoralization as evident among exhausted policemen as outrage was on the faces of the foreign journalists. The practical effect was to encourage defiance. Upwards of 60,000 people were in jail by the end of the month.

The abolition of the salt tax was only a headline demand, and Gandhi now spelt out ten others, including total alcoholic prohibition, a 50 per cent cut in land tax, a 50 per cent cut in military expenditure, a 50 per cent cut in the salaries of senior officials, the right for Indians to carry firearms, Indian control of the police and intelligence services, and a protective tariff against foreign textiles. However, Irwin was not prepared to dismantle the Raj on the spot, and the demands went unanswered.

Jinnah was very keen that the projected London Conference should not be derailed, but while he kept in touch with Irwin privately, he could not himself play peacemaker. India's most famous prisoner, therefore, received a deputation from two elder statesmen, Sir Tej Bahadur Sapru and M.R. Jayakar. No deal was forthcoming. Gandhi insisted that he, or anyone else, must be allowed to raise the issue of independence directly in London. This was not the remit of the Conference, so Irwin could not concede the point. The Viceroy's next move was to bring together the jailed members of the senior Congress leadership in the middle of August. Some, like Gandhi, were in the Yeravda jail in Poona, while the Nehrus, father and son, were detained in UP. The UP contingent was brought across the country by train and discussions commenced. The leadership did not buckle and civil disobedience continued.

LONDON CALLING

Attempts to resolve the situation petered out, with the Viceroy finally exasperated. The decision was taken to sideline Gandhi and assemble more biddable men in London to move the whole constitutional process forward. Irwin informed Jinnah on 1 September that there would be no more negotiations, and all invited parties then made their preparations. Jinnah was keen for Irwin to go to London, but he could not.

The promised Round Table Conference was finally convened in November 1930 in Westminster Hall. It met entirely without Congress participation, but there was substantial attendance from all other parts of Indian society, some of which were quite pleased to be rid of Congress interference. There were 58 representatives of British India and 16 from the princely states, which were included in the proceedings with a view to bringing them into an Indian federation. The Aga Khan led the Muslim delegation, but it was Jinnah who made the running. He refused to submit his opening speech to the authorities in advance, and immediately declared that Indians expected 'action' and looked forward to the creation of a 'new Dominion of India' to join the others in the British Commonwealth of Nations.[71]

The conference then lasted for eight rather desultory weeks from November 1930 to January 1931. Positions were sketched out, niceties were observed and committees were nominated – but no progress was made.

THE 'IQBAL PLAN'

While the Conference was sitting in London, the annual session of the Muslim League was held in Allahabad that December. With Jinnah away, it was chaired by the poet Sir Muhammad Iqbal, who proceeded to deliver a speech to an audience of less than 70, on the subject of a possible Muslim 'homeland' in northwest India. This speech made little impact at the time as the Indian public was more concerned with the fate of the imprisoned Congress leaders and the progress of the talks in London. Iqbal intended his remarks to feed into the general debate surrounding the London discussions, and his ideas were an attempt to put up an alternative to the Nehru Report and the Simon Commission's recommendations, neither of which paid any serious heed to the question of Muslim minority rights.

The subsequent importance ascribed to this speech demonstrates how the history of Pakistan has, in large measure, been written backwards. That this speech became influential can easily be seen now, but it took years before Jinnah was publicly displaying any influence from it, and at the time it was just one among many different proposals floating around within Indian politics. As a constitutional scheme it was vague and was more of a plea that the Muslims of India should be given some insulated cultural space in areas where they were the predominant community. Bengal was not referred to directly. Iqbal's main intention was to pull the Punjabi politicians out of their small corner, their 'ruralism', into a wider context related to India's other Muslims. In doing this he was not actually widely supported by opinion in Sind or NWFP; both areas harboured a degree of historical antagonism towards the powerful Punjab and would later express consistent misgivings about being submerged by such a dominant regional force. Iqbal's idea was, predictably, not well received in Punjab either.

Iqbal actually wanted this new homeland to be a 'Muslim India within India', which could fit into the federal schemes that had become fashionable as the Round Table Conference approached, so it would be incorrect to see his plan as envisaging anything closely resembling the eventual sovereign Pakistan of 1947. The 'Iqbal Plan' was more of a rhetorically expressed aspiration, something indeed that a poet might come up with. Iqbal was perfectly serious in his intent, but he was not a politician. His view of the Muslim question was heavily cultural and can neatly be opposed to the views of Maulana Azad, who preferred to stress the economic inequities in the status of India's Muslims. That is why Azad was in the Congress, not the League.

Iqbal was a complex man, and it would be a travesty to reduce him to a servant of a narrow cause. The 1930 speech marked one point in the evolution of a deep and subtle mind, and debate persists about the full meaning of what he said. He corresponded with Jinnah and met him several times throughout the rest of the decade until his death in 1938, during which time he remained Jinnah's staunchest supporter in the Punjab. Whatever he was thinking, he did not announce a demand for the creation of Pakistan in December 1930. India's high-profile politicians ignored him and carried on as before.

THE GANDHI—IRWIN PACT

The first session of the London Conference made no progress on any of the main issues, which indirectly confirmed that Congress participation was essential. Gandhi was therefore released from jail in January 1931, and entered negotiations with Irwin between 17 February and 4 March 1931, with the twin objectives of getting the Civil Disobedience campaign called off and a Congress delegation sent to London. The resulting document has been called the Gandhi–Irwin Pact. This did not give Gandhi all his 11 demands of the previous May, but it did state that Civil Disobedience would be terminated in return for the release of political prisoners, that the making of salt by coastal dwellers would become legal, and that peaceful picketing of shops selling cloth of foreign manufacture would be permitted. Gandhi undertook to attend the London Conference, but he also accepted that the British, in any future constitutional settlement, would retain control over external affairs, defence, minority issues and credits to foreign nations.

This illustrates how unconcerned Gandhi could be about the details within negotiated settlements. In this case, his overall objective was to get the Viceroy to have a dialogue with him on equal terms, and he accounted it a victory when the appearance of such a negotiation had been achieved. It seemed to be a move forward from the British attitude of late 1929, but on the other hand, the powers that Irwin retained strongly indicated that realities had not changed. This was the perennial weakness in Gandhi's style of negotiation: He was prepared to give up points that were very important to his opponents, provided his own principles were sufficiently acknowledged in return. He was not very concerned to 'win' in negotiations beyond obtaining what he wished to gain himself; he was not interested in the detailed comparison of his own winnings with those of others. Gokhale had sensed this in him, and Bose was quite outspoken on the subject, claiming in his memoir that the Mahatma was no match for 'an astute British politician' in these matters, and would always stick out for 'little things' while missing the large.[72]

Gandhi presented the Pact to a special Congress session at Karachi in March 1931, where the article about retained powers was rejected and the Mahatma was instructed to demand full and unconditional Independence. This was a stormy session, with the impeding execution of Bhagat Singh uppermost in the minds of many of the delegates. Singh, a wanted man for several years, had recently been apprehended and condemned to death for shooting a British official in 1928, and for throwing a bomb into the central Legislative Assembly from the public gallery in 1929, an act that had not killed or injured anyone. Many felt that Gandhi should intercede for Singh, and indeed he saw Irwin on 19 March to do so, and then wrote to him privately on 23 March, but to no avail. Despite the discontent that the Pact and Singh's execution produced, Gandhi was appointed sole Congress representative, and he set out for London later in the year, arriving for the new session in September.

GANDHI GOES TO LONDON

The arrival of Gandhi raised expectations that progress could now be made, but this proved a barren hope. The idea of sending one single person to represent the Congress was another piece of intuitive Gandhian theatre – how much more united could a party and the nation it represented be than in the body of one individual? It was a good strategy in theory, but it backfired; the Congress was rendered no stronger than Gandhi could be, and he was not a gifted negotiator. He had a genius for conciliation, but negotiation is not the same thing. Thus the Congress went to London armed with all of Gandhi's strengths, for which it had little use on this occasion, but also hampered by all of his weaknesses. He met and charmed everyone low or high, from poor East Enders and Lancashire mill workers to George Bernard Shaw, Charlie Chaplin and the Archbishop of Canterbury. His one notable failure was with King George, who was reluctant to entertain the 'rebel fakir' in his palace – the man who had been behind 'all these attacks on my loyal officers'. Face to face, the king was less than diplomatic, telling Gandhi that Civil Disobedience was 'stupid'.[73] Gandhi politely declined to argue with His Majesty.

Typically, Gandhi considered these outside contacts to be as important as his work at the Conference sessions inside St James's Palace. He wished to show he had no quarrel with the people of England. He wanted to tell them about oppression in India, about the destitution of its millions. This he did very effectively, even fitting in a live radio broadcast to the United States. Nevertheless, he was actually in London to work on a future constitution for British India, but that tedious task did not greatly appeal to him – and it proved beyond his capacities. As the sole representative of the Congress, Gandhi was alone and overworked. His general approach had always been to avoid close detail and to stick to generalities. This he tried to do, but the intensive schedule he took on weighed him down and the sessions were either too detailed to attract his passionate interest, or too formal and general to seem relevant. When awake and motivated, he opposed separate electorates for all minorities, but especially for the untouchables.

GANDHI AND AMBEDKAR: ROUND ONE

Gandhi's opposition to untouchability had developed over many years, and he believed the persistence of the practice to be the greatest stain on the record of Hinduism. However, he differed from Dr B.R. Ambedkar (1891–1956), the untouchables' leader, on several fundamental points. For a start, like all the other ills of India, Gandhi preferred to address it fully only after dealing with the Independence issue. Ambedkar, on the other hand, wanted immediate political recognition for his community, both in terms of electoral representation and legal rights. Apart from the timing of reform, the two men also profoundly disagreed on the very nature of the stigma of untouchability. Gandhi was acutely aware of how politically important it was that untouchables, or Harijans (Children of God), were considered to be Hindus. He was desperately afraid of an India not only divided between Hindus and Muslims but also between Hindus and Harijans. Ambedkar differed, and upheld that exclusion from caste status implied an exclusion from orthodox Hinduism. This matched his generally more radical approach, which led him to sense that the only possibility of advance for Harijans lay outside Hinduism, as Christians, Buddhists or Muslims. Ambedkar could see no prospect of caste Hindus having the generosity to end segregation – which it was in their economic interests to sustain – or to reform their theology – because preservation of the laws of karma and dharma absolutely required that they could not.

So Gandhi and Ambedkar argued through the Second Conference, at the end of which no agreement had been reached. All the other parties wished for separate electorates, and it was only Gandhi who did not.

THE CONFERENCE FAILS

The Round Table process was conceived by a sympathetic Labour government as a route to an agreed settlement, but it turned out to be a much more complicated and fractious business than anyone had expected. Most of the issues that were to bedevil the negotiations in 1945–47 were present in embryo at the three Conference sessions held between November 1930 and December 1932. These included safeguards for minorities, the structure of a possible federation, and the detailed terms upon which the princes might enter an Indian Union.

Apart from the complex subject matter, the Conference was also ill starred politically. After the abortive first session, the Labour government fell in August 1931, to be replaced by a coalition 'National' government. Prime Minister MacDonald survived the change, but the sympathetic Wedgwood Benn was replaced as Secretary for India by the imperialist Samuel Hoare. This change ensured that the Conference – a purely advisory body – was henceforth doomed to be ignored. Finally, Gandhi's own unwillingness to engage in details made it unlikely that a solid agreement of the kind the British wanted would be achieved.

Success may have been unlikely under such circumstances, but the difficulty of the task at hand should not be underestimated. The issues were extremely problematic, and approaching them within a framework of imperial control compounded all the difficulties thrown up by a long agenda and very diverse interests.

The most persistently thorny issue was one that underlay all of the others – the question of safeguards against possible misuse of the permanent Hindu majority in the country. This affected not only the Muslims but also the Sikhs, who had their own delegation, and, just as significantly, the untouchables, also present under their own leadership and keen to establish a separate identity from the main body of Hindus. This ensured that there was a strong demand for separate electorates from the untouchables, Muslims, Sikhs and Parsis. Eventually they got their way under the Communal Award, announced in August 1932 between the second and third Conference sessions, which gave different communities protected representation in all elected bodies.

The other main issue was federation. All federal systems involve conflicts of interest between the elements of the federation – states, provinces or whatever – and the federal centre. Every federal system in the world has developed its own version of how to handle these issues, but local protection of India's minorities rendered this problem doubly difficult. The most intractable problem of federation, however, concerned the princely states that were spread all over the subcontinent and came in all sizes and all religious mixtures. The difficulty of blending hundreds of hereditary rulers into an elective democracy was taxing enough, but it was also very hard to convince these traditional potentates that they really would be better off under the new system. Many of them were more terrified of the Congress than even the most fearful of Muslims, for while the Congress preached intercommunal harmony, it did not preach anything so pleasant about feudal rulers. The radical wing of the Congress was viscerally opposed to hereditary absolutism, which ranked alongside feudal landholding as an ideological and political anathema. The princes, accustomed to flattery and medals from the British, were likely to be saddled with a Congress government sworn to their destruction.

As the princes began to see flaws in the federal idea, so too did some Muslims, who did not want to come under a strong central government that would necessarily be dominated by Hindus. So they, too, spoke up for a system based on strong provincial rights and extensive autonomy. The one dissenting voice came from Jinnah, who at this stage was still attracted to the idea of a strong central presence in Indian affairs. He found himself appointed to a Conference subcommittee dedicated to examining the elements and subdivisions of a possible federal India, which put him in a position to promote his own preferences. A strong central government at the heart of a system of relatively weak provincial rights would allow him the greatest scope to find a position of leadership within the Muslim community, but this agenda placed him in a very small minority within Muslim opinion. As the proceedings developed he became increasingly disillusioned. The Muslim leadership at the Conference came from the Aga Khan and Fazl-i-Husain, and Jinnah exercised little influence on them. It occurred to him to quit Indian politics – a world in which he could trust no one and no one would follow him – and ease his way into British society, where he could expect his undoubted talents to assure him a good living and a degree of respect. Before the Second Conference began, he had taken a set of rooms in the Inner Temple and was settled in a house in Hampstead with his sister and daughter.

A third Round Table Conference was held between November and December 1932, but neither Jinnah nor Gandhi attended. Jinnah was not invited, and Gandhi was back in prison. A long period of detailed Parliamentary activity ensued, and the final result of the London Conferences was the Government of India Act, 1935. This carried the clear influence of a small band of Tory imperialists, including Hoare and two men who were to become Viceroy and India Secretary respectively, Lords Linlithgow and Zetland. Unsurprisingly, nothing was irrevocably given away.

GANDHI AND AMBEDKAR: ROUND TWO

In India, the period between the end of the Second Conference and the passing of the 1935 Act was much more eventful. Despite the Gandhi–Irwin Pact, unrest persisted across much of India, which was harshly dealt with by Irwin's successor, the former Governor of Bombay, Lord Willingdon. Gandhi returned in late 1931 and in the light of the failure of the Conference to grant Independence, he restarted Civil Disobedience in January 1932. Willingdon was nominally a Liberal but proved himself as vigorously imperialist as any of his predecessors. Gandhi was sent back to Yeravda jail and Congress was outlawed. Politics then ground to a halt, with Gandhi behind bars and Jinnah in London.

In September 1932, a serious dispute arose between Ambedkar and Gandhi about separate electorates for the untouchables, granted by Prime Minister MacDonald under the Communal Award of August 1932, which had also granted separate electorates to Muslims, Sikhs, Parsis, Europeans and Anglo-Indians. As soon as details of the Award reached India, Gandhi, still in prison, registered a strong protest, writing at length to MacDonald to explain the harmful consequences of separating Hindus and untouchables, whom he regarded as indivisible. Any formal recognition that the two were different was a mistake that would have serious ill effects, and the political strategy of effectively pitting one against the other could only lead to lasting damage. He was most concerned that the grievances of Harijans against caste Hindus would become the currency of Indian politics, something that could only be permanently divisive. MacDonald did not see the problem. He explained that every Harijan actually had two votes, one in the general constituencies and one in the reserved untouchable constituencies. This seemed recompense enough to him. However, he reminded Gandhi that as prime minister he was permitted to acknowledge any agreement freely made between Indian politicians. This put the ball squarely in Gandhi's court. So, to try to get Ambedkar to abandon separate electorates, Gandhi announced that he would undertake a fast unto death starting on 20 September 1932.

This announcement was sensational, for the Mahatma was now using a fast not to admonish the British, or even all Indians over an urgent matter of communal violence as in 1924. This time he was specifically reproaching Hindus over a deep, historic, social issue. He was also now relying on Ambedkar and the untouchable leadership to save him from death. Nehru could not take it on board, and wrote to Gandhi, questioning why he was getting drawn into a side issue when the wider battle for Indian Independence had yet to be won. The reason was that Gandhi felt that India would never be either one nation, or free from inhumanity, if the untouchables were driven apart politically from Hindus.

Ambedkar came to the Mahatma's side at Yeravda and negotiated, hard. Gandhi had already reluctantly accepted reserved seats for minorities as a necessary evil on the road to equality and reconciliation; the point of difference with Ambedkar was the manner of selecting candidates for those seats. A compromise drawn up by Sapru was acceptable to Ambedkar, but after some reflection Gandhi rejected it. Further changes brought the last point of disagreement down to whether the new Sapru system of 'primary' elections should last for five or 10 years. Gandhi, hating division, wanted five, to be rid of special measures as soon as possible. Ambedkar, knowing full well that untouchability would need decades to disappear from social practice, wanted the maximum term possible, and 10 was the longest he could get. Eventually, amid alarming reports of Gandhi's deteriorating condition, a deal was signed on the morning of 26 September. But the drama continued. Gandhi would not break his fast till the British had accepted the changes and altered the Communal Award. By 5.15 p.m. that evening, it was confirmed that the text had been approved in London.

THE POONA PACT

This agreement, known as the Poona or Yeravda Pact, set up a system of primary elections that effectively allowed the selection of all shades of untouchable opinion, not just the most conciliatory. The decision on the length of the special measures was deferred. In terms of provincial representation, Ambedkar more than doubled his original award, with the total of reserved seats rising from 71 to 147. This achieved a nice political balance. Gandhi had removed, or at least reduced to a short period, the official separation of the Harijan community from the Hindus, while Ambedkar had increased the standing of his people in the institutions of the nation. As a bonus, whether intentional or not, Gandhi had brought the Harijan issue to the forefront of India's attention and had charged the debate with a deep and personal emotion for a great many people. There are widespread reports of deliberate conciliatory gestures at this time towards Harijans throughout India, with the opening of temples, access to wells and general social fraternization. Nehru's orthodox mother, for instance, let it be known that she had accepted food from an untouchable. The willingness of the Mahatma to starve himself to death over the sinfulness and inhumanity of his own people was a shocking thing to contemplate. If he had died the guilt would be a permanent national disgrace on all who had not heeded his call, which was for nothing more demanding than the grant of legal and social equality to fellow human beings.

It has been suggested that Gandhi did all this deliberately, using the emotionally loaded method of fasting in order to teach his people that they must behave better, a lesson that they might learn from his personal ordeal in a way that they might not from a piece of dry legislation. Perhaps this is so. Certainly, the concept of untouchability never recovered from the blow it received in Poona; several bills were put forward to remove disabilities from Harijans over the next few years. Equally, there was deep resistance to the change from the more rigid caste Hindus and conservative brahmins – such men tried to label Gandhi a non-Hindu. Untouchability was an integral part of the concept of karma – that sins follow a soul into its next life. As such, the status of untouchability was not all negative, for if a person performed their prescribed duties well, then merit would accrue and promotion would be accorded in the next life. In the scale of eternity, life as a sweeper was a short interlude in a longer perspective. Seen like this, to abolish the practice of untouchability was in fact to deny that sweeper the chance for advancement by performing the dharma of a sweeper correctly. In other words, it was to turn the temporary disadvantage of untouchability into nothing but an unmitigated socio-economic catastrophe in a direct material sense, without any prospect of relief.

Shorn of its theological garb, untouchability was indeed sheer, unrelieved misery. This was how Ambedkar saw it and why, for his supporters both in and out of the Harijan community, it simply had to go.

Gandhi was consistently opposed to the concept and social practice of untouchability but he was not militant in the way Ambedkar was. He wanted to retain the integrated wholeness of the Hindu social system, of which he considered untouchability to be a perversion. Socially, he wanted a reform of general manners within the Hindu community. In religious terms he wanted to convert the Harijans into shudras – farmers or labourers – the fourth of the classical varnas, or caste groups. This went along with his view that all castes were equal and not arranged from first to fourth in an order of merit. The Bhagavad Gita encouraged all people to fulfil their duties as they were set out and not to do the work of another – which is dharma. This much was enough for the Gandhian vision of a better India. He was reluctant to take the theological arguments for or against untouchability on board. He had heard them many times, most famously in a formal debate with brahmins at Vaikam in 1924. He wanted untouchability abolished, and as soon as possible. There was no need to recourse to the shastras (scriptures), which he had examined and found no support for untouchability. It was unfair, degrading and in itself a kind of pollution. It was exploitative and morally indefensible. Gandhi's arguments and actions eventually won the day, and after his death Ambedkar, as minister of law, passed the legislation that abolished untouchability formally in the newly independent India on 29 November 1948.

GANDHI RETIRES

In the period immediately after the Poona Pact, Gandhi undertook three more fasts in quick succession for the sake of the untouchables. He also found himself in jail twice more because of Civil Disobedience. The movement had been faltering for some time, and was finally called off in April 1934, but he remained active in other ways. He abandoned the Sabarmati ashram on the edge of Ahmedabad and moved to a more rural setting near Wardha; the new settlement was named Sevagram (Village of Service). He started a new weekly publication, *Harijan*, to educate caste Hindus about the evils of untouchability. Not all were ready for this message, and many opposed him vocally whenever he appeared in public. In June 1934 someone even threw a bomb at a car, mistakenly believing he was in it.

By then he was exhausted and ill. Worse, he had almost nothing to show for all his efforts. Untouchable candidates did badly in municipal elections with open electorates in early 1933, demonstrating that reserved constituencies were probably necessary to ensure Harijan representation. His continued passion for the Harijan cause came between him and Jawaharlal Nehru, who could not understand why he was distracting himself from more important issues. Gandhi, of course, felt that national unity and the purification of individual souls was the only way forward to swaraj, but Nehru's Marxist sensibilities did not allow him to see the issue as anything other than part of a wider pattern of economic exploitation. This contrast was clear enough to Gandhi, who openly admitted that his presence in the Congress was probably alienating the intelligentsia. At the same time the party was to some degree repelling him. He found himself out of sympathy with the younger generation of socialist radicals, and he was personally disgusted by the corruption of other party members. In 1922 he had come to believe that Indians were not yet worthy of swaraj; by 1934 he had come to suspect that the Congress was not fit to govern.

He felt his presence in the organization was not helping anymore and that there was no work for him to do. Having announced via *The Bombay Chronicle* in September that he needed 'absolute freedom of action',[74] he officially left the party at the Bombay Congress in December 1934. He then went back to pursuing his rural 'uplift' work, but more significantly, he entered a long period of ill health that lasted till 1939.

JINNAH REGROUPS

Gandhi's disillusionment was mirrored in reverse within Jinnah, whose enthusiasm for politics had been rekindled. His life in London was not quite the success he had hoped for. He had nursed political ambitions, but British politics held no easier opportunities than Indian. He was too much of a 'toff' for the Labour party, and a shade radical or a bit too dark for the Conservatives. The fact that he approached both parties at a time when they were poles apart ideologically (especially with regard to India) does rather suggest that he was happier inside politics than outside, and not greatly concerned about what he was expected to support – in Britain at least. In the legal world he practised before the Privy Council, but the work did not stimulate him in the way that politics did. Threatened with insignificance, he was all too ready to receive overtures from Muhammad Iqbal and prominent Muslim League member Liaquat Ali Khan, encouraging him to return to India and lead a revived All-India Muslim League under the new Constitution. It seemed an attractive option; he stood for the Muslim constituency of Bombay again in October 1934, and was elected.

The Muslim League had healed its various splits in the years of his absence, with a truce between its two major factions in 1933 under which both agreed to accept him as leader. When an attempt by the Aga Khan and other loyalists to launch another Muslim party failed, Jinnah finally tasted a moment of vindication, standing forth unchallenged as the only national Muslim leader of sufficient stature and experience to unite the community.

In this strong position, he immediately showed that he had not yet abandoned the dream of a united nationalist front against the British, and he was soon in substantive negotiations with the Congress president, Rajendra Prasad, with a view to working out a joint approach to the new Constitution. Nothing concrete emerged, but Jinnah was still trying to promote a joint Congress–League platform at the League's Bombay session in 1936.

His willingness to re-engage so heartily with not only Indian politics but also the Congress demonstrates yet again that early readings of Jinnah's 'separatism' are unwarranted. The remark about 'the parting of the ways' attributed to him at Calcutta in late 1928 looks strangely unconvincing when one examines the next eight years of his life in their entirety. He had not, in fact, given up on himself, on the League, on India or even on the Congress.

THE GOVERNMENT OF INDIA ACT, 1935

India was looking at political change in 1935, with Gandhi out, Jinnah back, and a reformed political system. The 1935 Government of India Act split India from Burma, leaving British India with 11 'Governor's Provinces', now including Sind, NWFP and Orissa. The system of dyarchy was ended and responsible government with extensive autonomy was granted to the provinces. There were bicameral legislatures in the six larger provinces, and unicameral ones in the five smaller. Provincial ministries would henceforth be directly responsible to their legislatures. Overall powers in the areas of foreign affairs, defence and communication were reserved to the centre, where a new parliamentary-style body was to be set up. This resembled the old 1919 bicameral assembly, but both new chambers were based on a wider franchise and had more members. They were also to include representatives from the princely states, but how these were to be chosen was left to the discretion of the princes. The federal assembly was to have 250 members from British India, with 82 reserved for Muslims, and not more than 125 from the princely states. The upper house, or Council of State, had 156 members from British India, including reserved seats for Muslims, scheduled castes, Sikhs and women, and 104 members nominated by the princes.

But there were some glaring omissions in the 1935 Act. There was no grant of Dominion Status, nor any commitment to it, and there was no form of responsible government at the centre. India was still firmly in the hands of the Viceroy and his executive council, who were responsible solely to Westminster. Even in the provinces, where a degree of responsibility had been introduced, there were so many overriding powers reserved to Governors that at the slightest hint of trouble all the powers delegated to the ministries could be revoked and the Governor could rule by decree. Similar powers were provided for the Viceroy. This was a Constitution designed to sail only in fair weather with a following wind. Adversity would destroy it, as indeed it did.

The first blow was that federation never materialized in any shape at all. The provisions of the Act required at least half of the native states (by population) to come into a federal India in order to activate the new central assembly. But federation quickly lost whatever charms it had ever possessed for all the important princes, and they repeatedly delayed any decision to join. Negotiations on the federal issue, long deadlocked, were finally suspended with the outbreak of war in 1939, and were never revived. So, after 1935, the central government of India simply continued along the old lines laid down in 1919. For all the Conference talk, nothing of significance changed in terms of India's central political institutions.[75]

Much of the detail of the 1935 Act had been discussed during the Round Table Conferences, and it seemed a liberal measure to many on the British side; Churchill, however, thought it had given too much away. Indian politicians almost universally disliked it. Jinnah denounced it as 'humiliating'; Nehru called it 'a charter of slavery',[76] and was reluctant to participate in the new system. Gandhi, in one of his last political acts, insisted at Patna in May 1934 that the Congress should come into the new system. It duly did, but the cry was almost immediately raised for new arrangements to be drawn up, but this time by Indians in a constituent assembly.

The new Constitution had pleased no one who mattered in national Indian politics, though it was rather better received in the provinces. This was because the major Muslim demands of the late 1920s, many of them repeatedly voiced by Jinnah, had largely been achieved: the maintenance of separate electorates, the creation of the provinces of Sind and NWFP, provincial autonomy, and the allocation of one-third of the seats at the centre.

PROVINCIAL POLITICS

Provincial elections under the Act were set for early 1937 and the Congress enjoyed several enormous advantages over the League as the polls approached. The first was a pre-existing national organization, dating back to the early 1920s, that was largely Gandhi's work. It stretched right across the country and reached down to the village level. The second was a coherent national programme. At this point the more socialist wing of the Congress was in the ascendant, and a vote for the Congress represented a clear choice for agrarian reform, national self-government and intercommunal unity. The League had no such political machinery, much less money, and its platform was rather narrower – rights for Muslims and a rejection of Congress rule.

But the League could only gain limited advantage at this stage from fierce anti-Congress rhetoric, because the spectre of a Hindu raj had its most frightening effect only on those Muslims who lived in provinces where Muslims were in a permanent minority. In Punjab and Bengal, Muslims were in a majority and could look forward, under the 1935 Act, to permanent Muslim ministries. This conferred a degree of local security. As for their Muslim brothers in the minority provinces, the votes of Punjabis or Bengalis could not help them, beyond sending their own Muslim members to the central bodies.

Under the 1935 Act, provincial Indian politicians with powerful regional bases were in an almost perfect situation. It was easy for them to cast the British as the new Mughals – lofty perhaps, but reassuringly distant and uninterested. There was little incentive for any ambitious Muslim to become involved in all-India politics like Jinnah had done, and indeed very few did. The way forward in Muslim politics was not at the centre, where first the British, then the Congress stood squarely across the road to preferment. Instead, they could look to the provinces, where all the complex connections of family and clan and the vested interests of commerce and landholdings dominated allegiances. Fazl-i-Husain in the Punjab used his high standing in the Punjab Unionist Party to sustain his own all-India organization – the Muslim Conference. This organization was something of a vanity project, but it had helped him secure an invitation to the Viceroy's executive council in 1931. Status in the provinces could translate to the centre, but the reverse was not true.

When Jinnah visited the Punjab in 1936 he got the political equivalent of a bloody nose. He was shunned publicly, while privately the locals were uninhibited in their derision. Fazl-i-Husain wrote in his diary that Jinnah 'could not get on with anybody. He is no leader'.[77] For his part, Jinnah considered it a 'hopeless place'.[78] He was shut out of Punjabi affairs right up until 1947.

India's complicated regional politics tended to work against the purposes of the All-India Muslim League in terms of trying to establish a nationwide organization, programme or identity. In Punjab, the Unionist Party had been set up by a cross-communal alliance between large landlords, and it monopolized power in the area. Fazl-i-Husain led it until his death in 1936, whereupon Sir Sikander Hayat Khan replaced him. The Unionist Party was a class-based coalition of Muslims, Sikhs and Hindus, men whose prime concerns were not national but local, and none of whom wished to fall in behind either Congress or the Muslim League. If the British left them alone they were happy, and the British usually obliged. Why would such men welcome interference from Delhi by anybody else? In Bengal, local politics had divided on more communal lines, and there was no Sikh element to consider, but this did not simplify matters because neither community could clearly decide who was to be its representative party. Despite having had Muslim ministries since the 1920s, the Muslim League could not get a secure foothold there and Jinnah was forced to wait upon events and do deals as best he could. It was not until 1943 that he managed to construct a ministry led by the Muslim League in Bengal.

Jinnah's long-term strategy in response to this lack of influence in the provinces was to build an understanding that he could provide something that none of these local Muslim bosses had access to – a voice at the centre of Indian politics. This had always been his forte and from 1937 onwards he repeatedly emphasized the importance of such a voice. It was the appropriate and most effective place to talk to the British. The fact that he was, almost literally, the only man who could fulfil this role naturally recommended him for the job. It was then up to him to make good his claims that it was a job that needed to be done.

THE 1937 ELECTIONS

Matters did not start well for Jinnah when the Muslim League made a poor showing in the elections of 1937. Across the 11 provinces the League formed no governments at all, with a share in a coalition in Bengal with A.K. Fazlul Haq's Krishak Proja party. On the other hand, the Congress formed seven ministries. Five were in strongly Hindu regions: Bombay, Madras, the Central Provinces, and the newly separated Bihar and Orissa. The sixth was in the original backyard of the Muslim League, the United Provinces, where the old landlord class had fought fiercely to dissuade the electors from the 'radical' Congress. The seventh, remarkably, was in a Muslim-majority province, the NWFP, where the leadership of the Gandhian Abdul Ghaffar Khan excluded League influence. Assam was to follow as the eighth in 1938, but Punjab and Sind fell outside the Congress–League carve-up. Punjab was a dead-end for the League, while Sind, despite its Muslim majority, proved equally closed to Jinnah as the local Muslims split into multiple factions and none showed any interest in opening out their game to the wider world.

This was bad enough, but the actual detail of the individual contests revealed an even more discouraging outcome for the League. It had not only failed to win ministries in Muslim-majority provinces, but had also failed to win anything like a majority of the provincial assembly seats reserved for Muslims. Out of 482 it won only 109. The Congress, by contrast, won all the general seats open to it, plus nearly 60 of the reserved seats, making a total of 716. On this showing, with national support running at about 5 per cent, the League was not only not an all-India party, it was not even a party with much of an appeal among Muslims. It was Jinnah's astonishing achievement that within eight years he reversed all these perceptions, addressed all these weaknesses, and turned the League into a coherent and relevant political organ that was impossible to exclude from national politics.

JINNAH RETHINKS

The first help Jinnah received was from the Congress party, for after the 1937 elections the Congress went a long way towards proving the point he was trying to make – that Muslims needed organized protection. Had the results been closer then perhaps a different kind of politics might have resulted. But they were not, and in conventional democratic terms the Congress were clear winners. Jinnah, however, did not accept this, and he asked that some League members be brought into the new provincial governments. Congress leaders, in a position of strength, refused, which on a narrow view they were entitled to do. The determination with which they resisted Jinnah's requests suggests the influence of Nehru, the man of principle, rather than that of Gandhi, the conciliator. Jinnah appealed directly to Gandhi for help in May 1937, but Gandhi took no part in the daily management of Congress affairs and did not intervene. 'I cry out to God for light,'[79] was all he could offer.

The almost total exclusion from power in 1937 was a deep shock to many Muslims across the country. It seemed un-Indian, especially after years of power sharing, weightage and coalitions. The stark application of 'first-past-the-post' elections after years of minority safeguards did not augur well for the new politics. And the Congress had wider aims. Nehru's socialist influence inspired a 'mass contact' campaign that began in March 1937, in an effort to reach out to and politicize ordinary Muslims, bypassing their aristocratic leaders. Sir Muhammad Iqbal was well aware of what this threatened, and he had a plan to counter it. In a letter of 28 May 1937, he advised Jinnah that he must leave behind 'the old League' of the upper classes, or he would forever lose 'the masses who have so far, with good reason, taken no interest in it [the League]'. He advised an appeal to 'the law of Islam'.[80] This, of course, ran counter to Jinnah's entire career to that point, and at the time he was still warning off his more traditional supporters from using religious language for fear that others might think he endorsed communalist policies.

But Jinnah was standing at a crossroads in the middle of 1937. He could either wait for some change at the centre, or for some kindness from the main provincial Muslim leaders. Or, as the League had transparently failed to fulfil any of its basic purposes, he could retire.

It is clear that he made fateful decisions on a number of issues at this time and over the next two years, decisions that proved well judged in terms of resurrecting his own career and stature as a national politician. The fact that he was prepared to make these decisions is absolute proof that he was not deterred or demoralized by the elections of 1937 and that, in fact, he used them to embark on a new long-term strategy to win power.

First came his unsuccessful appeals to Nehru, then Gandhi, over provincial coalitions. After these rebuffs he opened negotiations with Sir Sikander Hayat Khan and Fazlul Haq with a view to his representing them at the central level. Negotiations proceeded throughout the middle of the year, and a deal with Sikander was finalized in Lucknow in October 1937. Jinnah got his authority to speak at a national level, but the price was that he remained permanently excluded from local influence in the Punjab. He also began to ramp up the anti-Congress rhetoric and he permanently abandoned Hindu–Muslim unity.

It had become uncomfortably clear that the closer to the Congress his platform was, the less there was any apparent need for him or his party in Indian politics. The Congress already stated that it stood for everyone in India. To do anything other than to distance himself from the Congress would therefore be to sign his own political death warrant. Political logic dictated that without demonizing his opponents he would attract no followers wanting protection. The Muslims in the majority provinces might feel safe, but there were plenty in the minority provinces who might not, and these were now his main target audience. And he could reach the others too if he could show that all of India's Muslims were in danger from the strength of the Congress at the centre. Who could stand and oppose them there? He had someone in mind.

THE GULF WIDENS

As Jinnah bent to these political imperatives, the communal content in Indian politics heightened, as Congress leaders hardened their stance against the League in response to the logic of their own beliefs. Nehru thought that to allow League members into government purely because they were Muslims was to perpetuate communalism, not dissolve it. And there would be Muslims in government anyway; it was just that they would be Congress Muslims. So Jinnah's basic argument was merely personal factionalism – an artificial, forced choice between 'his' Muslims and all-India Muslims.

From mid-1937 Jinnah began to play on semi-religious grievances such as the use of the Congress' 'national' anthem 'Bande Mataram', which in its full version pledged loyalty to the goddess Durga, and the use of the new tricolour flag, which he considered a Congress symbol. Gandhi suggested that neither song nor flag should be used if one single Muslim objected – an offer that brought forth no reply. More directly, Jinnah began to call the Congress 'authoritarian' and 'totalitarian'. Gandhi noticed the change, writing in February 1938 to say: 'I miss the old nationalist. Are you still the same Mr Jinnah?'[81]

From October 1937, Jinnah began to wear the sherwani and was seen less often in his immaculately tailored suits. Here, finally, was a man developing a message. What was the point of the All-India Muslim League? To protect India's Muslims, wherever they were. From whom? The Hindu Congress, who could no longer be trusted. Old-style intercommunal unity had to be abandoned as an ideal, because Congress obviously no longer believed in it. Now he was clear about how Muslim interests could be protected: under his wing, at the head of a strong League. That way equality, if not granted, could be demanded by an unashamedly Muslim organization. At a conference in Allahabad in January 1938 he stated clearly: 'I am proud to be a communalist,'[82] by which he meant that he was proud to have been fighting for the interests of the Muslims of India.

He also began to demand 'complete equality' with the Congress in all national affairs. This was vintage Jinnah. He had a superb way of asking for most when he was at his weakest. When his demands had been duly considered he could graciously accept rather less, which made him look good, and meanwhile he had advanced a little. Years of doing this built up his momentum until finally his bandwagon began to roll – for real. The Congress did not take him seriously at first, assuming that the people had spoken in 1937 and that Jinnah was simply ignoring their voice. He was not. But he was observing very closely the example of the Congress itself. He formed a new constitution for the League in early 1938, and in almost every respect it copied that of the Congress. The numbers varied a little, but the League became a party set up almost exactly as a mirror of its elder sibling. It had wards, divisions and provinces, all with their own organizations. There was a large central council of 465 members and a Working Committee of 21. As a final cheeky touch the annual subscription was set at 2 annas, half that of the Congress.

Two things had become starkly clear. Although the League had not picked up Muslim votes in the 1937 elections, those Muslims were still there and they still had votes. All they required was the right sort of leadership – which Jinnah set out to provide. At the same time, it became apparent that there was a game of national politics to be played. The very success of the Congress had ensured this. If it had flopped in the 1937 poll, losing out to all the small provincial special interest parties, then perhaps the centre of Indian politics might have become a deserted, echoing place dominated by the Viceroy's picked men.

But the fact that one party had scored a national success meant that national politics was real. And that meant that if the Muslims wanted to respond effectively, they too would have to have a national party and a national leadership, something that the Bengali Krishak Proja or the Punjabi Unionists were clearly unable to provide. The cards had finally fallen Jinnah's way, almost unnoticed in the apparent destruction of the 1937 poll.

JINNAH GATHERS MOMENTUM

The change did not go unnoticed among wiser Congress heads. This new, aggressive Jinnah, with a national organization and powerful provincial backers, did not look like the dandy quibbler of the 1920s. Feelers went out from the Congress in early 1938, and the mass contact movement was wound down, but Jinnah did not want to talk. He had had nothing to give the Congress a year before, and they had treated him with open disdain. Now he was prepared to bide his time until he could make new alliances on his own terms. In April 1938 he told an audience in Calcutta: 'In six months we have succeeded in organizing Mussalmans all over India as they never were at any time during the last century and a half.'[83]

Nehru began a correspondence with Jinnah in January that lasted till April.[84] In it Nehru constantly contended, or pretended, that he could not understand what Jinnah's function in Indian politics was. What were his points, his demands? Jinnah did not rise to the bait. From now on, virtually until Partition, he refused to enter into detailed discussions of what he was proposing or demanding. Here was the start of yet another highly successful tactic.

To further interrogate Jinnah, Gandhi went to Bombay in late April 1938 – Jinnah, this time, would not go to Gandhi. Jinnah demanded that the Congress accept the fact that he and his League spoke for all of India's Muslims. This demand was the central-level counterpart to his agreement with Sikander Hayat Khan, and it became a vital part of Jinnah's strategy, one he never gave up. Nothing was agreed, but it was now obvious that the Congress was doing the chasing. Gandhi, who was tired and ill, had put in a lacklustre performance, so in May Subhas Chandra Bose, then Congress president, went to see Jinnah. An attempt was made at negotiation in an exchange of letters, but Jinnah was immovable. In June he wrote to Gandhi demanding that no Muslims be appointed to the central Congress Committees without his consent. Gandhi, of course, refused, but the tide of demands was turning. That August Jinnah had a meeting with the acting Viceroy, Lord Brabourne, to discuss cooperation. The meeting was requested by Jinnah, which indicates that this was an alliance he was willing to make. He proposed that if the British accepted him as the representative of all India's Muslims, he would support the British at the centre. This would have been almost treason to the Jinnah of 1916, but times had moved on, and the deal as proposed was a perfect way for Jinnah to elevate himself to the level of a national leader at the same time as giving his party and his supporters a chance of official preferment. Brabourne declined, but this was the boldest step yet made by Jinnah towards the position he coveted. Deals with the Congress would never get him there – it was still too strong and its leaders were too jealous of the power they had won for themselves. There was little room on the opposition benches in Indian politics not already dominated by the Congress, and Jinnah made a clear attempt to find room on the government side.

This approach was both monumentally impertinent and politically very shrewd. What Jinnah was asking for was not that the British should acknowledge his influence, but that they should actually confer influence upon him. This was a self-fulfilling demand for political elevation. If the Muslims of India knew that Jinnah could get things done for them – that he had the ear of the British – then they would come to him and actually treat him as the leader he wished to be. This was the chicken and egg problem that Jinnah faced all through the late 1930s, when Muslims were heavily divided on a regional basis and he had, as yet, neither a united mass party nor an issue of real urgency with which to galvanize support. He was a man of marginal relevance seeking out ways to make himself centrally important to the life of Muslim India. Brabourne felt he did not need such a man; Lord Linlithgow, only a year later and with a war to consider, was to think differently.

Jinnah was gradually moving to a more active position, and this period marks the one genuine, abrupt change in his political career. He stopped trying to appease or ally with the Congress. Instead, he began to court the British against the Congress, something he had never done before. As part of this change he commissioned investigations into Congress misrule; in March 1938 the Raja of Pirpur reported detailed abuses and discrimination, and in early 1939 the Shareef Report followed in similar vein. The grievances these contained were largely examples of petty local bullying rather than active political tyranny, and when under Congress pressure the British offered to investigate them a few months later, Jinnah demanded no less than a Royal Commission on the subject. This betrays a rather less than confident attitude on his part, for he knew that the wartime conditions that were by then in place would necessitate a British refusal. The demand was, therefore, a skilful shot into the long grass. The complaints were never independently investigated, but meanwhile all the short-term propaganda value as was ever likely to accrue had already been extracted.

In December 1938, at the League conference in Patna, Jinnah made one of his least conciliatory, most revealing speeches. He told the League that the Congress was nothing but 'a Hindu body' and that Gandhi was planning a Hindu raj. The Congress had 'killed every hope' of a Hindu–Muslim settlement 'in the right royal fashion of fascism'. This was gloriously overstated, rough-and tumble-politics of a kind he had scrupulously avoided in previous decades. Then he moved on to reveal his method. Politics, he said, must be played 'as on a chessboard'[85]. He would ally with the devil if necessary to protect Muslim interests – a far cry from the fastidious Jinnah who had once believed that politics was essentially 'for gentlemen'. By this time he was being hailed as Quaid-i-Azam – the Great Leader.

In March 1939 he appointed a special subcommittee of the League to examine the many schemes for federation and/or Muslim autonomy that had begun to circulate. This was a helpful trend of opinion that he was determined to steer. It had to be set skilfully against the British scheme for federation contained in the 1935 Act, and also against the Congress's own determination to create a unitary India. And he went further than words and plans. By the end of March he had opened a back channel to Lord Zetland, Secretary of State, in London, via League leader Chaudhry Khaliquzzaman, to communicate a possible demand for separate Muslim areas outside a federal India. He then used a speech in the assembly to set out a strictly conditional support of the British, and to rule out any cooperation with the Congress at all. These moves were both designed to identify a distinctive place in Indian politics for the All-India Muslim League. He was declaring that his support would have to be earned – even bought, and that his position as an anti-imperialist nationalist was distinct from other Muslim notables like the Aga Khan, who was keen to promote some kind of all-India federation, or Sikander Hayat Khan and his Punjabis, who were relatively happy with the provincial autonomy granted to them under the 1935 Constitution.

Jinnah had now found a distinct voice and the political muscle to make it count.

THE COMING OF WAR

By the middle of 1939, the Muslim League had narrowed its focus and was more united and vigorous than it had ever been. The Congress, however, was experiencing its most serious split since 1907, which resulted from a tussle between Gandhi and Subhas Chandra Bose over the party's presidency. Bose had built up a devoted following on the Congress left, and was elected president in 1938. But he had also become increasingly impressed by the strength of European-style nationalist–socialist movements, and had tried to move the Congress both to the left and away from Gandhian methods. Having first met the Mahatma in 1921, he had never taken to either Gandhi's philosophy or his methods, and repeatedly criticized him through the 1930s, declaring as far back as 1933 that he was 'a failed leader'. Wishing to take a second term as president, against Gandhi's wishes, Bose stood again in February 1939 and was elected, but was immediately faced with mass resignations from his Working Committee. Gandhi finally got whatever revenge he would permit himself to enjoy when Bose was forced to resign in May. Bose then set up his own party, the Forward Bloc, with himself as its revered leader, or Netaji – an unmistakable echo of fashionable European titles, like Duce. The Bloc, predictably, was friendly towards the Axis Powers.

As the threat of armed conflict in Europe loomed, the British became increasingly worried about going to war with eight potentially disloyal Congress ministries in place, so the British Government amended the 1935 Act to give extra powers to the Viceroy and Governors. With no federal system and the possible end of provincial autonomy, the long debated Act of 1935 was, after only four years, a dead letter. Indian politicians now lost the power to intimidate the British, so that when hostilities finally opened in September 1939, Viceroy Linlithgow simply announced that India's 390 million were at war, without one word of consultation with any representative Indian. This was constitutionally permissible, but the political consequences were momentous.

All three main forces in India's political life now faced difficult choices.

The British had a straightforward aim – to bring India's full weight into the war, but an India wholeheartedly united behind the war effort might just as easily unite wholeheartedly behind demands for self-government. Indian unity was therefore a double-edged sword for the British, and the political concessions mooted over the next few years were all restricted by an underlying fear of loss of control.

The Congress had its own problems with unity too. The party was fragile at the time, as the strains imposed by government office and patronage began to work against internal cohesion, and the organization was still recovering from the upset over Bose's disputed presidency. In 1939 most Congress members were much more anti-fascist than they were anti-British, but there were obvious contradictions in supporting an imperial power to fight a war against other imperial powers in the hope of winning liberation from imperialism. And tactically, matters were not clear – what combination of co-operation, negotiation, or opposition was appropriate?

Jinnah was in a somewhat clearer position, but needed to proceed with care. He had distanced himself from both the government and the main opposition party, and could therefore choose with whom to ally and what to ask for in return. But he had to avoid looking either too close to the British, or of supporting the Congress to such a degree that he ushered in immediate swaraj and the dreaded Hindu domination it would bring. He had little actual power, in that he could not keep India out of the war, or commit her to it. But he could speak for the Muslims, and in that capacity he was determined to counter demands from the Congress for further constitutional reforms, and to take a substantial role in the government at the centre.

These priorities revealed themselves as soon as war was declared on 3 September 1939. Gandhi and Jinnah were summoned to the Viceroy's presence for consultation, where Gandhi pledged his moral support as an individual, and Jinnah immediately demanded that the Congress ministries be turned out. When Linlithgow quizzed him about some recent remarks that seemed to reject democracy, Jinnah reiterated his well-worn theme that democracy in India was not workable on the Western model, where parties took turn in government. This would not happen in India. When asked what his solution was, Jinnah suggested the partition of the country,[86] his first recorded espousal of the option.

A passage of intensive three-way negotiations followed, as the British tried to assemble the most support for the lowest political price, and Jinnah tried to steer a course between wringing concessions out of the British without alienating his own supporters. The Congress leadership – apart from Gandhi – simply wanted independence as quickly as possible. They wanted nothing to do with an imperialist war if it would not bring liberation to India. After an extended Working Committee meeting from 10–14 September, a 'manifesto'[87] was agreed, condemning Fascism and Nazism, but making clear that if the current war was simply to support the imperial status quo then 'India could have nothing to do with it'. If the war was for democracy, however, India could only be included by democratic means. The Congress was asking for democracy – self–determination, a Constituent Assembly, participation in executive government etc. – in return for the party's active support. 'No final decision' would be reached, however, until the British made a declaration of their war aims. It took a month for the Viceroy to reply. He consulted with London and found Secretary of State Lord Zetland unwilling to abandon the 1935 Act in any way. Linlithgow then met with no less than fifty-two Indian leaders, including Jinnah, and Gandhi – twice. Meanwhile, the Muslim League set down a marker on 18 September, offering support for the war if the British accepted the League as the sole representative of India's Muslims.

The Congress was the most active party at this time, and made a tentative approach to the League in hopes of forming a united front. Jinnah was invited to Wardha to participate in deliberations, but refused to attend. He did meet Nehru for talks from 16–18 October, which proved abortive, but he declined an invitation from the Viceroy to joint discussions with Gandhi. The Congress also ramped up the pressure on the British, with a resolution of the All India Committee of 11 October demanding that 'India must be declared an independent nation'.[88]

Gandhi and Nehru were drifting apart at this point. Nehru wanted to use the war as leverage in the cause of swaraj; a free India could then commit her forces to the anti-fascist cause. Gandhi, however, wanted nothing to do with the war and was determined to avoid the dilemmas that the previous global conflict had posed for him. He preferred to offer non-violent cooperation with the intention of placing the British under a moral obligation to make appropriate concessions.

Finally the Viceroy made a statement on 17 October, which made no concessions at all, while talking of the war as a 'common cause'.[89] It was greeted with very different reactions by the Congress and the League. The government's inflexibility was unacceptable to the Congress, and its Working Committee issued a statement on 22 October,[90] which stated that it 'could not possibly support Britain', and called on the provincial Congress ministries to resign.

The Muslim League response[91] welcomed the concern expressed by the Viceroy to give 'full weight' to the views and interests of India's minorities. Jinnah latched on to these words and took them to mean that the Congress did not speak for all India, as it claimed, and that the Muslim League had been given a veto over any post-war changes to the 1935 constitution. This was not quite what the Viceroy actually said; he made no reference to particular bodies or Muslims. Nevertheless Jinnah had seen the political reality clearly enough. He had been handed the chance to block all constitutional progress in India for the duration of the war.

As November opened, Linlithgow was still trying to get the Congress and League to agree on a joint approach, but Congress leaders were disinclined to promote Jinnah's importance, and Jinnah's demands – principally the formation of provincial coalitions with the League – were not acceptable. A series of meetings in Delhi failed to resolve any of the disputes between the three sides.

The Congress then had no choice but to follow through on its threat, and its provincial ministries all resigned by 10 November. The British were in small part embarrassed but in very large measure relieved. The running of such a complex country in time of war while in close partnership with dedicated opponents did not seem a good idea. The League members, however, were jubilant. This was the biggest advance they had made under the new Constitution, and it promised the opportunity of real power, if they could step into the newly vacant political spaces.

Had Jinnah endeavoured to make common cause with the Congress then the situation could have been grave for the British. The Raj had always relied to a great extent on disunity in Indian politics, and a golden opportunity was missed at this juncture. Linlithgow was relieved and wrote to Lord Zetland, on 4 November, that had Jinnah stood with the Congress the strain 'would have been very great indeed'. He further noted that he now had 'a vested interest in [Jinnah's] position'[92]. Thanks in part to Jinnah, the Viceroy was now politically stronger than he had been before the outbreak of the war.

Jinnah nominated 22 December as a day for the celebration of deliverance from Hindu 'tyranny, oppression and injustice'.[93] Where Congress had been celebrating an illusory deliverance 10 years earlier, the Muslims of India now celebrated a very real political opportunity that December day.

War: 1940–45

The outbreak of war left India militarily stranded, as a combatant nation with troops in the field but without a home front. For over two years there was no immediate external threat to India's borders but, as in 1914, British hands grasped power even closer than usual. The war years then slipped by with the Raj as a large passive force at the centre, strong enough to ignore the two less powerful forces ranged against it. Winning the war was all, and the British intended to do so with or without the Congress. Congress leaders found this difficult to comprehend and continued to beat their heads against a wall of imperial intransigence. In a system like British India the transfer of real power was always going to be a leap, and wartime is not a good time for such a manoeuvre. This left the Congress with nowhere to go except open rebellion, with its likely consequence – prison.

As France fell and bombs rained down on London through 1940, Viceroy Linlithgow continued to take a firm line in India: eight out of 11 provinces were being ruled directly by their Governors under Section 93 of the 1935 Act. But India was not quiet. In February, the Congress revived the threat of Civil Disobedience, and in March, at Ramgarh, passed its most radical resolution to date – refusing to support the war and demanding the immediate election of a constituent assembly. Meanwhile, the Muslim League was beginning to finalize an agreed line on some sort of separate political structure for the Muslim 'nation'.

JINNAH, GANDHI AND THE SECOND IMPERIAL WAR

The war was the making of Jinnah, politically. It debilitated his Congress opponents, made him newly useful to the British, and offered him opportunities to make demands that could not be swept aside as they had been in the late 1920s. The Muslims of India did not become more united directly because of the war, but they had fewer reasons to oppose it than most members of the Congress, who had a long list of objections to India's involvement in Britain's struggle to survive.

From the British viewpoint, Jinnah became their enemy's enemy. A useful ally, but not much more than a man they could pick up and put down at will. He could serve as the appointed divider while the British ruled on. How much of a force was he, really? He sat as member for a minority constituency in a decorative central legislature, a body that in its entirety could claim to speak for less than two million out of 390 million people. He led the Muslim League, which had several million members by the mid-1940s, but it remained unclear to what degree he truly represented these members or how keenly they would follow him. He would be hard to knock out of the game, but it was not a game he could dominate. Slowly, he established his right to speak for all of India's Muslims, mostly by repeating the claim that he was doing so. All the while his personal identity and that of the Muslim League were becoming inextricable.

With the return of war conditions, Gandhi was less ready this time to comply first and expect concessions later, but he suddenly found himself out of step with the senior Congress leadership. During the period of his meetings with Linlithgow from September 1939 to June 1940 he was able to be quite genuine in his claim to speak only as an individual, for he had little sympathy with the determination of the other members of the High Command to wring concessions from the British in their 'difficulty'. He was also completely opposed to the idea that a free India should commit troops to the war, or even that an Independent India should be wanting to have an army at all. These two points placed him at odds with Nehru in particular, who was passing through one of his most belligerent and radical phases at this time.

The Mahatma's isolation did not have significant political effects, because the Congress was in a weak position, vis-à-vis the Raj, that could not easily be remedied. Linlithgow persisted in consulting Gandhi because he felt that Nehru was 'doctrinaire to a degree'[94], and that the old man would be more amenable. This was a fairly safe bet with Gandhi, who was always keen to keep channels of communication open, and was dedicated to the principle that one's opponent should not become a permanent enemy.

Gandhi's political isolation, however, did have a marked personal effect. Deprived of influence in senior Congress counsels, he embarked on his least convincing period of national leadership. He was stranded politically, because he was reluctant to launch a Civil Disobedience movement against the beleaguered government, but neither could he support its war. His first public reaction to the conflict was to write of the need for Hindu–Muslim unity[95] at a time when it was receding faster than ever. If this could be recovered then perhaps the government could be persuaded to make concessions without the need for violence. By December 1939 this was a forlorn hope.

His next project was to try to end the war in Europe. He offered to go and speak to Hitler, but Linlithgow declined the favour. In July 1940 he wrote an open letter to the people of England asking them not to fight the Axis powers, but to let Messrs. Mussolini and Hitler have whatever it was they wanted. Britons should lie down and die as heroes of non-violence and then the war would be over.[96]

This idealistic exhortation is sometimes used to discredit Gandhi as a leader, and it is hard to defend as a serious political proposal. But he utterly believed in non-violence as a practical idea, and he knew people could hardly be expected to take it up if no one told them about it and suggested they practise it. Like his other similar suggestions in the pre-war period to Abyssinians, Czechs and Jews, it represents Gandhi the journalist as much as Gandhi the national leader. He held no power at the best of times, and 1940 was probably the worst of times for him. He was confronted with his own helplessness in the face of vicious global warfare. How could violence be stopped non-violently? He responded in a way that had worked well on other occasions, with an appeal to the higher moral faculties of everyone concerned, coupled with a simple plan of self-sacrificial action. And if the population of Britain *had* ceased to fight, then the war would indeed have been over. But his non-violent stance made it hard for him to thrive politically in violent times, and there was no easy way out. The logical course was to continue to condemn all violence, and he did exactly this, without partisan favour. As the war went on, he came to equate 'Hitlerism' with 'Churchillism', denouncing them both as equally violent.[97]

The Second World War, therefore, called forth a more characteristic response from Gandhi than had the First. Jinnah, however, repeated his earlier reaction. He immediately understood the political advantages on offer, but this time he intended to use them not to create national unity to strengthen the demand for Indian self-government but to create Muslim unity for the promotion of Muslim self-government. He was always more anti-colonialist than anti-British, so this shift did not greatly trouble his core beliefs. The main difference was that now he was in no hurry. Unlike 1916, he did not have a united, national movement behind him, and the promised self-government that the end of the war would bring was no longer going to be such a straightforward affair.

By 1939 Jinnah had mellowed towards the British. Gandhi, however, had hardened up. This time he was determined not to forsake ahimsa – the 'faith of a lifetime'[98]. The results of these shifts were very different. Gandhi produced a stream of idealistic letter writing, while Jinnah moved swiftly to produce a blueprint for separatism.

THE ROAD TO LAHORE

On 23–24 March 1940, the Muslim League passed a resolution in Lahore calling for the creation of 'independent states' for India's Muslims. With plentiful hindsight, this has become a critical event in the story of Partition. Though it certainly plays a part in that story, we must be careful not to credit the actors in Lahore with a prescience they did not possess. To read the inevitable creation of Pakistan directly into the unanimous passing of the resolution is to ignore the seven years of complex events that were to follow. This can be understood more clearly if we look at where the resolution came from, what it said, what it left out, and what it was intended to accomplish.

After Sir Muhammad Iqbal's speech in December 1930, the next important attempt to attract public support for a Muslim 'homeland' came from Chaudhry Rahmat Ali, a student in his mid-thirties at Cambridge, who published a pamphlet in January 1933 entitled *Now or Never*.[99] Rahmat Ali (1895–1951) was a strange, peripheral figure. A devout Muslim, from 1933 he came up with a series of geographical schemes for the expression of separate Muslim identity. His latter-day admirers have hailed him as the father of 'psychogeography', but he is better understood as a man in love with Islam, maps and neologisms, whose greatest achievement was the invention of the word 'Pakistan', meaning 'land of the pure' in Urdu. His original pamphlet does not spell out any of the acrostic readings since attributed to the word, although he does indirectly alert the reader to a deeper meaning by the way he sets out the constituent parts of the proposed state. He lists, in order: Punjab, NWFP (Afghan Province – labelled 'Afghania' on one of his maps), Kashmir, Sind and Baluchistan.

Several points spring immediately to mind. First, there is no mention of Bengal, so it would not be correct to claim that in 1933 Rahmat Ali was envisaging Pakistan as it later appeared. This omission also reflects the fact that the bulk of the enthusiasm for Pakistan at this stage was in the northwest, specifically in Punjab, his birthplace. His list also includes Kashmir, which at the time was a princely state, in charge of its own destiny. How it would be brought in was not specified, but nuts-and-bolts realism was never Rahmat Ali's strong suit.

Everyone remembers the name he created, but hardly anyone remembers his original plan, which confined itself to the northwestern area. He considered that entering any scheme of federation as discussed at the recent Round Table Conferences would be 'nothing less than signing the death warrant of Islam and its future in India'. Instead he wanted 'a separate federation' as 'a matter of life and death'.[100] His proposals seem rather reasonable in retrospect, even if his language was a little overwrought, but they were dismissed by Muslim politicians as a 'student scheme' and considered impractical.

The word 'Pakistan' has earned Rahmat Ali lasting fame, which is scarcely deserved if we also consider his later work, for he went on to dreams of a greater 'Pakasia' and, in 1942, to an ideology he called 'Pakism'. He followed this up with a demand for the complete rearrangement of India on religious lines, based on the familiar Two-Nation assertion that India was not a country but a continent. India would henceforward be called Dinia (land of 'Din', or faith), and divided up into 20 separate 'pure' religious island communities. Why not? Europe, as he pointed out, was divided into 31 little pieces. Any sizable enclave of Muslims was given its own -stan. The familiar Pakistan was to be joined by Bangistan (Bengal), Haidaristan (Delhi), Osmanistan (Hyderabad), Maplistan (Malabar) and so forth.

This polka-dot plan was one solution to the Muslim 'problem' and it had a certain democratic logic in solving the minority issue. Minorities are essentially defined by borders and can be turned into majorities if one isolates them by redrawing the map radically enough. Dinia was only one such approach. There were several others, some of which involved moving people (Muslims in or Hindus out) or adjusting boundaries. Theologian Dr Syed Abdul Latif proposed a federal India divided into cultural 'zones' rather than into hard, separate states. Other voices spoke against militant separatism. Muhammad Zafirullah Khan, a prominent Punjabi politician who combined membership of the Muslim League with a place on the Viceroy's executive council, rejected movements or divisions, and favoured autonomous regions, arranged by treaty around a British-dominated centre, which would be deputed to handle defence and arbitration of disputes. There was also a plan put forward by two Aligarh academics, Professor Syed Zafar ul Hasan and Dr M.A.H. Qadri, advocating the transformation of British India into two Muslim states, plus 'Hindustan' – which would include large Muslim enclaves – and a separate sovereign state of Hyderabad. Finally, there was also a proposal from Sikander Hayat Khan calling for the familiar Punjabi recipe of extensive provincial autonomy and a weak federal centre.

THE LAHORE RESOLUTION

With all these ideas jostling for attention we can see the context of the Lahore Resolution rather more clearly, especially in the light of the Viceroy's statement in October 1939 that any future proposals for constitutional reform would have to be considered by the wider Indian political public. This had been intended to counter Congress in any opportunistic dash for swaraj, but it doubled as an invitation to other parties to put forward their own ideas. Linlithgow had also privately asked Jinnah for constructive proposals in late 1939. In this situation Jinnah needed to make sure that at the very least there were Muslim counterproposals in the public arena to rival any Congress scheme. Meanwhile, within Muslim politics, he had to say something on the subject of separatism, partly to guide the leadership between all the rival proposals, but also because the idea of some sort of communal protection appealed to a wide range of Muslims, especially after the experience of Congress ministries from 1937 to 1939. This presented a gift-wrapped chance to forge some kind of wider unity. However, it did not promise to be easy because of the lack of broad agreement about what the Two-Nation Theory actually implied in practical terms. The solution was to keep all the specifics out of any proposals, and this is precisely what Jinnah did.

It is worth reproducing the text of the Lahore Resolution at some length, partly because it demonstrates just how elastic it was as a rope to tie the party together, but also because it is frequently quoted very selectively. The crucial passages are as follows:

'Resolved... that no constitutional plan would be workable in this country or acceptable to the Muslims unless it is designed on the following basic principles, viz. that geographical contiguous units are demarcated into regions which should be so constituted with such territorial readjustments as may be necessary, that the areas in which the Muslims are numerically in a majority as in the North-Western and Eastern zones of India, should be grouped to constitute independent states in which the constituent units shall be autonomous and sovereign.

'That adequate, effective and mandatory safeguards shall be specifically provided in the constitution for minorities in the units and in the regions for the protection of their religious, cultural, economic, political, administrative and other rights of the minorities, with their consultation. Arrangements thus should be made for the security of Muslims where they were in a minority.

'...providing for the assumption finally, by the respective regions, of all the powers, such as defense, external affairs, communications, customs and such other matters as may be necessary.'[101]

Immediately it can be pointed out that the word Pakistan does not appear. Nor does the word 'Partition'. Nor is there any mention of any kind of central body, or federating power, or of a time-frame for the execution of any of the provisions. Vagueness abounds, with the inclusion of a series of unspecified concepts – units, regions, areas, zones and states – all of which are undefined. There is positive reference to existing conditions, as in the words 'in this country', and the reference to 'the constitution', but these contrast starkly with the definitive words: independent, autonomous and sovereign. They also sit uneasily with the speech Jinnah gave to introduce the resolution, which stressed the international dimension of the Muslim demand: the detail of the resolution is constitutional, not diplomatic. In terms of timing there is the use of the word 'finally', which implies some kind of evolving process rather than a revolution. By comparison, Montagu's words in 1917 stand as a very model of lucidity.

To a master tactician like Jinnah this latitude was meat and drink, then and later. The immediate result, as intended, was broad unity. His main rivals in the provinces all backed the resolution. Fazlul Haq from Bengal, one of his more wayward supporters, moved the motion and it was passed unanimously, with Sikander Hayat Khan solidly in support. The text of the resolution was incorporated into the Muslim League's constitution the next April at Madras, and was not enlarged or changed until 1946, when the word 'Pakistan' was added and 'states' was changed to the singular 'state'. Meanwhile, it held the League together as a promise of a better tomorrow, the kind of marvellously enticing and universally adaptable idea that every politician dreams of finding. Jinnah managed, by leaving out much more than he put in, to attach his party to an idea that no one could gainsay in the general terms in which it had been expressed. He had still to bind all of his party to himself personally, but at last he had a Muslim issue that could define his organization, give it cohesion and, very importantly, a positive vision.

The key to the resolution, its content and its very existence, was that Jinnah had no power. He knew that any proposals he put forward had to get past both the British and the Congress, and neither would be amenable to pressure in the short term. He did not, therefore, have to live with the immediate consequences of the resolution. It was a shot to nothing; he was playing politics rather more than he was doing state formation. His primary purpose in 1940 was to hold the Muslims together, and to realize this aim the resolution worked quite, but not very, well. He had short- and long-term aims, and like all politicians, the longer term must fall by default if the shorter term is not attended to.

THE AUGUST OFFER

The Viceroy had asked the major parties to submit proposals for closer wartime cooperation, but he was also prepared to make suggestions of his own. In January 1940 he clarified that the Dominion Status to be awarded after the war would be the full independence version as laid out in the 1931 Statute of Westminster. Gandhi declared that he believed Linlithgow to be sincere, so a meeting was arranged in February. The Viceroy outlined a scheme to bring four Indians onto the executive council, but this was hardly enough. Gandhi wanted India to be free to choose her own destiny in the war, her own form of government and everything else. Minorities and princes should not be allowed to stand in the way. The minorities were a problem for Indians; the princes were a British creation and should be dealt with by plebiscites. In March, at Ramgarh, the Congress then demanded the immediate formation of a national government, with Indians in harness on the Viceroy's executive council. After talks through June and July the Muslim League fell into line with this demand, but with the stipulation that any Muslim League involvement in government would have to be on the basis of strict parity with the Congress.[102]

With agreement seemingly within reach, Linlithgow made his terms clear in his August Offer. He announced on 8 August 1940 that Dominion Status would be granted after the war with the 'least possible delay'.[103] Meanwhile, the executive council would be expanded to include 'representative Indians', and a War Advisory Council would be formed to include influential elements in India's national life, including the princes. No changes to constitutional arrangements were contemplated during the current 'struggle for existence', nor would they be adopted against the will of any minority – there would be no subsequent move 'to any system of government whose authority is directly denied by large and powerful elements in India's national life'.[104] No coercion would be used to enforce submission to any such government. This was a nod to the League, a guarantee that after the war the Congress would not be permitted to steal a march on them at the centre.

The Congress rejected the Offer outright, whereupon the League decided to accept, with conditions. These were: that the League would only come into administration with the Congress on a basis of equality and that all Muslims should be nominated exclusively by the League. This was asking that Jinnah be allowed to dictate whom the Viceroy could choose to appoint, and as such it naturally proved unacceptable. No progress, therefore, was possible.

The big loser was the Congress, whose leaders might have expected a more conciliatory approach from the Viceroy, but the mistrust that was to persist through the entire war was now solidly in place. So, to recapture the initiative, Gandhi launched a campaign of 'individual satyagraha' in October 1940, as a result of which Nehru was soon back in prison. By the middle of 1941 around 14,000 others had joined him. Subhas Chandra Bose nearly became one of them, but escaped from custody on the eve of his trial.

JINNAH STEPS UP

Despite the discontent, the British kept true to the August Offer, although they took their time about it. Through 1941, Linlithgow embarked on a number of conciliatory gestures. He expanded his executive council from six to 12, altering the balance from three official and three unofficial members to four and eight. In July 1941 he also set up the War Advisory Council and, without consulting Jinnah, invited three Muslim premiers of provincial governments to join it – Sikander Hayat Khan from the Punjab, Fazlul Haq from Bengal and Muhammad Sadullah from Assam. These three, who were all nominally in the Muslim League, were co-opted in their capacities as senior provincial figures, not as party members, but Jinnah chose to see the move as a direct challenge to his central position in Muslim affairs, and it proved a perfect opportunity for him to try out his strength. It went well for him.

On 24 August 1941, the Muslim League Working Committee demanded that the three premiers resign their seats on the War Council. Again, this was a bold step, but the turf war over the appointment of Muslims within the government had to be fought or Jinnah's standing would be undermined. Sikander, who over recent months had been following an increasingly independent line over Muslim 'separatism', proved surprisingly pliable and resigned as requested. He did this because it suited his purposes within Punjabi politics, where he was reluctant to appear either too communalist or too cooperative with the British. Fazlul Haq, on the other hand, was far less happy to feel the firm smack of leadership from Jinnah's hand. He resigned from the War Council but took matters further. He resigned from the League too, accusing Jinnah of 'arbitrary use of powers', and of seeking to rule 33 million Muslims in Bengal as an 'omnipotent authority'.[105] Now deprived of League support in Bengal, Fazlul Haq had to recombine his governing coalition, drawing in support from all available areas, including the Hindu Mahasabha and former Forward Bloc members. This could be counted as a blow to Muslim power locally, but in overall terms it was a massive boost to Jinnah's personal authority at the centre. The moral of the story was that from now on Jinnah would not be kept out of appointments to national office for Muslims and that he had just about enough political standing to make his interventions count.

It also served clear notice that the next few years of wrangling would be about the principle of 'parity', not about Pakistan – a word that Jinnah was still reluctant to use at that time, although he eventually came round to it when he found out how convenient and popular it was. The ideology of Two (equal) Nations would be enough to keep Jinnah afloat politically until the end of the war. The distillation of the Two-Nation Theory into parity at last gave him a perfect, practical issue for uniting India's Muslims. It had no weakness in its details – its strength *was* the details. It could run and run.

As 1941 drew on, India's political life was in a stalemate. Neither the Congress nor the Muslim League had access to any institutional leverage with which to pressure the British. Gandhi's individual satyagraha campaign, which had not been a notable success, was trailing away, while Jinnah was effectively standing on a sandcastle. He had proposed a separate formation of some sort for Muslims but the idea was not universally popular across moderate Muslim opinion. The British knew this, and were comforted by it. H.V. Hodson, the reforms commissioner, toured the country extensively over the 1941–42 period and found little overt enthusiasm for Pakistan. Indeed, not many Muslims would gain much by its realization. Punjabis and Bengalis stood to lose their autonomy, and Muslims in minority states would have to uproot themselves physically to take advantage of the protection a separate homeland afforded. Faced with that prospect, it must have seemed more attractive to stay within a united India and seek safeguards via a central government.

So Pakistan took on two meanings for two separate groups: the Muslim-majority communities hoped it would bring them autonomy away from the British and the Hindus, while the minority communities hoped it would be part of a rearranged Indian Union in which the Muslims had an equal voice in central government. The first vision, of course, had no natural place for Jinnah in it, whereas the second was tailor-made for him. But inconveniently, the real Muslim political clout rested with the Muslim-majority communities. These were the people that the British paid heed to, even so far as handing out places to them on the executive council. The minority communities had already been ignored by the Congress with impunity. This was always Jinnah's dilemma – that his most potentially powerful brigades had no real inclination to follow him into battle.

Jinnah's main prestige at this point was tied to his special relationship with the British, who chose to take him seriously despite his lack of political weight. If the leaders of Punjab and Bengal only behaved like members of the League when it suited them, then from where, precisely, was his standing drawn? If the strongly autonomous provinces did not fancy his Pakistan, then who would join? Would it even contain Sind, 77 per cent Muslim but without a League ministry? This was a pertinent question, for along with calls for Pakistan there were also calls for 'Azad Sind'. Jinnah could not push strongly for his separate state(s) because he had no way of knowing who would follow his call, while to start acting as the leader of a still imaginary country would be to promote himself to some invisible level above elected politicians, and potentially offend the grandees who ran the provinces he wished to represent. He had a formal standing at this point only in his life presidency of his own party and his seat in the legislature. In terms of the Muslim community he was the guardian and advocate of a rather vague idea; in terms of the British, he was a useful figurehead to counterbalance the Congress, a constant reproach to their pretensions to speak for the whole nation.

THE WAR BROADENS

Unhappy but stable, India was about to be overtaken by world events. Through 1941 the war was not going well for Britain, with German troops all over Europe, and on their way to Moscow. India was not directly threatened at this stage, but the entry of the Japanese into the Second World War in December 1941 changed local conditions dramatically. The fall of Singapore on 11 February 1942 represented the worst British military calamity in Asia since the retreat from Kabul a century earlier, and when the Japanese took Rangoon a month later,

Bengal became a prospective front line against the Axis Powers. The entry of the United States to the war also brought an intensified scrutiny of the Raj from Washington. Churchill and Roosevelt had concluded the Atlantic Charter in August 1940, calling for freedom and self-determination for the nations of the world, which sounded fine and noble as a rallying cry against fascism. But a month later, Churchill explicitly denied that such liberties were to be extended to India or Burma – a statement that rather compromised Linlithgow's many pronouncements on the same subject. And after Pearl Harbour, Roosevelt felt entitled, as a fighting ally, to question what the alliance was fighting for. In his mind he was not defending imperialism.

Some of the Labour members of Churchill's War Cabinet were as uncomfortable as Roosevelt, especially the deputy prime minister, Clement Attlee, who was keen to respond to requests from India for some gesture to be made to include Indians in their own government at a time of war, and he wrote a trenchant memo to that effect in February 1942. There was a military logic to this, in that it seemed better to recruit Indians willingly in the cause of their own defence than to leave them surly and disinterested. There was a paradox here, and Churchill well understood it. Britain was going 'to defend India in order, if successful, to be turned out',[106] as he put it. But above all, Churchill wanted to win the war. To reach an agreement with Indians might help to do that. The result was the Cripps Mission.

THE CRIPPS MISSION

Sir Stafford Cripps had been expelled from the Labour Party in 1939 for trying to make links with the far left, but by 1942 he was in the War Cabinet as a reward for successful diplomatic work in Moscow. In character he was as enigmatic as Jinnah. He was a brilliant barrister, an enthusiastic Marxist and a committed Christian, with a reputation for intellect and integrity. In spring 1942 he was given the job of bringing a draft declaration of future British intentions to India's politicians, with a view to enlisting their cooperation. He seemed especially suitable for this mission, having become friendly with Nehru during the latter's visit to England in 1938. He had also consulted with a wide range of Indian politicians on a private trip he made to India in 1939. The intention to bring a new deal to India was announced on 11 March 1942, but Churchill made it clear that the offer, which he called a 'declaration', had been agreed by the Cabinet, and that Cripps was going to India to secure 'acceptance' of it. Cripps arrived in Delhi on the 22nd.[107]

What followed is complex and confused. We know a great deal more about what the Conservative members of the government thought about it than Cripps did. This is because Leo Amery, the Secretary for India, and Linlithgow corresponded at length all through the Mission, which they both disliked. In this they concurred with Churchill, who was convinced that Indians, or at least the 'martial races' among them, would fight willingly for the King–Emperor but would never fight well for a bunch of cavilling Congress lawyers and the Hindu 'priest-craft machine'. Churchill knew that Cripps's errand was good public relations with the US, and he was politically astute enough to know that to reach out to India, through a Labour junior at Atlee's suggestion, put him in a win-win situation. He would get either a fighting India or a chastened Labour Party.[108]

There were two elements to the offer, which can be called the 'Later' and the 'Now' parts. The Later part covered what would happen at the end of the war and concerned the detailed shape of an independent India. This part of the offer was very much Attlee's baby, as he felt sure that Indian politicians would be more interested in long-term considerations than immediate admission to power. Dominion Status was promised (again), subject to details to be agreed by a constituent body, with a provision that any province would be able to opt out of the new Indian Union – the so-called 'local option'. A treaty would then regulate dealings between Britain and India, with the minority question provided for in that treaty.

INDIAN REACTION

Although the 'Later' provisions proved contentious, the Mission's overall package was rejected primarily because its short-term 'Now' provisions were simply not sufficiently attractive. They were essentially a repeat of the August Offer of 1940. No constitutional change was proposed, but Indian party leaders were to be invited to join the Viceroy's executive council, with the main portfolios – those of the home, defence and finance members – remaining with the Viceroy's nominees. Cripps proposed that the parties would take up the other eight non-official seats. Or did he? Maulana Azad later maintained that in their first meeting, on 25 March, Cripps had offered to fill the executive with Indians and reduce the role of the Viceroy to a position analogous to that of the King in London.[109] This the Congress would have accepted, but Cripps did not have the authority to offer any such thing. There had been sharp divisions in the War Cabinet over the concessions that should be made, and it is not exactly clear who drafted the text that Cripps carried with him, or what his detailed powers were precisely agreed to be. This was obviously a recipe for disaster, as was the fact that Linlithgow had not been properly consulted. Linlithgow's correspondence with Amery suggests that the politicians in London were at times as confused as Maulana Azad.[110]

Cripps made an effort to see almost everyone in Indian politics during his short stay, but despite his personal conviction that all was going well, he simply dug himself into a deeper and deeper hole. He started by reading out his prepared declaration to the Viceroy's executive council, the men his mission was intended to replace, and then fielded questions afterwards. The local option immediately drew dismayed attention. After he saw Azad on the 25th, he met Jinnah, who was 'rather surprised'[111] at how far the 'local option' went to meet the Pakistan case.

Next was Gandhi, who was implacably opposed to the whole idea. Having first pointed out that he held no official position in the Congress, he refused to bargain over portfolios, and instead demanded immediate full independence. Why had Cripps come with a 'cut and dried scheme', he asked, and told the envoy that he was sure the Congress would refuse the offer. Cripps then asked that if they did, and Jinnah accepted, what should he do? Gandhi told him to press forward, so as to let Jinnah feel the weight of 'responsibility' for a successful outcome.[112] This was the first time Gandhi fully expressed his willingness to give Jinnah a decisive role in shaping the structure of Independent India, or even the government of the country. This offer effectively lay on the table until Partition in 1947.

Gandhi's guess about the negative reaction of the Congress leaders was not entirely correct, because some were prepared to haggle over the details of power. But when pressed, Cripps could offer no more than the eight portfolios. Azad and Nehru demanded that at the very least the defence portfolio should be held by an Indian. They could accept that in a time of war the army had to be under the leadership of a British Commander-in-Chief, but they argued that a national war effort involved much more than combat operations. And, after all, it was the defence of their own land that was in question; British army, perhaps, Indian defence, certainly. But the British refused to hand over defence, forcing Cripps to spend a good deal of time trying to devise ways in which 'defence' could be separated from the army command. At this point the Americans took a hand and Colonel Johnson, Roosevelt's envoy to India, entered the discussions, much to Avery's and Linlithgow's annoyance. Churchill telegraphed Cripps to remind him that he had been sent to consult, not to negotiate. The whole affair was finally brought to a close after a letter from Azad formally rejected the offer on 10 April, and the Muslim League followed suit the next day. Cripps was forced to retire defeated.

FAILURE: LABOUR AND THE LOCAL OPTION

It is not difficult to see why the Cripps offer failed. It was not enough, and the threat of the oncoming Japanese invasion made it a good time for Indians to ask for more than was on the table. Gandhi was reported as saying that to accept the offer would be like taking 'a post-dated cheque on a failing bank', a very well known – and semi-apocryphal[113] – remark that illustrates how seriously the Congress underestimated British determination to win the war with or without their help. Yet it did seem a paltry offer, especially compared to the kind of language Cripps had used when he visited India as a backbench MP in 1939. At that point he had been prepared to explore exactly the sort of thing that the Congress was now asking for. But by 1942 he was very differently placed as a member of a wartime British Government.

This illuminates the fact that Labour members were generally much more generous in their constitutional outlook regarding India than their Conservative colleagues. They were the first British politicians who actually *wanted* to reach an Indian settlement, and this led them to a very different tactical approach. To ensure that an agreement could be reached, they were prepared to abandon the requirement that Indians had to agree among themselves to get their independence. This explains the inclusion of the 'local option' clause. This provision, allowing any province to drop out of a future Indian Union, has caused much argument since. Why was it put into the deal? It was guaranteed to upset the Congress, as indeed it did. The Congress Working Committee remarked that the 'novel principle of non-accession' was disturbing and clearly contrary to the spirit of a unitary India.[114]

So, if the point of the Cripps Mission was to unite India behind the Empire, the inclusion of this provision would seem to be gratuitously divisive. One explanation is that the opt-out was put into the deal as a way of guaranteeing that some future general settlement would not be scuppered by the reluctance of one or two provinces with special needs, a high-minded gesture that effectively threw away the best delaying tactic that the British ever discovered. The opt-out provision was therefore a pledge of good faith that the test of unanimity would not be a requirement held over the heads of Indian leaders.

LOCAL OPTION, JINNAH AND PAKISTAN

Another suggestion about 'local option' is that the British deliberately included it as a calculated step towards creating Pakistan. This interpretation is not correct. It simply acknowledged that the demand existed; no serious offer could ignore Muslim opinion. Jinnah publicly registered his satisfaction at this recognition in the 11 April statement, but the local option did not initiate one course or another, or help to realize any vision he may have had. To allow parts of British India to go it alone did not directly help Jinnah, because it did not necessarily collect all seceding provinces into one group. It could have been used by any part of India, even Hindu-majority parts, which felt they could do better on their own. In allowing for a splintering of this sort, it could actually destroy Jinnah's future as a politician rather than enhance it. 'Local option' was a green light for the large Muslim-majority provinces to secede if they so desired, but it gave Jinnah no power over them; in fact, it directly diminished his power over them. In 1942, Jinnah was no more than the leader who could represent Muslims within a united India. There was so little substance to the Lahore Resolution that it would have been an enormous leap for him to be perceived by anyone as the chief minister-in-waiting of a unitary, breakaway Muslim state.

Jinnah could see other obstacles that stood between him and Pakistan, and he eventually attacked Cripps's offer, pointing out that the post-war constitution-making assembly was to be chosen by an electoral college formed by the provincial legislatures – which were dominated by Congressmen – and it would decide on the new form of government by simple majority. This was a cast-iron guarantee of Hindu domination, and Jinnah, on behalf of the League, felt compelled to reject the whole package. If the Cripps offer was a back-door grant of Pakistan, Jinnah could not see it. It allowed not Pakistan, but secession.

CRUNCHING POLITICS, HIDDEN LOGIC

In the end, the Cripps Mission didn't so much show the disagreements among Indian politicians as highlight those between their British counterparts in the War Cabinet.

The Conservatives were hard-nosed about the whole issue of concessions, seeing no need to make any, and were happy to fight on as they were, putting down rebellion as necessary. This is in fact what happened; the Congress's bluff was called. It was the Labour members who were running against the tide of historic British policy in India. They wanted to foster agreement, and tried to put ideas in the offer that would do this. Above all they wished to deliver on the central point of sovereignty. This was to out-Gandhi Gandhi, and concede a point simply because it was right to do so. Attlee and Cripps sincerely wanted to reach a settlement. Attlee had written in his memo of February 1942 that the time was right 'to get the leaders of the Indian political parties to unite'.[115] But they misjudged the incentive value of their bargain, and failed to carry their Conservative coalition partners with them.

As a political initiative, therefore, the offer was never likely to succeed, because the people it was supposed to conciliate were unlikely to accept it, and some of the people that made it had no real desire to see it accepted. But there were levels of logic in the details.

The key is in the way that the offer of autonomy and separate accession was made on the basis of provinces. This meant existing provinces, not some new alignment dreamt up by Rahmat Ali. The main advantage of this was that the biggest provinces, the ones most likely to break away, were Punjab and Bengal. It was important for the British to conciliate these provinces as vital areas of India in the current war. Bengal was quite possibly about to become a battlefront with Japan, and the Punjab was a major recruiting ground for the Indian Army, and the most complex province in religious terms. Reassuring these areas that the end of the war would bring new possibilities was an easy thing to do, and calming them down was a good idea at any time. Both objectives were cost-free in 1942. This was because Cripps's offer allowed that secession would be by vote of the provincial legislature, but that minorities would have a right, in the case of a close vote, to call for a plebiscite. The rules were drawn to ensure that only large majorities would trigger secession, and large majorities in Punjab and Bengal absolutely required cross-communal cooperation. Meanwhile, most of the Hindu-majority states would not even consider secession. So offering the opt-out was not so damaging and could have two major benefits. It would steady communalism in the two main Muslim-majority states, and it might also curb Jinnah's ability to find common ground among a larger group of provinces aiming for some kind of Pakistan. Bengal and the Punjab were not contiguous so the likelihood of them joining in a unitary state seemed remote. It would need a titanic effort from Jinnah to meld them into a single political entity.

Cripps was endlessly questioned about the details of the offer, and he did his best to clarify what it all meant. But he struggled to reassure his audience, because much of the uncertainty in Indian minds stemmed from an inability to believe that the post-war arrangements were not some kind of imposition; Indians really would be as free to leave the Commonwealth as they were to subdivide India and make new arrangements between its parts. Cripps could thus only describe the union of non-contiguous provinces as 'impracticable' in his first press conference, though he allowed that 'two contiguous provinces may form a separate union'.[116] It would not, in fact, be his – or any other British politician's – choice.

The best explanation for local option is that the British, or at least the Labour Party, may have believed that in a post-war India, with imperial power out of the picture, it stood a better chance of holding a greater India together in some way than relying on absolute unanimity to emerge across the whole Indian political spectrum.

THE QUIT INDIA MOVEMENT

Once Cripps had flown home there were few options left on the ground in India. With hostile forces pushing through Burma, anything beyond what Cripps had offered seemed to be tantamount to inviting them in, especially as Gandhi expressed no desire to fight the Japanese, and stated that he believed it was the presence of the British in India that was provoking them.

Chakravarthi Rajagopalachari had not given up on political progress though, and in Madras that April, he proposed that Muslim provinces be allowed to secede as a positive move towards a Congress–League settlement, and that the Congress should re-enter provincial government. Both resolutions were heavily defeated at the All-India Congress Committee meeting on 2 May. Rajagopalachari then quit the party.

Cripps, Gandhi and Rajagopalachari had all tried to find ways forward, but none could find the right mixture to bring everyone together. With Cripps gone, the Congress had no obvious way forward. This proved to be the ideal moment for Gandhi to make his last great effort in the Independence struggle. The Congress was accustomed to seek leadership from the Mahatma, and as ever, when asked, he gave it. The result was the Quit India movement.

Gandhi's mood had been slowly darkening. His commitment to non-violence had made him reluctant to pounce on the British at the start of the war, but since then he had sincerely begun to believe that the British had no intention of ever demitting power to Indians. There would always be some trouble somewhere that would serve as an excuse to stay on. In May 1942 he wrote in *Harijan* that there was no longer any 'joint common interest' that bound Indians and British together, and that the time had come for 'complete separation'. The British should go, in a 'complete and immediate' withdrawal. This would put the Allied cause 'on a completely moral basis', and the long-term benefit to all parties was very apparent to him, particularly in erasing 'race superiority' from the world, and bringing a 'clean end' to imperialism, which in turn would blunt or even end fascism and Nazism.[117]

At this point he had little leverage at his disposal, since the Congress had both resigned its elected government posts and refused the post-dated cheque. After 22 years it was still a matter of taking to the streets. In July a last offer was put forward at a Congress Working Committee meeting, asking for immediate independence on the understanding that the British would be allowed to retain military bases in India. Failure to grant independence would result in renewed civil disobedience.[118] This motion needed the approval of the national AICC to become effective. On 8 August in Bombay the Committee, closely watched by government security forces, approved a new satyagraha, whereupon the entire Congress leadership was carted off to jail before dawn the next day. Nationwide disturbances followed, despite the fact that Gandhi had not yet officially called for action.

Violent resistance far beyond mere disobedience broke out all over the country; at the end of August Linlithgow cabled Churchill that it was the most dangerous rebellion since 1857.[119] It was certainly the most violent and widespread resistance movement of the Congress era, one supported by a much wider set of political elements than before, especially on the left. However, the government was more ready for it than on previous occasions and it was confronted much more ruthlessly by Linlithgow under wartime conditions than either Reading or Irwin had seen fit in times of peace. In a matter of weeks there were more than 60,000 protesters in jail and a thousand shot dead. The movement was stifled by these countermeasures but it was also starved of nationwide coverage by severe censorship of the press and radio. The army stayed loyal and gradually the movement lost momentum – by March of 1943 it was effectively over. The British, though shaken, were rulers still. A grim humour prevailed in the face of such clearly expressed resentment against the Raj. 'Quit India' had been scrawled and painted all across the country. 'We wish we could' started to appear underneath in reply.

Conservative diehards were proved right. The Congress was unable to oust the British, and the war could still be fought without their cooperation. Jinnah, as ever, seemed to be the gainer from an ill wind. The Congress was outlawed, and most of the Congress leadership stayed locked up until the end of the war.

Indian resistance, however, was not entirely crushed. It continued in the person of the exiled Subhas Chandra Bose who, after a circuitous journey via Berlin and Tokyo, had ended up in the jungles of Burma at the head of an army of his own devising – the Indian National Army (INA). Around 50,000 strong, this was a force mostly composed of Indians captured in Singapore, armed and supplied by the Japanese, and led by Bose himself. Assessments of the military effectiveness of the INA are a matter of partisan debate, but there is no doubt that it was strictly non-communal in its internal governance. What kind of India Bose could have fashioned after a Japanese victory is a matter of guesswork, but for his persistence and bravery he was hailed then, and often since, as a national hero.

GANDHI IN JAIL

From 9 August 1942, Gandhi was confined in the Aga Khan's palace at Poona and remained there for nearly two years. During this time he suffered two personal losses. The first was the death of his long-time secretary Mahadev Desai, who died only six days later on 15 August. Desai had been his personal secretary since 1919 and it is largely due to him that we have such extensive verbatim transcripts of Gandhi's conversations, set down in a multi-volume day-by-day account of his employer's life.[120] Gandhi was always voluble, and we have his weekly articles over 40 years to reveal what he thought on major issues; there is also the enormous correspondence he kept up with prominent figures in Indian and world politics. But it is to Desai that we owe much of the more intimate and casual glimpses of Gandhi's wit and wisdom. As a companion he was personally very close to Gandhi. He 'out-Boswelled Boswell'[121] was the Mahatma's tribute to him.

More distressing though, was the loss of his wife, Kasturba, who died on 22 February 1944. She had been confined with him all through this latest detention but eventually succumbed to chronic bronchitis and a series of heart attacks. He constantly reproached himself for the suffering he had caused her. They had married very young in 1882, he 13, she 10, and she had borne him four sons. She probably remained illiterate all her life, and was certainly no intellectual, but she was a devoted companion and helper. Gandhi always overplayed his dread of her anger to the amusement of visitors to their ashram. According to his *Autobiography* they jointly took a vow of chastity around 1906 when still in South Africa, and this played an important part in Gandhi's general outlook on the issue of love and service. If a couple are only in love with each other then they are not as able to serve the needs of others as those who have forsaken physical passion. More than this, Gandhi's celibacy was driven by the belief that sex with one's spouse was 'equally impure' as any other kind of lustfulness. His desire to rise above sinfulness meant that even his most intimate relationships were not unaffected. Nevertheless, the loss of his wife–companion was a great blow to him, and when he received a note of condolence from the new Viceroy, Lord Wavell, whom he had never met, he was genuinely touched.[122]

Prison, as ever, did not restrict Gandhi in many ways. He continued to spin and think and write letters. He was not allowed to engage in political organization, but he read the newspapers and talked with a wide coterie of Congress leaders imprisoned with him. He came under pressure from the British to condemn the violent resistance taking place across India, but he claimed that he had not called for it and that it was therefore beyond him to stop it. Unhappiness at the injustice of these persistent British requests, implying as they did that the violence was his responsibility, drove him to fast for three weeks in February 1943. The Viceroy had to decide whether to release him so that his death, if it occurred, would not be directly on the hands of the authorities. It was decided to release him only if his condition deteriorated dangerously. He survived, and was freed in May 1944 on grounds of malaria and general ill health.

GANDHI–JINNAH TALKS

Events had not quite stood still in the Mahatma's absence. Rajagopalachari continued to seek constructive ways forward, and had put a proposal to Jinnah in April 1944 concerning Pakistan. He suggested that opinion in Muslim-majority districts, not provinces, might be tested by plebiscite and, if found favourable to separation, such districts could be grouped into a new Pakistan. This would take some of the sting out of the problem of 'hostage' minorities, but it did flout Jinnah's insistence on respecting existing boundaries. He rejected the idea in July, famously comparing any possible Pakistan that might result as 'mutilated' and 'moth-eaten'. It was to pick up from here that the newly freed Gandhi asked for an audience in a letter of 17 July.[123] Gandhi wrote in Gujarati; Jinnah replied in English.[124]

The resulting Gandhi–Jinnah talks took place over 18 days from 9 to 27 September 1944. In many ways these conversations represent the high point of the relationship between the two men. They were completely alone, free of distractions of office or other pressing business. Wartime India had found its two senior politicians no better employment by 1944 than to speak to each other earnestly in private, to try to rediscover some of the spirit of earlier times. Electoral issues were not involved and the British took no part. Could the great conciliator find common ground with the former ambassador of Hindu–Muslim unity? Unfortunately, the answer was a definite 'no'.

The very foundations of the talks were not solid because Gandhi had asked to speak to Jinnah on his own behalf. Jinnah was then entitled to ask what binding force any agreement might have, and upon whom. If Gandhi were speaking purely as an individual then what influence would the discussions have on the Congress? While Gandhi was trying to reduce the import of the talks in order to get Jinnah to speak more freely, Jinnah, who was on the defensive, shrewdly picked out the weakness in such an approach – namely that by its very informality it reduced the discussions to so much chatter. Nevertheless, he welcomed Gandhi into his large house on Malabar Hill. He was not a man to miss a chance, especially with an adversary so keen to mollify him. He had actually been strengthened within Muslim politics by several factors over the previous two years, including the death of two prominent Muslims less than completely friendly to him. Sir Sikander Hayat Khan died in December 1942 and Allah Baksh, the Ittehad (Unity) Party anti-communal Sindhi leader, had been murdered in May 1943. And best of all, the great Gandhi had come to talk to him – as a supplicant and to him alone. If ever Jinnah had wanted recognition of his position as the sole spokesperson of the Muslim community, here it was.

We know what the two said to each other because Gandhi wrote several letters summing up their discussions, which were published when the talks were eventually broken off.[125] These letters illuminate Jinnah's detailed thinking on the Two-Nation issue, and also show how far Gandhi was prepared to go to conciliate him. The British took this as a clear indication that Gandhi was much more concerned to resolve their differences than Jinnah, and this must be true. Gandhi was very keen to find ways to form a united front within India with which to pressure the British. There had never been a joint Hindu–Muslim satyagraha sanctioned by the two party leaders, although of course, there were many Muslim Congress members. But Jinnah wanted to wait for the end of the war, while Gandhi did not. Gandhi stated publicly many times that the British could not win the war without Congress support, and this must count as one of his misjudgements. Jinnah was playing a longer game, and was in no hurry to see the British go. He always wanted the British to oversee the transition of power directly from their own hands to his. He had no confidence that any handover to the Congress would result in a share of power for Muslims. Gandhi was convinced that the war would last longer with the British in India, and he believed that the work of Indian renewal could not begin until the British were gone. So it was Gandhi who made the proposals and Jinnah who, as ever, counterpunched or blocked, as necessary.

The one concrete proposal that came out of the talks was the idea that six provinces should vote on secession, including Assam. This was a concession in itself because Assam, which had a League ministry thanks to 'weightage', had a Muslim population only about half that of its non-Muslims. If the six provinces voted to secede to Pakistan then a new Indian Union, positioned constitutionally above these provinces, would be set up 'after India is free'. Jinnah refused this offer on several grounds. He wanted any such vote of provinces to be conducted under British supervision, and he refused to have any unified administrative or governmental structure binding the Muslim provinces directly to India, or Hindustan. Most crushingly (and least reasonably) he also insisted that referendums in provinces should be conducted among Muslims only. This was a departure from any conventional idea of self-determination, for in a major province like Punjab there was only a small Muslim majority, of around 55 per cent. Essentially, this bloc would be allowed to determine the fate of the other 45 per cent, regardless of the scale of the majority. If, say, only about 75 per cent of Muslims wished to secede, then 41 per cent of the population could outvote everyone else. The closer to 51 per cent of the Muslim vote the proportion reached, the more absurd the result would be as an expression of national self-determination. If applied to Assam, this distortion would be even more marked. By any standards this was self-determination for one nation only.

Nothing was agreed and nothing was achieved. India, yet again, was becalmed. Jinnah felt no pressure to agree to anything; it was only the eventual victory of the Allies that would revitalize Indian politics.

Plans and Partition – The Nations are Born: 1945–48

To India the war brought repression, austerity and even famine. Several million people died in Bengal in 1943 when the Japanese threat led to a combination of requisitioning and hoarding that caused scarcity and raised food prices. The death toll soared when the relief effort proved incompetent and corrupt. Elsewhere shortages were widespread and inflation blighted the lives of millions. But by early 1945 it was clear that the Allies were going to win the war on all fronts. The Japanese were eventually driven out of Burma, and Netaji Bose is assumed to have died in an air crash in August 1945.

Victory, however, only posed more questions. How long would the British hold on to India? What was to follow the Raj? India had been promised independence by Cripps, but the war years had done nothing to resolve or discourage the Muslim demand for separate recognition. A post-war independent India, therefore, still had no 'natural' shape.

Time also became a major factor in all considerations. The later Raj tended to have a leisurely, eternal quality about it, but this vanished after 1945. From then on the British were not trying to set a time limit that suited the new government; they were trying to set up a new government in the time they felt they still had. This suited the Congress, whose leaders took every step they could to bring forward the transfer of power. But it was not helpful to Jinnah, who needed time to play a slow game, to get Muslim 'nationality' as fully recognized and protected as he could. Pakistan was still not a detailed proposal. It remained an aspiration.

What Jinnah wanted for his followers was security, but it was what he wanted for himself that complicated the whole process. The Two-Nation Theory ran alongside a One-Leader Theory, which he unabashedly promoted throughout the entire negotiating process. Muslims could have their protection only if they acted in concert. How would they do that, being so dispersed? By strong central representation, provided by him.

To win his approval, any constitutional scheme had to provide two things. First, there had to be no way that Muslims could be oppressed by other communities. This was readily achievable in Muslim-majority areas, but not in Muslim-minority areas without some connection with the wider political picture. Just to draw lines around all the Muslim-majority districts and serve that up as Pakistan was not acceptable, and he refused this offer from Rajagopalachari in 1944.[126] This rejection leads on to the second condition: in any scheme there had to be a 'centre' somewhere, free from Hindu domination, in which to concentrate political authority. An unspoken third condition was that he would be the one to wield that authority.

Jinnah did have constructive ideas. Early in 1946 he told a fact-finding Parliamentary delegation what he wanted, and he expanded his views to the Cabinet Mission that followed two months later. He envisaged two parallel states in India living under a weak central body, laid out on existing provincial boundaries. This would leave some Muslims in Hindustan and some non-Muslims in Pakistan, but he saw this as a healthy idea guaranteeing that each side looked after its minorities fairly. Ethnically and linguistically, the plural communities of Bengal and Punjab would be left in an undivided condition, although both would be in Pakistan. There would be a small, central executive authority above Pakistan and Hindustan that would be restricted to the business of defence and diplomacy, meaning that the army would not have to be split and defence would not become an increased burden; Jinnah remained adamant that he would not accept majority control of a shared army. There would be no central legislature, thus providing all the necessary communal safeguards at a stroke. Crucially, there would be strong executive bodies at the subsidiary level of Pakistan and Hindustan.

This would enable Jinnah, as chief executive of Pakistan, to impose some discipline on his disparate fiefdom, while not offending his sense of nationalism. He would be an Indian Muslim, ruling Indian Muslims safe from majoritarian interference. The many Congress objections to this scheme, and the working-through of its many limitations and internal contradictions, defined the end-game over the period 1946–47.

ROOTS OF PARTITION

It is commonplace to latch on to one particular event in the run-up to Partition and declare that such and such a moment was the point of no return, or that if only an agreement had been cobbled together at this or that stage then everything might have been different. This is an understandable temptation and all historians yield to it to some extent. But the uncomfortable truth about Partition is that the main parties were never very close to an agreement sufficiently founded in common interests to stick. The brief period in June 1946 when the major parties were clustered in support around the Cabinet Mission's proposals was a brief and exceptional moment when the British still had enough clout – and confidence – to push Indian politicians around. The moment did not last and the enormous gap between the sides that soon emerged, in words through July, on the streets in August, and inside the Interim Government from October, demonstrates how fragile the apparent consensus of mid-June really was. What little trust there remained between the major parties evaporated during this period.

As well as problems of interest and trust, there was often a very wide gap between the British, the Congress and the League as to the meaning of the most basic terms they were all using. To Jinnah, a nation was an abstract thing to be negotiated into existence whereas to Congress it was a pragmatic reality that had to be defended. Gandhi passionately believed that India was one country that the British had deliberately sundered, while Jinnah thought it was two that the British had artificially conjoined. These fundamental differences could not be reconciled. Meanwhile, neither the Congress nor the Muslim League conformed very closely to the British concept of a political 'party'. The Congress was a nation in miniature, actively and deliberately drawing together disparate strands of Indian life, conceived as the broadest oppositional force it was possible to unite. But the width of its pretensions made it highly vulnerable to a counterclaim such as the Muslim League's. Obviously the Congress did not speak for all Indians if Indian Muslims felt it necessary to set up their own organization. The Congress was as undermined by the Muslim League as the League was undermined by the presence of other Muslims in politics, particularly in the Congress. In the absence of a United Popular Front of All India there was little prospect of a comprehensive, even-tempered, negotiated settlement. Under such circumstances a straight handover would not be possible.

Even the concept of a 'coalition' took on a variety of meanings under Indian conditions. The British assumed that a coalition government, especially an 'interim' coalition government, would not present problems. In British terms, coalitions were a way out of trouble, but coalitions in India, whether at the centre or in the provinces, repeatedly proved to be a way into trouble as they failed to cooperate amongst themselves. The Congress–League central government, set up in October 1946, was not a success, and proved persistently unable or unwilling to address rising fiscal and public order problems, and thus helped to contribute to the increasing chaos in the country.

RISING DISORDER

It was the perception of rising civil disorder that drove the British increasingly hard after 1945, and this remained a crucial factor in compressing the time made available for negotiations. The British Empire stood on the verge of global military victory, but the Raj was underfunded and underfed. The mainstay of British rule, the famed Indian Civil Service, had suffered during the war from lack of recruitment and increasing demoralization as the European members began to contemplate careers elsewhere. The Indian personnel within the police service, who had done most of the work of repression, began to wonder if they could shake off their imperialist past in a free India.

Worse, the British leadership was unsure how to proceed. Viceroy Wavell firmly believed that Indians should be allowed to sort out their differences unaided, and he wanted to appoint a new representative Council as an opening gambit in a post-war India. Opinion in London differed. Amery, the Secretary of State, considered that a broad declaration of intent on the subject of independence would suffice to calm the situation and allow Indians to agree on their own future constitution at leisure. Churchill wanted to do nothing until post-war elections in Britain, which he fully expected to win. Newly mandated, he would then be in a strong position to decide the future direction of the whole Empire.

Wavell was invited to London in March 1945 for consultations with the Cabinet, but found little support for early concessions, especially from Churchill.

SIMLA

Wavell stayed on through April and May as the war in Europe drew to a victorious close for the Allies. Then, with wartime conditions at an end, all major decisions were deferred until after the general election, scheduled for July. He returned to India in early June to be confronted by demands for immediate independence and fresh elections. Neither of these had been authorized and neither, therefore, materialized. Instead, Wavell released all political prisoners and announced on the radio that he had set up a leaders' conference, to begin at Simla on 25 June.[127] His objective was to appoint a new executive council chosen from lists submitted by the main parties, which was to be an all-Indian body, except for the defence portfolio – since India was still at war. This was a bold idea, although flawed in detail, because he announced that he intended to establish parity in the council's membership between 'caste Hindus' and Muslims. This simplistic reduction of India's political disputes to a Hindu–Muslim polarity opened up a wide range of problem areas.

Gandhi was convalescing in the hills near Poona when he read a transcript of the broadcast, which included an invitation to him to attend the conference. He immediately entered into a correspondence with Wavell via telegram and letter,[128] seeking to clarify the multiple misunderstandings under which the Viceroy was labouring. The Mahatma distanced himself from the Congress, in which he held no official position, and advised the Viceroy to invite the party's president, Maulana Azad, and not himself. He objected strongly to the expression 'caste Hindu', and put Wavell straight on several points: that the Congress made no claim to represent only caste Hindus, and that not all caste Hindus were inside the Congress; the only party in India that claimed to speak for Hindus was the Mahasabha; the Congress was a purely political body, dedicated to harnessing the best Indians to the cause of the country's freedom; to treat the Congress as a denominational body was to deny the existence of Congress Muslims and would open up all sorts of problems about the representation of other groups, such as the untouchables. Wavell assured Gandhi that the arrangements for the new council would in no way prejudice further constitutional developments, and that delegates to the proposed conference were free to express their views when it met. Somewhat reassured, Gandhi agreed to attend, though in a semi-detached style that was to become familiar over the next two years.

Wavell undertook no preliminary soundings, so it was not until the night before the conference opened that Jinnah met the Viceroy. In an echo of his 1938 demand, Jinnah announced that he was not prepared to allow the Congress to nominate any of its Muslim members to the council. Wavell decreed this unacceptable. Jinnah, with admirable consistency, was also not prepared to allow any Muslim from any other party to sit on the council either, including any from the Unionist Party in the Punjab, whom he branded as 'traitors'. He supported this position by the extraordinary (and quite untrue) statement that the Unionist ministry in Punjab existed on his 'sufferance'.[129]

Next morning, Jinnah's position was revealed in public, and the arguments began in earnest. There was general agreement to the principle of overall Hindu–Muslim parity within the council, but the mathematics were all-important; five Congress nominees and five Muslim Leaguers would not guarantee Hindu–Muslim parity if the Congress nominated members from other faiths. Gandhi, from the sidelines, suggested that parity should be seen as a guideline and not a requirement; the parties could work within the general principle without one side seeking to dominate the other. In this view, the Muslim side of parity within the council could be topped up from the Congress side. Some Congressmen privately liked this angle, but the official delegation suggested extending the council membership to 15, to allow the inclusion of more minority representatives. Jinnah disliked the idea of general Muslim parity because it opened the door to his provincial rivals, and he continued to press for a narrow Muslim League–Congress parity, while banning all Congress Muslims from participation. Wavell made it clear this was not acceptable.

After two days, the conference adjourned for a fortnight for consultations. Nothing changed during the break, except that Jinnah, ever worried about being outvoted, demanded that the League be given full parity not just with the Congress but with all other parties combined. When asked to submit his list of nominees for selection, he refused, and the conference broke up on 14 July. Wavell diplomatically claimed the fault was all his own.

The issues highlighted at Simla made it clear that Jinnah had fundamental problems with the nature and purpose of the Muslim League. It had endured through desperate adversity, but under more favourable conditions, now that it was no longer cornered or outnumbered, he seemed to be conjuring problems from nowhere. It was abundantly evident that there were prominent Muslims all over India who were not in the League, be they in the Congress, like its president Maulana Azad, or in the Punjabi Unionists, like Khizar Hayat Khan, or neither, like the loyalist Muslims who had been sitting on the executive council, such as Sir Sultan Ahmed. It seemed that the League was paralysed unless it was allowed to deny the validity of the choices of any Muslim anywhere who refused to join it. Politics is not generally the process of getting your opponents to concede that your party is what it says it is. The claim to speak for all Muslims was a monopoly right that was neither freely granted nor yet enforced. It looked like overreach. And if this were true, then the contention that Pakistan was an irresistible demand was not credible.

Why did Jinnah make such an untenable and unhelpful claim – one that made him look like either a fantasist or a bully? Primarily it was because his ship would either float or it wouldn't, and he couldn't know till he launched it in earnest. The Simla meeting was a vital test of his claim that he was the spokesman of the Muslims. If he failed to establish that position now then he would never be able to recover it. And he did have a direct problem to deal with – in March that year he had lost control of Bengal to Governor's rule under Section 93, and in the same month a League ministry had been ousted in NWFP by Dr Khan Sahib, a Muslim Congressman. These reverses did not represent a major loss of support, but they demonstrated his weakness at a time when the real hard bargaining was about to start. The imperative was clear – he had to make good his claim. The implication, of course, was that he would have to chase all Muslims out of all other parties. Not for the first or last time Jinnah was trapped by the inexorable logic of his own positioning. The only factor that aided him in this situation was that the increasingly socialist-sounding Congress was beginning to frighten the Muslim landlord classes out of their apathy and into his camp, or sometimes to drive politicians directly across the party divide, like Mian Iftikharuddin of the Punjab Congress, and most spectacularly, Abdul Qaiyum Khan, deputy leader of the central Congress and a major player in the NWFP.

ELECTIONS

In late July the Labour party, to general astonishment, won a landslide majority. The old Tory diehards like Amery and Churchill were thrown out, and in their place was now a government led by Clement Attlee, who was committed to full consultations with Indian politicians over the terms of independence. Wavell was quite comfortable with this policy.

But the question remained: how to proceed? In India nothing had changed. Jinnah had put himself out on a perilous limb, but his luck held again. Khizar Hayat Khan of the Punjabi Unionists was prepared to prop him up, for to have no one to speak for the Muslims at the centre was to court chaos. In this the British concurred, so Jinnah's intransigence kept him in the game. He lived to quibble another day.

Wavell was recalled to London in August to consult with the new Labour Cabinet. Urgency was now deemed appropriate by all concerned, and elections were announced for both central and provincial assemblies. At this point, the initiative decisively passed to India's political elite. If they were determined to disagree then there was progressively less the British would be able do about it. Wavell was developing a generally poor opinion of Indian politicians, especially the Congress (and the feeling was mutual), but he and many others still believed that Pakistan was not a particularly popular cause among influential Muslims, and that as the realities of such a scheme became apparent, it would lose its appeal. Jinnah, however, took to the hustings intending to treat the poll as a plebiscite on the Pakistan demand.

The Congress remained determined not to abandon the principle of a unitary India, and Maulana Azad now proposed a federal Constitution with parity at the centre between all other parties and all Muslims, not just the Muslim League. The Congress did not adopt his plan but it showed that there was still a little room left for manoeuvre. Not much though, because the Congress leadership wanted and needed a unified India for the purposes of international relations, social reforms and economic restructuring, all of which were pressing concerns for the more socialistic Nehru, whose voice remained the strongest in the High Command.

Gandhi was again in retreat from the centre, drifting away from Nehru, with whom he acknowledged 'sharp difference of opinion'[130] on the usual range of topics such as industrialization, modernization, material welfare and the desirability of using force to expel the British. In the absence of direct talks about independence there was little to interest him in national politics. Instead he felt attracted to the countryside, to enjoy simple living, hand spinning and 'nature cures'.

The results of the elections, held across the winter of 1945–46, clearly established the Congress and the Muslim League as the only two national parties in Indian politics. Both had major reasons to be pleased. The

Congress won over 90 per cent of the non-Muslim votes and was able to form provincial ministries in six previous strongholds (Bihar, UP, Central Provinces, Bombay, Madras, Orissa) and even in Assam and NWFP. The League won all the reserved Muslim seats they contested, which at last put some substance to the claim that the League was the mouthpiece of the Muslim community. The Congress ended up with eight provinces and the League just two, with Sind under a minority League ministry and a nominally League government in Bengal. But, as ever in Bengal, the loyalties concerned were somewhat flexible, both among the rank and file and even in the case of the leader, Shaheed Suhrawardy, who remained something of a loose cannon over the next two years. So although Jinnah did very much better than in the 1937 debacle, he reaped a poor reward in terms of real power and influence. Importantly, the Punjab remained under Unionist control.

DETERIORATION

To keep the independence process moving, the British government now decided to send out a Parliamentary delegation under Professor Robert Richards, which spent a month gathering opinion through January 1946. It noted Jinnah's renewed strength and recommended that 'sovereign rights' be granted immediately. Jinnah outlined to Richards the clearest conception yet of his Pakistan and how he proposed to get it. He wanted the British to stay, at least temporarily, at the centre. His main outline – two constituent assemblies leading to two autonomous states under some kind of 'Union', with no central legislative and British supervision of the negotiation process – were his bottom line. Partition, of a formal kind, was not yet one of these demands.

Meanwhile, the situation in India continued to deteriorate. Food was in short supply and public order seemed increasingly fragile to British officials. From November 1945 some of Bose's INA veterans began to stand trial for 'waging war on the King–Emperor', but the proceedings soon developed into a focus for intense nationalist feelings. The defendants' popularity took the British by surprise, so although guilty verdicts were handed down it was considered politic to release them, in the teeth of opposition from senior British soldiers. This ominous sign was followed in February 1946 by an outright mutiny in the Royal Indian Navy at Karachi and Bombay, a situation resolved not by repression but by an appeal from Sardar Patel. The old assurance that the British could rely on loyal service from Indians was severely shaken. Time was now of the essence, and obstructions would have to be dealt with.

This is why, after the announcement in February 1946 that a three-man Cabinet Mission was being sent to India, Prime Minister Attlee told the House of Commons on 15 March that his government could not permit 'a minority to place a veto over the advance of the majority', regardless of how important that minority might be. This was significant. It marked an end to anodyne pronouncements in London about the difficulties of Indian politics, and an abandonment of the mentality behind the August Offer of 1940, which gave a veto to significant minority interests. Attlee was sending a clear warning that a settlement would be engineered one way or another. A constituent body was to be set up and an interim executive formed. In a further departure from tradition, there were no promises of Dominion Status. India was to be allowed to decide on Commonwealth membership for herself. Sovereignty really was on the way, and from now on obstacles would be removed, not introduced.

THE CABINET MISSION

The three-man Cabinet Mission[131] arrived in New Delhi on 23 March 1946, consisting of Lord Pethick-Lawrence, A.V. Alexander and Stafford Cripps. Pethick-Lawrence was the Secretary of State for India, but Cripps, though only President of the Board of Trade, was the real leader. They stayed for three months, spoke to everybody repeatedly, and struggled to find any commodious middle ground. Their attempts at conciliation are generally reckoned to have been India's best chance of avoiding Partition, and they did achieve some measure of apparent agreement. But they left three months later, exasperated, having outlined two plans, one in May on the Constitution, and one in June for the establishment of an Interim Government. This was a familiar two-part pattern of schemes for Later and for Now. Again, neither was to prove satisfactory.

Gandhi took little active part in the Mission's consultations. Their sort of work was not his forte, but he kept close by to help if he could, spending April in Delhi, then most of May in Simla.

Jinnah met the trio on 30 March and immediately laid down his markers. He wanted a 'viable' Pakistan, not one cobbled together out of majority Muslim districts wherever they fell. He wanted Pakistan to be 'a live state economically', including Calcutta. This amounted to the 'big' Pakistan, by which he meant Punjab, Bengal, Sind, NWFP, Assam and Baluchistan. This is sometimes referred to as the 'six-province' Pakistan, but technically Baluchistan was not yet a province and remained under direct central control. It was a Muslim-majority area though, unlike Assam which, despite being claimed by the League as a Muslim province, only had a Muslim majority in the area of Sylhet.

As part of the ongoing clarification of the Pakistan demand, the League met at Delhi in early April and altered the Lahore Resolution to demand one state for Muslims and not the unspecified 'states' in the 1940 wording. This headed off demands from Bengal for separate status and neatly converted demands for Bengali autonomy into an internal Pakistani issue. The revised resolution also specified all the areas to be claimed as part of Pakistan, and actually used the name, which had not appeared in the 1940 version.

When Jinnah put this demand to the Mission, he was told that he could have it, but that it would have to remain firmly inside a federal Indian Union. If he wanted more autonomy then he would have to part with Hindu-majority areas contained within his wider claim; in other words, he would have to lose West Bengal, Calcutta, East Punjab and most of Assam. The Mission also met provincial Muslim leaders and received a rather different impression of the realities of the Pakistan demand. G.M. Syed from Sind and Dr Khan Sahib from NWFP both expressed reservations about their provinces being absorbed into Jinnah's portfolio, and Khizar Hayat Khan laid out the problem for the Punjabis; a united Punjab inside Pakistan suited the Muslims but was flatly unacceptable to the other communities, while partitioning the province was bound to leave substantial numbers of people in the wrong place. All three leaders were therefore keener on provincial autonomy than on a tight-knit Pakistan.

Congress leaders were prepared to negotiate over the precise boundaries of any Pakistan, but insisted on moving as swiftly as possible to a British withdrawal and the formation of a sovereign constituent assembly to decide all the details of an independent India. Confident of their majority in that assembly, they wanted to jump first and sort out the landing while in flight. Jinnah, not unreasonably, was determined to know precisely where he might end up.

The three Cabinet delegates concluded that there was as yet no basis for agreement, and prepared proposals of their own. They decided on two broad models. Scheme A was a loose federal system – what became known as the 'three-tier' India, in which the existing 11 provinces would be collected into three regional 'groups'. Group A was the central Hindu-majority area, Group B the north-west Muslim-majority areas, and Group C, Bengal and Assam. These groups were to carry the bulk of the legislative and executive functions in the new Union, which would be held together by a federal government, responsible for defence, foreign affairs and communications. There was to be no central legislature. This scheme was a near match to Jinnah's demands, as it would have ensured that a Hindu raj could not be imposed on the Muslims, who would be left to decide all important matters for themselves locally in the fields of law, culture and religion. In addition, placing executive power at the group level also promised to give Jinnah a measure of control over his own provinces that a wider Union, especially one with a weak centre, would not give. The other proposal, Scheme B, was for a 'truncated' Pakistan, without Hindu and Sikh 'hostages' left inside its boundaries. It would be a fully sovereign state living alongside an entirely separate, sovereign Hindustan.

Having drawn up these alternatives, the Mission asked for guidance from London on 11 April. They were told unequivocally that they should attempt, if at all possible, to get an agreement to Scheme A, with the large Pakistan drawn within existing provincial boundaries and a federal Union. If this were not possible they were empowered to move towards Scheme B, with its smaller, sovereign Pakistan. The Mission's instructions made it clear that reaching an agreement was to be the highest priority. Conflict should be avoided at all costs, although Partition was a price that could be paid for a negotiated settlement. The fearfulness in this position is apparent, especially as the really complicated, multilateral negotiations were yet to begin. This is a clear indication that in London the idea that a settlement could be imposed had evaporated, and that the main priority was to ensure that there was no kind of breakdown that would result in division of the Indian Army. If this could be avoided then an agreed political solution might still be found. But the British did not expect to be able to stop the break-up of their own colonial army if local interests pulled it apart. By 1946 British politicians may have been willing to oblige Indians as far as they could, but they could not countenance civil war. That was definitely against British national interests, and also against the Labour Party's interests. Labour leaders could live with being seen as the men who gave India away, but they had no desire to be remembered as the men who reduced her to ashes.

THE MAY PLAN: THE CONSTITUTION

The three delegates explained alternatives A and B to the Indian politicians, and a conference at Simla from 5 to 12 May followed. This was a heated affair in which much turned on the nature of the proposed groups. In a crucial central moment, Jinnah managed to boil down the whole negotiation into one single issue. He is reported to have declared that if the Congress would accept the groups, the League would accept the Union. The offer was declined.[132]

The Congress sensed that Jinnah could use the groups to secede, and disliked the loose fit in the groups between geography, population and politics. For instance, the Congress did well in NWFP and had a ministry there at the time, while Assam, apart from Sylhet, presented a similar case – both provinces would be lumped into Muslim-majority groups. Gandhi did not like 'grouping' at all. He thought it divisive, and 'worse than Pakistan'.[133] Overall, there was a great deal of uncertainty about the system's details, and there were plenty of capable lawyers on both sides determined to tease them out.

Based on the Simla discussions, the Cabinet Mission announced their decision on 16 May as an 'award'. It plumped for a modified Scheme A, with a central legislature. An Indian Union was to be created, and it was to include the princely states. The Union would handle defence, foreign affairs and communications. It would have an executive arm and a legislature, with powers to raise finance. There was to be no parity between Muslims and non-Muslims within the central organs of government. All residuary powers were to be vested in the provinces, which were to be organized into the three familiar groups. All 11 provinces were to meet within the three groups to sort out detailed provincial and group constitutions, after which all the provinces, plus the princes, were to assemble to draw up a Union Constitution. The final transfer of power would not come until after this constituent assembly had completed its deliberations. Provinces could vote to drop out of a group, but not out of the Union. A review of the scheme was to be conducted after 10 or 15 years. Finally, an Interim Government was to be formed as soon as conveniently possible.

This was, in essence, a fairly loose one-state solution. It set out a more complex structure than that of any other state, and was perhaps not unreasonably intricate if there had been a will to work it. But it fell short of a number of key demands on either side. The Congress wanted the British gone yesterday, a sovereign constitutional assembly and extensive revisions to the powers of the federation and the rules for the groups. Jinnah, meanwhile, would have to settle for two Muslim entities, not a unitary Pakistan. He was also displeased that the central government had the right to raise taxes, and that the provinces were only given residuary rights, not sovereign. In addition there was no right of secession, and Muslims would be in a clear minority in the central legislature. Worst of all, there would be only one national constituent assembly. The Muslims were going to be locked into the process till the end.

Jinnah was potentially in trouble. He would have a lot of explaining to do to show his people how this was the Pakistan he had been promising.

And many of his less enthusiastic supporters were more pleased with the award than they could allow themselves to acknowledge. Some leading Bengali and Punjabi Muslims could see a convenient communal–national balance in it. In the end Jinnah fudged a public stance. He objected to the Plan's preamble, which explicitly rejected the idea of Pakistan, but accepted the move to the Interim Government; the League would come in on the basis of parity, with the long-term 'goal' of achieving Pakistan.[134] Armed with this wording he got a mandate from his Working Committee to continue towards his originally stated aims – and his supporters allowed him a second chance.

THE JUNE PLAN: THE INTERIM GOVERNMENT

After some discussion, and despite all his reservations, Jinnah and the League accepted the 16 May Plan in a resolution of 6 June. The Congress, however, held back.

Interest now moved to the precise make-up of the Interim Government. Wavell assured Congress leaders that he would treat the new executive as if it were that of a Dominion state – an assurance that the new government would not be just a replica of the outgoing Viceroy's executive council. But there were serious disagreements to address. Wavell wanted a 12-seat executive council with himself as chairman, but how many members of the major parties were to be included, and which portfolios would they hold? And the old Simla question about non-League Muslims had still not been resolved.

The second Cabinet Mission Plan was released on 16 June, initiating the formation of the new constituent assembly, with members to be chosen by the provincial legislatures. It also announced that the Viceroy would appoint a 14-member executive council. This would be a mixed, representative body whose exact composition was not to be taken as a precedent for the settlement of any other communal issue. The plan also provided that, in the case of either or both major parties being unwilling to join the new Cabinet, the Interim Government would be formed from among those 'willing to accept' the long-term plan as outlined in the 16 May Plan. This join-up-or-get-left-behind strategy was powered by a faith in momentum, but tactically it was a mistake. It upped the pressure without actually helping the main parties in any of their difficulties. And the Viceroy's list of nominations to the new government did not help either. Jinnah was not given parity, and the issue of non-League Muslims was not solved but merely avoided; Wavell did not invite any of them to join the new body.

The Congress leaders were unhappy for a variety of reasons. They had started out wanting a 7:4 Congress–League split in a 12-member Cabinet. Finally they had 6:5 in 14, which was unacceptably close to parity. They also insisted on the right to nominate Muslims if they wished. Gandhi felt it was an altogether mistaken approach to try to build a coalition government at this point, and that the British should ride one 'horse' or the other and not attempt to ride both. Maulana Azad offered to stay out of the Cabinet if it helped the Congress assume the reins of government; Gandhi insisted that he be included. Patel feared that if Congress failed to appoint any Muslims then the Muslim membership of the Congress could justifiably feel that they were not represented as promised, and might desert the party en masse.

Jinnah, meanwhile, was also holding back, waiting on the Congress lead. If the Congress went into the government, he would have to follow. If they stayed out he would certainly go in. The result might have been the same but the two potential outcomes offered very different political possibilities, and Jinnah was always keen to consider all available circumstances before acting. Presentation is all important in politics, and he was aware that in speaking last – especially as the weaker party – he could be sure to draw maximum advantage from the situation. He was ready to come in and the British had prepared him for the call. Then the Congress leadership pulled off a subtle manoeuvre. They did not like the long-term plan as it stood, but thought they could use their majority in the constituent assembly to amend it, so to accept it at a distance was not a disaster. However, they felt that they could not work in the Interim Government with restrictions on their right to nominate their own Muslims. Therefore they took the 16 June statement at its word and professed, in a resolution of 25 June, that they were willing to accept the 16 May Plan, and although this entitled them to join the Interim Government, they declined to do so.[135] To the leadership this felt like an important step towards Independence, while avoiding having to deal with Jinnah. Their eyes were on the more distant, but more valuable prize.

In theory this now meant that both parties supported the long-term May 16 Plan, but the complex reservations they had both lodged rendered that support highly conditional. Wavell might perhaps have dared to form a government without the League, but the prospect of doing so without Congress participation was too much. He quailed, telling Jinnah that the formation of the new administration was postponed. Jinnah, predictably, was very angry. The great manipulator of words had been out-twisted. The Congress was still going to get its constituent assembly – Jinnah's main bugbear – while the League had been robbed of taking up the reins of government. The British, however, had considerable sympathy for the Quaid, and Wavell made a last attempt to include him by offering to appoint an Interim Government on condition that Jinnah accepted Congress Muslims. Jinnah refused. The next day, the 26th, the Viceroy announced the appointment of a caretaker government. Two days later, the Cabinet Mission flew home.

JINNAH TAKES TO THE STREETS

In the League resolution of 6 June, Jinnah had made it clear that he was only staying on in the process because he saw the groups as of some help towards achieving Pakistan. The Congress's own reservations then appeared before the public. Nehru was elected Congress president on 7 July and came under attack at the meeting for giving away too much to Jinnah and of failing to resist British manipulation. He replied heatedly that the Congress was not restricted by its acceptance of the 16 May Plan, and that Congress representatives would be free to determine whatever they pleased in the constituent assembly. This sort of talk was of no comfort to either the British or Jinnah. Nehru then repeated and expanded these remarks at a press conference on 10 July.[136] This statement destroyed the last of Jinnah's meagre belief that the negotiations were in good faith, and is generally regarded as Nehru's biggest single political mistake.

The Quaid-i-Azam had just been robbed of government, and less than a fortnight later here was Nehru saying, publicly, that grouping would not work because Assam and the NWFP did not want it and would jump ship. The actual text of the Mission's plan said that no province could drop out of any group for a minimum of 10 years. Furthermore, the claim that no pre-existing undertaking would be binding because the constituent assembly was a sovereign body was not correct. Jinnah had been told, and all the public documents showed, that sovereignty would not pass until an agreement had been reached on the new Constitution. Jinnah had suspected British–Congress collusion over many years, and here was clinching proof.

On 28 July Jinnah himself made a mistake, or at least it is hard to imagine that he intended the consequences of what he did. With the unanimous backing of the Muslim League Working Committee he rejected the Cabinet Mission plan wholesale, and reverted to a straight demand for Pakistan.

He also announced a change of tactics. 'This day we bid goodbye to constitutional methods,' he said, and called for a day of 'Direct Action'.[137] The date named was 16 August, and Muslims were exhorted to stay away from work that day and to discuss the League's demands in the streets. Whether he foresaw the results of this call we do not know. He had never been an advocate of mass action and had repeatedly criticized Gandhi for using it. He may simply not have understood what was likely to happen. Others were more culpable for what followed. Shaheed Suhrawardy, the premier of Bengal, with Wavell's permission, called a public holiday on 16 August, which included granting the police special leave. What followed was mayhem; Calcutta exploded into violence. It is not clear whether Muslims or Hindus made the initial attacks, but all were soon repaid in full. For three days the city burned as killing and looting continued unchecked. Around 5,000 are believed to have died, and up to 16,000 may have been injured.

These events marked the start of a cycle of violence that escalated in unpredictable ways over the next 14 months.

INDIANS IN THE CABINET

Despite Jinnah's rejection of the Cabinet Mission plan, the Viceroy remained determined to include Indians in government. With the League in opposition, he invited the Congress into an Interim Government on 6 August. The Congress Working Committee, in consultation with Gandhi at Wardha, accepted on the 8th, and the ministry finally took office on 2 September. This left Jinnah in a very weak position and all political logic dictated that he had to come in. Eventually, a deal was brokered and in mid-October the League took five seats at the table, including the prized job of finance minister, which went to Liaquat Ali Khan. Jinnah himself did not come in. He wanted the defence portfolio, but could not bear to serve under Nehru, whom he seems to have disliked intensely by this stage. He would also have been abandoning the principle of parity, in that he would have been subservient to Nehru who, as vice-president, was premier in all but name. Jinnah suggested a rotating 'vice-presidentship' but Wavell ruled it out as unworkable. It soon became apparent that the new coalition was unworkable too. Whether or not the League joined simply to disrupt the government, this was what eventually resulted, introducing another unpredictable element into the situation.

GANDHI IN THE COUNTRYSIDE

While national political developments rolled on through the autumn, a dismal pattern of murder, rape and arson swept across large parts of north-east India. Thousands were killed as the Hindu minority in East Bengal suffered repeated attacks, especially around Noakhali, a district in the Chittagong area. These atrocities were then mirrored by similar violence against Muslims in Bihar. The suffering affected Gandhi deeply, and in October he set out to teach ahimsa amid the carnage.

He gave himself the strenuous task of walking on foot across the affected areas in an attempt to bring comfort and prevent further mass flight from the besieged communities. But the mission did not go well. Frightened villagers were not greatly inspired by being told they should lay down their lives rather than run away. As in 1918 Gandhi did not take this rejection well, but he did not collapse this time. Instead, he tried even harder to muster his full spiritual power, a process that involved sleeping naked with his young female disciples. By exerting complete physical control over his own body he hoped to empty himself of all violence and impurity, which would allow God to enter in their place.

The internal logic of this process was hard for some of those around him to understand, and his personal secretary resigned in January 1946. But to the Mahatma it was all perfectly clear, and in accordance with the 'inner voice'. The way he understood the interconnectedness of life always led him to approach larger tasks by starting with smaller ones. In this case the objective was to bring peace to India, so he would have to begin by trying to make peace within himself, by subduing his own base nature. Only when this had been successfully achieved could he hope to reconcile India's differences at village level, which was the key to the next task – national reconciliation.

But some local politicians felt he was doing more harm than good, and some of his admirers feared that others with less elevated intentions might be tempted to imitate his apparent fondness for sleeping with young girls without understanding the impeccably pure motivations behind the practice. Such criticism did have its effects, and Gandhi repeatedly asked his inner circle if they could detect any 'flaw' in his methods. No one spoke up.[138]

A combination of continued failure to quell the disturbances and the hostility of local notables persuaded Gandhi to transfer his efforts to Bihar in early March 1947, but only a few weeks later national developments drew him back to Delhi.

LONDON LOSES FAITH IN WAVELL

By late 1946, Wavell was coming to the end of his tether. He simply had no more ideas, but when his masters in London offered him the services of a specialist political advisor, he felt insulted. Instead, as a good soldier his mind had already turned to retreat and the protection of his men. Through October he drew up a Breakdown Plan, which envisaged a slow, phased withdrawal of British forces from the south of India to the northern edges, handing over province by province to whoever seemed best placed, while providing cover for the 100,000 British nationals during their progress to the last ports. This approach was not popular with Attlee, who was receiving messages from India that Congress leaders, including Gandhi, had lost faith in the Viceroy. As a last throw of the dice Wavell suggested that the two main parties each send two delegates to London for direct talks. Nehru, Jinnah and two others duly went west in early December, along with Wavell himself. A mini-conference with Attlee and senior figures in Downing Street lasted four days but produced nothing.

The constituent assembly opened on 9 December with no Muslim League delegates in attendance. Gandhi was opposed to proceeding without full participation of all delegates, but Nehru insisted on going ahead. This left a dysfunctional government running in parallel with a lame duck assembly. The League had joined the government with some political reward, but it simply could not go into the constituent assembly without opening up the certainty of being outvoted in the end. Wavell reacted to the deteriorating outlook by revising his plan of retreat, now codenamed 'Ebb Tide'. This second plan was politically no more acceptable than October's offering. It was defeatist, and a 'scuttle' par excellence. It was also superfluous because, unbeknown to the Viceroy, his Breakdown Plan of October had already cost him the support of the Cabinet. The politicians sensed that he had lost his nerve; Attlee already had a replacement lined up, and Wavell had to go.

MOUNTBATTEN

Enter Lord Louis Mountbatten (1900–79), and with him came a change in atmosphere and attitude. Where Wavell had lost support in London, Mountbatten was entirely secure. Where Wavell was an old soldier in retreat, Mountbatten was a new man with a fresh perspective, determined to sweep away obstructions. Energetic and self-confident, he was, in a word, undaunted. Attlee offered him the Viceroyalty in mid-December 1946 but Mountbatten only took the job after a round of negotiations, in which he asked for a time limit to the posting and full powers to negotiate with Indian leaders. He got both. Attlee then made a historic statement to the House of Commons on 20 February 1947, in which he finally set a definitive end date to British rule in India. He announced that the British would hand over power no later than June 1948, either to a unitary India, or to the provinces, or failing either of these, 'in such other way as may seem most reasonable and in the best interests of the Indian people'. The time for guarded words was now over. Privately, Mountbatten had his instructions to the same effect, with one important extra point, that if possible the successor state, or states, should be brought into the Commonwealth, to shore up British military and economic interests in South Asia. This he was specifically asked to accomplish by the king, who was his cousin. Commonwealth membership might not be too much of a problem in the case of Pakistan, which would need all the help it could get, but the Congress had been completely opposed to Commonwealth membership since 1930, and Mountbatten, therefore, considered securing it as a potential plum achievement.

Mountbatten had massive self-confidence and a fierce determination to manipulate or bludgeon his way to a settlement. He was not particularly young – he was 46 – but he acted young. Charm, speed and decisiveness were to characterize his approach. He was different; he was not sent out to manage or expand the Empire, but to wind it up in a blaze of goodwill.

The process for independence took on a deeply personal dimension with Mountbatten's arrival. It was his perceptions of people and issues that most directly affected the ultimate outcome, and his decisions that shaped the final details of the independence settlement. He arrived on 22 March and met all the major Indian leaders within a fortnight. His assessment of them was instant, decisive and fairly accurate. Gandhi, newly arrived from Bihar, he found charming and intriguing, but considered he did not need to pay him great heed. Nehru he liked, and the feeling was mutual. Jinnah struck him as distant, cold and difficult.

It took the whole of the first interview 'to unfreeze him', he told his press secretary.[139]

Gandhi had a simple solution, which was to give the central government over to Jinnah and the League. He suggested this to Mountbatten at their second meeting, on 1 April. Mountbatten did not take the idea very seriously, and his advisors convinced him that the other Congress leaders were unlikely to concur. The Viceroy revealed the plan to Nehru the next day, whereupon Nehru effectively removed Gandhi from the subsequent talks by labelling him 'out of touch'.[140] But when Mountbatten floated the idea to Maulana Azad, long the butt of Jinnah's contempt, the veteran Congressman considered it feasible; he thought that Gandhi's stature might get the Congress to accept it, that Jinnah might come round, and that it could end the communal bloodshed. Nor was the suggestion insincere on Gandhi's part. Ever since the Pakistan demand had been voiced, the Mahatma had been willing to give the Muslim leadership the whole running of India rather than break up the country. Muslim rule was still Indian rule, and he always expected concessions would bring the best out of his opponents. But not for the first time, Gandhi's radical ideas and his instinctive aversion to conflict were too far out of step with the political caste that so often recruited his moral authority when it suited their purposes to do so.

From then on, he hovered at the fringes of the negotiations, but took no central role in them.

THE WHIRLWIND BEGINS

Mountbatten appears to have decided almost immediately that there was little time left to the Raj and no progress to be made via negotiation. By 10 April he was telling his staff that Partition was probably the only way forward, and he put the idea to a conference of his provincial Governors a few days later. They were seriously concerned about the collapse of public order, especially the Governors of NWFP, Punjab and Bengal. But they did not recommend Partition; they wanted reinforcements. Mountbatten outwardly took this on board, but extra manpower was never a viable way forward for the expiring Raj. His solution was to push forward to Partition even more rapidly. This policy, however, was not untouched by doubt. Even in early May, as he was laying detailed plans for Partition, he was also privately deploring it, referring to the growing willingness among Indian leaders to accept it as 'sheer madness'.[141] The British Government had declared itself ready to give Indians what they wanted, and Mountbatten was following this line. But personally he feared for the consequences, and therefore constantly urged the need to show that the decision to partition the country had been an Indian one.

Jinnah was in favour of Partition along provincial boundaries, but had long been opposed to any internal partition of provinces, because he wanted Pakistan to include West Bengal and East Punjab. Congress leaders – but not Gandhi – had slowly been moving towards an acceptance of Partition of the country for some time before Mountbatten's arrival. A violent campaign orchestrated by the Muslim League against the Unionist ministry in the Punjab finally forced its resignation on 2 March, leading to serious three-way communal fighting. This prompted the Congress Working Committee to pass a resolution on 8 March calling for the 'administrative' partition of the province, a principle which, Nehru acknowledged to Wavell, would probably have to be extended to Bengal too. By 20 April Nehru was prepared to concede in public that the League could have Pakistan if whatever parts of India it wanted were willing to join. At the time this probably excluded the NWFP, which had a Congress ministry as embattled as that of the Punjab had been, and where the Pathan population might well opt for India over Pakistan, or even prefer sovereign independence, which promised to open up a sackful of further strategic considerations for the British. It was not yet clear how the NWFP would fit into any India–Pakistan settlement, and it was to be the NWFP that eventually brought up the rear in all the Partition arrangements because of this uncertainly.

Finally, the destiny of Bengal was also contentious. The Hindu Mahasabha, strong in West Bengal, had begun to call for the partition of the province from late February. This was seen as a way of curing Bengal's chronic political instability and of freeing the Mahasabha's own members from the local Muslim majority. Meanwhile a cross-party alliance in Bengal was beginning to float the idea of a united, completely independent Bengal, outside either Pakistan or India. Mountbatten knew of this and sounded out Jinnah on 26 April. The Quaid was not opposed to it; the Congress, however, was strongly against the idea.

All this was stopping just fractionally short of the acceptance that the entire country could only be pacified by Partition, while the continued violence in the Punjab merely enhanced the feeling that a definitive Pakistan–Hindustan division of territory was actually desirable. This was another point at which Jinnah's methods came back at him. At first only one side was hinting at Partition, as part of the Pakistan demand, but through 1947 both sides started to see its attractions. A scramble then began between the Congress and the League to recruit the support of the Sikhs, with the Congress as the slight favourites. Nervousness that this might change was yet another factor in pressing the Congress leadership towards an early settlement.

The fundamental political problem was that the Muslim provinces had not joined the constituent assembly, and there was absolutely no constitutional way forward unless they did. This avenue was completely blocked in April when the assembly's 'Union Powers' subcommittee recommended giving wide-ranging authority to the centre in independent India, something completely unacceptable to the Muslim League.

Mountbatten and his close aides now drew up a series of draft plans for a handover of power that provided choices for individual provinces, including internal partition and an option for Pakistan. The end product of this process became notorious as 'Plan Balkan', which sought to recognize the general impasse by offering the Muslim-majority provinces the choice of either coming into the existing constituent assembly, or forming some joint assembly among themselves, or standing out singly and acting as completely self-contained units. This plan was only capable of 'Balkanizing' Pakistan, not India, and it allowed for a united Bengal to choose either country or to remain independent. Lord Ismay, Mountbatten's chief of staff, flew to London with a final version for approval on 2 May, without it being shown to any of the Indian principals. The plan came back amended by the Cabinet's India subcommittee, who chose, as a matter of fairness, to extend the privilege of the three-way choice to all provinces, and by implication extended it to all of India's 565 hereditary rulers too.

PLAN PARTITION

On the night of 10–11 May Mountbatten showed the newly returned proposals to Nehru, who took strongly against them, whereupon the Viceroy's reforms commissioner, V.P. Menon, produced a rapid redraft. Menon, though a civil servant, had been following his own line on the independence issue for many months, and had submitted a memo in January 1947 suggesting a transfer of power to two successor states based on immediate Dominion Status – a plan that was ignored at the time. Menon was close to Sardar Patel, and must have been aware of how Patel and Nehru had recently come to see the military and constitutional advantages of immediate Dominion Status, and how they were only willing to accept Pakistan after the partition of Bengal and Punjab. All these elements now came together neatly when Mountbatten, shaken by Nehru's vehement rejection of the redrafted Plan Balkan, asked Menon to draw up a new set of Heads of Agreement, a task he accomplished in six hours. This second plan, soon christened 'Plan Partition', became the Independence settlement.

Plan Partition had several crucial new features. It was based on an acceptance that the Muslim League was not coming in to the current constituent assembly, and it therefore made provision for the setting up of two new ones, which would be treated as governments-in-waiting, or 'Provisional Authorities'. It allowed for a possible internal partition of Bengal and the Punjab, to be decided by the respective local assemblies, and it provided for a referendum on the membership of India or Pakistan to be held in the NWFP. It did not allow the main Hindu–Congress provinces the choice to opt for either India or Pakistan; they were to stay within the 'Union of India'. Nor was sovereign independence any longer on offer to the princes. Although it was not written into the document, the understanding was that the two 'Provisional Authorities' were to receive immediate Dominion Status. This bypassed all the potential difficulties of the constituent assembly stage of the transfer of power, as laid out in the Cabinet Mission plan. Now, with immediate Dominion Status in place, the successor governments could simply continue under the Government of India Act of 1935, and then secede from the Commonwealth if they desired. Meanwhile, both sides would proceed separately towards different constitutional models in their own time, within their own sovereign boundaries, and without immediate concern for the vexing constitutional questions that dogged the larger Indian polity. The whole transfer of power would be simplified and expedited.

Mountbatten flew to London on 18 May to explain the new plan. While he was there, the Congress leadership definitively crushed the idea of an independent Bengal.

PLAN GANDHI

Gandhi's lone pilgrimages in Noakhali and Bihar reflected his political isolation from the Congress leaders, and it had only been the arrival of Mountbatten that persuaded him to return his attention to matters of state. But he proved as eccentric as ever, hovering above the detail that all the others were so engaged with. His fervent opposition to any form of partition gave him little scope to contribute when all the other major players were wrestling with exactly this outcome. After his offer of the premiership to Jinnah he went back to Bihar, still calling for an official enquiry into the killings there. He saw Mountbatten again in early May, when he also met Jinnah alone, but made no progress with either. The only positive result of his discussions with Jinnah was a joint appeal to all Indians to remain at peace.

But he had not entirely given up. He had an alternative plan whose main points were: that a unitary government composed entirely of either Congress or League nominees should be sworn in; that the British should transfer power immediately without partitioning the country – any such decision was to be left entirely to Indians; that the constituent assembly should continue as it was; that a Court of Arbitration be set up to safeguard the minorities; and that 'paramountcy' – British authority over the princely states – should pass directly to the new Indian government and should not lapse, as it would under all other schemes.[142]

On 8 May he sent these ideas to Mountbatten, who thanked him politely. But by this stage Gandhi's opinions carried no sway with the Nehru–Patel partnership, so Mountbatten had little use for them. Gandhi spent the rest of May in Calcutta, trying to reconcile Hindus and Muslims.

Finally, on 2 June, he made one last appeal to Mountbatten. This was a Monday and therefore one of his days of silence. As India's fate hung in the balance, he wrote notes in pencil on the backs of used envelopes. As a distillation of his humility this seems almost perfect, but it also speaks of his powerlessness. While the continent lay awaiting 'vivisection', the old sage remained silent, knowing that no words of his would be of any use.

The reality was that the Congress had finally seized the political initiative, and that Mountbatten was looking for the easiest way forward that did least damage to British national interests. The law and order issue was extremely troubling and there was no solution. Even the police had begun to mutiny.

THE FINAL ACT

Jinnah was not happy when the details of Plan Partition became known. The partition of provinces struck at the viability of Pakistan economically, and threatened to give his new country a massive burden of defence expenditure with too small a fiscal base to support it. He began to develop new demands: over the army, and then for an 800-mile land corridor to join the two 'wings' of Pakistan. But his ability to obstruct and delay had vanished.

Mountbatten returned to India on 30 May with Cabinet approval for the new deal, which was then put to the leaders on the morning of 2 June. They were given time to digest the proposals, then Mountbatten told them that their formal acceptance would be required the following day. To avoid embarrassment, prior assurances of agreement to the plan were to be received by midnight. All but Jinnah indicated that they would approve the plan as requested. Jinnah felt unable to give his assent without referring to his Working Committee and to 'the people'. He went to see the Viceroy privately late that evening and, while he promised to do his best to carry the League with him, he could not formally consent to the plan without the authority of his All-India Council. Mountbatten was now trapped by the relentless pace he had set, and he extricated himself by hijacking Jinnah's authority. He said that he would speak for the League himself, and if it chose to contradict him later he would take the blame. Jinnah the bluffer was finally out-bluffed. Mountbatten specifically instructed him that when he was asked for the League's agreement the next morning, he did not have to speak, but must 'in no circumstance contradict', and should merely nod his head when the question was put to him. The meeting next day passed off as planned; Jinnah fulfilled his promise. Thus arose the strange circumstance that in the crucial meeting, Jinnah never verbally consented to Plan Partition.

Mountbatten, Nehru, Jinnah and Baldev Singh for the Sikhs each spoke on All-India Radio that night. Only Mountbatten was truly pleased; only Jinnah was downbeat. His language was sombre, and he appealed not for celebration but for calm, emphasizing that decisions had still to be taken, coolly and with earnest consideration. He represented the deal not as a final binding agreement but as another step in the process. In this he was actually correct. It should be noted that the agreement of 3 June was not an agreement to Partition; it was an agreement to enter a process to hand over power that might also result in Partition. There were still votes to be conducted in four provinces, two of which were voting on Partition as well as membership of Pakistan. There was to be a referendum in the NWFP and a Shahi Jirga, or grand tribal council, in Baluchistan. But Mountbatten was not deflected by these details. On 4 June he announced that independence would come on 15 August.

All the leaders had signed up to the plan, with the exception of Gandhi, who was still a wild card in the game. Mountbatten was aware that a strongly negative reaction from him might derail the process, so he pressed the Mahatma to call on him before his next public prayer meeting. Gandhi duly paid the visit on the evening of 4 June, whereupon

Mountbatten gave him a long flattering speech about how the plan's consultative elements had been inspired by his ideas, and should really be called 'Plan Gandhi'. Whether the Mahatma actually believed this gloss on events is not clear, but shortly afterwards he was prepared publicly to state that the Viceroy 'had no hand in the decision', and that the blame for Partition of the country should instead fall on Indians. It was primarily the intransigence of the Muslim League that determined India's fate, but he insisted that Indians could 'undo' Partition 'any time we want'.[143] He then stuck to this line through all the Congress party's approvals of the scheme, which he did not oppose. He was only prepared to say that the plan must be accepted unless the party could countenance even more conflict. This demonstrated his pragmatic side, but his acceptance of Partition as the fault of Indians also fitted into the long-term view he had set out in *Hind Swaraj* – that Indians kept the British in India through their own failings. He was never one to dodge self-criticism, and his eventually mild attitude to Partition can be seen as part of this tendency. It can also be viewed as inspired by the teachings of the Bhagavad Gita on the resigned acceptance of the unavoidable.

Formal approval of the scheme was then provided by official meetings of the AICC and the League, which cleared the political air, but left an enormous amount of detail to be arranged. Two Boundary Commissions, a Partition Committee and a Joint Defence Council were set up. The princely states had to be absorbed into the two new nations, and fierce arguments had to be resolved over the division of assets, military and civil. Mountbatten wished to be nominated as Governor-General of both the new Dominions for smoothness of transition, particularly in military matters. Nehru duly asked him to serve as such for India. Jinnah held back and it was only on 2 July that he announced that he himself would serve in the post for Pakistan. Mountbatten was furious. This decision has been seen as rampant egomania on Jinnah's part, or alternatively as an act of revenge against the puffed-up Viceroy for saddling the Quaid with the 'moth-eaten' version of Pakistan. Or it might have been grounded in a shrewd appreciation on Jinnah's part that sharing a Commander-in-Chief with the new neighbour was not in Pakistan's interests. As ever with Jinnah, the lack of a memoir means that interpretations of events tend to reflect preconceptions of the man.

JINNAH'S NEW NATION

The same is even truer of the great speech that the Quaid-i-Azam made to Pakistan's constituent assembly in Karachi on 11 August. This speech is very well known in Pakistan and is still a live issue. It is the only extended view we have into Jinnah's mind concerning the way he saw his new state, and it has been a matter of fierce dispute. On one side there are those who insist that in this speech he rolled out a secular, liberal manifesto for Pakistan, on the other are those who seek either to redefine or cherry-pick what he said, or to treat his words as some kind of aberration from his progress towards an 'Islamic' state. As ever, Jinnah is most easily understood when quoted selectively, and it behoves those who believe that he had some kind of Islamic vision to produce anything to that effect as explicit or as extended as the tolerant inclusion outlined in the 11 August speech. On other occasions he certainly referred to God, to Islamic principles and to the Qur'an, but when faced with the first sitting of the constituent body of the new nation, he unambiguously set out certain major founding principles of the new state, none of which are exclusively Qur'anic and all of which are familiar from the tradition of Western liberalism.

If he had wished to reveal the true extent of his 'Islamic' agenda then the opening session of the new state's guiding institution would surely have been a good place to do it. He could hardly have been politically damaged at this point by announcing something along those lines. And he would certainly have been in deep political trouble had he announced his commitment to wide tolerance on 11 August 1947, only to retract it a few months later, and replace it with a hardline vision of the Pakistan that some of his admirers have been trying to build ever since.

Primarily the speech is not about democracy, or law, or religion; it is about minorities. He was setting out his belief that Muslims could be trusted to rule Hindus and Sikhs wisely and fairly. It is worth quoting the speech at length. The passage below follows general remarks about the evils of black marketeering, corruption and nepotism, and forms part of a general discussion of the nature of the civic rights and religious peace enjoyed in Great Britain:

'If you…work together in a spirit that every one of you, no matter to what community he belongs…no matter what is his colour, caste or creed, is first, second and last a citizen of this State with equal rights, privileges and obligations, there will be no end to the progress you will make… We should begin to work in that spirit and in course of time all these angularities of the majority and minority communities, the Hindu community and the Muslim community…will vanish. Indeed if you ask me this has been the biggest hindrance in the way of India to attain the freedom and independence and but for this we would have been free peoples long, long ago… Therefore, we must learn a lesson from this. You are free; you are free to go to your temples, you are free to go to your mosques or to any other place of worship in this State of Pakistan. You may belong to any religion or caste or creed – that has nothing to do with the business of the State… Even now there are some States in existence where there are discriminations made and bars imposed against a particular class. Thank God, we are not starting in those days. We are starting in the days when there is no discrimination, no distinction between one community and another, no discrimination between one caste or creed and another. We are starting with this fundamental principle that we are all citizens and equal citizens of one State. The people of England in course of time had to face the realities of the situation and had to discharge the responsibilities and burdens placed upon them by the government of their country and they went through that fire step by step. Today, you might say with justice that Roman Catholics and Protestants do not exist; what exists now is that every man is a citizen, an equal citizen of Great Britain and they are all members of the Nation.

'Now, I think we should keep that in front of us as our ideal and you will find that in course of time Hindus would cease to

be Hindus and Muslims would cease to be Muslims, not in the
religious sense, because that is the personal faith of each individual,
but in the political sense as citizens of the State.'[144]

This is Jinnah finally looking over the ruler's desk from the other side.
He would not be the first to discover that things look rather different
from that perspective. Now he would have to make provision for his
own minorities, and the speech recognizes this fully. But there is an
extra layer to his words. He cannot have been so simple-minded as to
think that there would be no pressure from religious quarters within
the new Pakistan, and this speech is a bid to head off the most extreme
elements of it. He was laying down a marker about tolerance. How
secular the new state would be may not have concerned him unduly and
he must have known that there would have to be a religious element
in its fabric; he had openly accepted several times that Islam provided
a suitable ethical base for the social justice he hoped to nurture in the
new country. But this speech was another form of foundation. He was
declaring that he wanted to build a free, open and inclusive society.
Like Gandhi he wanted a tolerant state – not because he wanted secular
people, but because he did not want religious politics.

Three days later, on 14 August 1947, Jinnah finally took up his
first public office – as Governor-General of the new Pakistan. He was
beset with difficulties from the start. There were daunting problems of
administration, something he had never been concerned with previously,
and there was a desperate struggle with finance, another area in
which he had no experience. By the end of the year he had complex
responsibilities as a military leader in the fighting over Kashmir. There
was also a new Constitution to be written, and it is from his comments
during this period that most of the scraps of his 'Islamic' thinking have
been culled.

He seemed to find wielding real power a frustrating experience.
In some ways he was more questioned and less heeded as a ruling
Governor-General than he had been as a party leader in opposition.
This is well illustrated by his insistence that Urdu should be the sole,
official language of Pakistan, a diktat directly in defiance of the wishes

of Bengalis, who made up about half the population of the new state. Instead of uncritical adulation from all over India he now had to face dissent and criticism, and even direct defiance and abuse in East Pakistan in March 1948. He did not like it and it made him depressed and ill. By May 1948 he was rendered virtually an invalid, as what remained of his lungs finally dissolved.

GANDHI REVIVES

In stark contrast to Jinnah's garlanded path to high office and national glory, the Mahatma trod a dark and sorrowful road across the summer of 1947. His hopes for a free, united India had come to nothing, and he spent most of the months before Partition not amongst the chattering classes but amongst the suffering masses.

He had gradually been eased out of central power politics, a process he fully recognized and referred to repeatedly with sorrow and irony. His popularity at the local level gave him no joy. He was greeted with buntings made of the mill cloth that he abhorred, and he saw his image garlanded while no one listened to anything he said.

But even after 3 June Mountbatten still thought of him as useful. He asked him to go to Kashmir in early August to speak to the Maharaja and attempt to woo him into the Indian camp.[145] Gandhi went willingly but did not quite fulfil his brief as directed. He considered India's princes a British creation and a British problem to resolve. He therefore made little attempt to influence the Maharaja, and instead called for a plebiscite to ascertain the wishes of the people of Kashmir. Unsurprisingly, the mission failed – and it was the last piece of statesmanship that he undertook.

On 15 August he avoided the Independence celebrations in New Delhi. By then he was in Calcutta, where he stayed until September, working closely with Suhrawardy to quell the communal violence that still blighted the city. In this the two of them had a high degree of success, causing Mountbatten to remark that there were thousands of men deployed in the Punjab who could not stop the killing, while in

Calcutta just two men managed to bring peace. In admiration he called Gandhi a 'one-man Boundary Force'.[146] However, Calcutta descended into rioting again in late August and on 1 September Gandhi undertook a fast unto death, only abandoned on 4 September after receiving pledges of good conduct from all parties. On 7 September he travelled to Delhi where murderous hatreds were still untamed and he felt he could do some good.

He had not been a member of Congress since 1934 and he considered forming a new party dedicated to social reform now that nationalist issues were superseded. He was the 'Father of the Nation' but his political influence was at an end. Electoral politics and the accession of Nehru and Patel to supreme power rendered him obsolete. He had never been deeply involved in the daily detail of political affairs and he now lost such interest as he had ever had. Perhaps his last act was to champion the appointment of Ambedkar as law minister in the new government, a position from which the latter was able to write a number of social reforms into the legal fabric of the new India. One of these was the formal legal abolition of untouchability, an act which raised cries of 'Mahatma Gandhi ki jai!' in the assembly.

But politics would not entirely let him go. Murder and arson were still prevalent in Delhi through the autumn of 1947, and in January 1948 he decided to go on another fast to try to bring all the people of both India and Pakistan to their senses. He also targeted the new government of India, which was withholding a very large sum it owed to Pakistan. He began a fast on 13 January amid unprecedented media attention. There is newsreel footage of this fast as of no other, with Gandhi lying on a low bed in an annexe of Birla House, a cloth over his face, as thousands of people file past the open French windows. After only two days Nehru's government paid up the 55 crore rupees it owed Pakistan. More pledges of future good conduct came in, and eventually the Mahatma agreed to break his fast on 18 January.

Thus in his last few months he was able to rediscover and refocus some of his most elevated moral energy, with which he exerted an influence he had been denied for many years. Perhaps he saved more lives in these months than at any other time in his life.

He was certainly no longer the political force he once had been, but he was one of the world's most famous men, and as we know by now such men attract all kinds of unwelcome attention. While the West was finally beginning to understand and admire him, some deeply religious Indians were coming to hate him and to see him as a friend of Islam and a threat to the holiness of India, with his readings from the Qur'an and his apparent forgiveness of those who wished to kill Hindus. On the evening of 30 January he was shot at point-blank range on his way to his regular prayer meeting. A young Hindu named Nathuram Godse put three bullets into his chest, as an act of cleansing for Mother India. Such extraordinary ignorance and misunderstanding of the man defy belief, but a small provincial conception of God and a small weapon were enough to lay low the great spirit of the age. He had expressed the desire to die 'in harness' with the name of God on his lips.[147] Having been denied so many of his other wishes, this small request was granted him. His last word was 'Ram'.

JINNAH SLIPS AWAY

Jinnah slipped more slowly out of the world. He had been seriously ill for years with chronic bronchitis, then tuberculosis, an illness kept strictly secret throughout the turbulence of the independence negotiations. His breath became shorter and shorter and he was less and less able to tackle the work he wished to complete. His immense efforts to bring security and dignity to his fellow Muslims had burned out so much of his life force that he had little left to give when the moment of triumph came. He made mistakes more easily than he made friends, especially in later life, but he ranks highly among those who have served by leading. He died on 11 September 1948, to ascend shortly to the status of icon, incorruptible hero, a permanent friend and example to the citizens of his new nation. He was buried in a spectacular tomb and his reputation has been treated with enormous reverence. Whatever his real achievements, he was credited with even more. Jinnah, as both the real man and the legend, set such high standards that no one else has ever been called 'Great Leader' in Pakistan's history.

Part 3
Analysis

Quaid-i-Azam Jinnah and Mahatma Gandhi were undoubtedly the two most influential figures within the Indian Independence struggle. Jinnah shaped the final settlement by consistently demanding Pakistan, and Gandhi defined the largely non-violent nature of the campaign. Each made their contribution by taking over and refashioning a national political organization, which they came to personify.

Theirs would seem, therefore, to be a story of triumph, but such a view could only ever be a patriotic, not a personal reading of events, because for each of them the story ended in a kind of failure. Through 1946–47 neither the great tactician nor the great moralist managed to control events, and both were sidelined by the time the demission process came to an end, Jinnah by the Mountbatten–Nehru axis and Gandhi by his own party leadership. Neither got quite what they wanted in August 1947. Jinnah's Pakistan was not the large, viable state he had demanded; it resembled the 'mutilated' Pakistan he had refused several times before. Gandhi had to accept the vivisection of the country he had fought so hard to avoid, and found to his distress that he needed to fight brutality with selfless love even harder in liberated India.

Gandhi found no joy in the birth of the new state; while there were speeches and fireworks in Delhi, he was asleep in Calcutta. He awoke next day not to new life and freedom, but to a sense of continuing sorrow and an apprehension that violence was about to be unleashed on an unprecedented scale. Jinnah could take more personal satisfaction, but once freed from the fear of Hindu-majority rule, Pakistan seemed to have little deeper import for him beyond the lifting of that shadow.

Independence marked the end of the productive life of both leaders. Jinnah the doughty advocate–critic struggled to adapt to a new role as a problem solver, and failed to make much impact on the daunting practical difficulties he faced, which required much more than rhetorical skill or clever positioning. He lost allies and found himself arguing with people who had shortly before been fervently on his side. Gandhi lost even more. Once stripped of the nationalist cause and its moral high notes, he became just one spiritual guide among many in a land richly supplied with ascetics and holy men.

An unavoidable tinge of tragedy, therefore, attended the small lease of life the two veterans were granted after independence finally arrived, leaving Jinnah with too many momentous issues to decide and Gandhi with too few.

How did their separate dreams slip out of their hands? Why was it that the pessimistic mind of the lawyer and the hopeful soul of the mystic could not share a country? How did two nationalist Congressmen, admirers of and admired by Gopal Krishna Gokhale, come to take such different paths?

Gokhale the Guru

In 1912 Jinnah confided to a friend that he wished to become 'the Muslim Gokhale'.[148] Three years after Gokhale died in 1915 Gandhi wrote an introduction to a volume of Gokhale's speeches in which he acknowledged his personal debt to Gokhale's thinking and patronage, and referred to him as 'my political guru'.[149] Taken together, these declarations seem to place Gokhale at a central point in both men's lives, as model and teacher. But bearing in mind where the two erstwhile pupils ended up, how much influence did Gokhale really have, and what kind of a model can he have been? What did these tributes to him really mean? Was Gokhale the hinge upon which the Jinnah–Gandhi relationship hung?

Gopal Krishna Gokhale (1866–1915) was one of the most important Indian nationalist leaders in the pre-First World War Congress. His background was in education, and his political outlook was characterized by moderation and an emphasis on the duty of service. He was a brilliant yet modest man, in style and objectives conventionally contrasted to Bal Gangadhar Tilak (1856–1920). Tilak played the agitator where Gokhale was content to press for gradual change. Both men were deeply religious, but Gokhale's faith created in him a reflective and ethical outlook whereas Tilak's fired him to active protests driven by heightened regional and national identity. This pair of eminent Mahrashtrians ended up in 1907 heading the two tendencies within the Congress dubbed Moderate and Extremist, or Soft (Naram) and Hot (Garam) factions. The split between the two wings was only healed some nine years later, with Jinnah prominent among the peacemakers.

Even in such a short summary it is relatively easy to pick out elements of Gokhale's approach that might have appealed to either Jinnah or Gandhi. With Jinnah it was the moderate gradualism; with Gandhi it was the coupling of religious feeling with ethical politics and the call to service.

Gandhi's relationship with Gokhale was longer and deeper than Jinnah's. The two men first met in 1896 when Gandhi broke off briefly from his work for the rights of Indian immigrants in South Africa to bring his campaign to the attention of the Congress leaders back home. Gokhale took an interest in the cause, and in the man himself, seeing something of future greatness in him. Gandhi was still in the formative stages of his political development and he was reticent and unsure in his dealings with the Congress leadership, but Gokhale saw to it that the issue was given proper attention. Gandhi was entranced by Gokhale's gentleness and his air of spiritual graciousness; the two men formed a bond that kept Gokhale involved in South African issues for the next 18 years. Gandhi came to India again in late 1901 for a longer stay, and spent a month at Gokhale's side, all through the Congress session of that winter. Though Gandhi was deeply impressed by Gokhale's idealism, he was less enamoured of several other aspects of Congress politics. He disliked the lavish lifestyles of leading Congressmen, was repelled by their petty jealousies and frustrated at their part-time activism – how they talked incessantly for a week then 'went to sleep' for another year. He was disappointed by the emphasis on debate over action and he was disgusted by their lordly disregard of basic hygiene. The Congress compound was out of bounds to the lower castes that did the cleaning work, and the stench of the latrines seemed to him insupportable. Nevertheless, the wider causes of the party kept a strong hold on his allegiance. The two men corresponded extensively and Gokhale regularly sent funds to Gandhi for the furtherance of his work.

At Gandhi's insistence, Gokhale stopped off in South Africa on his way back from London in 1912 where he had been involved with the Islington Commission on Indian administration. The two men went on a triumphant tour of the Dominion, which included a meeting between Gokhale and General Jan Smuts, the interior minister. Gokhale was able to reassure Gandhi afterwards that the concessions he had worked for would soon be granted, as indeed they were, leaving Gandhi with the feeling that India was calling him to greater work back home. But before returning to India, Gandhi was requested by Gokhale to join him in London in 1914, where he was working on, ill and exhausted. Gandhi joined him there in August, and stayed in London for around five months.

The two men met for the last time in Poona in early February 1915, when Gandhi, newly returned from London, travelled inland to visit Gokhale's college-cum-ashram, from where he ran the Servants of India Society (SIS). Gokhale had formed the Society in 1905 as a body dedicated to rendering public service to all Indians, by bringing practical help and education to the masses. Gandhi wished to join the Society and Gokhale seems to have agreed to his admission. After a brief stay in early February, Gandhi then crossed India to visit Tagore's school at Santiniketan, and it was here that he heard of Gokhale's death, on 19 February. The secretary of the SIS, V.S. Srinivasi Sastri, now became its leader; he was much less keen on Gandhi's whole approach and refused to enrol him. Gandhi was thus left without his teacher and, having expected to live at the headquarters of the SIS, he was also without accommodation for himself, his disciples and his family. Shortly afterwards, he founded his ashram at Ahmedabad, by the Sabarmati river.

Gokhale also knew Jinnah well, and the young lawyer sided with Gokhale and the Moderates during the great schism at the Surat Congress session in 1907. Both were then returned as members of the Imperial Legislative Council in the elections held in late 1909. Jinnah agreed with Gokhale that the British presence was a guarantee of order and that without them there would be no progress for India. It was this view that drew them both into national, constitutional politics, and they collaborated closely over the next three years. It was during this phase that Jinnah made his remark about wishing to become 'the Muslim Gokhale', in a conversation with poet and Congress leader, Sarojini Naidu (1879–1949).

What did this remark really mean? If we examine Gokhale's general political philosophy it bears only a passing resemblance to what we know of Jinnah's outlook, even at this early stage. Gokhale wanted to work with the poor of India in a gradual and practical manner; by inclination, Jinnah was a haughty laissez-faire liberal, an advocate of improvement certainly, but through self-help. Gokhale was a devout Hindu while Jinnah was a casual Muslim. Gokhale believed, according to Gandhi, in the 'spiritualizing' of politics.[150] Jinnah would have wanted no such thing; he was wary of mixing religion and politics, as his reaction to the Khilafat movement was to show. So what was it that Jinnah could have wanted to emulate in Gokhale's life, beliefs or work?

Jinnah could have found much in Gokhale's career that he could aspire to, even if the gap between them in religious background and motivation was so wide. Perhaps we can understand the remark if we think of Jinnah as meaning not that he wished to follow Gokhale, or to replace him, or to emulate him exactly, but simply to be like him in his own way. He envied and admired Gokhale's eminence, intelligence, status and especially his non-communal stance. Jinnah was on course to become the senior Muslim in the Congress, and he was quite comfortable with the idea that religion should be relegated as an issue. But it must be said that there was no way in which he could ever have become the Muslim Gokhale; he was simply made in a different mould. Where Gokhale was a gentle persuader, Jinnah was a brilliant debater and an aggressive winner of arguments. Where Gokhale was a man sure of his standing, Jinnah was always in search of support. Where Gokhale's leadership was marked with diffidence and modesty, Jinnah would be a leader whose status had constantly to be reconfirmed. Gokhale was affectionately known as 'Baba Sahib'; Jinnah called forth nothing so mild. He became the Quaid-i-Azam and, according to M.C. Chagla, he loved it.[151]

Gokhale was impressed with Jinnah and supplied one of the best-known quotations about him. Again it comes via Sarojini Naidu, and in full it reads: 'He [Jinnah] has true stuff in him and that freedom from all sectarian prejudice which will make him the best ambassador of Hindu–Muslim unity.'[152] There is no reason to doubt that this is exactly how Jinnah presented himself. How better to rise in a broad church like the Congress? How better to live down a minority status? How else to muster all the available support that an outsider could hope to win? Jinnah's actions over the next few years readily bear out Gokhale's judgement. Jinnah was indeed the best candidate for the ambassador's job. It suited both his abilities and his wider purposes, and in such a role he could build a unique position in Congress politics. He could see a niche; there was no one like Gokhale on the Muslim side. There were loyalists and there were rebels, especially among the ulema. But there were few senior Muslims in the Congress in 1912, and Jinnah was definitely the brightest of them. But to play this sort of role would not have been quite the same thing as being the Muslim Gokhale, whose uniqueness was not the product of a minority status at all, except in the sense of his rare personal qualities. His inner strength was a religious one, and it underpinned his patient and conciliatory nature. Jinnah's strength came from elsewhere. He was a fireball of ambition and impatient energy, a man of action rather than reflection.

Gokhale was kind in his assessments of Gandhi too, at least in public. He praised him within Congress circles – 'indomitable...made of the stuff of which great heroes and martyrs are made',[153] 'immortal', 'a more exalted spirit has never moved on this earth'[154] – but he was less fulsome in private, and harboured a number of reservations about Gandhi's abilities. He considered that Gandhi's *Hind Swaraj* was flawed and showed signs of hasty writing.[155] He also had serious doubts about his qualities as a negotiator, and warned M.R. Jayakar, secretary of the Servants of India Society, 'Be careful that India does not trust him on occasions where delicate negotiations have to be carried on with care and caution.' He was prepared to concede that Gandhi had done 'wonderful work' in South Africa, but he feared that when the history of the negotiations came to be written with impartial accuracy, 'it will be found that his actual achievements were not as meritorious as is popularly imagined.'[156] This assessment is hardly what one would like to hear from one's beloved teacher. Nevertheless when it came to the art of negotiation he was probably right. Gandhi's preferred tactic was to push all the chips over to his opponent and put the onus on him to behave well in a position of power. This was the basic mentality that underlay satyagraha, so it should not come as a surprise that Gandhi took it with him to the negotiating table.

So what did the two Congress contenders take from the gentle Gokhale? The answer is that in practice they didn't take very much at all. Gandhi, who came from a similar philosophical background, actually rejected the mild gradualism of Gokhale and opted instead for mass movements and demands for immediate swaraj. Jinnah only ever shared a fraction of his political aims with Gokhale, and it is hard to see how he could ever truly have aspired to be a Muslim version of him in any sense that his contemporaries might have understood as significant. There was rather more to Gokhale than Home Rule, the primacy of law and constitutional methods. Popular awakening and the 'spiritualization' of the masses, two of Gokhale central tenets, were not ideas that Jinnah would have signed up to in 1912. Yet in 1943 Jinnah was still a professed admirer of Gokhale. In a speech to a Muslim League session at Delhi he praised him as a 'tower of intellect'. This is probably not the key quality of Baba Sahib that Gandhi would have chosen to single out.

As the two men's careers unfolded, it became clear, ironically, that it was from Tilak, the great mobilizer and stirrer, not Gokhale, the tower of intellect, that they both learned their most valuable lessons – Jinnah in the deployment of religion linked with nationalism, Gandhi in the effective use of popular symbolism.

Friends and Enemies

Jinnah and Gandhi were public figures involved in national politics for more than 40 years. This brought them into close contact with literally thousands of people, in relationships that were short or long, trivial or significant. Much of what we know about the two as characters comes from the testimonies of these witnesses. The picture that emerges is, of course, unclear, because although politics may be about trying to win friends, the result is often the making of enemies. Gandhi, it must be said, left a much better impression on most of his contemporaries than Jinnah, and this has heavily tilted the verdict of history in as far as it is influenced by personal memoirs. The chance to belittle and contemn Jinnah has scarcely ever been spurned by anyone well placed to do so, and this sort of criticism has stimulated a counterbalancing effort from Jinnah's supporters. The result has been a body of literature about him that is saccharine in the extreme.

The most sincere voices that speak up for him come largely from those impressed by his easy brilliance, and relate to his early years. Two British Secretaries of State for India were open admirers: Lord Crewe, who called him the 'best talker'[157] in the delegation that came to see him in London in 1914, and Montagu, who in 1917 watched him debate with Viceroy Chelmsford and tie him up in 'verbal knots' with his dialectical skill.[158]

Of hostile witnesses, pride of place must go to Lord Mountbatten. The range of critical remarks he made about Jinnah is quite striking. Officially, at the time, Mountbatten settled for 'cold', though afterwards he was rather less kind, calling him mad, megalomaniac, a clot, a bastard and, most famously, 'a psychotic case'.[159] He found Jinnah 'most frigid, haughty and disdainful', and cast him as 'the evil genius of the whole thing'.[160] This typifies the tone of much of what Jinnah's opponents habitually thought about him, but 'friends' sometimes concurred. M.C. Chagla described him as 'cold and unemotional'. Chagla states that Jinnah cultivated no relationships outside politics, and had 'no personal or human side to his character'.[161]

Foreign journalists often picked up on the same themes. G.E. Jones, who interviewed Jinnah for the *New York Times*, commented in his *Tumult in India* that Jinnah had 'hostile reserve, conceit and a narrow outlook'.[162] He also used pejorative words such as 'suspicious', 'withdrawn', 'isolated' and 'arrogant'. He did concede, however, that the man was 'a superb political craftsman'. Louis Fischer, another American journalist, was kinder. He met Jinnah several times and commented on his 'forbidding earnestness' and the fact that he 'rarely laughed'.[163] One notable enthusiast for Jinnah was British writer Beverley Nichols, who spoke at length with him in December 1943 and found him an impressive and appealing person – 'a giant'. However, much of this favourable attitude possibly sprang from Nichols's undisguised antipathy to Gandhi and Hindus in general. At the height of the Second World War it was easy to see the Muslims as 'loyal' and Hindus in the Congress as 'treacherous', a view that interlocked neatly with time-honoured imperial ideas about small, effeminate, untrustworthy Bengalis/Hindus as compared to tall, manly Pathans/Muslims. Nichols is rude and ignorant about Hindus to a quite embarrassing degree. His *Verdict on India* is said to have been favourite bedtime reading for Jinnah, with particularly lavish passages underlined in his personal copy.[164] Being called 'the most important man in Asia' would probably tickle anyone's vanity, but if Jinnah had paid attention to the rest of the book he would surely have perceived how lightweight Nichols was as a political writer. He had a waspish wit and a fine turn of phrase, but his métier was actually writing about gardening. *Verdict* is riddled with clichéd prejudices about India, and the interview Nichols obtained yields little real insight into Jinnah the man – Nichols incautiously admits that Jinnah had been 'good enough to edit it' himself.[165] He clearly admired Jinnah personally and approved of his outlook from an imperial standpoint, becoming an avowed convert to the cause of Pakistan across pages 188 to 194.

Friendlessness or isolation is a recurring theme in Jinnah's life. He was a solitary figure at several points in his career, but this characteristic seems to have attached to him regardless of his situation. Diwan Chaman Lal, a Punjabi Congressman who shared a passage to Europe with Jinnah in 1928, wrote of him as a man whose integrity was 'beyond question', but also remarked that Jinnah had been 'the loneliest of men'.[166] Stafford Cripps met him in December 1939 and characterized him as 'an intensely lonely man'[167] without confidants or advisors. This is more striking, because during the period in question Jinnah was absolutely at the centre of all sorts of collective activity. Whether he was consciously projecting an image or not, this kind of observation feeds easily into readings of Jinnah's character, both positive – that he was a man apart, carrying a crushing burden – and negative – that he was aloof and haughty.

Politics for most politicians is a serious business, and for Jinnah more than most. He never mastered the deftness of touch that Gandhi could employ. But there was once a lighter spirit discernible in him, captured for us by Sarojini Naidu. She was a close colleague of Jinnah's in the 1910s, when he was prominent in both the Congress and the Muslim League. Her extended description of him contains most of the well-known phrases applied to his early career and it deserves to be quoted at length on the subject of his character, if only to counterbalance much of what is found elsewhere. In 1918 she contributed an introduction to a collection of his speeches, in which she describes him as: 'Somewhat formal and fastidious, and a little aloof and imperious of manner, the calm hauteur of his accustomed reserve but masks, for those who know him, a naïve and eager humanity, an intuition quick and tender as a woman's, a humour gay and winning as child's…a shy and splendid idealism which is of the very essence of the man.'[168] Once upon a time he could be as likable as he was impressive.

Though he had a more attractive side as a younger man, it seems that this quality withered over the years as his political isolation increased and his frustrations multiplied. The hero-worship of later underlings is understandable – tied up as it was with the cause of Pakistan, Muslim identity and admiration for an older, wiser man – but their praise has a dreary worthiness, a flat dutiful tone concentrating on Jinnah's hard work, sagacity, dedication, self-sacrifice and so on. In *Qaid-i-Azam Jinnah: As I Knew Him*, M.A.H. Ispahani, a Pakistani diplomat and minister, praises at length Jinnah's 'glorious role', his 'matchless efforts', the 'magic of his name', the unquestioning loyalty of his followers, and so forth.[169] It may all be true but it is oppressive and uninstructive to read, with a faint air of unreality and over-compensation about it.

With age, Gandhi grew calmer and almost resigned to his loss of influence. The mature Jinnah, however, became increasingly intransigent, and the last 10 years of open warfare with Congress, from 1937 to 1947, took a terrible toll on his disposition and physical health, turning him into the tired, ill, truculent 71-year-old of 1947 whose rambling stories of persecution suggested to Lord Mountbatten that he was senile. By then Jinnah had learned that he had to fight his corner ruthlessly if he was to expect results, that lesser men could outmanoeuvre him, and that for all his brilliance he could be denied a place at the high table of politics – because he was a Muslim. After his estrangement from his wife in the mid-1920s, he can have found very little to cheer him. The road to Pakistan was very long and very stressful. Ultimately, even that journey failed to deliver quite what he had envisaged.

Gandhi had his share of frustrations and sorrows too, including three extended spells in prison, something that Jinnah's style of political activism always spared him. But the Mahatma's mild nature never failed, and there is very little contemporary criticism of his character to be found, especially not from his inner circle. This reflects the extraordinary reverence in which his contemporaries held him and the way that he seems not to have abused the space and authority this granted him. He was essentially the same in public and private. He never stood on ceremony, or hectored his opponents, no matter how far apart he stood from them on the issues at hand, whether he was addressing the king or a minor Raj official. His ability to reach out informally across political and social divides was extraordinary; during his trip to England in 1931, he managed to befriend the very mill workers that his hand-spinning was intended to condemn to unemployment.

Gandhi also enjoyed a much wider and warmer kind of political support than that which Jinnah constructed so painstakingly. His political aims were easily understood and generally shared. Just as importantly, his methods were thought to be correct; Indian freedom under Gandhi was to be won in an Indian way. To oppose him coming from within either orthodox Hinduism or broad Congress philosophy would have seemed either irreverent or un-Indian. Those who did oppose him found it difficult to remain in the Congress: Jinnah in 1920, C.R. Das in 1923, and Bose in 1939 had to leave and create their own platforms to oppose him at an all-India level. Criticizing the Mahatma was potentially a short cut to the political wilderness.

Contemporary critics of Gandhi were not usually close to him, mainly because he tended not to leave cast-offs, like the resentful Chagla. One exception was Jawaharlal Nehru, who frequently expressed his exasperation at the Mahatma's twists and turns. But through it all Nehru always admired him, and thought of him as a magician, capable of pulling off feats of political sorcery of which no one else was capable. In particular, Nehru recognized Gandhi's capacity to connect with the wider population in a direct and very Indian way. His unique ability to do this, and the unifying and empowering effect of that ability, was the main factor that pulled the Congress out of its middle-class youth, then anchored it as a powerful force at the centre of Indian politics.

Several senior members of the Congress did later write memoirs containing criticisms of Gandhi ranging from mild to severe. Kanji Dwarkadas, in *Freedom for India* (1966), is critical of Gandhi's inconstancy, his 'continuously changing moods and policies'.[170] This we might expect from a close friend and confidant of Jinnah's, but Dwarkadas himself has a different explanation. He lays claim to a degree of uncommon detachment about Gandhi because he never came under the power of his 'hypnotic influence'.[171] S.C. Bose was less restrained in *The Indian Struggle*. He criticized Gandhi for being, by unpredictable turns, 'obstinate as a fanatic' then 'liable to surrender like a child', possessing neither the 'instinct' nor the 'judgement so necessary for political bargaining'.[172] Bose became increasingly frustrated with Gandhi through the 1930s. He was a persistent doubter, and an inveterate opponent of Gandhi's chosen heir, Nehru. Bose's eventual resignation from the Congress in 1939 ended the dispute, and Bose's subsequent career as an authoritarian, militaristic, national-socialist amply displays his basic differences with Gandhi as philosopher and leader.

Among friend-critics, the most prominent was Rabindranath Tagore, who had a clutch of disagreements with Gandhi, most notably over the Non-Cooperation Movement of 1920. The disorder repelled Tagore; he called it 'the anarchy of mere emptiness'. He found it impossible to support the burning of valuable clothes and the denial of schooling to young Indians that the boycott required. Having publicly dubbed him 'Mahatmaji' in 1919, he was soon privately accusing Gandhi of 'a dangerous form of egotism'.[173] The two men remained on cordial terms, but were never close after the Non-Cooperation Movement.

Unsurprisingly, it was the British who went furthest in their failure to understand Gandhi. They thought he was a Bolshevik in 1919 and a fascist in 1942. They had, in fact, no clue what he was, because they had never encountered his like before. Nor, to be fair, had anyone else. He struck some on the British side as yet another strange, mystic fraud fashioned from the dust of India, begging while preaching repentance and abjuration. Yet this time the emaciated sadhu was actually a trained barrister. The confusion this induced in official British minds was not confined to Churchill, who latched on to his appearance in 1931 and famously expressed outrage that a 'semi-naked fakir of a type well known in the East' could come to bargain on equal terms with the King–Emperor's representative.[174]

These words exactly betray the mixture of contempt and bewilderment that Gandhi instilled in men who could only recognize traditional structures and symbols of authority. His comprehensive vision of a future India, his apparently light grip on power and the general unwillingness of others to speak out against him always baffled Raj officials, who initially assumed he was ridiculous and impotent, and later, that he was sinister and all-powerful. Misunderstanding of Gandhi led to comparisons between him and Hitler, a wild rhetorical leap that in hindsight seems sensationally misplaced. The travel writer Rosita Forbes (1893–1967), who met both Gandhi and Hitler, was prepared to make comparisons between them at a time when Hitler was still seen as the architect of German national revival, not a warmonger and mass-murderer. In *India of the Princes* (1938) Forbes makes a double comparison between the Fuehrer and the Mahatma. She considered that Gandhi had a 'mental isolation' similar to Hitler's and seemed to be without 'comparative knowledge'.[175] The kind of politics that Gandhi was promoting was never to the taste of establishment insiders, and a few pages later Forbes opines that both leaders 'feel too much'.[176]

There were also more serious political observers who made direct parallels between Gandhi and European fascists, and at the height of the Second World War it did at times seem that Gandhi was, if not in league with the Axis powers, then at least aiding their cause by undermining British military efforts in the Far East. It was the intimate connection between Gandhi and the masses that prompted these comparisons, and this is what sometimes made the Congress look like a fascist organization to the British. They added up the movement's mass popularity and multiplied it by the Congress's opposition to British rule and came out with a neat calculation that defined Gandhi as a nationalist demagogue and an enemy – in sum, a fascist. But what they mistook in all this was Gandhi's political awareness of the importance of inclusiveness in the service of national liberation. The British equated mass popularity with manipulation and hysteria, and this played along easily with the way they found it very difficult to believe in the unacceptability of their own rule. That all their hard work could be ignored, that all their selflessness, as they saw it, could be so misrepresented, seemed ungrateful and perverse beyond belief.

The British had not encountered anything like this sort of resistance among the Indian ruling elite over the years since 1857. Neither the princes nor the community leaders of the early twentieth century had exhibited such clear signs of uninhibited antipathy; the first 20 years of the Indian National Congress saw it fulsome in its praise for British achievements in India, and the original Muslim delegation to Lord Minto in 1906 was a loyal and decorous affair. Representative institutions had been added since then and promises of future self-government had been made. Commissions had been sent. Conferences had been held. But through all of this, no one stirred up the wider population in the way that Gandhi did. It was difficult to accept that he was expressing their discontents, and much easier to imagine that he was somehow causing them. Because of the attention he seemed to be able to attract, some went further and saw him as a sort of world rebel, which was rather how he saw himself. Sir Frederick Sykes, who as Governor of Bombay arrested him after the Salt March, spoke for many when he described Gandhi's foreign disciples as 'unbalanced young people from England and America'.[177]

Gandhi was especially gifted at opening channels of communication and sending the messages he wanted to get across. Although he did have enemies, they were not enemies he had set out to make. To oppose Gandhi was a choice, and because he constantly worked to break down barriers of hostility, not many of his opponents escaped his attempts to touch them personally. The enduring result of all these efforts is the overwhelmingly positive impression he left across countries and continents.

'Jinnah Studies'

There are surprisingly few books about Jinnah in English. This is probably because the Pakistan issue is not of great importance to many outside the subcontinent, and the technical issues about Jinnah's Islamic credentials are of interest primarily to Urdu speakers. To this day, the main biographical works are Hector Bolitho's *Jinnah: Creator of Pakistan*[178] and Stanley Wolpert's *Jinnah of Pakistan*. The first is neither current nor particularly objective. The second, despite its shortcomings, is widely quoted in general writings on the Quaid-i-Azam. This is especially true of one famous passage, which also appears at the start of the 1998 biopic *Jinnah*:

> Few individuals significantly alter the course of history. Fewer still modify the map of the world. Hardly anyone can be credited with creating a nation-state. Mohammed Ali Jinnah did all three.[179]

Well, yes and no. He did not really do three things. He did one thing, which Wolpert has chosen to describe in three different ways.

After this opening flourish of sonorous admiration, Wolpert adopts a more measured tone. Jinnah's life is duly recounted, but at crucial points the author repeatedly shies away from candid assessments and instead appears to show undue concern to appease the senior Pakistanis who granted him access to crucial materials. Nowhere is this clearer than where he chooses to dismiss the content of Jinnah's Karachi speech of 11 August 1947 by suggesting that Jinnah had 'simply forgotten where he was'.[180] As a serious analysis of a historic moment, this is surely inadequate. In a fit of forgetfulness Jinnah would hardly have presented a radical alternative to the staple political themes that had seen him through the previous decade. Nor was it a 'remarkable reversal',[181] and Wolpert must have known this. Five pages earlier he reports another speech by Jinnah, of less than a month before, in which all of the same themes about protection of minority rights, freedom of worship and equality of citizenship are included. Had Wolpert 'simply forgotten' what he had written? In belittling Jinnah's highly articulate address to the new nation, Wolpert comes very close to the line taken by General Zia ul Haq's government (1977–88), namely, that the 11 August speech, with its apparently liberal, secular themes, was 'a lapse' on the part of the Great Leader. There are many useful ways to explain what Jinnah said that day. Amnesia is not one of them.

From the point of view of consistency, the content of the Karachi speech cannot possibly have been an aberration. It not only reiterated ideas set out on 13 July in Delhi, but it also accords very closely with remarks Jinnah made on 21 May 1947,[182] and with a short speech he gave to the assembled party leaders at Viceregal Lodge in Delhi on 3 June, in which he stated that in the new Pakistan he intended 'to observe no communal differences'.[183] He only nodded his acceptance of Partition that day, but when it came to citizens' rights and the rejection of communal differences in the new Pakistan, he was vocal and definite.

Unless a substantial quantity of new source material comes to light, Wolpert's *Jinnah of Pakistan* will probably remain the standard popular work in the field. It is sympathetic to its subject but not slavish. Its main restriction is that it insists on foreshadowing impending doom at every step, from Gandhi's reception party in 1915 onwards, indulging in repeated unhistorical flights of fancy, such as asking whether Jinnah had 'his first premonition of Partition' in 1920 at Nagpur.[184] It also avoids delivering a satisfactory framework for Jinnah's motivations, and rests content to explain the apparent inconsistencies within his career by providing an extensive list[185] of around 18 possible factors, all general and most personal. This list starts with 'the cumulative weight of countless petty insults', then moves on to suggest, inter alia, 'Congress insults, stupidity and negligence', 'fatigue' and finally 'pride', although it is not clear whose pride it is. Wolpert opts for volume over accuracy and shirks clear explanation. In general, he seems to be trying to relieve Jinnah of responsibility for what he did, by showing him as a man more sinned against than sinning. As narrative the book is extensive, as history it is incomplete and indecisive.

There has been a strong desire in Pakistan, especially after 1977, to establish a clear line of Islamic succession from Jinnah to the present. This has led to the creation of a special discipline called 'Jinnah Studies'. The doyen of the subject is Professor Sharif al Mujahid, first director of Karachi's Quaid-i-Azam Academy, a government-backed institution founded in 1976. He wrote the benchmark *Jinnah: Studies in Interpretation* (1981), which first laid out the case for Jinnah's Islamic credentials.[186] Despite the Professor's efforts, no wider consensus has yet emerged about Jinnah's precise intellectual and political legacy. Other scholarly attempts to define the subject include *Quaid-i-Azam: Mohammed Ali Jinnah and the Creation of Pakistan*, by Sailesh Kumar Bandopadhaya, which focuses on a psychological interpretation of the Quaid,[187] and *Jinnah, Pakistan and Islamic Identity: The Search for Saladin* (1997) by Akbar S. Ahmed. This is a readable and entertaining book that wears its scholarship lightly. It is a good survey of the subject but of no great help in untangling Jinnah's thinking. Its main contribution is to talk up the role of Lady Edwina Mountbatten in the independence process, and to speculate at some length about her alleged affair with Nehru. Among the book's rather playful contentions is the idea that Edwina Mountbatten was 'Jewish'.[188] Edwina's maternal grandfather was a Jewish convert to Catholicism, which makes her a quarter Jewish at most – but her Jewishness is a necessary part of the author's explanation for Edwina's attraction to Nehru and her supposed sympathy with the Hindu-Indian cause, itself the result of Nehru's alleged characterization of Muslims as 'Nazis'. Despite its scholarly veneer, Akbar Ahmed's effort is inconclusive about the deeper workings of Jinnah's mind.

South Asians still feel compelled to write about Jinnah, and recent popular publications demonstrate that opinions are still deeply divided on the man. The most heralded of these was *Jinnah: India, Partition, Independence* (2009) by leading Bharatiya Janata Party member, Jaswant

Singh. He takes a highly critical line on Muslim political aspirations, with one eye very much on contemporary India, but he is surprisingly sympathetic in his assessment of Jinnah's personal qualities, setting small human failings against great political virtues. He is also prepared to place the blame for Partition not only on the Muslim League and the British, but on Congress leaders as well.[189] For blasphemies in the book against his own party's core beliefs, Singh was duly expelled from the BJP.

As a politician, Singh writes with insight about the difficult course of Jinnah's life. Unfortunately, this is rare, and amateur historians with more passion than skill are still regularly venturing into the field, producing works of ambitious revisionism, such as *Jinnah: Man of Destiny* (1999) by Prakash Almeida. Almeida's main contention is that Jinnah was somehow 'lost' to Indian nationalism, and the book is yet another example of the intellectual maze people can enter once they assume that Jinnah must somehow have 'changed'. According to Almeida, Jinnah could/should have been the great leader of an all-India state, but when he could not be, he chose to create Pakistan. Through the book, which is virulently biased against Lord Mountbatten, the discussion of Jinnah eventually becomes subsumed in a wider revelation that Partition was foisted on India as part of an (American) anti-Communist strategy to surround southern Russia with Islamic states. This produced Partition, regardless of whether anyone in India wanted it. If it had not been Jinnah, then the British would have found some other patsy to ask for Pakistan.

Detailed refutation of a book like this is largely futile. The numerous extraordinary claims it makes are partisan, under-researched and credulous. Nazi Germany, we discover, invaded Russia because Stalin 'refused to assist Hitler to attack India'.[190] The book's wider intention seems to be to relieve Indians completely of any responsibility for Partition, by showing reasons why the British somehow secretly wanted it all the time, and any evidence to the contrary must have been concocted.

Jinnah's career has attracted other exotic explanations, some of it even from academics, such as Professor M.N. Das. His *End of the British Indian Empire* sets out a detailed conspiracy between Churchill and Jinnah to create Pakistan, undertaken with the full knowledge and support of the British royal family.[191] The quite comical misunderstandings contained in this book are only exceeded by its extraordinary loopholes in logic. Churchill was out of government for the two years before Pakistan appeared, and he took no part whatsoever in the negotiations. Just because Churchill disliked Hindus does not mean that he loved Muslims so much that he wanted to destroy British India, which he considered the greatest overseas achievement of the British nation. And any theory that compensates for its almost complete lack of supporting evidence by claiming that an entire archive of Jinnah–Churchill correspondence has been deliberately destroyed does not deserve to hold our attention for long.

In the eyes of many it seems that Jinnah simply could not have been acting on his own behalf, but must have been doing the work of others. This is an untenable view, mainly because all his manoeuvrings are explicable in quite straightforward ways, and there is absolutely no sign of outside aid at any point. Quite the contrary. For long periods Jinnah was playing a lone and unpopular hand, even against some of his supposed allies.

His very evident liberalism has also been picked over by enthusiasts trying to turn him into a pioneer of Islamic government, such as Saleena Karim. Her *Secular Jinnah: Munir's Big Hoax Exposed* (2005) seeks to deny that Jinnah was a 'secularist', by discrediting an important quote used to support his secular priorities. This quote appeared in *From Jinnah to Zia* (1979) by Muhammad Munir,[192] and originally formed part of an interview given by Jinnah, on 21 May 1947, to an American reporter. In it Jinnah set out his vision of the new state of Pakistan, then only weeks away from its birth. The text seems to have been translated into and out of Urdu and then paraphrased (and misdated) by Munir. Saleena Karim believes that important subtleties of meaning were lost in this process, and proves her point about inaccurate translation very thoroughly. Her main revelations are that the word 'would' should have been rendered as 'will', and that the phrase 'a modern democratic state' should have been 'a popular and representative form of government'. The point of this meticulous analysis, though, is mainly to cast Munir as a dishonest man, the perpetrator of a 'hoax' and not the maker of a mistake. It then develops into a disquisition on Jinnah's Islamic intentions vis-à-vis the new state he was intending to create.

Jinnah, she claims, was always intending to build an Islamic state. As the main proof of his rejection of 'secularism' we are given the fact that he never uttered the word. Courageously, the author uses Jinnah's appointment of a Hindu to his first Cabinet as proof of his impeccably Qur'anic policies. She also allows herself the sweeping assumption 'that Jinnah's understanding of Islam was pragmatic, not religious'[193] – an obscure and unhelpful distinction that rather undercuts her central argument. However, it is close to the correct perception that Jinnah's understanding of Islam was primarily *political*. Throughout the book Jinnah's 'Islam' takes second place to Karim's. She refuses to discuss allegations that Jinnah was not a pious Muslim in his personal life, because 'this myth is slanderous and doesn't warrant a discussion'.[194] This is a jarringly weak argument alongside the book's general thoroughness. Could it be instead, that the mountain of evidence that Jinnah was no kind of pious Muslim in his habits is too inconvenient to deal with, and would spoil the neat picture the author has developed of his Islamic commitment?

Karim is also willing to claim ideas such as democracy, justice and the protection of minorities as Islamic concepts. Most would agree that they can be Islamic concepts, but they are hardly exclusively Islamic concepts. Arabic terms for them are not enough to establish exclusive ownership, and the problem remains that Jinnah might have come to any of these ideas via other routes than the Qur'an. If the definition of an Islamic state turns out to overlap so extensively with that of a liberal democracy, which appears to be the end result of the author's researches, then we are going to get precisely nowhere in defining where Jinnah stood on this issue.

Jinnah still fascinates writers; he also enrages them. For the case against Jinnah from a more liberal Muslim perspective we have *The Man Who Divided India* (2001) by Rafiq Zakaria, a prolific author who rendered distinguished service to the Indian Republic in the fields of politics, education and diplomacy. Zakaria takes an absolutely straight reading of Jinnah as a godless, ruthless, self-centred man who would stop at nothing till he had his own country to run. This version of Jinnah attributes no Qur'anic learning to him and portrays him as a man who enjoyed the blasphemous joke that his whisky-drinking made him a better Muslim than abstainers because it proved he had faith in the infinite mercy of God. Mullahs and maulanas bored and repelled him. He had nothing but contempt for the Muslim masses, referring to them as 'donkeys'. He was a rootless man, an outsider who shifted from platform to platform till he found unquestioning adulation and an open field for leadership. The text is littered with references to his arrogance, obsession, fanaticism and his 'monumental ego'. He hated Gandhi yet loved to be equated with him. Partition was his aim, his life's work and, in the end, his sole creation aided, the man boasted, only by 'his secretary and his typewriter'. Having built a Muslim homeland he then 'systematically discouraged every move to Islamize Pakistan'.[195] Jinnah, in this reading, was a very bad man who had very dark intentions.

Rafiq Zakaria has, it seems, collated all the available stories, accredited and unaccredited, that demonstrate Jinnah's rampant egomania. His points are not so much proved as paraded, rather like an endless line of Soviet rockets driven slowly past the reader's podium. Although the author can be absolved of any anti-Muslim bias, nevertheless by the time Jinnah is finally dead on page 170, one is forced to ponder whether the lack of balance is less in the deceased man than in the book.

The Gandhi Industry

Gandhi has been a much more popular subject for biography and analysis than Jinnah, compared to whom he is a safe option. There are literally thousands of books about the Mahatma, and they are generally positive in tone. This is because Gandhi-as-thinker can easily be extracted from his local context by foreigners, whereas Jinnah is of interest mainly to partisans or detractors of Pakistan. Gandhi was certainly a local politician with local aims, but he also took up issues that have a timeless, placeless feel to them. Almost all of his Indian causes can be converted into world causes – against poverty, tyranny and the evils of industrialization and its handmaiden, consumerism. His wider political creed was based on peace and love, ideas that are hard to oppose.

He also took up a great many themes of a more personal character, and his thoughts on sustainable living, thrift, diet, conciliation, personal devotion and self-respect have been echoed and amplified in thousands of books that now make up staple genres of the publishing industry, such as 'Self-Help', 'New Age' and 'Mind, Body, Spirit' literature. In these fields, even if you don't go to Gandhi, eventually he will come to you. This global Gandhi has become, in a sense, everyman's radical. Any kind of political protest movement can take lessons from him on mass mobilization and unarmed revolution; any kind of ecumenical outreach can find insights into toleration. Writers love Gandhi because almost anyone with a cause to promote – including vegetarianism, sexual abstinence, alcoholic prohibition, animal welfare, agrarian reform, dietary philosophy, alternative medicine, 'low tech' economics and rustic conservatism – can find something in his thinking to take for themselves.

This universality is only achieved at the expense of a certain selectivity, one to which Indians are rather less susceptible. The local view of Gandhi is much more varied. There were a large number of Indians, at the time, who opposed his politics in numerous ways, and many who took his religious views as a travesty of the Hinduism he claimed to profess.

Among the fiercest criticisms of Gandhi was contained in a relatively early assessment of his career. S.K. Majumdar, who never met the Mahatma, is strikingly caustic about the man in his *Jinnah and Gandhi: Their Role in India's Quest for Freedom* (1966). Majumdar opens by conceding that Gandhi was one of the greatest men who ever lived, but this tribute is soon followed by negative references to his 'boastful pride',[196] to his 'wishing to set up a Holy Gandhian Empire in India and to be its Pope',[197] and the accusation that he was 'a veritable destroyer who revelled in destruction'.[198] Majumdar believes that Gandhi had no vision for a modern India, and that Jinnah was a nationalist hero who stood up to Gandhi's 'authoritarianism' and 'obscurantism', but was driven out of the Congress. Gandhi then opened the door to Partition by wanting to crush all opposition within India, as a prelude to attempting 'to convert the whole world to the path of Gandhism'. This plan failed – twice: once with the Khilafat agitation and then again with the Quit India movement. This second attempt was a 'boomerang' that let the Muslims into power and allowed Jinnah to get Pakistan. Gandhi had the 'strategy of a Napoleon and the cunning of a Machiavelli',[199] but in the end his 'life's mission' to be a 'world saviour' was Jinnah's opportunity and India's undoing. Majumdar feels Partition was more Gandhi's fault than Jinnah's, and could be undone.

Majumdar bends all his material to serve his vivid and unconventional view of Gandhi as world conqueror in waiting. Spinning was the Mahatma's way to 'brainwash' his followers, and khadi was the 'battle dress of the "Swiss Guards"' of the Gandhian Papacy. Proof? That Gandhi liked to style himself 'Bapu', which is equivalent to the English 'Pope' (from Italian *papa* – father).[200] Gandhi did constantly refer to the world as if it were his parish, but this was because he thought of mankind as one and understood the spiritual instinct as a universal human dimension, not because he wished personally to become dictator of a world empire. All his other pronouncements on non-violence and the evils of tyrannical government should protect him from the charge that he was about to embark on a scheme of world conquest.

Majumdar feels let down by Gandhi and is not disposed to be kind about him, leading him to see a lust for power as Gandhi's main weakness. This draws him away from the standard criticisms of the Mahatma, which usually focus on his lack of realism or sound judgement. As a closely argued, negative critique of Gandhi-as-failed-dictator, Majumdar's book stands alone. It also serves as an object lesson in the dangers of trying to simplify history via selective quotation.

The most penetrating Indian criticism of Gandhi has always come from the left. M.N. Roy set out the basic argument in *Gandhism, Nationalism, Socialism* (1940), which accused him of taking a genuine mass revolutionary movement and handicapping it with exaggerated respect for social hierarchy, which blunted its impact and denied India a genuine popular democratic revolution.[201] This is a hard criticism to deflect because it relies heavily on a counterfactual assumption – that India would have had such a revolution if Gandhi had not refused to lead it on proper revolutionary lines. But this is really only to condemn Gandhi for not being a revolutionary socialist, which he certainly was not. He was in favour of social justice, but his general anti-consumerist stance took him away from the idea that equitable distribution of material goods was the royal road to happiness. Nor was he at all attracted to communism. In his idiosyncratic way he disliked it because of its obsession with secrecy.

Some on the left also contend that the British were always desperate to keep him in place as a leader, and alive during his fasts, in case someone more militant took his place. Gandhi, in this view, was an unsuspecting pawn of the British and a dupe of the capitalists, including Ambalal Sarabhai, Narottam Morarjee, Ganshyam Birla and Jamnalal Bajaj, who queued up to bankroll him. The conclusion is that Gandhi's prominence materially postponed the British departure, for which he can take no credit. Meanwhile he must take the blame for perpetuating the poverty of millions of Indians, condemned to live in an independent India run by landlords and industrialists.

The great historian of India's freedom struggle, R.C. Majumdar, was also very critical of Gandhi's non-violence, and discounted it as a factor in the winning of Independence. He set out a detailed argument to this effect in a lecture delivered in 1960,[202] pointing out that it was not Gandhi's non-violent mass movements that brought liberation. He quotes the Mahatma's concession that most Indians, even his Congress colleagues, did not understand non-violence, and his admission that so much had been attained 'even with our mixed non-violence'. Satyagraha was supposed to work by converting one's opponents; so, did the British attitude change? Majumdar sees no signs, and attributes the British departure to a series of global factors, and is even prepared to credit 'the humanity of British imperialism' before ahimsa as the bringer of Independence.

Gandhi's non-violence and his unconcern for strict religious norms have also prompted leaders of India's nationalist right to hack away at him to this day. V.D. Savarkar laid out this ground in the late 1920s and it has not greatly changed. During his lifetime Gandhi was mocked as a friend of Muslims – 'Mohammed Gandhi' – by a small ultra-nationalist Hindu clique, one of whose number eventually shot him. According to these zealots, Gandhi betrayed the martial tradition of Hindu warrior culture, as set out in the Mahabharata, and was insufficiently strict in his definition of 'Indianness'. Some modern nationalists blame him for not pushing harder, and speculate that the British could have been driven out earlier – with more bloodshed certainly – but that this would have been a price worth paying. They maintain that his failure to use his leadership to this end has permanently disadvantaged Hindu interests in the country, and allowed undesirable influences, both Muslim and Western, to gain undue prominence. Condemnation of his alleged reluctance to intercede for Bhagat Singh is still being strongly expressed in internet comment threads. For those who prefer their history tinged with glorious bloodshed, Gandhi will never be a satisfactory national leader. But he had no desire to leave behind a trophy mound of European skulls; he was not a man to make points by killing people.

A certain amount of sniping can be expected to continue from obscure vantage points for as long as the name of Gandhi still attracts the attention of the wider world. American writer Joseph Lelyveld has recently insisted that Gandhi was bisexual, at least for a short interlude in 1908.[203] This accusation is, of course, sensational, but it relies on very slender evidence, and its credibility depends on our willingness to see the Mahatma as a charlatan – a familiar Western reaction to the man, and one that requires the reader to ignore the whole of the rest of his long life and voluminous writings. Another recent book by an amateur Indian author was the result of 20 years spent scraping together enough material to 'prove' that Gandhi held racist views. This charge rests on his alleged contempt for black Africans, the odd unflattering reference to their backwardness and his apparent unconcern for their plight, but wilfully ignores all of Gandhi's voluminous writings on the oneness of humanity, the evils of racial pride, and so forth. To conclude that Gandhi was a racist on such selective basis is strange enough, but the logic of the book is rather obviously flawed from the outset, implying as it does that Gandhi was actually a *closet* racist – only revealed now by such skilful work. But if Gandhi knew that racism was wrong enough to need to hide it, how could his conscience permit him to do this? He was someone who willingly admitted to the tiniest failing, and if he thought something he said it; there was no dissembling in the man. So for the book to be correct, Gandhi's 'racism' would have to be the one deep belief he held but never avowed directly, because he knew it was wrong, and was therefore obliged to keep it under wraps, where he could not promote or act upon it. No wonder it took 20 years to make the case.

Non-Indian writers are generally much more indulgent towards Gandhi, especially those who actually met him. Louis Fischer, who spent time with him in 1942 and 1946, wrote *The Life of Mahatma Gandhi* (1950), a sympathetic and very readable account of the Mahatma's life and thought. Ronald Duncan, a British poet and playwright, spent time at the Sevagram ashram in the late 1930s and later edited a volume of selected writings by Gandhi with a fulsome introduction.[204] Professor Stanley Wolpert crops up here again too, with *Gandhi's Passion* (2001), an extended paean of praise from its author to the man who originally sparked his interest in India.[205]

Finally, perhaps the best recent interpretation of Gandhi as thinker and politician comes from Professor Anthony Parel, who edited and prefaced a centenary reprint of *Hind Swaraj* in 2009. Anyone who wishes to read a brief and lucid interpretation of Gandhi's political thought should seek out this slim volume.[206] What Parel has done, and done brilliantly, is to show how the link between the religious and the political Gandhi is entirely comprehensible, if only one starts at the right point. Parel lays everything out in precise Hindu terms, showing that Gandhi's political ideas bear only a superficial resemblance to the thoughts of Ruskin, Morris, Tolstoy or Thoreau. None of these thinkers meant anything to the Indian masses that followed him and who acclaimed him as an avatar and a saint. The reason they did so without the long explanations that Westerners required, and often still require, to understand him is because Gandhi was directly placing himself in a tradition of Hindu/Buddhist philosophy. All the ramified discussion surrounding him is reducible to his understanding of the four 'canonical aims' of life in the ancient Indian tradition: dharma (worship, spiritual duty), artha (the pursuit of power and worldly things), kama (sensual pleasure) and moksha (release, salvation, transcendence).

For Gandhi, politics was artha as a means towards moksha. Release, or self-realization, was both a political–nationalist cause and a personal–spiritual pilgrimage. This is the link. Gandhi's original contribution to Indian philosophy was in the way he insisted that the route to moksha was not through dharma – right practice, duty, obedience to religious precepts – but through artha – the pursuit of worldly power. The view that artha is not necessarily a form of degradation but could act as a dignified means to the end of moksha explains why Gandhi remained so uncontaminated by his political environment. He did not wish to indulge in politics for its own sake. For him, artha was to remain just artha; it was not to develop slyly into kama. *Hind Swaraj* is succinctly interpreted by Parel in these terms. The reacceptance of artha is for Parel a revolution, the greatest single development in Indian political thought since the Buddha.

Where ascetic Indian traditions tended to despise and mistrust kama, Gandhi concurred and this represents the most conservative part of his thinking. But he was also a radical in his attitude to dharma, which he did not regard in a technical or prescriptive way. This was very helpful in political terms and Gandhi did not think it disrespectful. It was this laxness that annoyed some traditionalist Hindus and lulled some Western observers into thinking that he was really some kind of Christian. It was simply that dharma was not a narrow thing for him, and he never sought to force the issue.

Gandhi was a renunciate pilgrim, hoping to become worthy of moksha through self-sacrifice and abnegation. His hope for India, then the world, was that others could share the revelation that artha was only one among the elements of life, that kama should be kept in check, and that dharma was not a matter of petty detail but of purity of heart. These elements made up his spiritual and political practice; all the rest is noise.

Jinnah: Lost and Found

Fringe critics of Jinnah sometimes find so many evil qualities within him that he appears to defy rational analysis. The only way out of this corner is then to label him as inconsistent or opportunistic. But there are ways to understand Jinnah without necessarily falling into blanket condemnation or uncritical praise. We can make a fruitful attempt if we simply bear three factors in mind – by temperament he was ambitious, by profession he was a barrister, by conviction he was a nationalist. It is the shifting ascendancy among these elements that motivated Jinnah the politician.

It is easy to see how Jinnah could rise to prominence. He cut an impressive figure, tall and serious. The younger Jinnah has been vividly drawn by Ian Bryant Wells in his *Ambassador of Hindu–Muslim Unity: Jinnah's Early Politics* (2005).[207] Wells shows how Jinnah's sharpness in debate, and his rather English habit of mixing up Parliamentary-style oratory with personal quips was not appreciated by other Indian public figures, who thought it aggressive and unmannerly. Above all, he was a man built for fighting causes, especially his own.

Jinnah was as ambitious as any politician anywhere, but ambition is not enough on its own to explain the whole dynamic of his 40 years in political life. Ambition is a staple in politics, affording no special insights into individuals, and Jinnah trod a more tortuous path than a man of uncomplicated ambitions would choose to follow. Although he approached the British to offer help and collaboration several times, it was always to enhance the general position of Muslims. When the approach was the other way around, and designed to promote British interests, he was quite clear. No less a person than Prime Minister MacDonald offered him a provincial governorship during the Round Table Conferences – but Jinnah indignantly refused.

Had he coveted government office he could easily have become a loyalist liberal; if he had simply wanted prominence among Muslims he could have allied with one of the established provincial leaders. Instead he spent many dismal years trying to broker difficult, detailed deals, especially through the 1920s. That period was significant. It drove him out of the established party system while leaving him dissatisfied with the constitutional provisions for Muslims.

The transformation in Jinnah, from the Indian nationalist of 1918 who confronted Governor Willingdon of Bombay with the Lucknow Pact in his back pocket to the communalist of 1938 who offered his services to the acting Viceroy, has always opened him to accusations of treachery and self-seeking. But this 'change' does not need to be reduced to a matter of baulked ambition. There were issues of principle at stake in Jinnah's move towards the Pakistan demand; the Muslims really were a minority in India, and Congress philosophy simply wished this fact into irrelevance.

The classic account of Jinnah's 'migration' relies on a supposed contrast between the early secular nationalist, 1906–20 'Congress' Jinnah, and the later communalist, 1934–47 'Muslim League' Jinnah. These two Jinnahs only look opposed if the Muslim factor is ignored.

The one major change that can truthfully be ascribed to him was the tactical decision, taken somewhere around 1937–38, to back the British as the most likely protectors of Muslim interests rather than the Congress. His explicitly religious attacks on the Congress were the result.

Throughout his career, his priority was the protection and promotion of Muslim interests. Other readings require us to believe the absurd idea that the early Jinnah ignored the Muslims of India only somehow to discover them and their needs in the late 1930s. They ask that we view the 'ambassador of Hindu–Muslim unity' as if he was not acting originally in Muslim interests, and only later took up their cause. To overdraw Jinnah at an early stage simply leads to errors of interpretation later. To exaggerate either his initial or his final position in Indian politics only serves to lengthen the journey he is supposed to have taken. We can easily read his journey as no more than a series of tactical adjustments, of which the last finally brought him what he wanted.

The one major decision that requires a detailed explanation is his leaving the Congress after the adoption of Non-Cooperation in 1920. The reason he did so was because the party had become a dead end for him, personally and politically. He knew he could not outrank Gandhi in the party's affections, but this need not be over-personalized. There were deep divisions between Gandhi and Jinnah on points of principle, and between Jinnah and the Congress on methods. And if Gandhi had died or retired, the organization would still have had a primarily lower-class Hindu membership. It was not just Gandhi; it was what Gandhi had done to the Congress that was at issue. From then on the party was never going to be an adequate vehicle for the protection of Muslim interests.

Jinnah never showed any willingness to return to the Congress leadership, and there is evidence that an element of personal resentment was involved – but not towards Gandhi. Jinnah's opposition to Non-Cooperation was actively encouraged by several senior Congress figures. Kanji Dwarkadas, an eyewitness, recounts how Jinnah was asked directly, by Motilal Nehru and others, to speak out against Gandhi on behalf of them all. Jinnah obliged, but Motilal and his supporters deserted him and voted with the platform on the day. This act of betrayal certainly isolated Jinnah among the Congress leadership and may have been a factor in his decision not only to leave but also not to rejoin.

After the Muslim position had twice been seen to be weak – in the splits of the late 1920s, and in the elections of 1937 – nothing less than a united Muslim front under a single leadership could have jolted the Congress out of its ideological unwillingness to recognize that a 'Muslim question' existed at all. From 1934 onwards, Jinnah was striving to establish his own standing, for he understood that only as an unchallenged leader could he get the deals he wanted, from either the Congress or the British. This was the ambition that drove him, and it was as much a tactical aim as a personal ambition.

Throughout the 1920s he refused to sign up to policies that he considered actively divisive. It took him a long time to come round to the full Two-Nation Theory. He certainly did not set off down that road in 1920. His method in the 1920s was to oppose the British when he thought it right to do so, while working to create some kind of Hindu–Muslim agreement that would bring more effective pressure to bear on the Raj. He was still living in 'one nation' till very late on, even referring to his belief in 'India for the Indians'[208] a year after the Lahore Resolution was passed. But he was firmly stuck with Two-Nation rhetoric by the time of his talks with Gandhi in 1944. By then his dual purpose, to find security for both himself and his community, had tied him up in his own dialectical knots. He could win all the points one by one, yet they were still not adding up to a neat solution. So no matter how well or how long he argued, he could not wish away the inconvenient truths of geography, nor reason away the enormous power of the Congress or how that power was regarded by the British.

Through the 1920s he remained committed to the traditions of the early nationalists, and it was in him that the spirit of Naoroji, Mehta and Gokhale survived. It was Gandhi who changed the Congress. This sort of thing goes on all the time in politics, and it is quite common to hear distraught politicians saying: 'I did not leave my party, my party left me. This is not the party I joined and I cannot stay in it.' This is exactly what happened to Jinnah – twice: firstly in the Home Rule League, then in the Congress, and it all but happened again in the Muslim League in 1928–29. Any full picture of him must include this aspect.

A major element in the confusion about Jinnah, and particularly the question of his 'consistency', is that there were three distinct phases in his mature career during which he was publicly addressing three different audiences. From 1913 to 1937 he was targeting the Congress, hoping to make an alliance against the British. During this time he thought that the advancement of Muslims interests was best served by the broad nationalist cause. In 1917, while still prominent in both all-India political parties, he issued an appeal: 'My message to the Musalmans is to join hands with your Hindu brethren. My message to the Hindus is to lift your backward brother up.'[209] With these words, Jinnah was directly exhorting Congress Hindus to share a self-governing India equally with their Muslim compatriots. But he never saw sufficient willingness to do this materialize. He made proposals; apart from the Lucknow Pact, they refused all of them. And the Pact was overtaken by events all too soon.

A second phase opened after 1937, in which he concentrated on the British in an attempt to make himself important, or useful, or at least *included.* With democracy and federation on the way after the 1935 Act it became necessary to convince the British of his case and of his credentials, because the Congress would not support him. Real power continued to lie with the British, and Jinnah's constant offers of loyalty and support were aimed at getting the best deal for Muslims out of the still-benign British. The Congress seemed determined to give him nothing.

Finally, from 1947 to 1948 he addressed the population of Pakistan, especially regarding the new Constitution. This is where his Islamic ideas appeared, as part of a newly opened debate within a country that had been set up on a virtually blank political programme.

Mixing up these three phases is bound to produce confusion, and will simply support the idea that Jinnah was unprincipled. His central aim remained constant, but his rhetoric and his tactics naturally changed with the environment in which he found himself. In all cases he was addressing the most important elements in the situation as he understood it.

The central core of consistency this reveals can also partially acquit him of the charge of egomania, because his career demonstrates that he believed in the representative principle and had a good grasp of what representative politics meant. In or out of the Congress, he spent his entire political career representing Muslims. Throughout he put forward views, especially through the 1920s, that were a reflection of wider Muslim concerns – on separate electorates and federalism for instance. He disliked the unrepresentative nature of the Muslim deputation to Lord Minto in 1906, and of the Raj in general. He withdrew from national politics after the second Round Table Conference in 1931 because he felt he had no support.

The relentless pumping up of Jinnah's negative characteristics only explains the Pakistan story if he is also granted an extraordinary power to turn wishes into reality. Such power he plainly did not have. Instead he made the best of what he did have, which was often little more than his native wits. Thus he always preferred to talk up the various problems that made the creation of Pakistan a pressing necessity rather than to discuss its precise details. As a politician he repeatedly placed himself in the privileged position of defining the question without ever adequately supplying an answer. The British saw him as a man who had got a long way by saying 'no' so often, but his negative stance was an ideal strategy for a man in a weak position who had carved out little more than a recognition that his views must be considered. He was much more trapped within circumstances than either his supporters or detractors admit. He worked very hard to get what power he could, yet it was still not enough to get him all that he asked for. Like the Pope, Jinnah had no divisions.

Even his friends sometimes prefer to rewrite his motivations rather than to accept him as he was. His most enthusiastic admirers like to insert Islamic ideals into his mission, despite the fact that all of his most extended and detailed statements are on the secular side. No matter what sympathetic remarks Jinnah may have made about Islam in his later years, those wishing to sacralize him will have to produce a masterpiece of special pleading to talk away all his liberal political statements.

It is almost impossible, on examining Jinnah's life, habits and writings, to find any grounds to assert that he was in any way an observant Muslim. In November 1939 he said on All-India Radio that he thought John Morley's *On Compromise* was indispensable reading for young people, but he never took any similar opportunity to recommend the Qur'an. This is an uncomfortable thought for those who can only see him moving in a straight line towards the demand for and creation of a separate, 'Islamic' state. Any such line can only ever be in the eye of the beholder. His main priority was to better the lives of Muslims by removing Hindu domination, not by imposing Islamic domination. Islam would come to a community of Muslims anyway, reinforced or not. His standard line was that Muslims would be 'free' in Pakistan and he repeatedly contrasted the dignified liberty enjoyed by Muslims with the restrictive nature of traditional Hindu social practices.

This issue has become clouded because before Partition his rhetoric was frequently anti-democratic. This was for two rather obvious reasons, neither of which is that he thought democracy incompatible with Islam. He needed to reject 'democracy' because that was what he was going to get in a post-British Greater India, and he did not want it. Therefore he had to put some distance between the idea of democracy and the need for Pakistan. This argument could be reinforced after 1939 by pointing to the global war and ascribing it to the 'failure' of democracy, which was a standard line used by anyone seeking to establish an extra-constitutional connection to the masses at that time. Furthermore, democracy, as he had seen it working in India, produced anomalies and distortions related to the structure of Indian society. For elections to have any meaning it must be assumed that there might be a different result from time to time. Jinnah could see that a communal, semi-literate, traditional society like the India of his era would never effectively change its collective mind sufficiently on any issue, whether divided into communal electorates or not. Clinging to separate electorates was clearly no way out of this stasis, and neither Jinnah, nor most other Muslims, had the courage to trust a general electorate to which politicians could appeal by promoting policies with the general welfare in mind. India has vote banks to this day, even with open electorates, and Jinnah was not prepared to live in an India like that, stranded in a permanent minority.

In wanting to move out of such a system Jinnah did not require an obligatory Muslim environment to receive his people. The move away from unwelcome domination – the negative agenda – was the crucial element. Where the idea got away from him was that the move to Pakistan could be presented as positive by sections within Muslim society, and Jinnah, as a shrewd politician, was not inclined to suppress this helpful tendency. But he himself, personally, did not need to have any strong feelings on the subject at all. This is the flaw within 'Jinnah Studies'. Jinnah as a critic of democracy deserves some attention; Jinnah as protector of Muslims – his people – is a recognizable figure; Jinnah as an advocate for the necessity of Islamic government is a chimera.

It is no easy matter to fit Jinnah into a wider Islamic context. He said a lot about Two Nations but very little about Islamic government, even if Qur'anic principles, such as justice and equality, can be found within his words. At the time, most scholarly assessments of his thought openly condemned it for being insufficiently Islamic, or for not being recognizably Islamic at all. The 'smoking gun' that would definitively place Jinnah somewhere in the matrix of Islamic ideas has yet to be found, and for every text or phrase taken to prove his Islamic credentials there are others to discount them. He was, for instance, a redoubtable advocate for the political rights of women. Above all, his actions simply will not bear the weight of a consistent religious interpretation. He seems to have made no effort to define or declare his Islamic agenda, and once in power he took no trouble to push through a religious programme. Granted he was ill at the time, and granted there were other calls on his attention, but if we can see no religious activity then it is hard to justify the assertion that Jinnah was a religiously motivated politician. As a religious leader his qualifications are essentially lacking in both word and deed.

Jinnah went into politics as an optimistic liberal. The young man who first attended a Congress session in 1904 was a bright and confident man, idealistic and broadminded. He was not just a rising star, he was arguably *the* rising star of the Congress. His hopes were for national self-government, a place at the top for himself, and economic and educational advancement for all Indians, with Muslims fully included. The optimist in him clung on to all of these hopes for freedom and advancement until the late 1920s. He worked extremely hard in and around the legislative assembly; on its committees, where he brought forward schemes and proposals, and behind the scenes, where he constantly tried to make personal contacts and alliances with prominent political figures, up to and including viceroys. Finally, by late 1929 all of these fronts were lost. The optimist at this point was not dead but only defeated, and was sparked back into life in 1934, when hopes of new leadership opportunities and a new Constitution brought Jinnah back to India. But the optimist seems to have died by 1938.

Jinnah had a complex personal and social nature, but he seems to have had a good understanding of the theoretical differences between himself as a private individual, his identity as a Muslim, and his overriding Indianness. He referred to these distinctions in his speeches: 'I am an Indian first and a Muslim afterwards'[210] (1931); 'I still remain a nationalist'[211] (1939). He was least of all a bigot in his private dealings. He had a coterie of Hindu friends throughout his life. However, within politics he gradually began to equate 'political' Hinduism, or at least Hindus in politics, with intolerance and unfair dealing. The Pakistan cause became completely associated in his mind with justice; it was right, it was necessary. Eventually he was unable, in practical political terms, to unpick his interests as a politician from his role as spokesman for the Muslim community. It would seem to be this confusion, above all, that led him into the eventual reality of Partition.

It has been suggested that for Jinnah Pakistan was actually more of a principle than a country, less of a rigid demand and more of a tactical 'ante', which had to be acknowledged before any serious discussion could begin. If negotiations had proceeded in a reasonable fashion and his general demands were attended to, then the full, real Pakistan need never have come to life. In the end it was about 'natural' equality, about levelling the playing field.

This is a pretty argument and has been adopted, among others, by Professor R.J. Moore.[212] The trouble with it is that this is simply not what Jinnah said, not even in the speeches referenced by Moore. Jinnah on the platform was always definite and assured. He was quite clear in April 1941 that he absolutely would not share 'one central government' with the Hindus. He explicitly denied that Pakistan was 'a bargaining counter' and he asserted that Muslims would 'if necessary, die' for the cause of Pakistan.[213]

So, it seems that we must either do Jinnah the discourtesy of believing that he did not mean what he said – that he would have Pakistan and nothing else – or that he did not say what he meant – that he was just setting out a negotiating position. But there is no need to be so clear-cut. There are ways to make coherent sense of the political position if we choose to accept Jinnah as a politician, not as some second Moses upon whom we must impose a burden of superhuman consistency, prescience and infallibility.

In 1940 he knew perfectly well that he would have to enter complex three-sided negotiations to obtain Pakistan, and that these could not start in earnest till the war was over. At that time he was more concerned that the Congress would do a deal with the British – he said so in May 1940.[214] To stop this, he set out a clear demand at Lahore that could not be ignored. Jinnah, we need to remember, was very much the weakest player in the game. Tactical considerations would suggest that a sovereign Pakistan was not his only possible objective, or the least he would accept. Jinnah must have known that once he had entered a bargaining process, all his positions would need to develop a degree of fluidity, especially since he was not in a position of strength. Or, to put the contrary case, Jinnah would have been ill advised to declare at the start: 'I will have Pakistan and nothing else, and that, gentlemen, is my bargaining position.'

The key to resolving this impasse is that the Pakistan demand was more flexible than it seemed, rather than a pure bluff or some kind of ritual prelude to the hard pounding. Jinnah *did* mean it, and he was preparing for all eventualities by remaining nimble with his definitions. He would not be pinned down until he had been taken seriously, that is, until he was recognized as the sole Muslim spokesman, sitting in substantive talks with proper authorities in a constructive, post-war situation. Until then there were elements of the detailed demand that changed. Jinnah was not in the same position during the Cripps Mission of 1942 as he was four years later. He was prepared to accept a limited form of Dominion Status in 1942 but he had moved on by 1946, as his strength had grown, and by then he wanted a full Dominion of his own. The point is not that he never wanted a separate political entity for Muslims, because he clearly did, and it would have suited all his purposes if he had got it. It was the precise details that were negotiable. He was very aware of the potential economic and military disadvantages of being given a small independent country, and he was therefore prepared to countenance some kind of loose federation with Hindustan. He did not want to wreck India, or lay claim to a blighted inheritance.

But he would not be locked into any system with a permanent Hindu majority. There is no mystery, unless we insist on viewing him as a robotic machine that endlessly demanded Pakistan in one form only, or as a devious careerist who would take any settlement that assured him of a large office and a fat salary.

Jinnah can be seen, if we allow him at least the virtue of sincerity, as an extraordinary and unique individual. He was a nationalist leader who actually invented his own nation. His was the first nation ever that any person could join simply by acknowledging its founding beliefs. Most of the nationalist struggles in the world have been based on old, or allegedly old, forms of ethnicity. Whether there really is a 'Serb' identity or what exactly 'Irishness' means are debatable subjects. There are people today trying to invent nationalist struggles based on the concept of 'African-ness', so Jinnah seems relatively modest in choosing Islamic heritage within India as a basis for nationality.

But his calling was not as a philosopher, his greatest virtues were principally those of an advocate, of a man who championed a principle. He shaped one particular political demand by talking it into being, but he seemed to have only a dim understanding of its wider implications. If he understood more he said nothing about it and offered no firm guidance on the absolutely vital further issues he was effectively raising. He did little to define his new country, before or after its creation, and it may well be that the relatively unoriginal and persistently negative cast of his mind was only really fit to oversee the basic initial act of separation.

The only cause that seemed to move him throughout his life was to ensure the protection and development of his own community. He never developed any vision much beyond these basic requirements. Call this 'justice', as he often did, and we can join up the lawyer, the advocate and the Muslim in him, and allow that he simply sensed a potential danger, alerted his people and argued their case. He did not seem to see his role as giving them much, if any, further guidance. As a leader he had a strong sense of direction but a weak imagination about the details of his destination. As a Moses figure he saw the promised land, but lacked commandments. Perhaps, rather than The Great Leader, he should more appropriately be revered as The Great Advocate – Wakil-i-Azam. This might make it clearer that, simply put, he was more of a great leader *to* Pakistan than a great leader *of* Pakistan.

The final move to Partition was not his sole work, and indeed he can be seen to be fighting against it until the very last. He could have lived as a Muslim Indian within India, as he had done all his life. That this option was finally removed was not only his doing. He bears a great responsibility for that removal because he had been seen to demand it eloquently and persistently over many years. But he would probably have settled for less, had he been given the chance.

He has frequently been cast as the Bad Fairy in the nursery of the Indian Union, but this portrayal is a caricature. Sadder analogies spring to mind. He was perhaps the apple that shrivelled on the tree, the milk that soured in the bottle, the favoured son who never inherited a promised bequest.

Gandhi: In the Round

The puzzle, when it comes to Gandhi, is not whether he meant what he said or what exactly his political objectives were, but how it was that a man who paid such scant attention to the norms of politics and who pursued a range of other-worldly aims, could ever have taken on the honorary leadership of an entire nation and been allowed to bargain with the holders of enormous conventional power.

A man like Gandhi would have been unlikely to succeed in politics anywhere other than India. His unwillingness to submit to party discipline, his insistence on the supremacy of conscience, his apparent scorn for traditional 'big power' elements of government – all this would have disqualified him from senior political rank in most other countries in the twentieth century. He would have been a reluctant runner in any race for preferment, and his adoption of absolute moral positions would have hampered him in the development of practical policy. He was an unconventional politician even by Indian standards, but it was only in India that his voice could have become so powerful, in a land that could make room in its concept of modernity for a man regarded as a living saint.

But it is misleading to think of India too broadly in this context. Specifically, it was British India that made him the figurehead he eventually became. By restricting the scope of political activity within a country as populous as India, the British simply forced political activity out into the streets and fields, areas where there was a public receptive to moral righteousness combined with direct action. The

British thus handed him the wonderfully powerful gift of mass Non-Cooperation, a potentially much more effective tool of opposition than any Parliamentary grouping.

The British did not directly create Gandhi, but once he appeared they had no conventional means to combat him. Jinnah they could deflect and neutralize because he was more than willing to stand in panelled rooms and orate, or sit in subcommittees and argue. This he did throughout the 1920s and the British were happy to keep him at it. To Gandhi they could offer nothing, and he used this to his advantage. Once he became prominent, the British had to remain wary of how they treated a man with such moral authority and such massive public appeal. But they also had an interest in not displacing him. As long as he preached non-violence he seemed a better leader to face than one who preached violence.

Granted that he was unconventional, but we are still obliged to ask: Was there any real coherence in Gandhi's political vision, or was it just cobbled together in whimsical or pragmatic ways, designed to appeal in any particular moment to as many ignorant and excitable people as possible? This harsh assessment was certainly a British view, but it coincided with Jinnah's. On 30 October 1920, before the adoption of Non-Cooperation by Congress, Jinnah wrote to Gandhi saying:

> Your methods have already caused split and division in almost every institution that you have approached hitherto, and in the public life of the country not only amongst Hindus and Muslims but between Hindus and Hindus and Muslims and Muslims and even between fathers and sons; people generally are desperate all over the country and your extreme programme has for the moment struck the imagination mostly of the inexperienced youth and the ignorant and the illiterate.[215]

The British liked to point out that the 'non-violent' protests sponsored by Gandhi were sometimes extremely violent. The hartal of 30 March 1919 featured the immolation of a Gujarati magistrate in Ahmedabad, and hundreds were to die in the Mahatma's three great protest movements. Gandhi's apparent refusal to accept responsibility for these lapses infuriated many British officials, who felt that he was purveying moral platitudes while deviously absolving himself of responsibility every time there was mayhem. He turned on the tap of disorder then walked away from the mess, without acknowledging that he really had no control over what befell the country in the meantime. As Governor Frederick Sykes put it: Gandhi's 'most dangerous habit was that of shutting his eyes to inconvenient realities.'[216]

It would have been extraordinary if the non-violent protests had been peaceful everywhere and at all times. The best that can be said is that where Gandhi or his main disciples were involved, the protests were non-violent, as at the Dharasana Salt Works. And it is not entirely true that he absolved himself of responsibility for death and destruction; he frequently punished himself by fasting, although as Sykes was ready to point out, a three-day fast was 'a somewhat inadequate penance'[217] for the murders of 30 March 1919. His notions about non-violence were dissected and ridiculed by the British on many occasions, and it was hard for him to keep a truly consistent line. He declared the armed Polish resistance to Nazi invasion in 1939 to be 'non-violent' because the Nazis were the aggressors, and the Poles were outnumbered. Of course, British critics had a field day with that statement, relating it directly to the perilously outnumbered situation in which the Raj subsisted. In an interview of September 1931, Gandhi appeared to contemplate with equanimity the potential bloodshed that would follow upon a British withdrawal, with the prospect of fighting between 'factions' and 'even whole provinces'. His willingness to say these sorts of things is a testament to his political honesty. It had its origins in his general indifference to death, but it tended to make him look irresponsible, even crazed, to British officials, who were well aware of the potential for disorder in India and were terrified of its possible consequences. Gandhi, by contrast, seemed insouciant.

But for all his quirks, he was not unconcerned about governability. His radicalism had political limits, and he was always specific in his use of resistance. He never raised revolt against taxation as a general principle; it was only against unjust, specifically British, taxation. He did not want to make it impossible for a future Indian government to levy taxes on its own population.

Nor, ideally, did he want the British to hand over a country in chaos, although he did actually say as much to assembled Congressmen at a private briefing in May 1942. His words that day got out and were widely quoted – 'Give us chaos. I say, in other words, leave India to God'[218]– and as often misunderstood. He wanted to be rid of the British and their war, along with all the exploitation and repression it was bringing. He did not mean he wanted to dissolve Indian society. His faith in 'the Congress mind' allowed him to see the potential chaos that might follow a British withdrawal as a small matter that would be overcome by free Indians without undue difficulty. He also believed that the end of British rule would also bring an end to the war, because the Japanese did not want to fight Indians – they wanted to fight the British, and they could then do so elsewhere. Accepting what he called 'the gift of anarchy'[219] from the British would be the best course, but he was not expecting to live in anarchy; nor did he want to. The whole sarvodaya project for self-realization and spiritual improvement in which he had invested his life's energies was designed to create a better kind of political and social stability. He had no desire to live in anarchy; no one can enjoy the fruits of spiritual fulfilment amid banditry. Nor did he think that anarchy would be what resulted if the British left. His faith in humanity, and in particular the genius of India, would re-order society, and for the better.

However, his apparent unconcern for bloodshed does require a little explanation. His beliefs tended to blunt his concern about potential fatalities, and he was always at pains to stress that it was braver and more virtuous to be killed than to kill. His creed of non-violence could make him seem curiously resigned to the prospect of Indians dying, and much more concerned about them becoming killers. If blood was to be shed, then let it be 'our own', he told the Nagpur Congress in 1920.[220] This he seemed to consider an integral part of yajna – sacrifice – something he referred to all through his life. In the run up to Partition he referred to having to 'go through the fire'.[221] Purification in the cause of higher goals remained his ideal.

By its nature, the entire Gandhian project was oppositional, not governmental. It relied on the idea that if men are good then government is unnecessary. He concurred in the classic liberal doctrine that the government that governs least governs best. He did not want to wish away every state role, but he envisaged that a minimal state would be required for the ruling of good, reformed people. Before 1919 he thought that the British Empire allowed him the most personal freedom among the models on offer and he supported it for its principles, not its practice. He then radically revised that view during the run up to Non-Cooperation and remained opposed to British rule in all its forms from then on.

Rebel though he was, there was always a sense of forbearance about his opposition. Violence and division worked against love, unity and truth, and this general view always set him against confrontation, something that to this day inclines revolutionaries and radicals against him. But he did not wish to win arguments so much as to dissolve them. In a sense, this made him a better leader of the nationalist opposition than Bose, because he took care to reflect back the failings of British rule rather than to construct a speculative vision of Indian superiority – as if his battle cry were: 'We can do better than this.' He made no promises about what the new India would be like, although he was convinced it would be more in tune with its traditions. This made him a conservative, pacifist nationalist and guaranteed that he would earn the contempt of the Bose school with its revolutionary militarism.

In the end, Gandhi did the least possible to set Indians against the British and, most importantly, the very least he could to set Indians against each other. He always strove for a unitary opposition, which is why Jinnah's separatism, and Ambedkar's, troubled him so deeply. All Indians should oppose the British, he thought, and the more we stand together the less we will have to fight. The final achieving of independence was free from state-sponsored violence, and for that he can take much credit.

Gandhi became a great popular leader, but he cannot truly be described as a democrat, because he was not particularly concerned about whether people agreed with him or not, or whether his ideas were widely supported. His conceptions of right and wrong were strong enough to push such thoughts away. In his own mind he spoke for the people – the 'dumb millions' – because he had taken the time to learn what their lives were like. Combine this knowledge with his intuitive feel for moral probity and you do not get a democrat but a leader who actually leads and does not follow the opinions of others as a 'representative' democrat would. He saw himself as a guide, as a man who pointed out the best road but could not compel anyone to travel down it. None of his exhortations to purer living were compulsory. Those that could should follow his precepts; those that could not were not condemned.

This attitude leads us into his highly eclectic version of religion. Unlike most people religion didn't go into him, it came out of him. He did his very best to exemplify and illustrate his ideals. The moral law, truth, non-violence, loving kindness – all these were the same. These were things he *did*. They were the only aims he thought it worth living for. He refused to be a 'slave' to things he did not understand, or could not defend. As a religious attitude this is surprisingly practical and anthropocentric, or even egocentric, rather than spiritual, traditional or authoritarian. He picked up what he wanted from wherever he could find it. He thought of Hinduism as the great repository of all the world's religious wisdom, and that all things of value and substance would be found within it. However, he was quite prepared to see those elements in other faiths.

There was a deep interconnection in Gandhi's vision between the concepts of God, truth, unity and the soul – for him, these were all one. This is a recognizable philosophical position within the Western tradition, but it is a deeply emotional connection in Hinduism, and it is this connection that made Gandhi, above all, a Hindu. Christians frequently commented on his ethical high-mindedness and thought they recognized it as Christian; but it was not. The Christian view of these issues is very different and stems from a God–Man distinction that is so complicated that not even Christians can explain it fully. Hindus have a simpler, more intuitive view.

Gandhi's ethics were not Christian. To think that they were is either chauvinistic, or to look at the flower and not the root. When he listened to his inner voice he was literally consulting God – within him. No orthodox Christian would put it quite that way. And the idea of unity in all things was what drove so much of his political thinking. India was one; we as humankind are all one. Violence is division and disorder; it comes from the flesh and not the spirit. Giving in to the flesh – be it sexual desire or craving for material things – is sin. The urge to consume and accumulate is sinful; it is to ignore the force of truth and love we hold inside ourselves. Salvation comes not from God having died for us all, as Christians believe, but from a struggle within ourselves, to perceive the truth and to find the strength to follow its voice fearlessly. This was a religious view, but it was the wellspring of all Gandhi's politics.

The resistance to oppression, the courage not to collaborate with one's oppressor, the self-reliance of swadeshi, the self-discipline of spinning, the refusal to sink into lust and the consequent ability to turn one's love towards the rest of the world – all these concepts added up to a political programme of self-government and rural, decentralized self-sufficiency, non-violence and chastity. All this led to spiritual elevation. Gandhi was not starting from the same points as the Western politicians who misunderstood him. For example, his interview with Benito Mussolini in 1931 lasted about 10 minutes. It would be difficult to imagine what the two men found to talk about that could have detained them even that long. If Gandhi had tried to 'convert' the Duce then the interview might have lasted weeks, but minds such as Mussolini's are not renowned for their receptiveness, and perhaps neither man developed much interest in prolonging the meeting.

Sometimes the question arises as to whether Gandhi was really a Hindu. He himself publicly denied it at the Second Round Table Conference. 'Not Hindu,'[222] he said firmly when described as such. But in this specific case he meant he was primarily an Indian, and thus more than a Hindu, while also making the point that untouchables, too, were more than the religious affiliation ascribed to them. If Gandhi can be allowed the last word on what he actually was, in 1924 he wrote that 'every fibre of my being is Hindu'.[223]

But our picture of him can become blurred if we listen too closely to everything he said. He was quite mischievous with descriptions of himself. His evident irony in referring to his 'dictatorship' during the Khilafat period opened him up to criticism from those determined to see the worst in him. He called himself 'an anarchist' in his address to the students of Benares in 1916,[224] which caused a stir because the word was associated with bomb-throwing at the time; he meant he was a freethinker. He even once described himself as 'a dacoit' in his Gujarati language paper, *Navajivan*. He meant he was opposing the government, but there is an unsubstantiated story that he soon received a letter from a real dacoit, offering to join forces with him to further their criminal careers together.

He was certainly more a Hindu than anything else. He believed that to melt into the ocean of existence is to find both oneself and God. To do this one must follow the path of the good, because God is truth and goodness. He enumerated the reasons he considered he was an orthodox, or sanatani, Hindu in the pages of *Young India* in October 1921.[225] These were: his acceptance of the orthodox canon of scripture (the Vedas, Upanishads, etc.), his belief in dharma bestowed by caste, his advocacy of cow protection and his acceptance of idol worship. He could hardly have been clearer.

Fasting was another aspect of his twin religious and political nature. It was not only a recognized form of devotional behaviour – even in Christianity – but, as dharna, it was also a traditional form of Indian coercion; any man with a grievance was allowed to sit at his oppressor's door and refuse food until he had been granted redress. The British loathed this tactic and considered it a type of moral blackmail, which it was. But in a wider Indian religious perspective it was acceptable because ultimately the only sufferer was the one refusing the food.

Moral force and a clear grievance were traditional elements of dharna, but Gandhi, by using his national prominence, added the full public gaze. If he had threatened to starve himself to death as an obscure mendicant then no one would have batted an eyelid. It was the status he had carefully accumulated that magnified and intensified the act. After all, people starved to death in India on a fairly regular basis. 'Old man dies in starvation incident' would not have been much of a headline in any Indian newspaper. But 'Mahatma dies in protest!' would. Of course, the expected result of Gandhi's death by self-denial was not simply one cremation; it would have been thousands of deaths from protests all over India. This was what the British hated so much. It was the connection between Gandhi and the masses, linked by bonds of great simplicity, that gave him such power out of such seemingly flimsy material. If anyone understood the power of solidarity in numbers, it was Gandhi.

Muslim writers have regularly painted Gandhi as a Hindu partisan, but he was not an advocate of denominational divisions or distinctions, and particularly not of sectarian bigotry. Again and again he went among irate and grieving communities who found themselves at the heart of communal violence in the run-up to Partition, begging all sides to lay down their arms and not to kill their neighbours. Some of his precepts were in fact anathema to orthodox Hindus. He was keener on goats than cows, because he felt that the overemphasis on cows was actually unfair to the wretched animals themselves, encouraging poor conditions and over-milking, which killed them 'by inches'.[226] He was utterly and implacably opposed to the practice of untouchability, which traditionalist Hindus positively approved of as a required element in any properly constituted Hindu society. Above all, he valued goodness above socially approved piety.

Salvation mattered to him, but not in the Christian sense. He believed that salvation, or union with God, was attainable, but that it came from self-denial, rejection of sensual gratification, inner discipline and selfless service to others. Where Christians emphasize the gift of grace, Gandhi saw only the obligation to work for the benefit of his fellow man. This made his concept of salvation into a political mission. He believed in salvation in the sense of saving everybody, not just himself. This took salvation away from personal doctrinal beliefs, and allowed him to wrest moral superiority out of Western hands, where the pale conquerors of India imagined it remained after God had spoken on the battlefield. Gandhi constantly showed up this vaunted superiority by emphasizing Indian virtues of abstinence, renunciation and suffering, unified in the concept of sacrifice. Neither good, nor even better government could counter this level of criticism.

The best way towards salvation, he believed, was ceaseless prayer. Prayer was self-improvement and was a constant comfort to him, especially in prison; prayer was 'the key of the morning and the bolt of the evening'.[227] Prayer was a way to hear the 'inner voice' that told him what to do, for he claimed he had no foresight, 'not the ghost of a suspicion' how his schemes would work out. That was a matter for God, who controlled these situations. To imagine that you, as a human being, could control the outcomes of earthly schemes would be to lose oneself, to 'come to grief'. The Gita teaches that man is the maker of his destiny by his choice of actions, but no man can control the results of those actions. God could be established and perceived through reason, but divine knowledge was primarily the sphere of the heart. Gandhi was very emotional and he equated emotion with divine action. This is what made him a philosopher of practical action.

Practicality was simply one end of the processes he felt he was engaged in. At root he completely believed in the interconnectedness of the entire world and the wider universe, in the realm of the invisible. This lifted him way off the rational, scientific plane, and he lived most of his mental life up there. He absolutely believed that the Bihar earthquake of 1934 was a punishment from God for the sins of Indians – specifically the practice of untouchability. This was not just colourful language or a device to motivate ignorant peasants, it was an entirely real and appropriate connection to him. He believed that celibacy, the rule of Brahmacharya, was not only good for society, in that it made more love available for all, but he also thought that in some way it gave him, personally, greater spiritual power. This was somehow linked with bodily fluids and sexual energy, and it was to enhance and energize these fluids and forces that he took to sleeping naked with various young female disciples.[228]

Modern biographies often concentrate on these practices too sensationally and without sufficient context,[229] and there has been a great deal of aggressive and unsympathetic treatment of Gandhi and his attitudes to sex. Essentially he was an anti-sensualist, appalled by the easy route to self-gratification offered by so much of human culture, and painfully conscious of his own struggle to resist it. He identified his personal inner space as the battleground of this struggle on the widest scale, with his own internal condition deeply tied to the fate of India. Only when he had purified himself would he be worthy and able to lead, so it was of vital importance that he developed absolute self-control. This was a form of egoism certainly, but we must remember that Gandhi believed absolutely that moral struggle was waged inside individuals. If he could not overcome his lower nature, then how could he expect others to?

This was all part of his self-consistent view that everything – personal and public, physical and moral – was interconnected, a view that included his belief that bodily illness was either a punishment from God for sin or a secondary result of straying away from the natural balance of Nature. Since Nature, God and truth were all the same to him, this should not come as a surprise. He was therefore as 'cranky' in this as any Christian Scientist, but without the 'science' or the Christianity. His constant talk of God and sin was not a garnish on his politics; it was his politics that were the garnish.

Conventionally, the political sphere is concerned with crude externals, while spiritual matters are much less visible or tangible. But for Gandhi the two elements always had to be there, for without a proper regard for truth within the whole there could be no meaningful parts.

In sum, he was an archaic, obscurantist, spiritual creature. This is the key to joining up so much of the alleged inconsistency we can read into his words or see in his actions. The utter self-possession his beliefs gave him, and the way this manifested itself as unpredictable egoism was completely real and integral to the wider beliefs he held. When he fasted he really thought that he, personally, must do penance. No one else's suffering would do. The inner voice inside him really was God. Indians responded to his political leadership, and that leadership was based on the self-confidence that this spiritual infrastructure gave him. There was not a trace of Western thinking inside him, a feature that Indians know and recognize, but which his Western admirers do not often acknowledge.

This then, was the substance of the passionate statesman and public figure. A certain coldness, however, haunted his personal family life, much as it did Jinnah's. The pressures of public life can often be a great strain for close relatives, as can very high moral example. Gandhi's close family and his intimate circle were open to both stresses, suffering by their proximity to a man of enormous fame, rarefied principle and moral severity. Being hard on oneself is difficult but it has a compensatory glow of achievement. Expecting the same high standards of one's close kin may be to impose, even if most gently and indirectly, a standard of conduct on them that they may not be able to attain. In this area, leading can sometimes be easier than following.

Gandhi's frictions with his four sons are well known but no less easy to explain for all that. He denied Manilal and Harilal the opportunity to pursue a professional education, such as he had had; why, we do not know. He may have been keen to avoid the perils of nepotism, or simply concerned that he would be viewed as a hypocrite for his fierce criticism of 'Western' professions if he allowed his own kin to join them. He also fought with his sons over his dislike of early marriage, by which he meant at any time before the age of about 30. Again, this was to deny to others what he had enjoyed. When Manilal wished to marry a Muslim girl in 1926, Gandhi refused to give his permission. His eldest son, Harilal, married against his father's wishes, but then lost his wife in the 1918 influenza epidemic, after which he fell apart, indulging in two rather half-hearted and essentially contradictory acts of rebellion, becoming both an alcoholic and a Muslim.

Gandhi, as a father, seemed to prefer his young cousin Maganlal to his own sons, and anointed him his personal heir. When Maganlal died in April 1928, Gandhi yielded to a rare moment of grief, describing him as 'dearer to me than my own sons', and as one who had 'never once failed or deceived me'.[230] The implied criticism is stark. But the lesson seems not to have been learned. His youngest son, Devadas, also encountered problems in his desire to marry Lakshmi, daughter of C. Rajagopalachari. In matters of the family, Gandhi appears uncomfortably tyrannical, but he would not be the first great thinker who found it easier to love people collectively in an abstract way than to love their nearest kinfolk in an individual way. He was much more comfortable on the wider stage of national politics, which allowed him the space for his expansive virtues while denying him shelter for his narrow failings.

What would the Congress have been without him? Could it have held together, or remained the extraordinary political object that it was, if united only by its opposition to the British? The evidence provided by the propensity of the Congress to split so repeatedly would seem to suggest that it could not have held together for long over anything contentious. When Gandhi was in prison from 1922 to 1924 there were splits; when he took a year out in 1926 there were splits. Such an unwieldy, uncritically inclusive political body was bound to suffer from both personal and ideological tensions. The Congress was conceived as a broad-based forum at a time when Indian politics was hardly real by normal standards; the way it survived into the era of more combative, divisive politics was a small miracle. That it was Gandhi who rose to its head was not the only reason for that survival but, once there, he was a powerful force keeping the Congress wide, moderate and sitting on a broad popular base. Gandhi was the great unifying force in Congress politics. It fell to him to eject the most troublesome members or to tame the wilder elements. He kept Nehru from leaving in 1936 and he drove Bose out in 1939. He persuaded the party to take the more emollient Nehru over the combative Patel as leader in the final stage of the independence process. He came and went as he pleased while managing to remain involved within the party's moral agenda, staying clear of the small, tricky issues that can taint and discredit leaders by generating perceptions of pettiness, favouritism and opportunism.

The Congress under Gandhi stayed together by not being too strictly led. He was even able to perform this service after formally leaving the organization in 1934. Though he may have seemed a divisive figure in 1920, he was mainly a force for unity. Remarkably, although he had no official position within the Congress in 1942, it was to him that the authority to launch the Quit India campaign was designated. No matter what historians may think on the matter, and no matter how unlikely a circumstance, Congress politicians themselves considered his guidance to be indispensable right up until 1947.

He retained this authority because he was proved right sufficiently often to seem wise, but just as importantly, the moral dimension in his outlook seemed unimpeachable. The breadth of his thinking and the moral content of his aims stood in for a great deal of detailed policy. These qualities made him very good at healing divisions. Perhaps if Nehru had been a different man he would have sidelined the Mahatma a decade earlier and pressed on with his own more socialist agenda. But he did not, realizing that the older man's connection with the peasant base of Indian society was hugely valuable to the Congress, and that he personally could not replicate it. Peasant and patrician alike found it hard not to acknowledge the Mahatma's unique qualities.

He preferred to call himself a 'practical idealist'. This might not be the best description of him, because with Gandhi it was always the fundamental view that was coherent, not necessarily the political programme. But as a phrase it does at least recognize that there were two strands to his philosophy, of spirit and matter. That, ultimately, is what made him a politician and not a hermit, a dreamer or a passive theorist.

Partition

It is hardly possible to write about these two great men without constant reference to the Partition of India in 1947. They were both old when it came about – Jinnah was 71, Gandhi 78 – so although they could only have hoped to outlive it a little while, the fact that they both died so soon afterwards means that Partition can easily appear to be the natural finale to their lives. This is understandable, but it creates unhelpful restrictions, especially in any discussion of Gandhi, who had so much to say on other subjects, and it can lend a false sense of inevitability to Jinnah's later career. The Pakistan demand virtually defined Jinnah for the last seven years of his life, but that does not mean that he was any more likely to achieve his aims than was Bose – and Bose had an army.

Partition was less directly connected with the careers of Jinnah and Gandhi than with the impending arrival of democratic forms into Indian government. It was this that forced Jinnah to insist on his own bespoke electoral system, regardless of whether he got a separate country surrounding it.

The British had been introducing small degrees of self-government to India for more than half a century before 1947, but when it came to the transfer of real authority they always held back, so that the effect of their reforms was always somewhat muted. This suited Jinnah before the Second World War, but the prospect of real independence at the war's end changed his outlook. Majority rule was always what he wished to avoid, and independence implied its certain arrival. The British Empire limped in over the winning line in 1945, and shortly afterwards Jinnah the demagogue appeared in full form.

Gandhi was also affected by the new situation. With the war over, he no longer seemed frightening to the British and instead, stood in danger of becoming an anachronism. Elections with real political power at stake had never been part of his standing, but once they arrived, in late 1945, his position as a moderating force within the Congress high command was weakened. His inclusive sort of problem-solving was suddenly less likely to appeal to partisan elements on the Congress side, and the shift away from generalities to details did not suit his approach at all. Instead, it placed technocratic and subtle men in a position to show their talents, while the prospect of government invited ambitious men to vie for real authority. The stage was set for Jinnah versus Nehru.

Partition was a complex process, and is not an easy story to tell. It is much easier to show why things went wrong than how they could ever have gone right. However, one simple question occurs repeatedly, as in many of the books referred to above: to what degree do either Jinnah or Gandhi bear responsibility for Partition?

Pakistan was the central element of Partition, and in this sense responsibility must fall on Jinnah, because even if he did not want exactly what he was eventually given, he asked for Pakistan much too often to deny his central role in the process. But the whole Partition saga was not exclusively about Jinnah. There were three parties involved, and they all had their own interests to protect. Matters would, of course, have been simpler if it had been a bilateral process, but the three-way negotiation was the result of internal Indian developments across the years 1937–42, during which Jinnah forced his way into the front rank of Indian affairs.

Jinnah can still correctly be seen as the main instigator in the process that led to Partition, for if he had reached agreement with the Congress then the dynamic that led to Partition would have been altered, or even avoided. It was in the person of Jinnah that the demand for Partition was concentrated. But there is now a long list of writers who are prepared to accept that it was the Congress that pressed for Partition in the final days, and that Jinnah was reluctant to accept the reality he had brought about.

Dr Ajeet Javed, in her *Secular and Nationalist Jinnah* (2009), helpfully lists a number of eminent writers and political memoirists who subscribe to variations of this view.[231] These include:

- M.N. Roy, who could not accept that an 'intelligent' man such as Jinnah could have intended Partition, with all its 'tragic consequences';
- Penderel Moon (*Divide and Quit*, 1961), who was an eyewitness to the events and claims that Jinnah confided to a few close friends in Lahore that the Pakistan demand was just 'a tactical move';
- Kanji Dwarkadas (*Ten Years to Freedom*, 1968), who reports a conversation in August 1942 in which Jinnah confessed that he did not imagine 'Pakistan would come into being' and was prepared to settle for less;
- Brian Lapping (*End of Empire*, 1985), who believes that Jinnah simply wanted an assurance of some major role in a united India and that, among the Muslim League leadership, 'Jinnah, at least, had never really wanted it [Pakistan]'.

There are other names that can be added to this list. Sikander Hayat Khan 'categorically' told Durga Das, the veteran journalist, that the Lahore Resolution was 'essentially a bargaining counter'.[232] From a more academic angle, S.S. Sokhey, in a letter to *Economic and Political Weekly*, dated 22 November 1968 and published that December, stated that he knew Jinnah 'intimately' from 1926, and that 'I can say positively that to the very last day he was against the division of India and tried to prevent it.'

Ayesha Jalal, in *The Sole Spokesman* (1994), also has first-hand testimony that Jinnah would have accepted less than Pakistan, as eventually granted. She interviewed the Punjabi grandee Mian Mumtaz Daulatana in 1980, who told her that Jinnah was 'all in favour' of accepting the Cabinet Mission plan, and didn't want Partition.[233]

Jalal's book treats Jinnah as a politician rather than as a fervent separatist, and her central insight is that Jinnah was making a shifting set of general demands with the objective of making some kind of provision for India's Muslims, either inside or outside a unitary India. Specific structures were less important to him than the assurance that political power would somehow be shared at the centre. Only if this were not possible within one Indian state would he insist on a definitive division of power by setting up another state. She also shows how Jinnah and his closest colleagues were trying to slow down the process of Partition right up until the announcement of 3 June 1947, while the Congress leaders (apart from Gandhi) were trying to speed it up. Jinnah could have lived with a unified India, provided there was enough willingness to share power and ensure fair treatment for all. As he said at Aligarh in late 1942: 'Mr Gandhi wants the whole, whereas I only want a share.'

Ayesha Jalal understands Jinnah as a tenacious but flexible politician, and not as an inconsistent opportunist or a thwarted visionary. This helps to unify the earlier and later Jinnah, showing that he can be seen as a nationalist and an 'ambassador for Hindu–Muslim unity' over a long period. Crucially it explains why, with all his reputation for intransigence, Jinnah actually accepted the Cabinet Mission plan of May 1946, which he would not have done had he been inflexibly set on a separate, sovereign Pakistan.

As a view of Jinnah, this will be of no comfort to Pakistanis who might not like to think that the creation of their country was not Jinnah's sole objective. But Jinnah, in Jalal's view, did not necessarily need his separate state if the Muslim 'nation' had been sufficiently recognized in some way within a united India. If this had been done, if what he described to Kanji Dwarkadas as 'a gesture' had been made, he could have been personally and ideologically satisfied.

What the British gave him was a literal interpretation of a demand he had been making in the service of a wider, longer strategy. He got his bargaining position – a sovereign nation – not his bottom line. In some circumstances this would be accounted a triumph, but we know that he opposed the internal partition of provinces, which he was eventually forced to accept. This and the vacuum that followed in

Pakistani constitutional affairs, which sprang from Jinnah's apparent unreadiness for detailed nation-building, combine to suggest that his achievement was a disguised failure.

Partition arose from a combination of three crucial elements: a long period of intense competition and mistrust, an elaborate series of bluffs by Jinnah and the British, and a pragmatic realization by some Congress leaders that giving up a unitary India, though painful, was probably inevitable and might, if brought about swiftly, yield a range of immediate benefits.

The British repeatedly emphasized to Jinnah the weakness of any possible version of Pakistan, expecting him to refuse it. In the end he did not refuse, but was hustled away from the negotiating table by the Congress, who suddenly changed tack. Having remained opposed to giving Jinnah anything like a sovereign state, Congress leaders suddenly showed the British the green light in late April 1947, and insisted on the immediate carve-up of India along lines of their own choosing. Mountbatten duly obliged. After one false start he had an acceptable plan in draft form by 13 May.

M.A.H. Ispahani was very clear about these moves in his memoir. He believed that the British pushed the Muslims to accept a weakened Pakistan, hoping that they would be unable to survive independently and would therefore soon be back. He also believed that Mountbatten was actively 'in league' with Nehru to this end.[234] The Cabinet Mission had already attempted a similar strategy when it offered Jinnah a 'small' sovereign Pakistan, with the partition of Bengal and Punjab, or a 'large' semi-autonomous bloc of six undivided provinces. Jinnah was hemmed in. He knew the weakness of a small Pakistan, especially in military terms. He had considerable defence experience, having sat on the Skeen Committee on 'Indianizing' the army in the 1920s, and on the Round Table Conference's Defence Subcommittee in 1931. He would have preferred the larger Pakistan, naturally, only with rather more autonomy than the Cabinet Mission was prepared to offer. Eventually, Jinnah and the Congress between them rejected all the Mission's constitutional schemes.

The resulting delay, from mid-1946 onwards, proved more damaging to Jinnah than any other party, and this marked another turn. Extended negotiations had usually strengthened Jinnah's standing, especially when he made aggressive demands. His intransigence at the Simla Conference in July 1945 was rewarded by a huge boost in the elections of the following winter. Hard bargaining gradually turned into a way for him to advance his own position, if only by inches. But by mid-1946, the process was taking so long that the weight of expectation on his own side placed him in a position where he became unable to delay indefinitely. As soon as the Congress sensed that they could force him into accepting a weak Pakistan, they pounced.

Nehru and Patel had moved a long way towards accepting Partition through the spring of 1947, and had come to see that it could be a rather better outcome for them than for Jinnah, in terms of their overall political aims and their eventual shares of the military assets, set at roughly 82:18. On 25 April, Patel told Mountbatten that the Congress would accept Partition if the Muslim League would not come to terms, and on 1 May Nehru wrote to Mountbatten accepting Partition under the principle of self-determination in defined areas. By 8 May, the Congress was prepared to reverse its long-held aversion to Dominion Status.

In the end, Congress leaders were simply pleased to do a deal whereby they got a compact state, having wrested the vital areas of East Punjab and West Bengal, including Calcutta, from their smaller rival. And they were finally freed from Jinnah's obstructive influence. In Nehru's pithy formulation, they were happy to 'cut off the head to be rid of the headache'.[235]

The British, meanwhile, managed to leave behind two states inside the Commonwealth, and almost no casualties on their own side. The former imperial rulers were desperate for the whole process to be over, and Mountbatten wrapped up the proceedings as quickly as he could. In the end Jinnah could not refuse, just as the worst offer yet was on the table. That offer was a fully independent sovereign Pakistan of three complete and two half provinces, without Calcutta.

To the League leaders the grant of Pakistan represented opportunities, long awaited, that could not be passed up. To the Congress, Partition was an ideological defeat, but it suddenly felt like a political victory. By the end there was not nearly enough resistance to the idea in responsible circles. Jinnah, therefore, did not quite dominate the proceedings as his fiercest critics have often imagined.

Gandhi took almost no part in these later dealings. He confined his efforts to calming the communal violence in Bengal and Bihar. He was ready to give advice if asked, but he was not asked. Mountbatten was aware of this and chose to speak to him occasionally. But the Viceroy well understood that in the new climate of representative politics, the old eccentric now really didn't represent anyone but himself. He may once have spoken for the masses, and he may have had the most genuine claim to embody India's unique virtues, but all that counted for nothing in the kind of process that was under way. Faced with either trying to balance the positions of Nehru and Jinnah, or of somehow following Gandhi's guidance, Mountbatten inevitably chose to deal with elected and representative men who were prepared to sit in government. The unique voice Gandhi possessed had kept India together until that point. Now it literally disappeared, as he sat silent in Mountbatten's office the day before Plan Partition was announced.

Partition may or may not have been a mistake. Opinions usually run along predictable lines of religion and nationality. The mass murder that accompanied it, though, was definitely a mistake. Could it have been foreseen, and who would be to blame if it had been? It is not difficult to see the Partition massacres as inevitable now, but at the time the Congress leaders did not. Almost no one did, with three exceptions.

The most clear-eyed about the potential for violence were British officials, including Mountbatten, but they did little to stop it, either before or during the carnage. A second cautionary voice was Jinnah's, as he warned of bloodshed and confusion in early May 1947. But here again, we can see him playing politics because he was seeing problems not in Partition itself but only in the subdivision of provinces, and he was therefore attempting to deter the British from that course. After 3 June, however, he set about selling the deal, and from then onwards he downplayed the problems and denied that there would be trouble, or any need for an exchange of populations. This was the period in which he most earnestly presented Partition as the end of intercommunal tensions.

The third voice was Gandhi's. After the August killings of 1946, he was convinced that the division of India would bring bloodshed, especially if imposed by the British. His preferred route to any settlement was always that the British should go and leave all the post-independence details to Indians. But he had little leverage within the senior Congress leadership by then. Before Partition was announced, the Congress leaders were preoccupied with speeding up the transfer of power to prevent Jinnah making further demands. Once the plan was announced, there was a new country to organize at breakneck speed. Precautions were neglected, and much faith was placed in the restraining influence of 'hostage' minorities. In this nervous climate, to be seen to be taking steps to prevent migration, or to prepare for civil conflict was considered to be more likely to alarm than to reassure the population.

None of the leaders actually wanted there to be any violence at all; they stood to gain nothing from it after the negotiations were over. All of them appealed for it to stop once it had begun. It would be unfair to blame national leaders for local violence that they had no wish to prolong. For their part, the British were the responsible power up until 15 August 1947, but after that it was the two successor states that held responsibility for law and order. To a great extent, the Partition massacres grew out of a power vacuum. It would be very harsh to blame either Jinnah or Gandhi for the detailed course of events.

Jinnah, however, definitely played the more significant role in the background to Partition. It was Jinnah who made the historic step of not only insisting that India's Muslims should be seen as a nation and not a community, but, most importantly, that they could only be protected as *one group*. These ideas led to Partition once they had fully interacted with, and helped shape, another set of new developments in the Congress. Gandhi always thought of the Congress as a parliament, but gradually other leaders began to treat it as a party. This was not his doing, nor in line with his thinking, but once it had happened it became very difficult to recombine or adequately represent India's diversity in political terms within one organ.

Indian politics in the later Raj thus developed two centres of political gravity, which became increasingly mutually exclusive. Most, if not all, Indians welcomed both democratization and British withdrawal, but these developments worked in unhelpful ways against the historic diversity of India, which was suddenly frozen into antagonistic modern variants with tragic results.

No matter who must atone, only a very thick-skinned Pakistani could insist that Partition was a success. The state of Pakistan has been poor, and deeply divided within itself. It has been neither a nationalist democracy nor a principled theocracy.

Sixty-five years later, the magnitude of the disaster of Partition appears greater than ever. And sadly, where writers of 40 years ago used to express pious hopes for some kind of reunification of the subcontinent, this note is entirely missing from recent literature on the subject. The long-term consequences for the region have yet to work themselves out. If there were only one nuclear power in South Asia today then international relations would be very different. If a democratic Greater India had had a border beyond Peshawar in 1979 then perhaps the Russians would never have dared intervene in Afghanistan, and the next two decades would not have been a prelude to the Afghan and Middle-Eastern wars of the twenty-first century. The enormous sums spent on armaments to defend the Indo–Pak border might have been used for other more constructive purposes. Hindu nationalists now live in fear of a 'third' partition. And so forth...

Meanwhile, Muslims within India have been practising their religion freely and living under their own personal laws. They do not have Islamic government, or full Sharia law. But neither do Pakistani Muslims. Many Muslims are still poor and underprivileged in India. They were before and they still are, but now they have to struggle without the bulk of their former coreligionists to give their voice more weight. It is not a straightforward issue of paradise and hell, but a strong case can be made that the entire situation would have been much better had the splitting of British India never come about. This is a standard Indian position, and it has some merit.

The Congress cannot evade a measure of blame. Nehru made two subsequent admissions about Congress misjudgements. In 1956 he told his biographer Michael Brecher that Congress leaders had viewed Partition as a way of ending the violence, and that they had consented to it because they did not want to accept a weak federal Indian Union with strong regional units that could push the central government around.[236] In 1960 he confessed to Leonard Mosley[237] that Congress leaders were tired of arguing with Jinnah and considered that Partition was most likely to be a temporary arrangement. They had no inkling of how bitter relations were to become, making reunion impossible.

The Congress leadership played politics with Partition. They wanted to give Jinnah as little of what he asked for as possible, so they denied him Calcutta, and his corridor, and they held back the share of assets. This was all simply hardnosed realpolitik. Of course, they can hardly be blamed for not giving Pakistan the best possible start in life. That was not their brief, nor was it in their direct power, and it was certainly not in their interests. After all, the two new countries were involved in a straight zero-sum game, in which any form of gain for one was a loss to the other.

Ultimately, everyone was implicated in the decision, because everyone eventually endorsed the settlement: the League on 9 June and the Congress on 14 June. So did the Sikhs, who then suffered severely. Even Gandhi, who had probably worked harder for unity than any of the others, also finally urged its acceptance as an inevitable compromise, unless the Congress were prepared directly to move to a 'big revolution'.[238] Rather unfairly, unlike any of the leaders who had hurried to clinch the deal, he was made to pay for it with his life.

There is an illuminating side issue here. Neither Gandhi nor Jinnah carries the faintest whiff of corruption on their persons. This is partly because neither enjoyed any long spell of responsible executive power, which is always the greatest test of any politician's probity. Public office never came to Gandhi and only for one year out of 45 in politics to Jinnah, and that too at the very end of his life. But there is no need to assume that either would have weakened in a position of power. Gandhi did not need money nor did he value it; Jinnah had plenty already. The downside of this was that by the mid-1940s the major nationalist elements were perhaps a little too in love with their own high-mindedness. This effectively hid the likely effects of Partition from them, and as a consequence made it more likely to happen.

To assume that responsible politicians readily agreed to a Partition scheme that they knew would produce mass murder is unreasonable. This accusation is usually brought against the British, prompted by the idea that the former colonial masters wished to destroy the country they had ruled for nearly two centuries in an act of general spite. Such a charge may be emotionally satisfying to some, but it has no basis in documentary evidence. Or even self-interest. Would it have bestowed any conceivable strategic or economic benefits on Britain to have left chaos behind them? What political advantage could the Labour government responsible have possibly imagined it would gain?

The British really did not want Partition as a solution. To insist that they did is to believe that mountains of official documents were no more than a smokescreen for some deeper purpose, and that officials spent literally years lying to each other in private. The British were extremely concerned about a two-state solution for two reasons. First, because of the direct military implications of suddenly having two new, potentially hostile armies mixed up all over the subcontinent, with no way of keeping them apart. Second, because there would assuredly be a period in which the country would be unable to defend itself from external aggression; there was real fear in senior military circles that the Russians would somehow exploit this vulnerability by invasion. Military thinking had even gone as far as to express concern over how this would affect communications between Great Britain and Australia. In an internal memo of 4 March 1947, drawn up by the India Office in London, it was set out that government policy should be to hand over power to as few separate authorities as possible – preferably two. Furthermore, a Partition like the one laid out three months later was listed as the fourth, and least preferable, option available to the government.[239]

But tragically, the British did not have enough concern to deny Partition to Indians if they said they wanted it. And by 1947 enough of them seemed to. The British did not have the political will or the military strength to resist, so the question became one of management and manoeuvre. None of the parties to Partition was mad or evil, but at the end they had all in different ways become narrow and self-serving. This is the root of the tragedy – that all parties, in the quest for crumbs of comfort, found them in sufficient quantity.

Of course, things might have gone differently at crucial moments. Had Wavell handled Jinnah more firmly in June 1945 at Simla and formed a Cabinet without him, then Jinnah would have had to come in or be left behind. Jinnah was not impervious to political persuasion, and in October 1946 he proved to be ready to come in after an Interim Government had been formed without the League. A similar approach in 1945 might have eventually recruited a chastened Jinnah to the Viceroy's council, willing to work with Congress. Or if the reverse had been done in June 1946, and Jinnah had been allowed to form his own Cabinet without the Congress, then perhaps a similarly bracing effect might have been produced on Nehru.

But in truth these things were never likely to happen, mostly because the British Government had decided that the ideal settlement was an agreed one. British politicians, to the very end, took what Indians wanted as the main guiding principle of their search for a settlement, and remained desperate to find a consensus among India's political leaders. But this approach had serious drawbacks. One was that there was so little agreement available that schemes had to be introduced from outside, which were therefore essentially alien in conception, and too easily became friendless within India. Another was that the policy rested on an unrealistic view of unanimity; the bar was set too high. Unanimity is an ideal political condition that states may strive to achieve once formed, but no state is formed amid perfect unanimity. The British were suddenly trying to build a country out of unity, rather than building unity within a country, as they had been before. The two new Dominions in South Asia were both, as it were, carts before horses; they were states formed before their borders were drawn, as political entities built to express consensus, not impose it. This fetish for unanimity could only have sprung from imperial guilt, that after imposing decisions for so long the British were at last going to stoop to consultation. When they did so it was with the fervour of a convert, not the wisdom of a parent.

Partition looks the way it does and casts the shadow it does because it has persistently been the belief of some in India that the whole event was a British plot, either to appease Jinnah or to fool him into splitting up India. Such ideas are too warped in their details for easy refutation, but there is one extra point to be made. These ideas have found fertile ground because of another central British mistake. The British consistently assumed that the major problem with Partition would be the military issue – how to split up a very large army into two new units, with new loyalties. In the event this was not even a minor problem within the Partition process, which turned into an informal war conducted locally by civilians, not a civil war conducted nationally by soldiers. The division of the armed forces went completely smoothly. There is no record of serious strife or any loss of life in the division of the Indian Army, a process actually accomplished in under 12 months, where senior military planners had predicted it might take anywhere from five to ten years to reassemble the Indian Army as two effective, separate fighting units. On both time-scale and potential disorder, the British were proved conclusively wrong.

This has left its mark. The fact that there was a profound military calm actually makes it look as if the British had a plan to hold the armed forces back from the situation. Had there been serious fighting amongst the newly segregated army, then the whole nationalist picture of British intentions would be different. Perhaps after a short war, some kind of unitary India, loose and suspicious, might have been formed. Or a decisive victory for the much larger Hindu-Indian force could have created a very different situation, and perhaps Pakistan might never have been formed at all. But certainly the idea that the British imposed Partition as a calculated, smoothly executed plan would never have taken hold.

In sum, the fact that Partition produced so many civilian casualties is at the heart of the conspiracy theory that Partition was a successful British plan that ran to its intended conclusion. Those deaths provide a motive to find reasons, and can also serve as 'proof' that a malign intention was always present. But it was the calmness and professionalism of the British-led army that have granted a permanent right to any aggrieved Indian patriot to invent any scenario for Partition he or she might wish to dream up. Books on the subject are still appearing. The army's good luck, or good behaviour, was eventually a propaganda gift to anyone wishing to malign the colonial power.

Partition is perfectly understandable without the need to introduce hidden British perfidy. The failings of the British were on public view throughout, as were the parallel failings of India's politicians. It was the Congress that definitively decided to partition India, in a way that most suited it in a situation it had not chosen. And it was Jinnah, for all his spokesmanship and careful representation, who could not save his heartlands from dissection, as the two largest Muslim provinces of British India were sliced apart. He had never held sway in either Bengal or the Punjab but had used them to give himself mass and momentum. The Bengalis were poorly repaid for the loan of their weight, for they were the greatest losers of all in the whole Independence saga. They now live in two states and have had to pay a double blood price to do so.

The Congress rejected Gandhi's advice, foiled the Bengalis and ignored the Sikhs, while none of the provinces included in the freshly formed Pakistan would have opted for the new country over all other choices, especially not at the price of internal subdivision.

All political careers, they say, end in failure. Gandhi believed that the Congress could unite India, Jinnah built the Muslim League to unite the Muslims, but the raw power at stake in the endgame of imperial India brushed aside both Gandhi's ethical principles and Jinnah's nuanced views on democratic equity. The minds that had set out the whole terrain of Indian Independence found no way to keep the debate at the rarefied level at which they excelled.

But their careers also mark out the limitations of leadership and fame. Popularity, even combined with integrity, is sometimes not quite enough, as the map of South Asia still reminds us. In the end, neither the practical idealist in a loincloth nor the sharp-dressed realist had the answers.

Conclusion

Jinnah and Gandhi have each been acclaimed as the 'father' of a modern state, but parenthood was not kind to either of them. Jinnah was robbed of his health by overwork, and Gandhi, the most recognizable Indian figure in history, was shot dead for creating a country that was less 'Indian' than one 'patriot' deemed appropriate. National paternity cost them their lives, but over time it also resurrected them and gave each an iconic afterlife, praised on their own sides of the border that came between them. Nationality and religion have been reliable predictors of attitudes to both leaders ever since.

Can we say that Pakistan is Jinnah's legacy? It is certainly hard to see how Pakistan could have come into being without him. There are those who contend that the demand for Pakistan was so overwhelming that it would have come anyway, but this is fanciful when one considers the Herculean task Jinnah undertook in trying to unify and discipline the Muslim political 'nation'. Why did he have to work so hard if the whole thing was already running on rails?

Without Jinnah's efforts, a federated India would have been rather more achievable. None of the Muslim provincial bosses had much difficulty with the idea. It suited them. Had they felt the need for collective protection they might have joined together under the leadership of one of their number, but there were never any signs of this happening. At the Round Table Conferences none of the major figures ever looked like taking on the unifying role that Jinnah was so keen to play. It was Jinnah who adapted and promoted the idea of Muslims as a nation, even though at the start it had a distinctly limited appeal and almost no natural followers. Scholars generally disliked it; Maulana Azad objected politically to it, and it did not serve any essential purpose for Muslim provincial leaders who were already safe in their status at the head of their own little nations, such as the Nizam of Hyderabad and the major Punjabi and UP landowners. Bengali Muslims never showed much sign of wanting to join a larger grouping; to the end, they wanted to go their own way. Jinnah imagined a protective superstructure that none of the provincial leaders actually needed. In the 1930s it was always the academics and the fringe enthusiasts who were asking for a separate Muslim homeland. Just because Muhammad Iqbal advocated something like this in 1930 does not mean that the idea was either feasible or popular. It was Jinnah's efforts that made it so.

The point is clearer if, for a moment, we remove Jinnah from the picture. If he had died at some point before 1937, the poor showing in the elections of that year would probably have killed the Muslim League forever as a national party. If Jinnah had died just before the arrival of the Cabinet Mission in March 1946 then things might also have turned out differently. The complex Cabinet Mission plans were difficult enough for Jinnah to navigate as undisputed leader. With him out of the way the likelihood of splits in the ranks of the Muslim League would surely have been high. Jinnah actually did a very good job of uniting his team and holding it in check. He did not get the settlement he wanted, but he had a genius for holding his own side together at crucial moments. Had he been taken out of the equation at almost any time, the likelihood of Pakistan's creation would have diminished enormously. There were few Indian Muslims capable of tackling the difficult double liberation, from the British and the Congress, that Pakistan represented.

Jinnah managed to oppose a powerful empire while keeping his major potential ally – the Congress – at arms' length. This was a remarkable feat of political positioning, to piggyback on the big beast and jump off at exactly the right moment. No other independence movement against a major power has had this double feature. Sadly for Jinnah, this extraordinary feat of nerve and judgement has brought him little critical approval. Quite the contrary. The unique character of the liberation he achieved means that he is either perceived as an especially good or an especially bad man, and not often as anything in between.

Is the Indian Republic Gandhi's legacy? He certainly did not choose its borders, but he played an enormous role in consolidating the demand for independence into a coherent, viable form – democratic and non-discriminatory. Many, especially on the political extremes, would not have subscribed to his thinking about personal liberation, but they could still agree with him that India should be free, whether as part of a process of self-determination, or a step towards a more egalitarian or even a more purely Hindu society. No other Indian leader, even Bose, could have held together the range of views that Gandhi managed. More people instinctively agreed with Gandhi's methods than with Bose's. And for all Bose's care to ensure that his army was as non-sectarian as possible, the trouble with a Bose-style liberation of India is that it inevitably contained Bose. Gandhi's India did not have to be ruled by Gandhi personally. This helped to keep major politicians within the Congress and assured the wider public that the India he wished to deliver would be better, but also familiar. Unlike so many other former colonial countries, India's bid for freedom was not led by an ideologue with standard allegiances. In this sense, the Indian Union of today, which has its own unique character, owes a great deal to Gandhi's eclectic blend of method and political tastes. His influence on Nehru is hard to define, but surely he can be credited with at least a small role in the development of the non-aligned foreign policy pursued by Nehru's India, which bore the recognizable stamp of two Gandhian principles: a diffidence towards power, and a determination to stand outside conflicts and, if possible, to dissolve them. This was the best of Gandhi, and Nehru's respect for him meant that there was a sympathetic but powerful heir to shepherd the Mahatma's ideals and priorities into the modern world.

In domestic terms it is harder to see the consumerist, hypermodern, nuclear-armed India of today as a legacy that Gandhi would relish. In the end, most Indians decided that the remedy they preferred for their ills was not greater spiritual elevation but straightforward material prosperity. That is what their leaders offered them, and they were no more able to resist the blandishments of cars, fridges and TVs than the rest of the world. Gandhian purity remains an option in the private sphere, but India, as a mass democracy full of poor people, simply could not sustain its public affairs on an ambition to stay poor.

Two central questions about Jinnah and Gandhi can now be given short answers. One: did Jinnah 'change' at any point in his career? Not really. The world changed around him more than he changed his personal and political objectives. Two: how could the unlikely figure of Gandhi ever have attained such power and prominence? Because he offered a unique blend of ethical living, religion and liberation to a country denied conventional politics.

A third remains: what of their relative greatness, in both personal and historical terms? Both were from Gujarati merchant families, both were lawyers trained in London, both were nationalists. These well-rehearsed parallels, however, were entirely superficial. The two could hardly have been more different, and not just on a simple Muslim–Hindu basis. They took very different approaches to the whole area of human development and politics. Jinnah wanted to lead from above, Gandhi from below. Jinnah was happy to leave the personal lives of his followers alone; Gandhi placed personal concerns at the very centre of all his schemes. Although Gandhi's approach might seem more ephemeral when described like this, his mission was actually much more radical in scope and scale than anything Jinnah deemed possible, or appropriate.

Gandhi's political and spiritual legacy must emerge as of greater significance. Jinnah may have created a country but he settled no arguments. On the contrary, he started rather more arguments than he finished. We can also see ways in which Gandhi influenced Jinnah, in dress and party organization, for instance, but there is no discernible way that Jinnah influenced Gandhi. This is because Gandhi's ideas came from within himself. Though respectful of tradition, he was an idiosyncratic originator and synthesizer of abstract concepts and practical ideas; there has been no one like him since. Jinnah took his ideas from those around him, as a politician does. He soaked up the aspirations and distilled the needs of his community, and turned them into recognizable political demands. Gandhi created his own 'narrative' from within, whereas Jinnah found his around him.

As a man, Jinnah was the greater in determination, for Gandhi would shy away from difficulties. When he did not get his way he either fasted or, as in the final run-up to Partition, he simply stood aside. What could he do against the will of the people, he asked. This was typical of the turns he could take when he wanted to.

But when it came to true consistency of principle, Gandhi must be said to hold the crown. Having laid out his spiritual and political aims in *Hind Swaraj* in 1909, he never resiled from any section of it, with all its eccentricities, including its blanket condemnation of Western medicine. One notable exception to this impressive consistency might be the surgery he underwent at the hands of a Western doctor in 1924. However, the discomfort of appendicitis can sometimes work a dramatic, if temporary, change in people's views on medical care. But in his condemnation of untouchability, in his commitment to non-violence, and in his insistence on a unitary India, he was perfectly consistent. His views on the importance and the nature of swaraj never changed, and his willingness to hand over the entire country to Jinnah in order to preserve its unity were the same in 1942 as in 1947.

Jinnah seems to have had less overall consistency, partly because he was forced into much more tactical manoeuvring than Gandhi, but also because the arrival of Pakistan as an idea so late in his career – after more than 30 years in national politics – gives a misleading impression. Pakistan was the completion of his project, not an aberration. It had become the only form in which he could achieve the freedom and security he had always sought for his people.

Jinnah was more the warrior and Gandhi more the sage; one essentially urban and technical, the other rural and instinctive. Jinnah couldn't walk past an argument without wanting to win it; Gandhi wanted to abolish conflict. Both made politics personal, but in different ways: Jinnah by emphasizing what you are and Gandhi by emphasizing what you do. Most importantly for the story as it unfolded, Gandhi was an optimist who remained an optimist. Jinnah was an optimist who despaired.

They occupied different spaces in Indian public life and it was difficult if not impossible for them to flourish at the same time. Gandhi had his peaks of influence in 1919–22, 1929–34 and 1942–45. Jinnah had his in 1913–18, 1927–29 and 1945–48. Gandhi was the first to establish a mass following, and it took a long time for Jinnah to find anything as large for himself. Finally, by the early 1940s the Indian public had been sufficiently politicized across enough issues to give both men a secure grip on national politics.

But from 1945, the increasingly conventional style of the negotiations effectively excluded Gandhi from prominent involvement in the endgame of Independence. From the Simla Conference onwards there was increasingly less room for his kind of leadership, so the element of individual confrontation that can sometimes be detected in crises like 1920, 1931 or 1939 gradually disappeared. Gandhi and Jinnah had private talks in Jinnah's bungalow in Delhi in May 1947 but this was not a summit meeting; nothing significant was expected to emerge from it by then. As Gandhi sat silently in the Viceroy's office on 2 June 1947 it must have been clear how far India had travelled, and how eccentric his whole approach had become. From then on, India's politicians would not walk barefoot along dirt roads or live in ashrams miles from a railhead. Appeals to moral high principle were no longer enough to provide the materials for a new nation. Jinnah once described Gandhi and his policies as 'utterly unsuited to modern times and the realities we have to face in India'.[240] When he said this in 1929, it was not true. By June 1947, it was.

It is tempting to pick out Western parallels and analogues in the two leaders but this is not helpful. Throughout, the versions of Western philosophies they developed were recognizably Indian and were shaped by the local dilemmas they faced. Because of the British presence, both were forced to wrestle with conflicting principles while working towards what were essentially post-British solutions. Gandhi accepted democracy, but he was never permitted to use it. Instead he employed every Indian device he could think of: hartal – a development of customary mourning, fasting – a familiar Indian religious act of purification, dharna – a traditional way of publicly demanding justice from an oppressor, and ahimsa. He was a nationalist in British eyes but in his own thinking his nationalism was only a box in which to put the drive for a morally purer society. He once wrote: 'My patriotism is subservient to my religion.'[241] He was sincere in his rejection of all Western influence, and apart from brilliant use of the newsreels, he was relatively consistent in his rejection of Western inventions. It is simply too facile to berate him for travelling in cars. Circumstances were forced upon him and he was realistic enough to accept that the world he lived in carried a heavy British stamp. To undo the distortions of the moral framework of Indian society that this caused was his mission, and provided that the means did not unduly affect the outcome, he was prepared to make compromises in the cause of ridding India of her imperial masters. Cars and trains could be made to serve a good purpose.

Jinnah was an Indian faced with another impossible choice. To protect Muslims within a wider Indian state, he could not accept British-style Parliamentary democracy. Yet to lean on any other crutch, such as nationalism or Islam, was to open up complicated and unpredictable areas. He was not the sort of man to tackle these problems. He worked within the existing rules, which is what lawyers do. He was noticeably reluctant to invent new rules. The Pakistan he seems to have envisaged had all the contradictions within it that have haunted it ever since – a state defined by its Muslim population, but in which he hoped Islam would eventually disappear as a distinctive political element. Islam and nationalism are not ideal bedfellows, and if, as in Pakistan, there were also wide regional variations and an asymmetric economic base to cope with, then we can see that Jinnah had a serious set of problems to navigate. These issues, though, were left for later attention. Jinnah's great mission was to protect the political rights of Muslims. Until this initial aim was secured, all the rest was detail.

Gandhi's great task was to liberate Indians; Jinnah's was to protect Muslims. Gandhi already had a national unit, whereas Jinnah had to separate a new country from an older one, a formidably difficult task requiring political virtues of the first order, including determination, energy and organization. All of these qualities directly aided the creation of Pakistan, an extraordinarily unlikely event if viewed from many points in Jinnah's life. But these virtues, real though they were, did not amount to the wider gift of vision – a quality that Gandhi had. This distinction needs to be explored further.

It is easy to see Jinnah as a lawyer who argued and won a case for India's Muslims, just as he argued and won many others. It is even easier to see him as a politician who wished to create a job for himself. But in both these views, neither of which is entirely devoid of merit, the man is judged by only one aspect of his political career – Pakistan. And our views of Jinnah are still heavily conditioned by our views of the country he sired. Until we can all agree that the creation of Pakistan was a Himalayan blunder – or at least a blunder with some Himalayas in it – this linkage means that definitive judgements of the man who brought the country into being are still awaited, and remain partisan. If he had chosen another cause, we might find more to praise him.

Gandhi has been lionized and has even posthumously won Oscars, but a shadow still falls darkly over the principal architect of Pakistan. Unlike Jinnah, who is venerated in Pakistan and almost nowhere else, Gandhi is admired all over the world. The Mahatma somehow managed to convey universal truths in an inclusive way that also suited his immediate political objectives. In this he represents a very rare conjunction of actor and thinker. Jinnah, trapped within the stunted politics of British India, and dwarfed by Gandhi's expansive thinking, has never been seen as a leader of vision outside Islamic communities. This situation is highly likely to continue, and scholarship will not change it. While Gandhi is regularly compared to Buddha or Jesus Christ, Jinnah's name is coupled only with Kemal Ataturk, or Mazzini at a stretch.

The fact that Jinnah left no blueprint for Pakistan can be taken to mean that he had no hard and fast conception of what lay at the end of his demands. But across his final days his reticence may also have been because he understood that it was not his responsibility to decide what exact form the new Constitution would take; it was up to the Pakistani constituent assembly. This is exactly the kind of 'constitutional' excuse he gave to Mountbatten on 2 June 1947 to avoid hitching the Muslim League to the Partition plan – he always had a politician's sensitivity in adjusting what he said to the moment and to his audience. His post-

Independence statements about Islamic principles and the Constitution were generally made to religious listeners, and were vague enough to have cost him nothing while helping the general cause of unity. None of these statements are strong on specifics. Jinnah was a master of avoiding the detail when it suited him.

But those who assert that he did have definitive ideas need to explain why he never revealed them. If the birth of his new country was not a propitious moment to do so – then when would it have been? It can be reasonably suggested that he would have found it difficult to plan a detailed Constitution, in advance, for a country he was not sure he would get and whose exact extent, jurisdiction and powers he could not know. Such an undertaking would have been a colossal waste of the precious energy he still possessed. Perhaps. But this view can only partially excuse Jinnah for neglecting the main duty of a great leader, which is to see further than his followers. The absence of a definitive plan for Pakistan was a crippling omission. It can be viewed as a tacit admission that he feared the coalition he had created might dissolve if he spelled out to his supporters where he thought they were all heading under his guidance. Seen like this, Pakistan was essentially a suggestion – never a plan that could have been set out in detail. If his actual views were not what others believed they were, or if he did not have the courage of his own convictions, then he was not the leader he pretended to be, and does not deserve the mantle of statesmanship that many have been keen to award him.

In the longer view, it was Gandhi who set out a whole series of interlocking abstract beliefs. His destiny was not to create the modern Indian state in detail, but to invent and popularize a way of proceeding that allowed it to come into being and gave it many of its most distinctive characteristics – principally its diversity.

But his espousal of non-violence, and the scale to which he magnified it, have changed the world. Before Gandhi there had been wars of liberation, struggles accompanied by large-scale bloodletting in the name of nationality and freedom. Gandhi correctly discerned that these struggles pass on a legacy of violence and division, a legacy he wished above all else to avoid. He was determined to ensure that the new India would be born peacefully, would pass into the hands of responsible leaders, and would inherit a credit balance at the Bank of Karma. The moral high-mindedness of this approach still seems audacious, and even more astoundingly, it proved successful.

The liberation of India was a remarkably peaceful affair. No battlefields and, relative to overall population, very few casualties, though there were deaths on both sides in all three of his great protest campaigns. The desperately tragic element was that in the end it was not the British as departing colonialists who were directly responsible for the principal bloodshed – it was the liberated colonial subjects themselves, and here Jinnah has to take a great deal of the responsibility for so relentlessly terrifying Muslims about the perils of Hindu raj, for unleashing 'Direct Action' without adequate discipline, and for failing to control the very extensive campaign of violence employed to unseat the Khizar Unionist government of Punjab through 1946–47, which he knew of, and appears to have sanctioned.[242]

As an example of the triumph of superior moral values, the Indian Independence movement was, broadly speaking, a success. Gandhi converted weakness into strength by defying the powerful to use their power without proving their own moral bankruptcy. If all the British could do was to shoot unarmed protesters then the mission to civilize and 'uplift' was clearly a sham. In terms of the stark light this threw on the colonial overlords, it was a brilliantly effective approach. The wider world could not fail to understand the iniquity of soldiers and policemen thrashing defenceless protesters.

It was this vision, not of a country but of a liberating moral purpose, that marked Gandhi out as the superior campaigner. Jinnah had a powerful local efficacy in what he was doing, and his tactical skill was unquestionably of a high order. His sometimes outrageous claims about his own authority to speak for a group of 90 million diverse people, and his repeated tactic of making exaggerated and exasperating counterclaims when cornered, exemplify his talents as a negotiator. But it has to be said that, despite all his efforts, history shows that Jinnah was not a particularly good deal-maker. He loved to negotiate, but after the Lucknow Pact of 1916 he never managed to close out the deal he was trying to make. In 1927, 1929, 1937, 1942 and even 1947, major deals went astray and he failed to get what he wanted. Sometimes his opponents did not believe he represented anyone but himself. At other times he was asking too much, or unwilling to concede enough. But we might also ask: was he simply not very good at actually working out how to reach agreement, and that he was actually more comfortable prolonging a dispute in the hope of improvising a victory?

He was at his best as an advocate, which implies an appeal to a higher authority – in law a judge, in politics the British. When faced with a more level playing field – that is, a negotiation – his judgement may well have been less unerring. When given supreme power in Pakistan, with no higher authority above him, and no equals, when his long career of opposition, competition and minority status was finally behind him, he seemed bereft of purpose.

In some ways he was a local man struggling with local issues in a fairly conventional way. One cannot fault him on his grasp of the details, but when it comes to Gandhi, one enters another level of perception. Gandhi was never good at detail and he never shared the concern for ego gratification to be found at the centre of so many political lives, including the Quaid-i-Azam's. When he wanted to offer the Interim Government wholesale to Jinnah in April 1947 he illustrated this faith in full measure. He genuinely thought that to give Jinnah the supreme office was the best way to prove, definitively, that the Congress did not have an anti-Muslim agenda. Where he was mistaken was that his colleagues would simply never permit so drastic a concession, having waited for years, many spent in prison, to wield real power; in Nehru's case it was more than 3,000 days of such waiting. Gandhi was aware of Jinnah's probable reaction to his radical offer. When Mountbatten, surprised at Gandhi's proposal, asked him what he thought Jinnah might say if he was informed of the source of the offer of the premiership, Gandhi suggested he would say 'Ah, it is the wily Gandhi again'.[243] The Mahatma understood many aspects of high political strategy, but his instincts led him to placate his declared opponents, in order to show how little he cared for power, and to allow his adversaries an opportunity to become better people. He did not share the career politician's acute awareness that one's most dangerous enemies are often to be found on one's own side.

It is this breadth of vision that explains why we have Gandhism, Gandhigiri and the adjective 'Gandhian', while we have no recognized 'Jinnahism'. This is because Jinnah's main admirers tend to interpret his beliefs in established Islamic terms, and thus have no separate name for them. Whenever the word 'Jinnahism' does appear it is usually with heavily negative connotations, for his enemies have allotted him a special place in the pantheon of political thinkers, as the archetype of token religiosity adopted for political purposes. It is not national visionaries, but whisky-drinking politicians that wrap themselves in Islamic identity who are the Jinnahists. This is a cruel fate for an intelligent and sincere man. For he was sincere. There is no need to deny him that defence and solace. He would hardly have burned his life out in a cause that so often seemed hopeless had he not been. In 1948 he described himself as 'a fanatic' in the cause of Pakistan.[244] And, of course, to be sincere does not necessarily mean that you are not wrong. For it is hard to absolve him of having massively overstated his case in order to win it. Muslims, and Islam, were never in the kind of danger he described – certainly not at the hands of either Gandhi or Nehru.

Perhaps the real legacy of Jinnah's political life is much less than an -ism, and is merely the cautionary lesson that unity in opposition cannot be expected to outlast the winning of power. Figuratively, he led an army to war with the sole aim of winning its first and only battle. There would be no need for any further fighting, and afterwards matters would somehow take care of themselves. But his was an army that was all in the mustering. The Muslim League was never a deep and wide stream like the Congress. At its very core, and even in its very name, it was an exclusive body. It was a one-off organization for a one-off purpose. Jinnah was not interested in or involved with the liberation of Muslims in any other country. He was, at least according to his former colleague M.C. Chagla, not even concerned with the fate of the Muslims left behind in India.[245] Nehru may have had an international vision for the Third World, away from European domination. Jinnah never did.

He had little use for political vision that went further than the immediate process in which he was engaged. He found a way to build a diverse alliance – his own mini-Congress – and keep it together with himself at its head, by under-specifying everything to do with the movement, apart from his own leadership of it. This makes him a very successful politician, and is a tribute to his ability to inspire others to serve what, in some ways, amounted to his personal purposes. But it also helped reduce him to a figurehead, leading a coalition that was at least as opportunistic as he was. The Pakistan movement contained far too many people uninterested in, or actually opposed to, many of his views and objectives. He became the liberal leader of a movement that had some very illiberal members.

Gandhi, too, was deeply submerged in his own political process, but he could see it as a thing in itself, a thing that had to be right in the moral sense, not just pragmatically fit for purpose. Gandhi also had a deep concern about the distant results of his actions. This is what makes him the visionary of the two.

Gandhi has never been judged by his achievements so much as his principles and methods. He did not usher in the ethical world revolution he hoped to see, but his admirers indulge him in his noble failure. One thing that has greatly helped his posthumous reputation is that he never presided over an organized, official project of any kind. He was the oppositional politician par excellence. He never held office, and thus avoided the burden of high expectations, and never had to live down the realization of his own vision.

Even if we cannot hold Jinnah responsible for everything that has since happened in Pakistan, the granting of his wish that it be created has given him a great deal to live down. In the interests of balance we need to play a counterfactual game and imagine: if Gandhi had won his India – of villages and spinning wheels, celibate marriages and no alcohol – what would we think of him? Or worse, if he had suffered, as Jinnah did, in getting a curtailed, 'moth-eaten' Gandhian India, with all its potential faults and none of its promised benefits? Fate was kind to the Mahatma. He never achieved his dream, and so, unlike Jinnah's, it has remained unsullied by failure.

LEGACIES

For a spiritual leader, social critic and oppositional figure, Gandhi's main achievement, surprisingly, was political. He took the Indian National Congress, an organization founded on Western concepts, and turned it into an unmistakably Indian institution. Its indigenous culture of inclusiveness and collective leadership enabled Indians to pick out the best of the ideals that Gandhi had to offer. Nehru, Gandhi's anointed heir, oversaw this process so well that now Gandhi can take credit for creating a new kind of Indian. Jinnah as a leader was never capable of doing anything similar, for he was always more a warrior than a lawgiver. The Muslim League was a party sprung from exclusivity and privilege, and leading it gradually made an aristocrat out of him, while the demands of the Pakistan cause constricted his broader liberal beliefs. He could not create a new form of Islam; most of his followers were quite content with the kind they already had. This was Pakistan's tragedy in waiting – that its creator was so preoccupied with processes rather than outcomes that he never developed locally appropriate guiding principles. Meanwhile, his ego ensured that there was no Nehru figure on hand to protect the best of his liberal aspirations.

Jinnah garnered the widest possible support base, but his was the leadership of momentum, not of foresight. He sacrificed one essential element in nation-building – the laying out of common ground for the future. Islam was politically too undefined, and Muslims were too diverse to have clear, common aims. Perhaps he thought that liberalism – the love of freedom – was enough, but liberalism requires security to function as a social and economic code. Pakistan had serious problems of insecurity – militarily, economically and financially – that Jinnah was reluctant to acknowledge and did not address. He missed the large point for a lesser one. The result was a paranoid country, too small to sustain its own defence without compromising its other obligations. Jinnah was told this repeatedly – and it was immediately proved true; the country's first budget announced a disproportionately heavy military spend based on a disappointingly low tax yield. But he forged on, buoyed up by a following that was looking for an immediate uplift in their lives, which many of them expected Islam to provide. This is what makes Jinnah a less astute and less successful leader than his admirers like to think.

Gandhi had the right kind of virtues to found a nation. Jinnah, ultimately, did not.

Bibliography

Akbar, M.J., *Nehru: The Making of India*, London: Viking, 1988.

Akbar, M.J., *Tinderbox: The Past and Future of Pakistan*, New Delhi: HarperCollins, 2011.

Attlee, C.R., *As It Happened*, London: Heinemann, 1954.

Ahmad, J., *Speeches of Quaid-i-Azam*, Lahore: Sh. Muhammad Ashraf, 1946, 2 volumes.

Bence-Jones, M., *The Viceroys of India*, London: Constable, 1982.

Bose, S.C., *The Indian Struggle*, London: Whishart, 1935.

Campbell-Johnson, A., *Mission with Mountbatten*, London: Hale, 1951.

Chagla, M.C., *Roses in December*, Mumbai: Bharatya Vidya Bhavan, 1974.

Close, H.M., *Attlee, Wavell, Mountbatten and the Transfer of Power*, Islamabad: National Book Foundation, 1997.

Collins, L., and Lapierre, D., *Freedom at Midnight*, New York: Simon and Schuster, 1975.

Coupland, R., *The Constitutional Problem in India*, Madras: Oxford University Press, 1945.

ed. Coward, H., *Indian Critiques of Gandhi*, Albany: State University of New York Press, 2003.

ed., Duncan, R., *The Writings of Gandhi: A Selection*, London: Fontana/Collins, 1983.

Das, Durga, *India from Curzon to Nehru and After*, London: Collins, 1969.

Dwarkadas, K., *India's Fight for Freedom 1913–1937*, Bombay: Popular Prakashan, 1966.

Dwarkadas, K., *Ten Years to Freedom*, Bombay: Popular Prakashan, 1968.

Fischer, L., *The Life of Mahatma Gandhi*, London: Granada, 1982.

Forbes, R., *India of the Princes*, London: The Right Book Club, 1938.

The Collected Works of Mahatma Gandhi (Electronic Book), New Delhi: Publications Division Government of India, 1999, 98 volumes.

Gandhi, M.K., *Autobiography: My Experiments with Truth*, New Delhi: Penguin, 2001.

Gandhi, M.K., *Hind Swaraj and Other Writings*, ed. A.J. Parel: Cambridge University Press, 2009.

Gandhi, M.K., *Gokhale: My Political Guru*, Ahmedabad: Navajivan, 1955.

Glendevon, J., *The Viceroy at Bay*, London: Collins, 1971.

Golant, W., *The Long Afternoon*, London: Hamish Hamilton, 1975.

Guha, R., *Makers of Modern India*, Cambridge, Mass.: Belknap Press of Harvard University Press, 2011.

Hamid, A., *Muslim Separatism in India*, Karachi: Oxford University Press, 1967.

Hasan, M., *Legacy of a Divided Nation*, London: Hurst and Co, 1997.

Hodson, H.V., *The Great Divide*, Karachi: Oxford University Press, 1985.

Ispahani, M.A.H., *Qaid-e-Azam Jinnah: As I Knew Him*, Karachi: Forward Publications Trust, 1967.

Jalal, A., *The Sole Spokesman*, Cambridge University Press, 1985.

Javed, A., *Secular and Nationalist Jinnah*, New Delhi: Kitab, 1997.

Jinnah, M.A., *Jinnah, Speeches*, ed. J. Ahmed, Lahore: M. Ashraf, 1968.

Jones, G.E., *Tumult in India*, New York: Dodd Mead and Co., 1948.

ed. Kazimi, M.R., *M.A. Jinnah: Views and Reviews*, Karachi: Oxford University Press, 2005.

Keay, J., *History of India*, London: HarperCollins, 2000.

Khairi, S.R., *Jinnah Reinterpreted*, Karachi: Oxford University Press, 1995.

Lall. A., *The Emergence of Modern India*, Columbia University Press, 1981.

Lapping, B., *End of Empire*, London: Granada, 1985.

Majumdar, S.K., *Jinnah and Gandhi: Their Role in India's Quest for Freedom*, Calcutta: K.L. Mukhopadhyay, 1966.

ed. Mansergh, N., *The Transfer of Power 1942–7*, London: H.M.S.O, 1970–82, 11 volumes.

Masselos, J., *Indian Nationalism–A History*, New Delhi: Sterling, 2002.

Merriam, A.H., *Gandhi vs. Jinnah*, Calcutta: Minerva Associates, 1980.

Misra, M., *Vishnu's Crowded Temple*, London: Allen Lane, 2007.

Moon, P., *Divide and Quit*, London: Chatto and Windus, 1961.

Moore, R.J., *Churchill, Cripps and India*, Oxford: Clarendon Press, 1979.

Naidu, S., *Mahomed Ali Jinnah, An Ambassador of Unity: His Speeches and Writings 1912–1917*, Madras: Ganesh, 1918.

Nanda, B.R., *Gandhi and His Critics*, New Delhi: Oxford University Press, 1985.

Nanda, B.R., *The Making of a Nation*, New Delhi: HarperCollins India, 1999.

Nehru, J., *The Discovery of India*, London: Meridian, 1946.

Nichols, B., *Verdict on India*, London: Jonathan Cape, 1944.

ed. Pirzada, S.S., *Foundations of Pakistan*, Karachi: National Publishing House, 1969, 2 volumes.

Rizvi, G., *Linlithgow and India*, London: Royal Historical Society, 1978.

ed. Roy, A., *Islam in History and Politics*, New Delhi: Oxford University Press, 2006.

Saiyid, M.H., *Mohammad Ali Jinnah: A Political Study*, Lahore: Ashraf, 1962.

Sen, E., *Testament of India*, London: Allen and Unwin, 1939.

Sharma, M.S.M., *Peeps into Pakistan*, Patna: Pustak Bhandar, 1954.

Singh, A.I., *The Origins of the Partition of India 1936–1947*, New Delhi: Oxford University Press, 1987.

Singh, J., *Jinnah: India–Partition–Independence*, Karachi: Oxford University Press, 2010.

Sykes, F., *From Many Angles: An Autobiography*, London: Harrap, 1942.

Wells, I.B., *Ambassador of Hindu–Muslim Unity: Jinnah's Early Politics*, Delhi: Permanent Black, 2005.

Wolpert, S., *A New History of India*, Oxford University Press, 1977.

Wolpert, S., *Jinnah of Pakistan*, Karachi: Oxford University Press, 1993.

Wolpert, S., *Shameful Flight*, Oxford University Press, 2006.

Wolpert, S., *Gandhi's Passion*, Oxford University Press, 2001.

Zakaria, R., *The Man Who Divided India*, Mumbai: Popular Prakashan, 2001.

Ziegler, P., *Mountbatten*, London: Guild, 1985.

Notes

1. *Collected Works of Mahatma Gandhi (CWMG)*, New Delhi: Publications Division, Ministry of Information & Broadcasting, 92 volumes.
2. All references below are to the online electronic book version, available at http://www.gandhiserve.org/cwmg/cwmg.html
3. John Morley, *On Compromise*, London: Chapman & Hall, 1874.
4. *Young India*, 'A Morning With Gandhiji', 13 & 20 November 1924: *CWMG*, vol. 29, pp. 262–71.
5. Mohandas Karamchand Gandhi, *Hind Swaraj, and Other Writings*, ed. A.J. Parel, Cambridge University Press, 2009, chap. 4, p. 27.
6. *Harijan*, 'Conundrums', 30 September 1939: *CWMG*, vol. 76, pp. 355–9.
7. *CWMG*, vol. 78, p. 104.
8. *CWMG*, vol. 17, p. 22.
9. ed. Ronald Duncan, *The Writings of Gandhi*, London: Faber and Faber, 1971, p. 69.
10. *Harijan*, 'Source of My Sympathy', 16 September 1939: *CWMG*, vol. 76, pp. 320–2.
11. *Harijan*, 'Discussion with C.V. Raman and Dr Rahm', 30 May 1936: *CWMG*, vol. 68, pp. 424–6.
12. Stanley Wolpert, *Jinnah of Pakistan*, Karachi: Oxford University Press, 2007.
13. Beverley Nichols, *Verdict on India*, London: Jonathan Cape, 1944, p. 189.
14. Arthur Lall, *The Emergence of Modern India*, New York: Columbia University Press, 1981, p. 93.
15. M.A. Jinnah, Delhi, March 22, 1943: QAP, file 561, p. 66.
16. *Young India*, 'To The Members Of The All-India Home Rule League', 28 April 1920: *CWMG*, vol. 20, pp. 245–6.

17. Ramachandra Guha, *Makers of Modern India*, Cambridge, Mass.: Belknap Press of Harvard University Press, 2011, p. 184.
18. *Young India*, 23 August 1919: *CWMG*, vol. 18, p. 220.
19. *Young India*, 10 March 1920: *CWMG*, vol. 19, p. 449. ibid. 17 March 1920, *CWMG*, vol. 19, p. 467.
20. Guha, *Makers of Modern India*, p. 216.
21. Mushirul Hasan, *Legacy of a Divided Nation*, London: C. Hurst and Co., 1997, p. 91.
22. full text available at http://www.pakistani.org/pakistan/legislation/constituent_address_11aug1947.html
23. *CWMG*, vol. 14, p. 395.
24. M.H. Shahid, *Quaid-i-Azam: Speeches*, Lahore: Sang-e-Meel Publications, 1976, p. 82.
25. Wolpert, *Jinnah of Pakistan*, pp. 337–40.
26. *Young India*, 'Interrogatories Answered', 29 January 1925: *CWMG*, vol. 30, p. 158.
27. K. Harris, *Attlee*, London: Weidenfeld and Nicholson, 1982, p. 552.
28. Louis Fischer, *The Life of Mahatma Gandhi*, London: Granada, 1982, p. 157.
29. *CWMG*, vol. 76, p. 356.
30. Gandhi, *Hind Swaraj, and Other Writings*, p. 69.
31. The *Times*, London, 7 February, 1921, issue no. 42638.
32. *New York Times*, 5 May 1946.
33. Letter to Henry Polak, 14 October 1909, quoted in Gandhi, *Hind Swaraj*, pp. 128–29.
34. Arthur Read and David Fisher, *The Proudest Day: India's Long Road to Independence,* London: Jonathan Cape, 1997, p. 107.
35. Abdul Hamid, *Muslim Separatism in India*, Lahore: Oxford University Press, 1967, p. 75.
36. Sankar Ghose, *Mahatma Gandhi*, Bombay: Allied, 1991, p. 94.
37. ed. M.R. Kazimi, *M.A. Jinnah, Views and Reviews,* Karachi: Oxford University Press, 2005, p. 5.
38. I.B. Wells, *Ambassador of Hindu–Muslim unity: Jinnah's Early Politics*, Delhi: Permanent Black, 2005, p. 30.
39. Jaswant Singh, *Jinnah: India–Partition–Independence*, Karachi: OUP, 2010, p. 71.
40. Sarojini Naidu, *Mahomed Ali Jinnah, An Ambassador of Unity: His Speeches and Writings 1912-1917*, Madras: Ganesh, 1918, p. 11. Three famous Jinnah quotes are all on this one page.

41. M.K. Gandhi, *Autobiography: My Experiments with Truth*, New Delhi: Penguin, 2001.
42. ibid.
43. *CWMG*, vol. 14, pp. 342–3.
44. Gandhi, *Autobiography*, part V, chap.1, p. 339.
45. Wolpert, *Jinnah of Pakistan*, p. 38.
46. *CWMG*, vol. 15, pp. 148–55.
47. *House of Commons Debates*, vol. 97, cc. 1695–7.
48. Wolpert, *Jinnah of Pakistan*, p. 62.
49. Arthur Herman, *Gandhi and Churchill*, London: Hutchinson, 2008, p. 255.
50. Gandhi, *Hind Swaraj, and Other Writings*, p. 110.
51. Wolpert, *Jinnah of Pakistan*, p. 56.
52. ibid, p. 59.
53. *CWMG*, vol. 17, Appendix 1, pp. 464–5.
54. *CWMG*, vol. 19, p. 137.
55. M.R. Jayakar, *The Story of My Life*, Bombay: Asia Publishing House, 1958, vol. 1, p. 318.
56. *Young India*, 'To The Members Of The All-India Home Rule League', 28 April 1920: *CWMG*, vol. 20, pp. 245–6.
57. Wolpert, *Jinnah of Pakistan*, p. 70.
58. Fischer, *The Life of Mahatma Gandhi*, p. 257.
59. *CWMG*, vol. 18, p. 183.
60. Wolpert, *Jinnah of Pakistan*, p. 87.
61. *Young India*, 'Hindu Muslim Tension: Its Cause and Cure', 29 May 1924: *CWMG*, vol. 28, pp. 43–62.
62. *Young India*, 'Statement Announcing 21 Day Fast', 25 September 1924: *CWMG*, vol. 29, pp. 180–1.
63. Wolpert, *Jinnah of Pakistan*, p. 95.
64. H. Montgomery Hyde, *Lord Reading*, London: Heinemann, 1967, p. 382.
65. *House of Commons Debates*, vol. 210, cc. 1821–51.
66. Wolpert, *Jinnah of Pakistan*, p. 97.
67. M.J. Akbar, *Tinderbox: The Past and Future of Pakistan*, New Delhi: HarperCollins, 2011, p. 183.
68. Singh, *Jinnah: India–Partition–Independence*, p. 142.
69. Reginald Coupland, *The Constitutional Problem in India*, Madras: Oxford University Press, 1945, p. 87.
70. Fischer, *The Life of Mahatma Gandhi*, p. 330.

71. Wolpert, *Jinnah of Pakistan,* p. 120.
72. S.C. Bose, *The Indian Struggle,* London: Whishart,1935, pp. 158–9.
73. William Golant, *The Long Afternoon,* London: Hamish Hamilton, 1975, p. 101.
74. *CWMG,* vol. 65, p. 8.
75. For the 1935 Government of India Act, see R. Coupland, *The Constitutional Problem in India,* Madras: Oxford University Press, 1945; P. Spear, *Penguin History of India,* London: Penguin, 1965; H.V. Hodson, *The Great Divide,* Karachi: Oxford University Press, 1985.
76. B.R. Nanda, *The Making of a Nation,* New Delhi: HarperCollins India, 1999, p. 266.
77. ed. Waheed Ahmad, *Diary and Notes of Mian Fazl-i-Husain,* Lahore: Research Society of Pakistan, 1977.
78. Ayesha Jalal, *The Sole Spokesman,* Cambridge University Press, 1985, p. 22.
79. *CWMG,* vol. 71, p. 277.
80. Jalal, *The Sole Spokesman,* p. 42.
81. *CWMG,* vol., 72, p. 446.
82. Rajmohan Gandhi, *Eight Lives,* Albany: State University of New York Press, 1986, p.151.
83. S. Wolpert, *A New History of India,* Oxford University Press, 1977, p. 326.
84. Wolpert, *Jinnah of Pakistan,* pp. 157–9.
85. Syed S. Pirzada, *Foundations of Pakistan,* Karachi: National Publishing House, 1969, vol. 2, pp. 304–6.
86. John Glendevon, *The Viceroy at Bay: Lord Linlithgow in India (1936–46),* London: Collins, 1971, p. 138.
87. 'Working Committee's Manifesto', *CWMG,* vol. 76, pp. 433–7.
88. *CWMG,* vol. 76, pp. 437–8.
89. *CWMG,* vol. 77, pp. 408–13.
90. *CWMG,* vol. 77, pp. 414–5.
91. AIML/File No. 128, p. 116, in Jalal, *The Sole Spokesman,* p. 48.
92. Anita Singh, *The Origins of the Partition of India 1936–1947,* New Delhi: Oxford University Press, 1987, p. 52.
93. Wolpert, *A New History of India,* p. 329.
94. John Glendevon, J., *The Viceroy at Bay,* London: Collins, 1971, p. 148.
95. *Harijan,* 'Hindu–Muslim Unity', 7 October 1939: *CWMG,* vol. 76, pp. 366–8.
96. *Harijan,* 'To Every Briton', 6 July 1940: *CWMG,* vol. 78, pp. 386–8.

97. Speech of 12 October 1941: *CWMG*, vol. 81, pp. 186–93.
98. *CWMG*, vol. 81, p. 396.
99. Rahmat Ali, *Now or Never: Are We to Live or Perish for Ever?*, London, 28 January 1933.
100. ibid.
101. *Indian Annual Register* 1940, i, p. 312.
102. Jalal, *The Sole Spokesman*, p. 62.
103. Glendevon, *The Viceroy at Bay*, p. 182.
104. ibid.
105. Jalal, *The Sole Spokesman*, p. 68.
106. S. Gopal, *Churchill*, Oxford: Oxford University Press, 1993, p. 466.
107. For the Cripps Mission see *Transfer of Power (ToP)*, vol. 1, and Coupland, *The Constitutional Problem in India*, Part 2, pp. 263–86.
108. For Churchill's attitudes, see R.J. Moore, *Churchill, Cripps and India*, Oxford: Clarendon Press, 1979.
109. Maulana Abul Kalam Azad, *India Wins Freedom*, Calcutta: Orient Longman, 1959, pp. 51–2.
110. ed. Mansergh, N., *The Transfer of Power 1942–7*, London: H.M.S.O, 1970, vol. 1 passim.
111. *ToP*, vol. 1, p. 480.
112. *CWMG*, vol. 82, pp. 384–7.
113. M.J. Akbar, *Nehru: The Making of India*, London: Viking, 1988, p. 339.
114. Coupland, op. cit., p. 279.
115. *ToP* vol. 1, p. 110.
116. ibid., p. 539.
117. *Harijan*, 'One Thing Needful',10 May 1942: *CWMG*, vol. 82, pp. 256–8.
118. *CWMG*, vol. 83, pp. 86–88.
119. *Transfer of Power*, vol, 2, p. 853.
120. Mahadev Desai, *Diary*, Varanasi: Sarva Seva Sangh Prakashan, 1968–9.
121. http://yabaluri.org/TRIVENI/CDWEB/TheTripleStreamjul42.htm
122. Fischer, *The Life of Mahatma Gandhi*, p. 491.
123. *CWMG*, vol. 84, p. 199.
124. ibid, n. 4.
125. *CWMG*, vol. 84, pp. 369–71, 373–4, 379–85.
126. Rajagopalachari to Jinnah, 8 April 1944, in *Indian National Register*, 1944, vol. 1, pp.129–30.

127. For the Simla Conference see *ToP.* vol. 5.

128. *CWMG,* vol. 87, pp. 132–64.

129. *The Transfer of Power,* vol. 5, pp. 1153–4.

130. *CWMG,* vol. 88, p. 118.

131. For the Cabinet Mission instructions, plans, deliberations etc. see *The Transfer of Power* 1942–7, London, HMSO, 1977, vol. 7.

132. Notes of meeting, *ToP,* vol 7, pp. 436–8.

133. Wavell, *The Viceroy's Journal,* pp. 259–60: *CWMG,* vol. 90, p. 436.

134. Jalal, op. cit., pp. 202–3.

135. *ToP* vol.7, p. 1037.

136. Akbar, *Nehru: The Making of India,* pp. 379–80; A. I. Singh, *The Origins of the Partition of India,* pp. 176–7.

137. Pirzada, *Foundations,* vol. 2, pp. 557–60.

138. S. Wolpert, *Gandhi's Passion: The Life and Legacy of Mahatma Gandhi,* Oxford: Oxford University Press, 2001, pp. 224–31.

139. A. Campbell-Johnson, *Mission with Mountbatten,* p. 56.

140. Wolpert, *Gandhi's Passion,* p. 232.

141. *The Transfer of Power,* vol. 10, p. 540.

142. *CWMG,* vol. 95, pp. 44–7.

143. *CWMG,* vol. 95, pp. 203–6.

144. M. Munir, *From Jinnah to Zia,* Lahore: Vanguard, 1979, pp. 29–30; *Speeches of Quaid-i-Azam Mohammad Ali Jinnah as Governor General of Pakistan,* Karachi: Sind Observer Press, 1948, pp. 4–5.

145. Wolpert, *Gandhi's Passion,* p. 239.

146. Ziegler, P., *Mountbatten,* London: Guild, 1985, p. 436.

147. *CWMG,* vol. 95, p. 76.

148. Naidu, *Mahomed Ali Jinnah,* p. 11.

149. *CWMG,* vol. 16, pp. 265–9.

150. *CWMG,* vol. 22, p. 157.

151. Chagla, op. cit., p. 107.

152. Naidu, *Mahomed Ali Jinnah,* p. 11.

153. Gokhale's Speeches, p. 744, in S. Wolpert, *Tilak and Gokhale,* New Delhi: Oxford University Press, 1961, p. 250.

154. D.G. Tendulkar, *Mahatma,* Delhi: Publications Division, Ministry of Information and Broadcasting, 1969 vol. 1, p. 137.

155. Fischer, op.cit., p. 159.

156. Jayakar, op. cit., vol. 1, p. 405.

157. Wolpert, *Jinnah of Pakistan,* p. 36.

158. E. Montagu, *An Indian Diary*, London: Heinemann, 1930, pp. 57–8.

159. L. Collins and D. Lapierre, *Freedom at Midnight*, New York: Simon and Schuster, 1975, p. 105.

160. ibid.

161. M.C. Chagla, *Roses in December: An Autobiography*, Bombay: Bharatiya Vidya Bhavan, 1974, p. 107.

162. G.E. Jones, *Tumult in India*, New York: Dodd, Mead, 1948.

163. Fischer, *The Life of Mahatma Gandhi*, p. 493.

164. R. Zakaria, *The Man Who Divided India*, Mumbai: Popular Prakashan, 2001, p. 148.

165. B. Nichols, *Verdict on India*, London: Jonathan Cape, 1944, p. 188.

166. Wolpert, *Jinnah of Pakistan*, p. 96.

167. R. J. Moore, *Jinnah and the Pakistan Demand*, Modern Asian Studies, 17, 4, (1983), pp. 529–61.

168. Naidu, *Mahomed Ali Jinnah*, p. 11.

169. M.A.H. Ispahani, *Qaid-e-Azam Jinnah: As I Knew Him*, Karachi: Forward Publications Trust, 1967.

170. K. Dwarkadas, *India's Fight for Freedom 1913–1937*, Bombay: Popular Prakashan, 1966, p. 62.

171. ibid, p. 89.

172. S.C. Bose,, *The Indian Struggle*, London: Lawrence and Wishart, 1935.

173. ed. H. Coward, *Indian Critiques of Gandhi*, SUNY Series in Religious Studies, Albany: State University of New York Press, 2003, p. 113.

174. W.S. Churchill, *Complete Speeches*, London: Chelsea House, 1974, vol. 5, pp. 253–4.

175. R. Forbes, *India of the Princes*, London: The Right Book Club, 1938, p. 40.

176. ibid, p. 49.

177. F. Sykes, *From Many Angles: An Autobiography,* London: Harrap, 1942, p. 383.

178. H. Bolitho, *Jinnah: Creator of Pakistan*, London: John Murray, 1954.

179. Wolpert, *Jinnah of Pakistan*, p. xx.

180. ibid, p. 340.

181. ibid, p. 339.

182. *Transfer of Power*. London, HMSO, 1981, vol. X, p. 929.

183. Bolitho, *Jinnah*, p. 186.

184. Wolpert, *Jinnah of Pakistan*, p. 70.

185. ibid, p. 162.

186. Sharif al Mujahid, *Jinnah: Studies in Interpretation*, Karachi: Quaid-i-Azam Academy, 1981.

187. S.K. Bandopadhaya, *Quaid-i-Azam: Mohammed Ali Jinnah and the Creation of Pakistan*, New Delhi, Sterling, 1991.

188. A.S. Ahmed, *Jinnah, Pakistan and Islamic Identity: The Search for Saladin*, New York: Routledge, 1997, p. 150.

189. Singh, *Jinnah: India, Partition, Independence*.

190. P. Almeida, *Jinnah: Man of Destiny*, Delhi: Gyan Books, 1999, p. 264.

191. Manmath Nath Das, *End of the British Indian Empire*, Cuttack: Vidyapuri, 1983.

192. S. Karim, *Secular Jinnah: Munir's Big Hoax Exposed*, Exposure Publishing (on demand), 2005; M. Munir, *From Jinnah to Zia*, Lahore: Vanguard Books, 1979.

193. Karim, *Secular Jinnah*, p. 3.

194. ibid, p. xii.

195. Zakaria, *The Man Who Divided India*, p. 228.

196. S.K. Majumdar, *Jinnah and Gandhi: Their Role in India's Quest for Freedom*, Calcutta: Firma K. L. Mukhopadhyay, 1966, p. 67.

197. ibid, p. 73.

198. ibid, p. 94.

199. ibid, pp. 187–8.

200. ibid, p. 73.

201. M.N. Roy, *Gandhism, Nationalism, Socialism*, Calcutta: Bengal Radical Club, 1940.

202. R.C. Majumdar, *Three Phases of India's Struggle for Freedom*, Bombay: Bharatiya Vidya Bhavan, 1961.

203. J. Lelyveld, *Great Soul: Mahatma Gandhi and His Struggle With India*, New York: Alfred A. Knopf, 2011.

204. ed. R. Duncan, *The Writings of Gandhi: A Selection*, London: Fontana/Collins, 1983.

205. Wolpert, *Gandhi's Passion*.

206. Gandhi, *Hind Swaraj, and Other Writings*.

207. Wells, *Ambassador of Hindu–Muslim Unity: Jinnah's Early Politics*.

208. Guha, *Makers of Modern India*, p. 220.

209. Naidu, *Mahomed Ali Jinnah*, p. 46.

210. *Bombay Chronicle*, 15 September 1931.

211. A.G. Noorani, 'Assessing Jinnah', *Frontline*, volume 22, issue 17, Aug. 13–26, 2005.

212. In M.R. Kazimi, *M.A. Jinnah, Views and Reviews*, Oxford: Oxford University Press, 2005, p. 62.

213. ed. J. Ahmed, M.A. Jinnah, *Jinnah: Speeches*, Lahore: M. Ashraf, 1968, vol. 1, p. 259.

214. J. Ahmed, *Speeches of Quaid-i-Azam*, Lahore: Sh. Muhammad Ashraf, 1946, vol. 1, p. 184.

215. Saiyid, *Jinnah*, pp. 264–5.

216. Sykes, *From All Angles*, p. 343.

217. ibid, p. 344.

218. *CWMG*, vol. 82, p. 283.

219. ibid.

220. *CWMG*, vol. 22, p. 147.

221. Interview to Reuters, 5 May 1947, *CWMG*, vol. 95, p. 26.

222. Fischer, *The Life of Mahatma Gandhi*, p. 364.

223. *CWMG*, vol. 29, p. 212.

224. *CWMG*, vol. 15, p. 153.

225. *Young India*, 'Hinduism', 6 October 1921: *CWMG*, vol. 24, pp. 370–375.

226. Letter to the *Statesman*, 16 January 1918: *CWMG*, vol. 16, p. 209.

227. Fischer, *The Life of Mahatma Gandhi*, p. 380.

228. Wolpert, *Gandhi's Passion*, pp. 227–28.

229. See V. Mehta, *Mahatma Gandhi and His Apostles*, New Haven: Yale University Press, 1993; p. 260; J. Adams, *Gandhi: Naked Ambition*, London: Quercus, 2010; Lelyveld, *Great Soul: Mahatma Gandhi and His Struggle with India*.

230. *CWMG*, vol. 41, p. 452.

231. A. Javed, *Secular and Nationalist Jinnah*, New Delhi: Kitab Publishing House, 1997, pp. 271–8.

232. D. Das, *India from Curzon to Nehru and After*, London: Collins, 1969, p. 195.

233. Jalal, *The Sole Spokesman*, p. 202.

234. Ispahani, *Qaid-i-Azam Jinnah: As I Knew Him*, pp. 263–4.

235. Alan Campbell-Johnson, *Mission with Mountbatten*, London: Hale, 1951, p. 98.

236. Michael Brecher, *Nehru: A Political Biography*, Oxford University Press, 1968.

237. Leonard Mosley, *The Last days of the British Raj*, London: Weidenfeld and Nicolson, 1961.

238. Das, *India from Curzon to Nehru*, p. 248.

239. *Transfer of Power,* vol. IX, pp. 840–50.
240. S.S. Pirzada, *Collected Works of M.A. Jinnah,* Karachi: National Publishing House, 1969, vol. 2, p. 421.
241. *Young India,* 'A Taxing Examiner', 6 April 1921: *CWMG,* vol. 23, pp. 5–9.
242. A.I. Singh, *The Origins of the Partition of India: 1936–47,* New Delhi: Oxford University Press, 1987, p. 211.
243. A. Campbell-Johnson, *Mission with Mountbatten,* p. 52.
244. Quoted in A.S. Ahmed, *Jinnah, Pakistan and Islamic Identity: The Search for Saladin,* London: Routledge, 1997, p. 32.
245. M.C. Chagla, *Roses in December,* Mumbai, Bharatya Vidya Bhavan, 1974, p. 80.

Index